# Darling

## LOVE LETTERS
### *from* WWII

# Peggy O'Toole Lamb

Print ISBN: 978-1-09830-565-9

eBook ISBN: 978-1-09830-566-6

*Dedicated to my Uncle Frank and Aunt Catherine*

# TABLE OF CONTENTS

# PREFACE

"Words are like the god Janus;
they face outward and inward at once."
*"Anam Cara, Celtic Wisdom"*
John O'Donohue.

Frank has been dead for over forty years, Kitty died five years ago, but the letters Frank sent to her during World War II remain alive, his words seeping bits of information out of the inferno of war. His words encrust a bitter time, yet his letters contain love and hope that he would return safely to his young wife and their newborn son, John.

As I write Frank's story, I know the ending, but I keep wanting his story to be different. I don't want him to lie shivering in the muddy slit trench while artillery and bombs drop around him, I don't want him to see the barn filled with Jewish corpses, I don't want him to trudge through the mud and muck of war watching his friends die, knowing he has to kill or die. I don't remember this uncle, not my Uncle Frank, the one I knew as a child, the one who slept in his reclining chair, spoke very little but made sure his children had well-made clothes, a swimming pool, and good food.

Frank's letters remained folded in a tin box, which was typical of the era. Letters bound in rubber bands holding the past together, yellowed love letters that kept Frank and Kitty bounded during his long two-year absence, letters that revealed his pain of separation from his wife and newborn son. His words on the page hold Frank in eternity, words that echo a past and reverberate into the future. Words unread may as well be words unspoken, so I read my Uncle Frank's love letters to my Aunt Catherine.

I read between the lines of what he said and could not say. It was wartime, and missives took days and weeks to arrive if they arrived at all. Letters were opened and censored before crossing the ocean, words were transcribed to photographs and sent V-mail (Victory mail) on microfiche to reduce the cost of transferring an original letter, words expressing a longing we can only imagine.

First Lieutenant Frank J. Foster looks at me from his photo amidst the stack of his letters on my desk, his eyes stare into mine, he sees me, he whispers to me, he assures me he's safe and not to worry, but I am worried about him so young, so far from home. He's barely thirty. His lips form a sweet bowtie, his clean-shaven face and brushed back hair expose his prominent ears. His right ear cocked towards me causes me to pause. I feel he is listening to my thoughts, guiding me as I dig through his past. He is leading me to England, to France, to Germany, to Austria, to places he's been, sending me on a mission to find out what he couldn't tell Catherine, what he couldn't speak about after the war.

Frank is a handsome man, tall and thin with a friendly face, light brown hair, and intelligent eyes. There is a softness about him that gives one confidence that he wouldn't leave a man to suffer, and he would stop to help a child in need, friend, or foe. He has a softness that must have made war unbearable for him as he mopped up the French towns. The French greeted him, screaming, "Vive les américaines!" throwing flowers at him, blowing kisses, tears flowing, a vast difference from the days before where dead bodies of farmers, women, and children, and soldiers laid by the roadside, mutilated and shot by the Germans.

His military portrait taken before all that happened shows his innocence is intact, his face smooth, no brows furrowed. I follow his journey, letter by letter, knowing his words are written in real-time, the action not yet completed. Like seeing the light from a star billions of years away, I read Frank's letters as if I'm in with him in actual time while he writes daily to Catherine, unaware his words will be read long after he is gone, unaware that his light is still shining.

# CHAPTER ONE

# Letters Home

Frank tucked Catherine's letter in his shirt pocket, a habit he would keep throughout the war. Her letters would always be close to his heart. Pale pink washed over the desert mountains and night rose in a misty blue. The sky had turned to indigo by the time he reached his wooden-floor tent tucked among hundreds of pyramidal tents along the dirt roads of Camp Young. The desk he shared with the other lieutenants was vacant, and he took the opportunity to write.

> *Dear Kitty,*             *Friday, April 7, 1944*
> *I just received the letter you wrote while you were in the hospital or rather the day you were leaving. You sound so proud of the baby. I wish I could have been there to share some of the joy with you.*

Catherine had been alone in the hospital with their newborn son while Frank was in the desert playing wargames. He reminded himself he had a duty to his country and for the free world. But how sad, Frank had held John for only an hour after birth while on a brief leave. The baby's eyes had barely opened, the color still indistinguishable, and his face scrunched in a sour smile. Struck by a love he had never felt before, Frank rocked his baby back and forth, cooing and awing at the little guy, a string bean of a baby at 22 inches long, weighing under eight pounds, a mere hummingbird in comparison to the100-pound shells he loaded in his big gun earlier that day.

*Kitty, you will be the best mother in the world.*
*I only hope I can be as good a daddy. It's pretty tough*
*being a dad since I have not yet learned how to*
*change diapers.*

\* \* \*

George Jr. Foster, George, Harriet, Anna Duffy Foster
Marshall (Frank), Ralph

Frank was apprehensive about babies and having a family, but eager to get started and change what he had experienced as a child. In his early years, he lived in a Cleveland tenement with three siblings, his English immigrant father who worked in a metal factory, and his Irish immigrant mother, a domestic and factory worker. His parents died of the flu in the 1920s, and the grandparents could not afford to take all the children. George, the oldest son, was sent to a wealthy family and treated as a child worker. He later told Frank he felt abandoned and resented his siblings. Harriet, his baby sister, disappeared from his life, adopted to another non-related family. Unable to find a better placement, the grandparents sent Frank and his younger brother Ralph to the Catholic diocesan orphanage, a three-storied brick building that housed 200 boys and was run by the Sisters of Charity. His birth certificate had his given name as Marshall Eugene, which did not contain a saint's name, so the nuns changed it to Francis Joseph Foster. The boys all called him Frankie.

The day his little brother Ralph left the orphanage, Frank put on his best clothes to walk him to the train station. Little Ralph, in his dungarees, his cap askew, holding a small bundle of his belongings, held tight to his big brother until they arrived at the station. A nun scurried over and helped him climb aboard the orphan train bound for parts unknown. Frank, barely ten years old, stood on the side of the tracks waving good-bye, then returned alone to the orphanage.

* * *

*We are preparing to move, but the when and where are the unknowns. Kitty, this little trip can't last forever, and soon we can enjoy our son together.*

What if he didn't return from overseas, leaving his new son fatherless, making a widow of his wife? Both his parents had died, making him an orphan, and hundreds of thousands of soldiers had already lost their lives fighting this war. What were his odds?

What Frank didn't know was that *this little trip,* as he called the war, was going to last a long time, six years in all, his time being in the army over four years. Not only miles would separate him from his family, but the war would change him and how he saw the world. After World War II, no one seemed to talk about the war, least of all the soldiers. The returning men and women kept the horrors locked inside, unwilling to burden their loved ones, and afraid to relive the hell they survived. Frank buried his feelings and never talked about his war experiences in his letters or when he returned home. The funny, tender man didn't come back; instead, a stoic, hardworking father returned, determined to make a good life for his family.

Frank signed his letter as he would for the next two years, "*Love to you and our boy John,*" and sealed the letter. In his Catholic school handwriting, he wrote his return address, *Camp Young 546th A.A.A., Battalion B, Indio, California,* then addressed the letter to Mrs. Frank J. Foster in Silver Lake, Los Angeles. In the left-hand bottom corner, he signed his official signature, *Frank J. Foster, 1st Lt.,* having the privilege of self-censoring his letters and the duty to censor the enlisted men's mail.

The next day he posted his letter and checked the outgoing basket, scanned over the enlisted men's correspondences for restricted information, signed the envelopes, and put them in the outbox. Every soldier had received the pamphlet from the Secretary of War, George C. Marshall, and knew the strict rules controlling the content of the letters they sent home. The guiding rule was not to give the enemy any information, and if they failed to follow the rules, the consequences were dire: demotion, the brig, and even court-martial.

The War Department Pamphlet stated there was to be no mention of location, strength, material or equipment, no writing of military installations or transportation facilities, convoys or their routes, the time en route, of war incidents en route. No disclosure of movements of ships, naval or merchants, troops, or aircraft; no mention of plans or forecasts or future operations, known or guessed. No word to be written of the effect of enemy operations or casualties nor formulate a code system, cipher, or shorthand to conceal the true meaning of your letters.

Throughout the war, Frank wrote home about the weather, the U.S.O. Shows, his comrades, finances, and always asked about the baby conjecturing what he must be doing. He pleaded with Kitty to send photos each month so as not to miss out on his son's stages and growth spurts. He kept a photo of them folded in his breast pocket, easily accessible to show others, or to contemplate in solitary. In his letters, his loneliness was palpable, his fear rarely surfaced, and his future was always in question. He protected Catherine from the horrors of war, perhaps out of duty, but also not wanting to hurt her or unduly scare her more than she was from the newspapers back home. Letter writing was a touchstone to normalcy, never sure when it would all end.

# CHAPTER TWO

# The U.S. Enters the War

The whir of sirens signaled lights out, shades closed. In a small bungalow on the outskirts of Los Angeles, in the darkened bedroom, a mother pinned the diaper to her baby girl's flesh, and the ensuing cries echoed in the living room where the men gathered around the radio listening to the news. December 7, 1941, the Japanese bombed Pearl Harbor.

It was early in Frank's courtship with Catherine. They were visiting her sister Mary, celebrating the baptism of her second child, Mary Nola. The father, Horace, and Frank discussed what would come after the attack. Would Frank be drafted? He was thirty-one, not yet married and no children, whereas Horace and Mary had two children and another one on the way.

Four days later, the United States declared war against the Japanese Empire. Germany immediately declared war on the United States. Within hours President Roosevelt signed the declaration of war against Germany, fully committing the country on two fronts: the Pacific theater and the European theater. Less than a week later, Uncle Sam required every healthy man from 18 to 64 years of age to register with the Selective Service to serve his country for the duration of the war, plus six months.

Frank registered and was conscripted into the army in early 1942 and sent to Camp Callan, La Jolla for a thirteen-week training in Coastal Artillery with emphasis on long-range weapons. Gun positioning took more than eye-hand skill and brute strength. It took brains.

Frank had a keen eye for shooting varmints and rattlesnakes, having lived in the desert, a sharp mind for numbers, and a competitive spirit. After a series of tests, the army yanked Frank from the rank of private and sent him to officer school in Richmond, Virginia, where he further trained for combat duty as an officer.

Before leaving, he was sorely in need of seeing Catherine.

*Dear Kitty,*                                              *August 24, 1942*

*Just a short note to tell you that I am trying to get a weekend pass, and if I do, I will be in Los Angeles early in the evening Saturday. Hold both thumbs. I won't know till Friday whether I will get it. It was sure good seeing you again, and I haven't gotten over it yet.*

*Love, Frank*

Frank and Catherine 1942, Palm Springs

It hadn't been that long ago since Frank caught Catherine peeking through the rectory kitchen curtains to watch him standing outside. He'd noticed her around the church grounds and wondered why a beautiful young girl was working at the Catholic rectory here in the forgotten desert? She questioned what this handsome man in boots, freshly pressed pants, and a sweater vest could be doing coming by the rectory every Sunday afternoon?

At twenty-one, Catherine had left her Los Angeles home for Palm Springs to help her ailing Aunt Mary Agnes, who was the housekeeper at the rectory of the Church of Solitude Catholic Church. Mary Agnes hailed from New York, having had work at St. Patrick's Cathedral. The Irish priests at St. Patrick's had a priest friend in the desert and thought it would do Mary Agnes some good to get out of the cold, so they sent her to the warmer climate due to her crippling arthritis. Her hands could barely hold the pans taken from the oven, so Catherine took over the hard work allowing Mary Agnes to stay on as housekeeper, even if just in name.

Frank, a devoted Catholic, having been raised by the nuns and priests, visited the rectory most Sunday afternoons with his friend Bert Ripple. The church was Frank's family. It wasn't long before Frank asked his pastor, Father Gallagher, about Catherine. Father checked with her aunt before introducing Catherine after dinner one night. The shy girl from behind the curtain accepted Frank's invitation to go out the following week. The priest called Catherine's parents and assured them that even though Frank was only half Irish, he was a hardworking man with integrity.

Well, Frank never did get over Catherine. She occupied his thoughts night and day. He thanked God for the day he met her, an angel that would bring him love and a family. He asked Catherine to marry him before he went off to war, and within a short time, on March

17, 1943, they were married at St. Francis Church in Los Angeles, where Catherine and her three sisters had received all their sacraments. In their photo, Frank stands tall and erect in his formal uniform. He has that little boy look, the crooked smile, and shy eyes, while his face beams, *I'm the luckiest guy.* Catherine's Irish beauty radiates through her smile, her high cheekbones touched with pink, her face framed by brown curls. Frank clasps her hand, their fingers intertwined in a bond that will last forever.

\* \* \*

By the time Frank finished officer training, the U.S. military had recognized the terrible damage the Luftwaffe, Germany's air force, was inflicting on the United Kingdom and North Africa. The focus turned away from Coastal Artillery to Anti-Aircraft Artillery. First Lieutenant Frank J. Foster was relocated to Camp Haan in Riverside then on to the Desert Training Center to prepare for battle in the northern Sahara. The War Department had ordered General Patton to locate, create, equip, and command a desert training area to get the troops to fight against the Nazis in North Africa.

Flying with his staff officers over the Mojave Desert covering parts of Arizona, Nevada, and California, Patton scoured the area for signs of human settlements but found only a few crisscrossing roads and a few deserted gas stations.

"This godforsaken land is perfect," Patton declared. He established the Desert Training Center stretching from southeastern California to western Arizona, encompassing the Mojave and Sonora Deserts, and touted "the greatest maneuver training area in the U.S. history, eighteen thousand square miles of nothing but a desert designed for Hell."

\* \* \*

Frank was no stranger to the desert, having moved to the Coachella Valley in 1931 to join Bert Ripple his good friend from Campion High, a boarding school in Cleveland. After waving good-bye to little Ralph, he lived in the orphanage until high school. Frank impressed the nuns as a responsible young adult caring for the younger boys who also had lost their parents or were left on the roadside to fend for themselves. Frank was quick-as-a-whip smart, and the nuns felt he needed more academic challenges than they could offer him. Fortune smiled upon Frank when the Jesuit priests accepted all responsibility for raising Frank and enrolled him in Campion High School, a boarding school for boys from wealthy and influential families. His high school yearbook praised him: "Frankie is one of our best in sports, especially in basketball. His four-year record at Campion is probably the most clean-slated of anyone, as well as he is full of wit and humor."

Excelling was innate in Frank, who had to fight to survive since his early years in the tenements. Being streetwise, he knew how to be chameleon-like and fit in with this elitist group while not changing who he was. Well aware of the other boys' family backgrounds, he kept his past in the past, never mentioning his difficult childhood, and adapted their style of talk and dress. He already had the intelligence to keep up on his studies and the athleticism, the first to be picked on any team. As with all holidays, Frank had no home to go to, but Frank never let on.

On the evening before everyone left for the Christmas holidays, Frank packed his suitcase. In the morning he donned his best suit, like the other boys, said his good-byes and wished them all a Merry Christmas. He walked to the train station where he bought a ticket and rode the train for as long as he could, often days. Once he knew the dorms would be empty, he took the train back, walked to the dorms, unpacked, and spent Christmas at the rectory with the priests, his only family.

By the end of high school, Frank earned a full scholarship to the Jesuit college, Marquette, where he enrolled in Dentistry, taking premed and science classes. Once again, he excelled, but he wasn't satisfied. Like any young man, Frank wanted to break away and explore what was beyond the priests' protective circle. He was no longer the vulnerable orphan, nor did he ever want to return to that life of not having a family of his own. After two years of college, his buddy, Bert Ripple, lured him to the desert to work with his father in agriculture on date farms and citrus orchards. Life opened up for Frank in the vast desert plains and the rugged mountains. The warm air-filled Frank with hope as he shed his past along with his eastern wardrobe.

After working during the day in the fields and on the date farm in the heat, Frank and Bert, would ride their horses, winding through the brambles, cactus, and thorny greasewood trees, climbing up the steep rocky ravines to the coolness of Mount San Jacinto. From their mountain top advantage point, they looked over the vast desert dreaming of future agriculture on the barren land. There was lots of open space, an oasis with the water below the desert floor. The rich people from Hollywood drove around in their fancy cars, heading to the Salton Sea, with the tops down on their convertibles, scarves blowing in the dry wind. Bert had an idea. *They must get thirsty just like we do.*

Bert opened up a date stand under a palapa along Highway 111 and sold cold drinks, dried dates in fancy packaging, and the famous date shake. With his scientific mind, Frank veered his career path toward making fertilizers to enrich the soil and make the fruit grow better.

They were only twenty-one years old when they set out to conquer the desert, planting date gardens, growing citrus fruits, and vegetables. Little did they know that within ten years, tanks, artillery, and soldiers would fill the valley, detonating bombs, firing howitzer guns, and playing war games. Frank would be among them.

* * *

After Frank's training along the coast of California with cool summer breezes, Frank found himself stationed in the Coachella Valley at Camp Young, as First Lieutenant in the 546th A.A.A. (Anti-Aircraft Artillery), Battalion B. Their unit specialized in the 155-millimeter field gun, nicknamed "Long Tom," which fired 100-pound shells with a maximum range of 14 miles. Frank referred to it as his *peashooter.* His battalion prepared to ship out with Patton to the battlefield in North Africa in a few short months.

155 mm "Long Tom" Anti-aircraft Artillery, Desert Training Center, 1943

In Patton's words, "The California desert can kill quicker than the enemy. We will lose a lot of men from the heat, but training will save hundreds of lives when we get into combat." Patton gave the orders to every U.S. Army officer under his command across the United States to move all troops by rail to California.

The Army Corps of Engineers cleared the brush, greasewood, and cactus and erected over 3,000 pyramidal tents without electricity or running water. Rows of metal beds with flat mattresses and no sheets lined the canvas sides with footlockers at the end of each bed for their issue and khaki musette bags. Temporary wooden structures housed administrative offices, hospitals, and warehouses.

Trainloads of men and supplies, tanks, and army trucks descended on the Coachella Valley overtaxing Indio, a small town of migrant workers and farmers.

During the training period, Patton pushed his troops as hard as humanly possible. Some men died from exposure, heat exertion, and dehydration, as well as from other illnesses and accidents. In heat above 120 degrees, soldiers, including officers, were required to be able to run a mile in ten minutes wearing a full pack and carrying rifles and ammunition. Ignoring the Metropolitan Water District of Los Angeles, Patton refused to have his men build water storage tanks, saying, "the men are here to learn to fight in tough situations. If you can work successfully here, in this country, it will be no difficulty at all to kill the asshole sons-of-bitches you meet in any other country."

The fine sand and dust mucked up the weapons and equipment, and the dirt clung to the soldiers' sweaty shirts. As hot as the summers were, the winter temperatures were equally brutal at night, dropping to below freezing. Before retiring, the soldiers checked their beds for scorpions and rattlesnakes that curled in the dark corners. Despite Patton's harsh and unreasonable demands, Frank and the men had respect for their Commander because Patton led by example. He stayed in the same primitive accommodations, ate the same food, and put in long hours checking on his troops, while his wife, Beatrice, lived in a comfortable adobe home on the Whittier Ranch nearby in Indio.

Frank wasn't so lucky to have his wife nearby. By then, Catherine had already moved back home to her family in Los Angeles.

For days and weeks on end, the men trekked or drove in trucks across the sand, at times as far as a hundred miles into the desert on field maneuvers, eating rations and sleeping on their bedrolls. Patton had chosen the training area because it was large enough to simulate war without the risk of shooting or running into each other. The men received daily canteens of water, food rations, and a sleeping bag when out in the desert, but rarely did anyone have water left to wash up. At one point in training, Frank dispensed only two canteens of water for his fifteen men to test their stamina in the desert. He doled out the precious liquid twice a day. To survive dehydration, the soldiers cut the tops off a barrel cactus to squeeze the water out or to chew on the pulp.

When they arrived at their destination, Frank and his battalion set up their long-range anti-aircraft weapon, the "Long Tom." Tractors towed the gun on an eight-wheeled carriage with fat tires across the sand into position. The gunner climbed to his seat. It took two men to ram the shell into the back breech of the gun and another two men to load enough gun powder bags to reach the desired range.

A private closed the breech plug and locked it. Frank set the position as the soldiers rotated the base of the gun. Frank located the target in the crosshairs. He gave the command to fire into the seemingly endless desert at targets set up over thirteen miles away to test the accuracy of the shell hit. From sunup to sundown, the men marched and fired, following their orders to attack, destroy, and move-on. By late afternoon, the men trudged across the sand, towing their big gun back to a temporary camp, only to find their foxholes filled with sand and their tents collapsed and hanging off the cactus and Joshua trees.

Out on bivouac, night fell abruptly across the desert floor with its sagebrush and prickly plants casting ungodly shadows in the moonlight. The wind whistled through the smoke trees, and tumbleweeds tossed about like nighttime burglars. Under a makeshift lean-to, the men crawled into their bags, their clothes smelling of the day's sweat and gun powder, and soon drifted off to sleep.

Under the stars, Frank pulled out Catherine's letter and wrote back.

*Dear Kitty,*                *Monday, March 27*
    *Did you get yourself that anniversary present I promised you? It's our first anniversary, and I hate to miss presenting it myself. How are John's Aunties doing? Is he spoiling them with his good manners?*

When they got back to Camp Young, the men looked forward to passes into town and other distractions. Throughout the war, big time entertainers came to the troops both on the home front and overseas, and one of the best was The Bob Hope Show.

Buses pulled into the staging area where men had their assemblies. Sweeping across the desert floor was a sea of soldiers sitting on their helmets, knee-to-back, chanting until Hope strolled onto the large wooden stage. In his opening monologue with a deadpan look on his face, Bob asked the soldiers to check their boots for scorpions and to shake the sand out. "Don't want to dirty things up around here."

His wry jokes got the men laughing, laughing at themselves and their situation of constant rules and regulations, the demanding officers, K-rations, army food, the heat, and, of course, the lack of women. From backstage, two skimpily clad girls walked up behind Bob, who acted as if he hadn't noticed. The guys whistled and cat-called. "I hadn't expected that reaction." Bob knew he had hit a nerve, and he called out the dancing girls.

On Saturday nights, dances were held in the town or at Camp Young when the usually forbidden female could enter. Aware of the shortage of single women, the Hollywood elite, who called nearby Palm Springs their second home, organized the Desert Battalion. These young ladies paid their way to the camps in chartered buses. Filing down the steps, the girls waved to the boys, blowing kisses, all of them dressed to the nines in heels and form-fitting skirts and jaunty hats. Matrons and officers chaperoned while the young couples danced cheek to cheek to the sounds of the Big Band blaring over the speakers. The girls felt it was their duty to socialize with these men who were away from home, often for the first time, and possibly would not return.

Other citizen groups saw the influx of soldiers into their towns as an immoral disruption and wanted to stop the appalling soldier's behavior of whistling at the young girls. The Indio Women's Club met with Patton, who dismissed their objections by saying, "If I were you, I wouldn't worry if they whistled at me. If I went into the street and they didn't whistle at me, then I'd worry."

Patton was rough in many ways, and he didn't mince his words. The men respected him, his work ethic, and his honest, straight talk. Daily, Patton traveled by jeep visiting his troops across the vast expanse of the Desert Training Center but always ended up back at Camp Young headquarters by evening. Frank surmised the only way he could cover that much ground in a day was to fly back in his Army plane landing in the nearby Shaver's Summit Army Airfield, a single landing strip adjacent to Camp Young. Here is where the Army Tactical Air Command (T.A.C.) trained alongside the ground troops in preparation for wartime reconnaissance and bombing raids used to clear the way for tanks and artillery during the war. Patton would depend heavily on the T.A.C. working in conjunction with his armored and artillery divisions, as his Third Army raced across France and Germany to end the war.

Within six months of opening the Desert Training Center, General Eisenhower called Patton back into action to command 33,000 men in North Africa to fight the Nazis. Frank and his battalion continued to train in the desert while waiting for deployment to the Great Sahara, but the Allies won the war in North Africa sooner than expected. Frank was relieved to spend more time in California, closer to Catherine. Even though there was no longer the need for desert training, Frank and his battalion stayed training under the hot sun until the closure of the D.T.C. in the Spring of 1944 when the troops were shipped overseas. Patton's directive was to train the men in the worst conditions possible, so even if they met snow, sleet, and subzero temperatures, they'd know not just how to survive but how to fight the enemy, beat him at his game, even if in his backyard. Taking over command was Major Walker, nicknamed Patton's bulldog, who knew just how to train men to fight anywhere.

In such grueling conditions, one soldier commented, "You'd have to be a coward to leave here and volunteer for the war on the frontline."

On April 8, 1944, along with thousands of other troops, Frank and his battalion prepared to leave for overseas. The spirit of Patton echoed in the desert wind, *you're heading out for the real war, and I'm in charge of you son-of-a-bitches!*

# CHAPTER THREE

# Last Stop U.S.A.

Orders came Saturday afternoon: *Prepare to depart by train at 0700 Monday, April 10.* Frank crumpled the paper, tossed it in the wastebasket as if shooting hoops, then walked outdoors to the open tents to let his men know.

Frank found some of his men in their tents. From the looks on the boys' faces, Frank knew that he didn't have to say much. "We're moving out Monday early. Have your gear packed and ready for the trucks by Sunday evening at 2100. We depart at 0500 from camp and on the train at 0700. Be prepared for confusion." He joked, "as usual, F.U.B.AR." He walked over to the baseball diamond, and just his presence froze the players. "Game's up, boys. Pack the fun stuff. We may have time to use it overseas."

All guns, tanks, and any material that would be needed to ship overseas had to be in good working condition. Everything had to be cleared out of the tents, which took no time at all. The difficult task was sorting through personal belongings, keeping only the necessities, and contacting loved ones. It was getting in the right frame of mind to meet the enemy that took more thought, more heart, more courage. Fighting in the desert had toughened these soldiers. The imminent war created a euphoria, a sense of pride, and the fruition, of all their hard work. Now they had a chance to kill the enemy, to rid the world of Nazism, and possibly, be the one to kill Hitler.

Frank returned to his office and packed his personal belongings, a photo of Kitty, her soft brown curls, deep-set blue eyes, high cheekbones, and a smile to melt his heart, their wedding photo with Frank in uniform, tall, thin, with a child-like face of innocence, his lips forming a sweet bowtie, his clean-shaven face and brushed back hair exposing his ears, and a snapshot of John a week old in his arms taken by his brother-in-law Steve. Frank reflected on the one day he got to hold his child in the hospital, not knowing then, it would be the last day he would see him before going overseas. If only, he had gotten a pass to see them one more time before shipping out or at least to have called. But there was no time.

On Sunday morning, Frank attended Mass in the outdoor chapel, his eyes settling on the blue hills in the distance behind the stone altar. He felt connected to Catherine because she too would be at Mass with her parents.

Early Monday, the train station was a flood of uniforms, moving in a wave, jostling into position to board the train. Excitement electrified the air, energized by the movement, and feeling a part of something bigger than each man, a unit, a corps, a battalion, an army, all going into the unknown.

The town of Indio was emptying. The last two years had seen the population explode with soldiers and those supporting the burgeoning businesses. The bars, the restaurants, the dance halls would be a thing of the past, as would the street fighting, carousing, and young girls waiting to dance.

The Red Cross girls set up their tables on the platform under the shade of the arcade and passed out donuts and coffees to the soldiers as they filed by. One young man asked for a kiss instead of a donut. A sassy girl replied, "You can have both," and leaned over and kissed the young man good-bye. Wives and children lined the quay waving and blowing kisses, straining to see their men hanging out the train windows. Every man returned the blown kisses, waving their hats, saluting, flailing their arms, shouting, bellowing last words of love.

The train whistle blew a few, sharp blasts, the gears clanked into position, and the troop train slowly moved out, stretching across the desert, passing through hamlets below the beautiful Shadow Mountains. Frank caught a glimpse of Mount San Jacinto now topped in snow and envisioned his earlier days riding across the desert to the pine forests. *So much has changed in twelve years.*

* * *

After her two-week hospital stay, Catherine returned to her childhood home, where she and her three sisters grew up playing hopscotch on the deck. They walked to school past Walt Disney's first studio and mixed with the kids of the Hollywood folk. It was a glamorous time, the Roaring Twenties, and the schoolchildren imitated the movie stars and entertainers, especially Peggy, the youngest sister, who practiced switching her hands across her knees, shimmying and singing the musky piano bar songs. Sarah, their Irish mother, scolded the girls for doing the Charleston. "That's the devil's work."

Catherine took ahold of her father's elbow as they climbed the seventy-six stairs to their white bungalow tiered against the hill. Her mother held baby John tight, careful not to drop him, which worried Catherine. "Mom, I'll hold John."

Her mother looked offended but gently passed the baby to her daughter. Sarah suffered from back problems, and possibly overdid the morphine and nips at the bottle, an issue long hidden in the household.

Catherine settled in her rocking chair with John asleep in the tiny crib next to her. She opened Frank's letter that had been placed that morning on the table beside her.

*Dear Kitty,*       *Monday, April 10*
*We don't know yet where we are going to be located*
*and probably won't be able to say when we find out. As*
*soon as we're settled, I'll call you if I can.*

She put her hand on the baby's back and rocked. Her faith in God would have to get her through this time. She trusted that Frank would call, he would write, and he would come home. She finished reading the letter.

*Good night, darling, see you as soon as I can.*
*Love to the family and all my best love to you and*
*John, Frank*

* * *

Frank returned to his private cabin on the train with the other officers, who had already started drinking.

"Have a shot, Frank."

He obliged, lit a cigarette, and joined the conversation. "Have you heard any news about where we're heading?"

No one knew any specifics as to where they were going.

"Most likely Camp Shanks, or somewhere in New York," Captain Howell guessed. "It's near to where the troopships are docked." They didn't even know when they would ship out to Europe.

First Lieutenant Hubbard, a handsome man with a receding hairline and a grin like a cat who ate the mouse, entered the room and shouted, "Let's play." They lowered the table and brought out the cards. "A little stud poker, anyone?"

The men cut the deck, high card dealt, and the dealer passed out five cards each. The game lasted most the day and into the night, with poker recruits coming and going.

By morning they were crossing Texas. Frank wrote:

*Hello Darling,*            *Tuesday, April 11*
    *I won't be sending this letter till we stop, which I*
*have no idea when that will be. I'm starving for a word*
*from you, Kitty. I have not had mail since Sunday, and*
*it will probably take time for the mail to catch up to us*
*again. Keep writing, even though the letters are old, they*
*are still good.*
    *If you sent any to Camp Young, I'm hoping they'll*
*be forwarded. I hope you have my new A.P.O. number*
*by now, but in case you don't, my new mailing address,*
*which will stay the same for the rest of my duty overseas,*
*is: "Battery B 546th A.A.A. Battalion, A.P.O. 654 c/o*
*N.Y. N.Y."*

Even though Frank, as an officer, had the privilege to censor his letters, other military personnel could double-check the content and often sent his letters zigzagging across the country, and at times they were never delivered. Kitty's letters arrived in irregular intervals too. Sometimes weeks passed without a word from her. Then Frank would hit "*payday,*" as he called it when several letters came in a bundle. The importance of mail to a soldier was only second to food, but for Frank, it came first.

The train slowed as it wound its way through a farming community in rural Texas. Frank heard a commotion flare-up in the passageways and opened his door to find soldiers hanging out the windows, shouting and hollering at the passing houses and fields.

*You'd have to see this to believe it, Kitty, we're passing through Texas, and those Texans are really whooping*

*it up! Many of them went right through their hometown,*
*and one kid almost fell out the window.*

Things settled down, and Frank went back to his cabin to finish his letter.

*I suppose the baby will be baptized next Sunday.*
*I will be offering up my prayers here and will be there in*
*spirit. I bet he's lots of fun now and getting cuter every*
*day. I wish I could get some pictures of him, but I will*
*wait patiently until you can get around to having them*
*made.*

Catherine had John baptized at their local parish, St. Francis of Assisi. The family gathered around the baptismal font, her parents Thaddeus and Sarah, her sisters, Agnes, Peggy with Steve, her fiancée, and her older sister, Mary, and her husband Horace with their three young children, Shereen, Mary Nola, and Terence. The priest recited prayers while he poured the holy water on the baby's head, then blessed John with oil on his forehead, mouth, and heart. The godparents vowed to protect him and make sure he followed the rules of the church. Going back to the house, they celebrated with tea and Irish bread, a little whiskey, and a late dinner of roast beef and potatoes. Dada, as they called their father, played the fiddle, and for a moment, life seemed orderly. Catherine shared what news she had heard from Frank and read his letter aloud.

*If I get out on pass in New York, I will try to look*
*up Aunt Mary. And as soon as we are settled again, I will*
*get permission to call you. I imagine there will be at least*
*a two-hour delay for a call, but I will keep trying.*
*Good nite darling, see you as soon as I can.*

Four days after leaving California, the U.S. Troop train pulled into New York City, but neither Frank nor any other soldiers got off. The train lurched forward as they attached more cars. The Red Cross girls had set up on the platforms with their donuts and coffee, sending off more soldiers who crowded aboard. Men leaned out the window, calling to the girls, "Donuts and coffee, Miss." A flurry of white-aproned ladies with the iconic red cross on their hats gladly obliged the soldiers, hoisting trays of donuts and cups of coffee, the least they could do knowing these boys may not see home again. A band played 'Over There' as the new enlisted men marched to the train cars waiting to take them off to war. The train continued north, 30 miles up the Hudson River from New York City to Camp Shanks.

Camp Shanks was the largest Army port of embarkation in the United States from 1943 till the end of World War II. Over 3.1 million troops, mostly those troops who would take part in the invasion of Normandy in 1944, left from there. The G.I.s knew they were headed overseas on a possible one-way ticket, which is why they named the camp, "Last Stop, U.S.A."

# CHAPTER FOUR

# At Sea

Morning Report: *April 18, 1944: "Breakfast at 0500 Camp C.P. Shanks. Report to New York Port of Embarkation for permanent change of station."* Frank read the orders, crushed the paper, and went down the hall to muster his men to prepare for an early departure the next morning. Most troops had two to three weeks to prepare for overseas at the debarkation camps. Why were they being rushed out? After fifteen months of training, his time was being cut short on his last leg in the U.S. *Kitty, it's like the old saw, hurry up and wait, but this time it's wait and hurry up!*

The three short days in Camp Shanks had not been enough time to get passes into the city, only time to get ready for an indefinite stay overseas.

> *Hello Darling,*                *Tuesday, April 18*
>
> *I have been too busy these last few days to write to you (the old alibi), but it is really true. Still no word from you, Kitty, that mail is sure taking a long time to catch up to us.*
>
> *At present, I'm stationed on the East Coast. Have been trying to get out on pass in order to call you. Unfortunately, I don't think I will have any chance to call as we leave tomorrow in the early morning.*

*How's the baby Kitty? I keep reading your last letters over and over every day. Your descriptions are swell.*

Frank never had the opportunity to leave camp or call Catherine or meet up with Aunt Mary, as he had hoped. Even worse, Catherine's letters did not get delivered. He had expected to talk to her before going overseas, where calling her would not be possible. The lump in his throat remained as he got ready for an indefinite time abroad.

During those precious last days in the states, Frank, along with thousands of other soldiers, queued up for medical exams and vaccinations against T.B., diphtheria, tetanus, hepatitis, and meningitis. The line snaked through the different stations where new uniforms, combat boots, and heavy overcoats were issued. Frank, like the other soldiers, was combat loaded with a rifle and handgun in the event of hostile seas or enemy take-over at the ports of entry.

That evening, Frank organized his duffle bag with khaki shirts and pants, officer dress uniform and jacket, and a soft dress cap, long underwear, army-issued underwear, and socks. He placed his toiletries, shoelaces, aluminum mess kit, a cup, and canteen, eating utensils, flashlight, and a gas mask in his rucksack. Clearing his desk, Frank grabbed his letters to post them and prayed for news from Catherine before leaving for war. His mood dampened not receiving any word from her that evening or the next morning at breakfast. He conjured images of her and the baby, tried to see them in the living room with her Dada playing the violin, and Sarah, her mother, wearing the same blue flowered apron, her hair piled high, fussing about the baby. He worried about his single sister-in-law Agnes and wondered when Peggy and Steve were getting married and what gift to give them. *Kitty, you'll have to get them a wedding present from us and get yourself that anniversary present. How is Agnes? Any new boys hanging around the house?* It was tormenting to think about home, so he went back to the business at hand.

The officers met after dinner to discuss the orders of deployment. Frank had fifteen subordinates to get aboard the ship, to assign cabins, and to go over the rules. Before turning the lights out, Frank and his buddies, Kuret, Carlson, and Hubbard, managed to fit in a hand of poker and smoke a few cigarettes. It seemed that was the only way to stop thinking about home.

Dawn broke over the Hudson River as the soldiers, in their olive-colored uniforms, steel helmets strapped under their chins, and a field pack and carbine swung across the shoulder, filed aboard. Frank stood at the gangplank in his officer uniform and accounted for each member of his platoon then boarded the *R.M.S. Queen Elizabeth.* The military commissioned her for the war and stripped the ship of her luxury fittings for transportation of troops, tanks, artillery, and other war supplies. Heads strained to look up at the behemoth hull painted a dull steel gray that blended with the sky and water, so as not to be easily detected by the German reconnaissance planes.

There was no fanfare at the docks. No farewell bands, no family, and no friends waved hankies, and not even the Red Cross girls were there to offer coffee and donuts. As the war intensified, a high level of security and secrecy surrounded the embarkation of troops and artillery to prevent sabotage en route.

The soldiers funneled past guards and through security checks before being assigned to their berths in the bowels of the ship, darkened by blackout windows with only faint lights on the floor leading the way down narrow halls. The solitary bell in the harbor clanked, the waves splashed against the hull, and voices echoed off the walls. It was a maze of hallways and stairwells, the soldiers' voices echoing, calling to each other when they found their assigned bunkrooms, ten to twelve in a room on canvas hammocks hanging from the ceiling to the floor. The men hoisted their bags and gear onto the beds, and the room filled with men vying for space. The once luxurious liner now carried twice as many soldiers than was planned for civilian passengers. There were over 15,000 troops jammed into the hallways and rooms, even the grand staterooms now had canvas hammocks hanging from ceiling to floor, and the emptied swimming pools held sleeping quarters.

Frank, like the other officers, shared the larger staterooms rather than the crowded quarters of the enlisted men. Two bunks lined along both walls and a common work area with a desk and chair for their official duties.

Once aboard, Captain Lyle Howell briefed his officers on the ship rules. The captain was in charge of 172 men, while Frank and the other officers each oversaw between fifteen and thirty enlisted men. They all had worked together in the 546th Anti-aircraft Artillery battalion since the early training days at Camp Young in the Desert Training Center. They were a reliable team: Captain Howell and First Lieutenants Hubbard, Carlson, Foster, and Second Lieutenant Kuret, along with several other officers.

Captain Howell began. "First, no one is to be on deck when we leave the harbor. All soldiers are to remain in their rooms. All the windows and portals are blacked out to prevent light from being seen outside. Once we're in the open sea, the men will be allowed on deck, but only at certain times of the day."

Every soldier received a colored-coded card to be carried or worn around his neck throughout the transit. The card restricted their movement to certain times of day and night and designated areas of the ship they could use, as well as their mealtimes.

"Be sure your men follow these rules. You're responsible for reporting all transgressions. Army rules apply while at sea. You're dismissed."

Frank thought about the young kid from Kansas, George Littlefoot, who hadn't returned to camp on the eve of debarkation and was put in confinement on the train across the states. Frank wrote A.W.O.L. (absence without leave) on the Morning Reports next to his name. Once in Camp Shanks, he escaped again in an attempt to get home, away from the army. In many ways, Frank understood his desire to quit, to be with his family. Once again, Littlefoot found himself in confinement on the ship.

The deckhands threw off the thick mooring lines onto the pier, and the ship eased out of her berth. Tugboats banged against the side bumpers jolting the soldiers back and forth in their bunks. The men down below joked and horsed around, like kids on the first night at summer camp, hiding their homesickness and fear. *The Queen Elizabeth* moved slowly down the Hudson River, past lower Manhattan and the Statue of Liberty, through the Verrazano Narrows, until she reached the open ocean. The engines fired up, and the stench of gas and oil seeped into the hull. Shouting and stomping could be heard overhead on the deck as the seaman pulled the ropes through cleats, tightened down the rescue boats, and pulled up the side bumpers. The great ship sounded her horn three times in deep sonorous blasts.

After leaving the harbor, the ship's captain opened a set of sealed orders that revealed the course, the speed, and the circuitous pattern to follow. As was practiced throughout the war, no one, not even the captain nor upper brass, knew the passage route before leaving shore. This practice prevented any leaks to the enemy over the wire, by word, or other transmissions of information.

*The Queen Elizabeth* could outrun enemy hazards, particularly the German U-boats, while crisscrossing through the Atlantic, never taking the same route. Once the ship left the harbor, she was on her own to navigate across The Pond.

H.M.S. Queen Elizabeth troop ship 1943

Frank climbed the metal stairs to the open deck and watched the skyline of New York fade in the distance. He never did get to visit the Empire State building nor the Statue of Liberty while in port as he had wished. He wistfully thought about Catherine's parents, who had entered the United States thirty years earlier, landing on Ellis Island. His grandparents had left England and Ireland for the United States in the late 1800s. It seemed strange to him that now he was going to the old country to defend the places his family had left.

The first evening had its share of confusion as the soldiers lined up for meals. The ballroom held rows of folding tables, enough places to serve over 2,500 at a time in three rotations for breakfast, and three rotations for dinner. The kitchen staff shouted and clanked pans and dishes as they made thousands of meals, cleaned up, and got ready for the next round throughout the day. Due to the numbers of soldiers, meals were only served twice a day, which concerned the young soldiers whose appetite clearly demanded three square meals. Each soldier was responsible for bringing his mess kit to every meal and cleaning his plate and utensils afterward. Cold cuts, bread, and condiments lined one wall for those who wanted to make sandwiches for a snack later. The canteen sold cokes, candy, and cigarettes. The only thing missing was the alcohol. The troopships were dry ships.

Frank passed the long line of enlisted men and entered the officers' mess hall in a smaller tourist class lounge that didn't necessitate queuing up for meals. The officers also brought their mess kits, ate the same food, and cleaned their plates and utensils. Bob Hope often made jokes about the officers and their perks, giving the enlisted men a few laughs at their superiors' expense. In the army, the officers had benefits and privileges, but also extra responsibilities. To maintain control, the officers had the authority to dole out punishment and prison time. But in the end, they were comrades in battle.

The days at sea consisted of early morning calisthenics, classes, and emergency drills for evacuation in case of fire, torpedo attack, or other casualties to the ship. Under the ship's Firing Director, both American and British anti-aircraft artillery (A.A.A.) units had the additional practice of manning and shooting the anti-aircraft guns mounted on the side of the warship. The practice shooting sharpened their skills and assured the equipment was in good working condition. Two privates loaded the gun, three swiveled the turret into position. The first lieutenant checked the crosshairs and set the bubble to hit the target dead center. He raised his hand and shouted, "Ready!" The crew backed away from the recoil of the barrel. "Fire!" The shells screamed across the sky, the noise deafening. The rat-a-tat of machine guns added to the cacophony with the bullets grazing the water and disappearing. The men cheered from the upper decks, as if at a rousing football game.

Throughout the day and into the evenings, lectures and classes covered topics such as military tactics, equipment, personal hygiene, and venereal diseases. For entertainment, the ship had a library of movies playing throughout the day, and the soldiers mingled in large rec rooms for conversation or table games.

Even though gambling was strictly forbidden, the officers overlooked poker games and craps. Frank walked past a bunkroom with guys hanging off their berths betting on the card players below, the telltale bets of cigarettes and coins piled in the middle of a makeshift table. He ignored them and continued down the hall to his own friendly poker game with the officers.

Somewhere in the middle of the Atlantic, five days after the *Queen Elizabeth* pushed away from the dock, mail was finally passed out. Frank received word from Kitty. He immediately wrote back even though he knew he couldn't send it until they were in port, and then it would be weeks before she would receive his letter:

> *Hello Darling,*                      *Sunday, April 23*
> *Received three letters from you today. They were put on board ship the day we sailed, and I didn't get them until we were well out to sea. It was as soothing as candy to a baby. Speaking of baby, he's one-month-old tomorrow. I wish I could have seen him just once more.*

It was a common soldier's lament, wanting just one more day, one more moment with their loved ones. The joy of letters, even old ones, kept the soldiers' morale up.

*I'll write at least one letter a day for the rest of this trip. When we dock, I will send one letter by regular airmail and one by V-mail, and you can let me know if there is any difference in the length of time they take to arrive. Love, Frank*

V-mail (Victory mail) was a letter written on a form, photographed onto film, and sent on microfiche overseas, thus reducing the cost of transporting the regular-sized letters across the ocean.

\* \* \*

Catherine received his V-mail. She borrowed her father's magnifying glass and read the tiny words on the small paper:

> *Hello Darling,*           *Monday, April 24*
>     *Another day down and many more miles between us. It doesn't seem possible we can be so far away from each other in so short a time. I'm starving for word from you. I keep conjuring up pictures of John, wondering if my pictures of him are true. I never realized that I could get so homesick. Have been doing an awful lot of sleeping, a little poker playing, and some work. Will write again tomorrow, Kitty, but there is very little we can discuss. I will save all the tall tales for our friends.*

Catherine was disappointed that Frank hadn't received her letters till in the middle of the ocean. She had written faithfully every day, sometimes twice, and so had her sisters before he left the desert. Her heart broke that he was homesick.

On John's first month birthday, Catherine dressed him in a white suit with a little bowtie and took him on the streetcar with her mother to Jose Reyes Studio in Hollywood. It was almost May when Catherine received the finished photos. She carefully wrapped a small portrait in a velvet pocket, slipped it into a cardboard sleeve, and brought it to the post office to be sealed and posted. Frank's address never changed, but his location did, and she never knew where he was.

\* \* \*

The majestic ship rose high on the waves and slid down the backside. Many of the men stayed in their cabins, puking and groaning, the stale air only making them feel worse. Those who braved the deck had to wear lifejackets and hitch themselves to the rail. Without warning, the ship lurched and rolled to the port side, sending books and letters skidding across the floors, then righted itself and continued in a new direction zigzagging to avoid detection.

Ten days after they had set sail from New York, the men on deck sighted islands dotting the horizon and what seemed to be birds flying in formation above the skyline. As the ship approached, it became apparent that those were not birds but planes heading towards them. The *Queen Elizabeth* had crossed the Atlantic without protection from the air and sea until the American bombers and Coastal Command aircraft escorted the ship from twelve miles off the coast of Scotland.

The War Department had kept the location of disembarkation a secret until the tugboats met the *Queen Elizabeth* and towed her into the harbor in Firth of Clyde, Scotland, on April 28.

A Royal Air Force aircraft circled the ship, as a salute to the American soldiers. As the men filed off the ocean liner, local officials welcomed them, and service members handed out ration packs to tide them over for their next leg of the journey. Tenders ferried them across the broad Clyde River to the small city of Gurock, where army trucks waited to take them to interim camps or to the troop trains that transported them from the north to south of England to more permanent posts.

Dressed in drab olive-green uniforms with their standard steel helmets low over their eyes, carbines over one shoulder, and stuffed duffle bags in hand, the soldiers walked down the docks and through the gates. Local citizens, who had been waiting since early morning, erupted in cheers, waving American flags and the Union Jack, throwing flowers and kisses. The long journey across the ocean had ended. A feeling of euphoria spread over the soldiers, proud to be an American soldier, and eager to win the war. Shoulders straight, boots in unison, they marched down the cobblestone street.

Frank's battalion remained in a temporary camp near Glasgow before transitioning to a more permanent location. In early spring 1944, Patton met his newly arrived officers and staff of the Third Army in Glasgow, Scotland. If he was unable to greet them personally, he sent them a letter.

> *"Welcome. You're here to fight. Ahead of you lies the battle. You cannot afford to be a fool, because, in battle, fools mean dead men. It's inevitable for men to be killed and wounded in action, but not because of the incompetence and carelessness of some stupid son-of-a-bitch.*
>
> *We're here because some crazy Germans decided they were supermen and had the right to rule the world, looting, killing, and abusing millions of innocent men and women, and children. They were ready to do the same thing to us. It takes guts and brains to win wars. We're going to lick those son-of-bitches in Europe. The Germans don't know I'm here, so keep it a goddam secret. That's all. Good luck."*

How could the Germans not know the whereabouts of the most famous or infamous general in the U.S. Army? Eisenhower, the

Supreme Commander of the Allied Forces, had given General George S. Patton Jr. the command of the Third Army in early January 1944 but kept it a secret from the Germans, the media, and the general public. As far as the enemy knew or even the press, Patton was greeting the First United States Army Group (F.U.S.A.G.) in Scotland, a fake army to deceive the Germans on Patton's next mission. *Operation Fortitude,* as the plan was named, was created to mislead the Germans into thinking Patton would strike the coast of Normandy at Pas de Calais with his fictitious army, F.U.S.A.G.. Churchill remarked, "In wartime, the truth should always be attended by a bodyguard of lies," hence the codename *Bodyguard* described the deception.

Frank was now officially part of Patton's Third Army, but not even Catherine would know for months, and the rest of the world was equally confused as to the whereabouts of Patton and what his mission was.

# CHAPTER FIVE

# Somewhere in England

A few days after landing in Scotland, Frank's battalion moved to temporary barracks that were drafty wooden structures near the port. The men lived in close quarters without the right to move freely. The soldiers unloaded boxes, checked their equipment, tagged and marked every piece, then checked and double-checked the inventory. Daily drills and training continued while they tended to their weapons, unpacking the ammunition, guns, gun mounts, trucks, tanks, and other machinery all packed in grease that had sealed them for the journey.

The first night after dinner, the men stampeded to the mail depot. The mail had finally caught up with them. The postmaster called out the names, and each soldier ran forward, took his mail, and retreated to a quiet area to read in private. The news from home wasn't always pleasant: a death in the family, jilted by a girlfriend, left by a wife. But the worst was no mail at all. *A soldier could march for three or four days without food on the strength of one letter from home*, a soldier wrote in his diary. Frank flipped through a bundle of letters passing over one from Mrs. McGuire, another from Father McGuire, and a pink envelope from his sister-in-law that put a smile on his face. When he got to Catherine's letters, he tore them open and read them as he walked back to the barracks. He wrote back to Catherine that evening, knowing none of his letters had reached her since they left New York, and she would worry.

*Hello Darling,*                *Friday, 4-28-44*

    *I missed writing to you yesterday, but I'll try to do better in the future. I'm sending this by V-mail to see if it's faster than airmail. We arrived safely yesterday after a very pleasant trip, and at the present stationed "somewhere" in England. The letter you wrote on the 19th arrived yesterday, that gives us eight-day service, which is pretty darn good.*

The next letter from Catherine landed as if a bomb had dropped. She had moved, so Frank thought. He quickly replied.

*Dear Darling,*               *Friday, April 28*

    *I received your letter telling me about going to Ontario, California. It left me in a fog. I wish you would tell me more about it. Do you intend to find an apartment there and live alone? That would be kind of rough Kitty. It would be swell if you were with someone, but alone it is not good.*

    *Well, good night, darling. Keep up the ole chin.*

With mail coming irregularly, he couldn't ascertain if Catherine had to leave home, if the baby was well, or if something happened to Catherine's mother who had been ill. Five days after the ship had docked, another letter from Catherine arrived. The situation had changed. Catherine had gone to visit her older sister Mary. It was a respite for the two sisters to have each other to confide in. Both were concerned about their mother's illness that kept her bed-ridden at times and often more of a burden than help for Catherine. They talked about raising children, changed diapers together, fed the children, and kept each other company. Horace, her brother-in-law, worked in his gas station during the day and volunteered for the war effort as a fireman at night, so Catherine was a help to Mary as well. Frank sighed a sigh of relief and wished he were home to help raise his child.

Top left to right: Peggy, Mary, Sarah (Mama) with Terence, Thaddeus (Dada) with Shereen: Bottom: Agnes, Horace with Nola, Catherine, and Frank

The next day the men were given time to take care of business on the British base but were sequestered from civilians.

*Hello Darling,*                                        *Saturday, April 29*
*I just finished changing money into British money. The monetary system seemed complicated at first but have gotten it straightened out now. Have spent only 20 cents (or shilling) since I've been in England, at that rate I won't need any money here! We are all restricted to our area, but I hope to start getting passes soon. I have yet to go into an English pub to try out their beer, but soon.*

*The weather is very much like our California winters, but cooler and invigorating. Problem is there are no heaters in our building, and in order to keep*

*warm we wear our heavy clothing. Now I understand*
*why the English are into tweeds and woolens!*

 *It is now 9 o'clock in the evening, and the sun*
*is still up! It doesn't get dark till 10:30 — Goodnight,*
*darling. I'll see you in my dreams.*

During the war, the number of daylight hours was a game-changer. The Allies could now bomb longer into the evening, which meant Frank and his team worked longer shifts operating their guns. The U.S. Army Air Force bombed only in the daylight and in good weather, which was statistically more effective and less dangerous than night air raids that the Germans preferred. Patton's anti-aircraft artillery battalions worked in conjunction with the U.S. IX Army Tactical Air Command (T.A.C.), now stationed next to the Royal Air Force base tucked in the center of England, away from the ports. All activity was shrouded in secrecy. No one knew for sure when the "big day" would arrive, the invasion of Europe.

The German Blitz became more of a nighttime bombing campaign. The psychological effect of night bombings riveted the English people to their radios, attentive to the air raid sirens, ready to seek safety in basements at all hours. The Germans had already bombed London and other cities, killing tens of thousands of civilians, even though the Nazis had denied intentionally attacking civilians.

It had been less than twenty-four hours since the 546th troops landed in Great Britain. Frank's unit had spent fifteen months in the desert, training in the dry heat. Now, they were billeted in cold, damp barracks, bundled in all their clothes, trying to stay warm in the wet English weather.

In the morning, the men went through their daily routines, reveille, cleaning barracks, drills, and three meals a day. *No change* reported. The men didn't get passes into town, and their boredom created problems, fights broke out, disputes over personal space, complaints of the rotting smell of unwashed clothes, and bad food. The coughing and snoring in the unheated sleeping quarters made for a terrible night's sleep, not to mention the difficulty with the change in time zones. It was military purgatory waiting for orders from the Commanding General to move on to a more permanent station.

On May 2, the 564th battalion moved to Staffordshire in central England. Staffordshire was the staging area before shipping out to the continent, as well as the place where the wounded came in from the front for rehabilitation and medical care. Prisoners of war stayed in separate guarded barracks for questioning.

As First Lieutenant, Frank's duties included reconnaissance, additional classes, and advanced training, which took him out of the confines of the base. To fulfill his duties, Frank had a driver and a jeep at his disposal throughout the war.

> *Dear Kitty,*                    *Tuesday, May 2*
> *I was out to visit an old castle today. It is sup-*
> *posed to be a thousand years old and it sure looked it,*
> *but the grounds around it are really beautiful. The cas-*
> *tle is built on a hill and commands a view of the whole*
> *area. I would enjoy visiting this area under more favor-*
> *able conditions.*
> *We are still allowed no passes, but I have lined up*
> *some U.S.O. Shows and a movie for tomorrow, which*
> *helps the situation some.*

Idle men only led to more drinking and gambling, so the officers kept the enlisted men busy when not on duty. Luckily, the men were eager to see the shows or watch an American movie. Big names, like Bing Crosby, Mickey Rooney, Judy Garland, andMarlene Dietrich

entertained throughout the war as well as roughly 7,000 other perform-
ers who brought a little bit of home and comfort to the men overseas.

> *Dear Kitty and John,*          *Wednesday, May 3*
> *We had the U.S.O. Show today and it was
> the best I have seen to date! We're going to work up a
> dance too for the boys. A few of the officers and I had a
> walk-about in town and the people are cooperative and
> friendly about the dance. It seems we are in a position
> to sell tickets to the girls instead of to the boys. That is
> an unusual situation. Tell Peggy, she would have to do a
> little more work here to get her man on this side of the
> ocean. But that job is evidently over with now that she's
> with Steve. I hope we're able to let our men out on pass
> very soon or they'll be singing the prisoners' song.*

Once passes were issued, the American soldiers flooded into
town, filling the void of men left by those who had gone to war. Some
G.I.s behaved poorly, but for the most part, they were gentlemen. The
M.P.s patrolled the city, and if they caught misbehaving soldiers, they
put them in confinement.

As with the other men, letters from home were like an umbilical
cord. Frank needed the sustenance of knowing his small family was
doing well, surviving and thriving, as he approached the unknown.
Letters wound their way through an unsteady postal system.

> *Dear Kitty and John,*          *Saturday, May 6*
> *Funny this writing to two people instead of one. I
> wish that little stranger could talk back. I can't wait to
> hear him laugh, maybe even cry a little. Kitty, I wonder
> where your letters are wandering. You can't imagine how
> much a letter from home means now. I have been writing*

*every day, you ought to get a steady stream now, except I addressed them to Ontario, and now you are back with your parents.*

*We were paid yesterday. If I have any money left over at the end of the month, I will buy bonds and send them home. If things continue at the present rate it will be a good sum. Please send photos. Goodnight Darling.*

*PS I'm hoping to hear from George, still haven't had a word from him in two months*

The headlines and news clips provided Catherine with information about the war, but if Frank's letters didn't arrive daily, she worried that something had happened to him. The newspapers back home shouted in bold letters on front pages, **50 LOST IN LONDON ATTACK; ARMY SAYS ALARM IS REAL; AIR WAR RAGES OVER BRITAIN.** Only his letters could reassure her.

Throughout the war, Frank wrote to his estranged brother George who left to fight in Africa and Italy. With no word from George since he shipped overseas six months earlier, Frank could only guess if he were alive or dead, or even somewhere nearby in Europe. Grasping and longing for news of loved ones only got worse as the war progressed.

*Darling Kitty,*                              *Friday, May 5*

*Could you please send a subscription to the Los Angeles Times? I'm not sure they will be permitted, but the English papers don't cover anything about home, or how Americans see the war.*

*You look a little thin, Darling. How much do you weigh? The photos are swell, but you didn't show enough of the baby.*

Photos of Catherine and the baby laid on the corner of Frank's desk along with her letters. He propped up his favorite pictures on his desk and went back to work. During the next couple of weeks, Frank traveled to ports and towns across England. He took advanced training, familiarizing him with methods used by the Allies, coordinating with other troops during battle, and communicating with the air force.

Frank traveled fifty miles north for a briefing on the war. Of course, he could not tell Catherine restricted information so, he made it sound like touring.

> *My Darlings,*                              *Sunday, May 7*
> *I miss hearing from you and looking forward to a letter when I get back to the barracks tonight. I took a trip this morning and saw some of the results of the Battle of Britain at Birmingham. Also saw some German bug bombs on exhibit in the main part of town. I would sure like to get a pass into London and look around, maybe soon. I thought we would get away from the rules and restrictions, but it's worse here than in the states. Can't leave our post without a blouse on (U.S. issue uniform coat) etc. etc. Well, goodnight. I miss you darling.*

Birmingham and London had borne the brunt of the Luftwaffe bombing campaign between July 10, 1940, and October 1940, the Battle of Britain. The Germans had attempted to disable Birmingham's manufacturing of tanks and weaponry to bring England to its knees after the surrender of France on June 22, 1940. The British Royal Airforce claimed victory over the skies of England at the end of the battle. Still, the Blitzkriegs continued till April 1943, sending the "Brummies" (citizens of Birmingham) into shelters nearly daily.

Frank saw the immense destruction of factories, churches, halls and cinemas, civic buildings, and thousands of properties and homes.

The German "buzz bomb," also known as a "doodlebug," on display in front of a small war museum, had hit the town months earlier. Frank's aversion to the long sleek body of the doodlebug was akin to coming across a rattler in the desert. The British had an advantage with a sophisticated radar system that could detect the German bombers coming in. Still, the Luftwaffe kept bombing the citizens, using tactics that violated the Geneva Convention.

The prescient words of Winston Churchill posted at the entrance to the war museum was written before the Battle of Britain yet punctuated the duty that lay ahead:

> *The whole fury and might of the enemy must very soon be turned on us. Hitler knows that he will have to break us in this island or lose the war. If we can stand up to him, all Europe may be free, and the life of the world may move forward into broad, sunlit uplands. But if we fail, then the whole world, including the United States, including all that we have known and cared for, will sink into the abyss of a new Dark Age made more sinister, and perhaps more protracted, by the lights of a perverted science. Let us, therefore, brace ourselves to our duties, and men will still say, this was their finest hour."*

# CHAPTER SIX

# The Countryside

*Hello Darling,*               *Thursday, May 11*

> *Traveled over 120 miles today on these narrow English roads, and that's a lot of miles! I have been lost so many times. Just because an English road starts in the direction of north doesn't mean that it isn't going south, or for that matter, if it's going anywhere at all. I found a place to have fried eggs, a real treat, the first I've had since we landed. To look out the window here, you would never dream there was a war going on within a million miles. People strolling in the streets, soldiers courting the young misses, people playing tennis, it's an idyllic scene, but the war is still on they tell me.*
>
> *John will be two months old by the time you receive this. Maybe his daddy will be home to bounce him on his knee, along about Christmas time. It's a swell idea to have a little sister for him. That is going to be a day, Kitty. I'm living in my daydreams.*

Of course, it was daydreaming, or wishful thinking, that Frank would be home for Christmas, but at the time, there was hope. The United States had entered the war two years earlier, and the Allies had begun to gain on the Nazis having U.S. tanks, guns, ammunition, airplanes, and an almost infinite supply of workforce. In 1943 Bing

Crosby crooned, "I'll Be Home for Christmas," a song written to honor the soldiers who longed to be home at Christmas time. Propaganda in the U.S. touted the Allies wins and promoted patriotism, alongside the gruesome reality. Families back home needed to hear some good news, not just the number of casualties. That sunny day and country roads made daydreaming almost real.

As for the confusing roads, it may have been partly due to the rural layout, but something else was afoot. When England entered the war, and the invasion of the Germans by air and sea was an imminent threat, the road signs were either switched or taken down.

The weather stayed clear over the next few days, and the soldiers' spirits were high now they could wander into town, visit the pubs, talk to the ladies, and the older folk still left in town. The beer was expensive, the bars crowded, and Frank found himself window shopping. He had promised Catherine lace and perfume. Frank wandered the streets in his uniform, stopping in at a small lace shop, his hands touching the delicate edges of a doily. The matronly storekeeper put down her needle and asked, "Do you need help choosing something pretty for your girl back home?" She was used to these men with the faraway look in their eyes, tall men with rough hands, fighting men sneaking past the raucous pubs to take a moment to be in the presence of feminine softness. Different patterns of lace cloth hung on the wall behind the counter, reminding Frank of the Irish lace tablecloth in Catherine's home.

"No, thank you, Ma'am. I'm just looking." Frank left, put his hand in his pocket, and grabbed a roll of bills, flipping through them, he thought better of spending too much on lace.

Down the road, he ran into some of his officer friends who invited him to have a beer with them. Kuret, Captain Howell, and Frank's roommate, Hubbard shared a few good stories around the wooden benched table in the dim light of the seventeenth-century pub with its stained-glass windows, low ceiling beams, and a fireplace in the corner, the smoldering wood competing with the pipe, cigar, and cigarette smoke.

Frank pulled out a photo of John, his big ears dominating a thin face, a funny picture he lovingly referred to as Lil' Dopey.

Hubbard chuckled. "He looks just like you! You must be Big Dopey!"

The next photo was of Catherine with the baby in her arms at his Baptism, the classic Madonna and son. "This is where he looks like me!" The men were looking at Catherine's portrait, her innocent loveliness apparent. "Your wife is a beauty. You can tell by her eyes what a good girl she is."

The rest of the men took out their photos. Kuret had his wedding photo and a cute picture of his wife in her apron, holding a wooden spoon like she was about to hit Kuret. "My wife was waving that spoon telling me I better come back home. It was our last dinner together with her family before I shipped out."

Grinning, Captain Howell said, "I asked my wife to send me a pin-up of herself. I thought it would be funny." He took out the photo his wife sent. It was an old photo of her in a bathing suit, only from behind. "I snuck up behind her at the beach one day and snapped this photo. She was so mad, but she got the last laugh now!"

The men roared. "Better pin that one on the wall."

Frank wrote to Catherine that evening, having missed a few days of letters from her.

> *Darling Kitty,*          *Monday, May 15*
> *Miss you, Darling, especially tonight. I guess it's*
> *just the case of the blues. No letter for three days-I do miss*
> *my dessert. The mailman has been coming after dinner,*

*so all the guys call their letters from home dessert. I'm still rooming with "Hub" who is as crazy as ever! Have you written to his wife, Iris? Or to Mrs. Howell or Mrs. Kuret yet? We're still pretty much the same old crew. I hope we can all stay together for the rest of this show. There's little news to tell you, and if there were, I wouldn't be able to tell you anyway.*

*We're having another class this evening, getting mighty darn sick of these extra hour night classes. It would not be bad if we gained something in knowledge or experience from them, but no, a silly waste of good time.*

The weather turned cold again, and the dampness settled in the soldiers' lungs. Pneumonia and bronchitis spread through the barracks. Captain Lyell spent a few days in the hospital suffering from a lung disorder. Luckily, Frank reported having gotten over his cold.

A few days before departure to a more permanent base, the officers had a stag party at a typical English club.

*Hello Darling,*                    Wednesday, *May 17*
*I really enjoyed the party tonight. It was held at an expensive Bowling Club. We had a tournament of bowling played on the lawn and it was a lot of fun. In between games we went into the clubhouse and drank a few beers and sang a few songs. Honey, don't miss any day of writing to me, cause your letters have to fill a large gap. I miss you Kitty and it's going to be hard to keep missing you.*

By May 20, the captain, lieutenants, and enlisted men were ready to roll. The 546th battalion shipped out via trucks and train to Cottesmore, Rutland.

# CHAPTER SEVEN

# Restricted

At the train station in Staffordshire, the enlisted men crowded into the boxcars, sitting on their duffle bags, some hanging out the doors. The U.S. Quartermaster drivers operated the trucks carrying the weapons and supplies, forming a convoy heading southeast. Only the drivers knew where they were going. The fewer people who knew and the less they knew, the less likely information would leak to the German spies, or over the airwaves, or intercepted through the mail. From now till the end of the war, all Company Morning Reports and official communications were labeled *Restricted*.

Frank, Captain Howell, Hubbard, Carlson, and Kuret drove in open jeeps alongside the convoy. All of them were armed. The military convoy drove seventy miles along the winding country roads, passing through villages with bombed-out church steeples and weapon factories laid in ruin among the rubble.

The 546th arrived at the Royal Air Force Station in Cottesmore, Rutland, once used as a training airfield. But as the war intensified and the Luftwaffe attacks continued in the south of England, the R.A.F. became operational. They first dropped propaganda pamphlets in occupied France to encourage the French to defend their country. After 1940, the R.A.F. became active in direct combat with the Germans. The United States Army Air Forces took over the facilities in 1943 for flying troop transport aircraft and delivering Horsa gliders for storage in anticipation of the future use by airborne forces to carry soldiers and supplies to the Continent.

The barracks at Cottesmore proved to be a haven for the men, much better than before, and from Frank's letters seemed a bit like a country club.

*Hello Darling,*                      *Wednesday, May 24,*

> *I've been gone almost two months since I saw our little boy that morning in the hospital. I'll bet he's a lot of work. I'll be home soon to help.*
>
> *I haven't got a pass yet, but with the facilities here, I don't think I'll care to. We played baseball this evening, so I'm a little pooped out. If we keep up at the rate we are going, I will be getting back in shape, what with walking all day and baseball and badminton in the evening. I'm still eating like a horse and putting on some weight. I'm enjoying the life over here, plenty to eat, sleep, and exercise, the only thing missing is you. The old bromide is true; absence makes the heart grow fonder.*

Frank's letters were beginning to sound like summer camp.

> *I'm a bit weak from laughter, have been watching Hubbard cut Kuret's hair, he really did a job. I finished it by doing the trimming and shaving. Poor Kuret, his wife would never recognize him now.*

The men bantered back and forth, pulled practical jokes on each other, gave out nicknames, and used code words and acronyms for everyday events — the sound of the anti-aircraft guns firing designated the A.A.A. men as *Ack-Ack gunners.* The endless chores around the barracks and in the kitchen were *chicken shit* or C.S. in polite company.

When orders went awry, F.U.B.A.R. was slashed across the paper, indicating *Fowled (or fucked) Up Beyond All Recognition.*

Hubbard snipped the wavy black hair, and when Kuret caught a glimpse of his haircut in the mirror, he howled. Frank and Hub knew they'd have to watch their backs, or Kuret would get them back. But for now, Kuret was *S.O.L., shit out of luck.*

Back on duty, Frank checked the skies with his binoculars. The Dakotas and C-47's were returning from practicing lift offs and landings while towing the Horsa gliders. With skill and accuracy, Frank took a reading so that the four guns in his battery would be aligned and shoot parallel with each other. He positioned the 155mm howitzers towards the sky in the event an enemy plane followed the planes back in. His orders had to be precise, and the soldiers ready to load their guns even though the landings were usually uneventful. No enemy planes strafed the airfield, which was now heavily fortified with bombers, anti-aircraft artillery, and infantrymen. The "Ack-Ack gunners" were some of the most highly skilled personnel in the U.S. Army, and the army depended on them to clear the skies of enemy planes. They honed their skills daily, so in the event of a strike, they would be ready.

Days became a pattern of getting household chores done, drills and fitness exercise, entertainment to keep the boys occupied, playing a few ball games, and writing home. P.X. Rations came weekly, another diversion from the *No Change* Frank wrote on the Morning Reports.

*Darling,*         *Saturday, May 27*

 *Tonite, we were allotted 7 packs of cigarettes, 3 bars of candy, a couple razor blades, a bar of soap, two packs of cookies, some mints. We can buy toothbrushes and creams and shaving stuff and sundries on the side. So, you see, we get about all the essentials, except writing paper. I wish you'd keep sending some. Still waiting*

*for the L.A. Times, did you get the subscription? I can't*
*believe what we hear over here.*

The lack of information and mixed messages kept the soldiers on their toes. The news from the frontline was top secret until the B.B.C. or Algeciras got ahold of it, and then it was often misleading. The units didn't know when they were going to the Continent. They just had to be ready. The generals and commanders spent hours and days in the war room, creating elaborate ruses and secret plans leading up to D-Day. The soldiers were not privy to this information; they only knew what their battalions needed to know.

One officer showed up in camp with a radio, and the men crowded around to hear the news and hoping for some entertainment. The reception was pretty sad on the whole because both sides were jamming programs. Music started playing, coming in swell then all of a sudden in comes the jam, a long monotonous overtone. After toying with the radio, they picked up some American music and listened to Bing Crosby, Dick Todd, and a few others.

*Everyone is walking around humming the songs*
*we picked up. We also picked up some German propa-*
*ganda news. It was really good. Some of the boys heard*
*Lord Haw Haw.*

"Germany is calling, Germany calling," Lord Haw Haw, a.k.a. William Joyce, spoke over the radio waves in his melodious voice, broadcasting Nazi propaganda across the U.K., jamming other programs and spreading lies and insults. Joyce, an American born of Irish immigrants, moved back to Ireland as a teenager later crossed the channel to England, then moved to Germany and became a naturalized German citizen. He knew both cultures and how to demoralize the British and American soldiers. At first, the British viewed his program as a joke, and the electrifying fabricated news was a welcome diversion from B.B.C.'s dreary options of organ music and sedate broadcasts. But as the war escalated, the citizens found his misinformation alarming. Many thought Lord Haw Haw had inside information about where and when the bombings would strike, thus causing uncertainty and anguish, leading to false preparation with citizens running to bomb shelters, and gun crews becoming jittery. Frank said Lord Haw Haw only infuriated his men, giving them more reason to finish off the Nazis. The U.S. soldiers weren't buying his lies.

After Joyce enjoyed his moment of fame and affluence in Germany during the war, he was hung in London on January 3, 1946, for betraying England.

The build-up of troops in England created a buzz around Cottesmore, suggesting that the invasion of the Continent was imminent. The Supreme Commander of the Allies Eisenhower and the British General Montgomery had started strategizing "Operation Overlord," the invasion of Normandy, in late November 1943. By early June 1944, the soldiers' nerves were raw with anticipation. At times, they felt the army brass was crying wolf.

Even Patton didn't know the exact timing of the Normandy invasion. His orders were to put together his Third Army and join the Allied Forces after the invasion. As a foil to deceive Hitler, Patton continued to act as Commander of a fictitious army, F.U.S.A.G., the First United States Army Group. German spies sent the false reports to Hitler that Patton would lead the invasion, and the most likely, the attack would be Pas-de-Calais, the northeast coast of Normandy.

In the spring of 1944, Patton secretly visited the U.S. troops in Northern Ireland. Frank flew over to Northern Ireland in late May, to meet with the Third Army's anti-aircraft men at the airbase. *I had a* chance to fly over to Ireland yesterday but unfortunately could not get away to see more of the country.

His mother and Catherine's parents came over on the boat, as the Irish liked to say. *John's three-quarters Irish,* Frank bragged to the other officers, *and I'm half Irish.*

In the short time since Frank landed in Great Britain, he had toured on military assignments to Ireland, Scotland, and England, writing home about the countryside, the farmers who raised dairy cows, and the ancient towers and churches which he found new and pleasant to witness. *I wish we could see the countryside together, Kitty, of course under a better situation.*

Frank's relatives lived in England, but he had no way to contact them, no addresses, just their names that his estranged sister, Harriet, had sent in an unsatisfying letter.

> *Hello again Kitty,*               *Saturday, May 27*
>         *I wrote this morning but had a chance to write again. Tonite I had a letter from my sister, she has been hearing regularly from George. I can't understand why I don't hear from him. In regard to looking up the Gilberts, I would if I had their addresses and if I could get off for more than a few hours. Harriet gave me the names of a few more relatives, but she also neglected to tell me where they live. It would be interesting to see these people. It would probably give me a good idea of what I would be doing and where I'd be living if my grandmother had not struck out for the good old U.S.A. Thank God she did.*

After the family was separated, the siblings had not developed strong ties with each other. Still, Frank couldn't figure out why their brother George kept in touch with Harriet yet never bothered to write him. Both of them were fighting in the E.T.O., George in North Africa and Italy, Frank in England and soon France.

*Kitty, two days of warmth and sunshine in all of this previous damp, seems unbelievable. Everyone is out enjoying the freedom and freshness of the country, walking, riding bicycles, hitchhiking. There is one thing I will always remember England for, and that is its beautiful countryside, perfectly orderly, and always clean and above all no billboards.*

*If only I would be stationed permanently in England, then I would get a bicycle. a far more rational way to get around, especially in the crowded cities, and think how much gas a country could save. And it would be good exercise!*

One evening in late May, when the sunlight bounced off the distant hills, Frank walked over to the vacant field to join a baseball game with the boys, the young enlisted men, full of testosterone and pent up energy. Frank took the batter's box and swung, sending the ball into the left-field and ran like a son-of-a-bitch until he collided with the first baseman. Something twisted and sprung in his foot. He couldn't get up. With help, he limped off the field.

The next day he made light of the injury, telling Catherine, *I'm chair bound for a couple of days. I pulled a ligament in my foot yesterday and can't do any walking around. Don't amount to nothing. I spent the last three hours censoring mail and have just five minutes to write you.*

Frank had broken his foot. The doctors put on a heavy plaster cast and kept him in the hospital. He didn't tell Catherine, only lamented he didn't get his pass to go to London. *It will be a long time before I get another chance to go to London. Actually, I'm better off staying on the Post than going to town. There is little or no food in the cafes, and the shows are already overcrowded.*

Life was bleak for the citizens during the raids and war. With the able men sent to war, women had to work in the factories and run the businesses. For safety, they sent their children to the countryside to avoid the air raids. By war's end, the relentless Blitzkrieg had killed over 30,000 Londoners.

As the days pushed nearer to the invasion, Frank's letters became folksier, with no mention of the military, just weather and small talk, which he had always said he was no good at. The contrast of what was happening in Europe and what he wrote home was like night and day. Either Frank followed the military rules of secrecy so that no German or wife had any idea what was about to happen, or he didn't know anything about the imminent invasion. Worried that he may have crossed the line, he wrote to Catherine.

*Dearest Kitty and John,*         *Friday, June 2*

*Has anything been blacked out in my letters? As First Lieutenant, I censor my own letters, but at times the base censor goes over them.*

*The mailman came and brought your letters of the 23rd and an American magazine from December 4, which means it must have traveled several times around the world in six months' transit! I can't think of anything I need but you, and I'm afraid you wouldn't fit in a shoebox.*

*P.S. They're playing our song on the radio "No love, No Nothing." How true.*

Radio brought the outside world into camp connecting Frank and Catherine with songs they both knew and could relate too. "No love, no nothing until my baby comes home, no sir, nothing as long as my baby may roam," crooned Marlene Dietrich. The song played over and over in Frank's head.

Soldiers were coming back from the war in North Africa and Sicily, Italy, and filled the Cottesmore base, bringing back stories of victory and personal tales of loss. *What stories they can tell! I'd like to hear from George, not a word in two months. It's possible he may be sent here or even back to the States since he has put in twenty months.*

Frank searched the faces of the returning soldiers, hoping to find George. It had happened that one soldier who was living on the base found out his brother was two barracks away! If only that would happen, and George was nearby.

On June 4, the hospital released Frank after he had spent the last week in bed due to his broken foot. Frank hobbled down the hallway and headed back to the base to report back to duty. Captain Howell briefed him.

"Good to have you back, Frank. The boys need you out there. More flight activity going on now."

"Yes, sir, been bored just lying in bed with this darn foot. Any more news?" Captain avoided the word invasion. All military communication was in writing, then destroyed.

Captain Howell made small talk then handed him an envelope. "Hubbard has the rest you need to know."

Frank turned to go when Howell added, "By the way, Frank, I told my wife you'd been laid up in the hospital for a week now."

"Well, Captain, I didn't tell Catherine, didn't want to worry her. It's just a broken foot. Didn't want to make a mountain out of a molehill."

"Yeah, and it happened while playing ball. That doesn't sound too heroic either, no purple heart."

Frank grinned. "Nah, that's nothing. I met a paratrooper in the hospital who had come through the Italian Campaign without getting hurt, and the first week in England, he broke his leg at a dance!"

They both got a laugh out of that.

"Guess I better fess up and tell Catherine. Don't want her hearing it from somebody else."

> *Hello Darling, Sunday,*             *Sunday, June 4*
> *It's raining again in Merry Old England. Feels like it might turn to snow any minute, I wanted to let you know, I actually broke my foot last Sunday, so I spent the week in the hospital. My foot will be in a cast for the next five weeks. Anyway, I'm back on the job now with my leg full of plaster.*

At 1600 on June 4, Frank returned to duty. The anti-aircraft guns pointed to the skies, positioned to protect the U.S. aircraft that hauled the paratroopers over the channel in preparation for the invasion. Frank scanned the skies in the hazy light and noticed dark clouds to the west.

# CHAPTER EIGHT

# Patton's Speech to the Third Army

On Monday, June 5, the soldiers of the Third Army assembled en masse, dressed sharply in clean uniforms and polished boots. The side of the hill filled with U.S. Army soldiers, some standing, others were sitting on their helmets, or crouching on their knees, waiting in anticipation. The officers were seated up front in rows of folding chairs. At the back, Captain Howell stood up with the other top brass, something big was about to happen.

General Patton

At 1300 hours, a klaxon blared in the distance announcing the arrival of a jeep with three stars in the front. An undertone of comments passed like a wave through the crowd as the vehicle came to an abrupt stop. A tall, well-built man rose from the passenger seat, climbed on the running board, and surveyed the men. He had a bulldog look under his highly polished three-starred helmet beaded with rain drop-lets. Stepping down, he slammed the door and strode to the stage, MPs and special forces lining the way. At six-feet-two-inches tall, he demanded attention. He wore a fitted coat decorated with badges and medals, khaki riding pants, and high cavalry boots, and carried an ivo-ry-handled Smith & Wesson Magnum in his studded holster. Frank recognized him immediately. Every soldier stood up to attention and saluted the general.

In return, he saluted precisely and asked, "Any of you people know who I am?" No one spoke. Either the new soldiers didn't know who he was or wouldn't say, intimidated by his stature. "I'm General George S. Patton, and all of you sons-of-bitches are working for me now." There was a hush. He was about to speak to his newly formed Third Army, a group of inexperienced young men who were about to go into battle.

"Be seated." Looking directly into the eyes of one soldier, he nodded, then scanned the crowds of helmeted soldiers. "Men, this stuff that some sources sling around about America wanting out of this war, not wanting to fight, is a crock of bullshit."

Frank straightened his shoulders. Old Blood 'N Guts hadn't changed much since the Desert Training Center, maybe just a little tougher after whipping those Nazis in North Africa and Sicily.

"Traditionally, Americans love to fight, love the clash of battle." The soldiers bumped each other's shoulders and socked the guy next to them in approval of what this man was saying.

He paused and raised his voice, building a crescendo. "Americans love a winner. Americans will not tolerate a loser. Americans despise cowards. The very idea of losing is hateful to Americans. Battle is the most significant competition in which a man can indulge. It brings out all that is best." Patton smiled, his half-smile as if containing his enthusiasm.

The men hooted as if their team had scored a touchdown.

Patton grew serious, almost fatherly. "You are not all going to die. Only two percent of you right here today would die in a major battle. Death must not be feared." He let his words sink in deep. The thought of one's death and the tragedy to one's own family sobered the soldiers, and their heads bowed, not wanting to look at one another.

"But a real man will never let his fear of death overpower his honor, his sense of duty to his country, and his innate manhood." His voice rose an octave as he shouted, "Remember that the enemy is just as frightened as you are, and probably more so."

His body dominated the arena as he paced and looked directly at the officers. "All through your Army careers, you men have bitched about what you call 'chicken shit drilling.' That, like everything else in this Army, has a definite purpose. That purpose is alertness. Alertness must be bred into every soldier. I don't give a fuck for a man who's not always on his toes."

Frank wasn't one to complain, but he didn't like unwarranted criticism either and had grumbled to Catherine, *had an inspection this morning, and it seemed everything was wrong, so we had our ears properly knocked down. If they keep that up, I'll put in for a 'yard bird' rating and like it.* And he said a few other negative things about the night classes, *wouldn't be so bad if we learned something,* and he had to admit he criticized the drills, and boredom of repetition of maneuvers. Now, his commander had laid it on the line, no more bellyaching.

Patton looked over his new Army of clean-shaven faces, young men probably pissing in their pants and praying every night to go home. "An Army is a team. It lives, sleeps, eats, and fights as a team. Each man must not think only of himself, but also of his buddy fighting beside him. This individual heroic stuff is pure horse shit. We have the finest food, the finest equipment, the best spirit, and the best men in the world. Why, by God, I actually pity those poor sons-of-bitches we're going up against."

The crowd roared, tossed their helmets, and pumped their fists in the air. Patton felt their new energy, a corner of his mouth turned up, pleased he was winning them over.

"Every single man in the Army plays a vital role. Don't ever let up. Don't ever think your job is unimportant. What if the truck driver decided that he didn't like the whine of the shells and turned yellow and jumped headlong into a ditch?" Heads nodded.

"The quartermaster is needed to bring up the food and clothes for us because where we're going, there isn't a hell of a lot to steal. Every last damn man is important…even the one who boils the water to keep us from getting the GI shits."

The men shouted approval, loving the profanity and the honest, straightforward delivery.

"We'll win this war, but we'll win it only by fighting and keep moving, showing the Germans that we've got more guts."

He stood silent and lowered the tenor of his voice. "War is a bloody business, a killing business. The Nazis are the enemy. Spill their blood, or they will spill yours." His voice bellowed, "Shoot them in the guts. Rip open their bellies. I don't want any messages saying, 'I'm holding my position.' Our plan is to keep advancing."

Patton promised to kill any yellow cowards under his command like the rats they were, rather than to send them home to breed more cowards. He softened for a moment. "Sure, we want to go home. We want this war over with. The quickest way to get it over with is to go get the bastards who started it."

The men chanted, "Hooah! Hooah!" They heard him, they understood, and they agreed.

The Lieutenant General, the Major General, and the Corps General stood up and clapped in support of Patton. With the timing of a professional, Patton waited until the audience sat back down and fell silent. "Don't forget, you men don't know that I'm here. No mention of that fact is to be made in any letters. The world is not supposed to know what the hell happened to me. I'm not supposed to be commanding this Army. I'm not even supposed to be here in England. Let the first bastards to find out be the goddamned Germans. Someday I want to see them raise their piss-soaked hind legs and howl, 'Jesus Christ, it's the Goddamned Third Army again and that son-of-a-fucking-bitch Patton.'"

The silence broke with an eruption of laughter and hoots. Patton's voice bellowed over the microphone, echoing across the hills, "We want to get the hell over there! We're not going to just shoot the sons-of-bitches, we're going to rip out their living goddamned guts and use them to grease the treads of our tanks. We're going to murder those lousy Huns by the bushel-fucking-basket. Someday, maybe twenty years from now, you'll be able to tell your grandson, 'Your Granddaddy rode with the Great Third Army and a Son-of-a-Goddamned-Bitch named Georgie Patton!'"

The men of the newly formed Third Army whooped and yelled and belly-laughed, the air electrified by Patton's words." All right, you sons of bitches. You know how I feel. I'll be proud to lead you wonderful guys in battle anytime, anywhere. That's all."

# CHAPTER NINE

# D-Day

"A good day for bombing," described those clear days in 1944. With adequate visibility, the Allied planes flew late into the evenings. But on June 5, the weather changed, turned to more clouds and rain. A storm was brewing in the Atlantic, funneling through the English Channel, picking up strength.

Anxious to be back on duty and with his adrenaline pumping, Frank didn't let the plaster cast on his foot inhibit his movement. His gunners scanned the skies in the hazy light as planes and gliders returned to their stations at Cottesmore to line up on the runway, waiting for orders to come in at any time. The anti-aircraft guns pointed to the skies, positioned to protect the Allied aircraft that would soon haul the paratroopers and equipment over the English Channel. The planes lined up on the runway while the pilots waited for their orders.

On June 5, Supreme Allied Commander General Dwight D. Eisenhower was up at dawn, preparing to give the orders to attack and proceed with *Operation Overlord*, the invasion of Normandy, despite warnings that bad weather could hamper the landings and the ability of planes to fly. By afternoon when the weather still looked bleak, he scribbled a note. "I accept full responsibility for the decision to launch the invasion and full blame should the effort to create a beachhead on Normandy coast fail."

In the early morning hours, 0430 of June 6, the Army Rangers preceded the attack. Once on the shores of Normandy, the Rangers scaled the sheer 100-foot cliffs west of Omaha Beach and mounted ropes and ladders to disable the cannons facing the sea. From the ocean, the U.S. Navy Frogmen glided through the turbulent waters detonating obstacles and clearing landing paths through *Rommel's Devil Garden,* a maze of booby traps, barbed wire, and sharp metal jaws capable of ripping open the bottom of landing craft. Under the cover of night, the paratroopers dropped behind enemy lines and waited for the reinforcements to land along the sandy beaches. By morning battleships and carriers crossed the channel with soldiers in full combat suits, loaded with grenade belts and rounds of ammunition strapped across both shoulders, machine guns on their laps. The extreme low tides in the morning would be ascending by noon, giving the army of men time to disembark and the landing crafts the ability to return to sea on the rising tide. Precision maps and aerial photos of the shoreline showed the exact location of where to go ashore and the precise timing of the tidal flow.

On the eve of the invasion, Eisenhower distributed the printed "Order of the Day for June 6, 1944" to the 175,000-member expeditionary force:

> *You are about to embark upon the Great Crusade. The eyes of the world are upon you. You will bring about the destruction of the German war machine, the elimination of the Nazi tyranny over the oppressed peoples of Europe, and security for ourselves in a free world.*
>
> *Our air offensive has severely reduced their strength in the air and their capacity to wage war on the ground. Our Home Fronts have given us an overwhelming superiority in weapons and munitions of war and has placed at our disposal significant reserves of trained fighting men. I have full confidence in your*

*courage, devotion to duty, and skill in battle…good luck
and the blessings of Almighty God upon this tremendous
noble undertaking.*

By 2130 on June 5, night fell, and the full moon slid in and out
the clouds, and everything became eerily quiet. Frank and his men
remained watchful for German planes. Once it started getting light,
Frank set the elevation of his 155mm. He peered into the crosshair and
set the angle for a bullseye should an enemy plane came into sight. At
the base of the gun, the men were ready to swivel the barrel to follow
any foreign aircraft.

Earlier the night before, the Allies clandestinely painted black
and white stripes on their planes so as not be mistaken for enemy aircraft. The commanding officer spread the word to the gunners *if it ain't
got stripes, shoot it down.*

One of Frank's men recorded the event. *Our 155mm guns were
about 150 feet from the middle of the airbase, from that center point,
we'd make sure nothing followed our planes back in. It was all C-46's and
C-47's and the Horsa gliders that hauled paratroopers over to the channel
for D-Day. The army knew they weren't getting the gliders back because
they didn't have a motor.*

By dawn, the planes had towed the tubular steel-framed Horsa
gliders to the runway. Fifteen men in combat uniforms mounted each
glider through a flap door under the wing, sitting shoulder to shoulder
on rough-hewn benches that lined both sides, their feet resting on a
plywood floor. Army loadmasters frontloaded the soldiers' guns and
gear into the glider. Two pilots climbed in last, and the loading door
closed.

One after another, the C-47s took off, pulling the Horsa gliders
into the air, their only purpose was to carry the troops to Normandy

before crash landing on the occupied soil. In-flight, they looked like dragonflies made out of balsa wood.

By 0930, the weather cleared, and the sky filled with thousands of planes and gliders heading across the channel from all points in England, like black and white-winged predators in V-formations.

Horsa gliders being towed on D-Day

On the other side of the channel, the Germans had stuck poles and tree trunks in the ground, so when the gliders hit them, they would end up crashing.

*More than a few guys got hurt in the landing, and every one of those gliders and a few planes crashed. Our job was to protect the airbase at Cottesmore.*

On the other side of the channel, the 6th Airborne Division Captain told about landing in a Horsa glider:

*"The landing was ghastly. Mine was the first glider down. We were not quite in the right place, and the damn thing bucketed along a very upsy-downsy field for a bit and then broke across the middle - we just chopped through those anti-landing poles as we went along. However, the two halves of the glider fetched up very close together, and we quickly got out ourselves and our equipment and lay down under the thing. Other gliders were coming in all-round, and Jerries (Germans) were shooting at them and us, so it wasn't very healthy to wander about. Our immediate opposition - a machine gun in a little trench - was very effectively silenced by another glider which fetched up plumb in the ditch and a couple of Huns (derogatory for German) - quite terrified - came out with their hands up!*

That next night Frank wrote to Catherine:

*Darling Kitty and John,*            *Wednesday, June 7*
      *I'm going to have to plan my days better. I let yesterday slip by without writing to you. It has been a beautiful day here today, the first in a week or two, but this evening it has started in to rain again with lightning, thunder and all the trimmings. Why these people keep fighting for this country is beyond me, with all the rain and cold weather. I believe I would sell it cheap and find a land that is not quite as beautiful, but more livable. I should change my attitude because we see a lot of thatched roofs around here and slate roofs grown thick and blossoming with moss, really lovely.*

For days following D-Day, Frank and his boys surveilled the air, guns mounted and positioned with orders to protect the retuning Allied planes and shoot enemy planes. Army pilots came in low, low enough that the men on the ground could count the bullet holes. After completing his mission of dropping soldiers into Normandy, one pilot had swooped over the hedgerows of Normandy, and enemy bullets blasted him. Frank counted forty-seven small arm bullet holes.

\* \* \*

On June 6, the radio waves world-wide carried the news of the invasion, and the papers heralded the Normandy Battle. Catherine read the banner headline in the Los Angeles Times: **INVASION!** *Allied troops attacked five beaches in Normandy earlier today. The invasion gave the Allies a foothold in France, at the cost of more than 4,400 Allied dead on June 6.*

What did she think? What did she know? Frank's letters had always consoled her, but the last she had heard from him was days ago, and the letter in her hand was already over a week old. Several scenarios played through her head. Was he still in England? Was he part of the invasion? Would the Germans now counterattack in full force? Was he safe? Her parents and sisters consoled her, but no one knew for sure if anything had happened to Frank. All Catherine could do was pray. No letters arrived for weeks. The mail had been stopped for security reasons prior to D-Day and didn't resume till many days after. The world seemed to hold its breath.

\* \* \*

During this time, Patton was ensconced in England, chomping at the bit to get over to France to kill those *bastard Germans.* Keeping Patton from fighting infuriated him. He resolved to get his Third Army in shape and blast across Europe to Berlin, and personally kill *the son-of-a-bitch, Hitler.*

Sadly disappointed, on the evening of June 6, 1944, Patton wrote to his son:

> *At 0700 this morning, the B.B.C. announced that the German radio had just come out with an announcement of the landing of Allied Paratroops and large numbers of assault craft near the shore. So that is it. This group of unconquerable heroes whom I command is not in yet, but we will be soon. I wish I were there now as it is a lovely sunny day for a battle, and I'm fed up with just sitting.*

Patton had long wished to be the commander of the First Army in the invasion of Normandy. Due to the public outrage over the "slapping incident" of a soldier in Italy and his misspoken words alienating Russia, Eisenhower passed over his unpredictable friend for the less talented but widely respected and dependable General Omar Bradley.

The Supreme Commander enacted a simultaneous plan, "Operation Fortitude," to misinform the Germans into thinking Norway was at risk of another Allied invasion. Chatter on the radio disclosed false weather reports and warned of tanks freezing up and the need for snowshoes to defend in the far north of Norway. It worked, drawing Hitler's attention away from the strategic areas in Northern France. Both sides jammed the radio waves, and no one could believe what he heard. Frank warned Catherine not to rely on everything she read in the newspapers or heard on the radio either. *We never know what's happening till it's over, and if I did know I couldn't tell you.* He begged her not to worry about him or look for him in the newspapers. *Keep praying, Kitty, and I'll be home soon.*

The Germans feared Patton all along; they believed he was going to lead the invasion of Europe by crossing the channel at Pas de Calais, France, the shortest crossing of the English Channel and the quickest route to Germany. The Nazis fortified the port of Calais along the *Atlantikwall,* a defense system that extended from the Arctic Circle in Norway to the northern border of Spain.

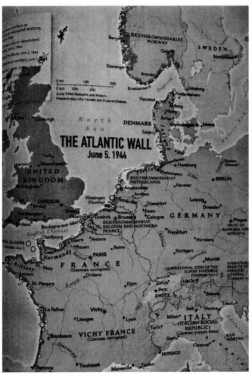

Weakening his position, Hitler ordered more troops and tanks to Calais, opening his flanks on the east, where Russia was fighting to defeat Hitler. As part of the Allied ruse, a massive troop build-up appeared on the southeast shores of England. The Allies positioned life-size inflatable tanks in a field near the docks, a fleet of dummy landing craft in the harbor, and fake aircraft on the runway, all fabricated in Hollywood by set designers.

Hitler was caught off-guard. While the invasion of Normandy took place, Allied airplanes flew towards Pas de Calais as if attacking or dropping off troops. The pilots swooshed down and dropped clouds of aluminum strips disrupting radar readings, making it seem like a massive attack was taking place. Other aircraft flew into enemy territory to the south of Normandy and dropped hundreds of dummy paratroopers wired with recordings of rifle fire, soldiers' voices, and grenades. The ruse was working.

The Allied bombardment of the northern coast of France continued to flush out the Germans and weaken their defenses. The bombings also took a toll on the French citizens, their terror escalating as bombs exploded on their cities and towns. Bombs shattered century-old stained-glass windows and toppled the cathedral towers, and homes lay in rubble.

Sirens blared early the morning of June 6. U.S. fighter planes came in low strafing the streets and buildings of Caen. People did not know if it were safer to stay in their homes or to run to bomb shelters. Many hunkered down in basements without electricity and with only a small amount of food and water. During the days that followed, over 2,000 citizens died in Caen alone. Despite their loss, the French garnered strength, knowing the Allies had landed on the continent. A glimmer of hope shone on that sunny day of June 6 amidst the wreckage.

Late in the evening of June 6, Frank finished writing his letter, not mentioning a word about the invasion. Censorship had been tightened.

> *I hope we can settle down to a steady schedule,*
> *after all this. I haven't had a letter in five days, seems like*
> *five years. I can only imagine what John looks like now,*
> *but I only conjure up the impression of the first time I*

*saw him. Another officer, Lt. Hamilton, had a baby girl recently while overseas. I'm glad I had a few hours with you and John before leaving. Kitty, it would have been really sad not to have been there at all. Even though I censor my own letters, there is further censorship before it actually leaves the post.*

*Doc caught me limping last week and threatened me with a sore foot the rest of my life if I didn't get my cast back on, which he did while I was in the hospital. It isn't serious enough to stop me from getting around.*

*Doc cemented iron into the cast, but I'm afraid they will have to put on a new cast pretty soon, I've got the bottom almost pounded out this one. Funny what trouble a little bone can be.*

By June 8, the news of the invasion was no longer classified, and Frank wrote:

*Hello Darling,*                  *Thursday, June 8*

*Well the Big Day is here and gone, let's hope the results are quick and favorable. This war can't end soon enough for me. Things have worked out pretty well for you and me, Kitty, now all we have to do is get this war over in a hurry so that we can get set up in our home. You mentioned a little sister for John. I like that idea and will keep thinking about it till I see you.*

For a moment, Frank forgot about the war and talked about ordinary life, civilian life, and the future.

*There will be quite a hole in the family when Peg moves to Riverside. Are you paying the folks anymore?*

*I hear from Mary Ripple there is plenty of room in Riverside. It's a place I'm thinking we might move some-day, maybe soon. I'd like to change some of those diapers, hate to miss out on all the fun. It seems like years since I kissed you good-bye, Kitty. Good night darling, see you soon as...*

From D-Day on, the days were numbered D-1 to the end of the war on May 8, 1945, or D-335.

# CHAPTER TEN

# Propaganda

*Darling Kitty*                      *Sunday, June 11*
*I've been listening to a few German news pro-*
*grams, and we are really taking a beating, according to*
*them. Heard Axis Sal the other day. She's quite a gal. She*
*plays the best in modern music, then pours it on with*
*a honeyed tongue. She has a large audience among the*
*soldiers, but her effect is in reverse.*

The soldiers gathered around the one radio as Captain Howell twisted the knob back and forth till the station came in loud and clear. The train whistle blew, big band music filled the air, and the rich voice of Axis Sally took to the airwaves, "Home Sweet Home," one of the most listened to radio programs during the war by the servicemen longing for the music they loved back home. The men huddled around the one radio, static noise, then:

*Berlin calling, Berlin calling. Hello fellas, when*
*Berlin calls, you must listen. Do you love the British?*
*Do they love us? Of course not. This is a Jewish British*
*war, fighting for all the kike friends of Roosevelt and*
*Churchill. I've been talking to your wives and girl-*
*friends, and they won't want you back, especially if you*
*come back mutilated. I heard just yesterday that your*

*little wife is seeing someone else, someone home sitting by
the fire in that rocking chair you left behind. Well, boys,
I've got something for you.*

She flipped on a vinyl disc and played the sultry sound of jazz
that mesmerized the G.I.s. When Axis Sally's voice returned, she dealt
out more propaganda telling the soldiers they were fighting on the
wrong side. *Listen up, men. I'm a true American girl who loves America.
You're fighting alongside the Bolsheviks, not for freedom. Germany is fighting for all of us. Stop fighting that kike war and dying for Roosevelt and
his cronies.*

The jitterbug started up, and the men shook off their lousy feeling, guffawing *what a wench*, but all agreed she sure played great music.
To what extent did she affect the men? No doubt, she got under their
skin and in their heads.

The next day Frank wrote to Catherine:

> *Hello Darling,*　　　　　　　　　*Monday, June 12*
> *I have dawn shift and have that early morning
> taste in my mouth from too many cigarettes before break-
> fast. I dozed off for a few minutes and dreamed I cap-
> tured Hitler and all his cohorts. I didn't say a word to
> them, just let my Tommy-gun do all the talking. What
> a morning! I guess what brought on the dream was the
> fact that I was listening to the German propaganda and
> news broadcast. The stuff they put out serves only to dis-
> gust me. They really don't understand anything about
> America or Americans.*

Axis Sally waged a propaganda war in America as well, calling
out to wives and mothers of soldiers overseas. *Women of America, listen
to the truth! Are you waiting for the one you love? Waiting and weeping in*

*the secrecy of your room? Thinking of your husband, your son, your brother who are being sacrificed by Franklin D. Roosevelt, those boys perishing on the fringe of Europe?*

The cruelest programs were her visits to the P.O.W. camps in Germany, where she interviewed the American soldiers.

*Now please tell us your name, nice and loud so your wife can hear from you. Tells us how you're being treated.*

The captured men were forced to say they had good food, exercised, and had never been tortured, which of course, were lies. Axis Sally read a list of soldiers' names who were either wounded or dead. Her voice dripped with sarcasm and demeaned the young men in captivity. *You see ladies and gentlemen, all these stories about mistreating the P.O.W.'s, and refugees and such, is all Jewish propaganda. These men, women, and children are getting ideal treatment.*

Axis Sally's real name was Mildred Gillars, a failed American actress living in Germany since before the war. Her melodious voice and acting experience earned her a job as a radio announcer. While working at the radio station, she fell in love with a Nazi whom she later accused of brainwashing her and forcing her to sign an oath of allegiance to Hitler. Her attorneys claimed she was coerced into broadcasting lies to mislead the Allied soldiers. When the Third Reich fell, she escaped, literally out the back door of the studio, only later to be caught and tried on ten counts of treason. She was convicted on only one of the counts, making and broadcasting, "Vision of Invasion," a play she aired one day before D-Day. On the morning of June 5, her voice stretched across the English Channel and the Atlantic Ocean, broadcasting a mother's nightmare that her son had died a horrific death on a ship in the English Channel while attempting to invade "Occupied Europe." One wonders, was it just irony, or did she have inside information on the attack of Normandy?

# CHAPTER ELEVEN

# Second Wave of Normandy Invasion

Frank and the other officers met with Captain Howell to debrief after the invasion and to prepare for their deployment to Normandy. The captain was feeling optimistic.

"Men, we've made a good dent in the German forces, and they're retreating and regrouping. Hitler sent a bunch of old Krauts from the Russian front to France, not too many young Jerries left. I've got great optimism that this war will be over in two months."

"You willing to bet on that, Captain?"

"As a matter of fact, I already have a few wagers going."

Frank wasn't going to bet against winning in two months, even though he thought he could win the bet.

Captain Howell and First Lieutenant Hubbard

*Hello Kitty,*                    *Friday, June 9*
*Another day closer to the end of this war. I wish I*
*could share Capt. Howell's optimism. He has a number*
*of bets that the war will be over in two months. Anyway,*
*when it's over, we will have a lot of catching up to do,*
*won't we Kitty. Let's see, we have our first anniversary*
*last March 17 to celebrate, the baby's birthday, and Peg*
*and Steve's wedding.*

Frank limped away from the meeting. His foot was still giving him problems, but even worse wearing the cast.

*I'm afraid they're going to have to put a new cast*
*on because I have this one beaten to a pulp. It's funny to*
*wake up in the night and find that darn thing in bed*
*with me. It's like sleeping with a wet mackerel! I walk*
*out in the yard, and the walker bottom picks up mud,*
*and I have to spend a half-hour cleaning it before getting*
*into bed. It's so tiresome.*

Frank looked forward to his special assignment at Bomb Reconnaissance School in Over Court, Bristol, one of the worst cities to have been hit by the Germans before the Normandy invasion. When the Allies destroyed the launchpads on the Cotentin Peninsula during the initial attack, Hitler withdrew his troops from the cliffs and stopped launching bombs at Bristol and the English seaside. The location was perfect for the Bomb Reconnaissance School, which trained special forces to identify and deactivate bombs. The 546th would be traveling roads on the continent laden with booby traps and unexploded explosives, and each unit needed troops to know how to handle the situation alongside the engineer bomb squads.

Frank's broken foot hobbled him in more ways than poor sleep and walking stiff-legged in a cast.

> *Kuret just came in out of the rain whistling like a meadowlark. He has to make my tour of duty. And I have spent most my day censoring mail and is that ever boring.*

Much to Frank's disappointment, Kuret took his place in Bomb Reconnaissance School.

> *Kitty, I haven't been out on pass for three weeks! Anyway, it's easy on the pocketbook. I only spent two pounds in the first fifteen days, and half of that was lost on a flip of the coin!*
>
> *I'd like to finish this letter, but Hubbard is distracting me, arguing about where to live after the war. He claims it won't be California, but I'm willing to bet he ends up there. I'd like to move to Riverside and definitely won't go back to the desert.*

Hubbard walked away, and Frank finished his letter.

> *It's 10:30, and I can see the sun setting slowly in the west, the sky is slate gray, and only two-thirds of the sun is showing through the gray, the sun is orange-red. It is the first sunset I have noticed over here, and it is really beautiful. I miss you, darling.*

Now that the Allied military lodgment had been established ashore in Normandy, the Third Army geared up for deployment. These men of the Third Army had not been in action, only war games, and Patton had to shape them up. The new divisions were untried and still green, as well as the staff echelons who were also inexperienced in battle. Patton started from scratch to mold his army into a "hell on wheels" outfit.

Frank felt the crunch complying with frequent inspections to determine the status of their training and the condition of their guns and equipment. The chief staff of the artillery critiqued each unit. Patton meanwhile made personal inspections of his troops throughout the United Kingdom, visiting all the main units and talking with the officers.

Getting back from touring the North, Frank wrote to Catherine:

*Hello Darling,*                                    *Thursday, June 15*

*I just returned from a trip over to the North Sea, so now I've been from Scotland to the south of England. I hope I can get over to Ireland before this business is over, but I won't be able to see any but the North until the war ends though.*

*I hope your parents are getting used to John's middle name, Marren. It keeps his Irish lineage going. I bet by the time he starts to eat solids, your dad will be giving him potatoes.*

*I am still waiting to hear about Peggy and Steve's wedding. I wish I could have been there to help with the celebration. I could dance a riotous set with this leg in a cast, anyway I could do a lot of pivoting. I hope they are able to be together for a long time. Looks like your sister Agnes will have to carry the U.S.O. or should I say the soldiers' burden now with Peggy out of circulation.*

*That Tokyo raid was surely good news. I hope they can keep them dropping every day now. Maybe it won't be so long till we get together again, Kitty.*

The bombing of Tokyo continued throughout the war. They kept score of the number of dead and destruction of tanks and arms. Frank gleaned news about the war from what he heard on the radio, or what he read in the *Stars and Stripes* Army newspaper, the London edition of world news, and the occasional L.A. Times.

Not having news of his estranged brother, George, for almost a year made him speculate *it's just possible they are moving so fast thru Italy that George didn't get time to write.* The unknown was the hardest.

When Frank returned to Cottesmore, he had three letters from Catherine waiting for him. Catherine bragged about John to the point that Frank wrote back, *you make me envious with your descriptions of the baby. I hope he is half as good and cute as his mother claims he is. Could it be that she is prejudiced-- maybe. Well, you will have to prove it to me with some pictures of him.*

With good weather and long days, Frank's routine now included more night watches and around the clock surveillance of the skies.

> *Kitty, there is little new to report to you today, it has been beautiful and warm today, but I was too tired to enjoy it. Was up till after midnight last night checking our guns, then had to get up again at 4:30. I didn't even realize today was Sunday until noon. Everyday just runs into another. I could have gone into town on a pass tonite but couldn't see going. Carlson, Hubbard, and Capt. Howell went last night, spent two pennies for a trolley ride, took a long walk, then came back to camp.*

The clear nights brought out the Germans planes, which continued bombing the English cities. During the day, the Germans shot V-1 pilotless bombs across the channel. The job of the anti-aircraft artillery was to intercept the planes and weapons.

*Kitty, I suppose you have heard about pilotless*
*planes. I haven't seen any as yet, and nobody seems too*
*excited about them. Looks to me that the Germans are on*
*their last leg. Keeps us on our toes all night.*

In early July, Patton clandestinely activated his Normandy headquarters near Nehou while keeping up the façade of the fake First U.S.
Army. The slow progress and pace of deploying troops worried him
that without a push, the warfare could turn static as it did in WWI. He
settled into his well laid out Command Post in an apple orchard as his
troops slowly moved across the channel throughout July, amassing an
army of six corps and forty-two divisions. It wouldn't be until mid-July
that the 546th would deploy.

Eventually, Frank used his pass into town and missed writing
Catherine a letter.

*I went out on a pass from noon till midnight and*
*had a tolerable good time. First, I got myself a haircut,*
*then hobbled around and took a look at the town. I went*
*to a department store trying to find something to buy,*
*but most everything takes ration points, and of course, I*
*am without them. I'm still trying to pick up some little*
*trinket for you, just a souvenir.*

The department stores were half-destroyed, and what was left on
the shelves had no use to Frank, ironing boards, a mismatch of clothing
and sizes, a few shoes, and a sundry of household goods. Frank wandered down the street.

*I had dinner in town, met a captain there who*
*volunteered to show me around. We went to the opera*
*house and saw a stage show, which wasn't too good and*

*yet not too bad. British humor is considerably different than ours. After the show we went to the pubs—but I got back early and in good shape. The pubs here are only open from 6 pm to 10 pm, and you have to get there early or not at all. They have one to two, sometimes even three, to a block, and it's almost impossible to get a seat in one!*

He got back early to camp and was surprised to find the L.A. Times.

*I finally received the first edition of the Los Angeles Times. It's nearly a month old, but the familiar pages really strike a home note. I'm tickled to get it anyway because it gives a slant that the English papers don't. Kuret nearly tore a table down, trying to get to the comics. We all miss the U.S. newspapers. Us kids have to have our comics.*

A week later, Frank got a 24-hour pass to London, a place he had long wanted to see.

*I had a quiet and enjoyable weekend in London. I saw the site of all the Robin Hood tales and got to Mass in an old cathedral. The town was so crowded that I had to stay at the Red Cross Canteen. I met up with officers from another battery and toured around, got tickets to a movie which we all had unfortunately seen on the base. We tried to get our money back. The Brits think Yanks are a little crazy anyway, and they make allowance for it. The best they could do was get tickets for next week's show.*

Except, by next week, Frank would be in France, fighting.

CHAPTER TWELVE

# Move to the Continent

*Hello Darling,*                    *Tuesday, July 4*
    *Today is the fourth of July. I missed writing to you*
*yesterday, just couldn't help it, I was too busy to sit down.*
*As a matter of fact, too busy to go to bed last night, and*
*I'm just about to hit the hay as soon as I finish writing*
*to you.*

Frank had spent all of July 3 in meetings, overseeing the packing of the 155mm guns, preparing his men, and carrying out orders from the General to move to the south of England in preparation for debarkation to Normandy.

The plans to ship the Third Army to the Cotentin Peninsula were underway. Vehicles to transport troops and equipment assembled in Southampton. The U.S. Army sent over 10,000 new guns, scabbards, and bayonets and outfitted the men for war, for the changing weather conditions, and survival. Besides rifles with bayonets, handguns, and grenades, the soldiers carried canvas tents, bedding, and shovels to dig trenches and foxholes when in the field.

The Germans had no idea that Patton had established his Command Post on the Cotentin Peninsula. Even seven weeks after D-Day, Hitler was still waiting for him to land in Calais, keeping an eye on what he thought was the First United States Army. Fake ships and airplanes remained in their positions along the southern coast of

England. Rommel left his post in Normandy and returned to Germany to speak with Hitler and to report no action. All the while, the XIX Tactical Air Command established its headquarters adjacent to General Patton's Third Army Headquarters in Nehou, far from Calais, and detailed their plans for air-ground coordination

Upon Patton's arrival at the Army Headquarters on the continent, orders from the Supreme Headquarters of the Allied Expeditionary Force (SHAEF) placed heavy emphasis upon security to conceal the presence of Patton and his Third Army. SHAEF imposed radio silence and safeguarded all documents and telephone transmissions. The Military Police protected the surroundings until the Sixth Calvary, and the Anti-Aircraft Artillery Battalions arrived.

Exchanging his comfortable English manor for a canvas tent in the Norman orchard, Patton activated his headquarters, naming it "Lucky Forward." Over the next three weeks, more than five hundred units of the Third Army in England mobilized. The units arrived on the Cotentin Peninsula in waves, unloading on Utah Beach while the Germans erringly expected the Third Army to invade Pas-de-Calais.

At 0600 July 4, Frank and his battalion left Cottesmore in a convoy of trucks, jeeps, and tractors pulling the guns for the long haul of 162 miles to the north of Southampton. Other units joined the long procession as the convoys wound their way through villages and along the verdant country roads. People lined the streets in the small towns, waving the Union Jack and American flags, throwing fruits, vegetables, and flowers to the men packed shoulder to shoulder in the open trucks. Planes flew overhead in defense of the movement.

Frank, riding in his open-air jeep, kept his eyes forward and occasionally ducked a flying peach. When the enlisted men arrived at Lobscombe Corner, they dismounted from the backs of trucks and assembled in the large dirt lot as orders came over the loudspeaker.

"Men, you will be billeted in the tents assigned to you by your captains. We're shipping men out daily, so don't get too comfortable. We have no canteen, so pick up your K rations for breakfast, lunch, and dinner." Other units milled around, some soldiers returning from battle, others preparing to deploy.

Frank looked around and questioned a few men from the other units where they had been and where they were going. He couldn't shake the feeling that his brother George was nearby.

> *Hello Darling,*                    *Monday, July 10*
>     *One of our officers accidentally ran into his brother. They walked by each other, and neither recognized the other. The second time they met by chance, they connected. I wish I could run into George that way. I think though that he is in the thick of it in Italy. That's the only reason I can think of that he doesn't write.*
>     *Another dull Monday after another dull Sunday. Went to early Mass and intended to get up early and go again today, but slept thru it.*
>     *I miss you more each day I'm away Kitty. Keep up those prayers to bring this affair to a rapid close. From the news, we hear over here people in the states are very optimistic. I hope they don't carry the optimism too far, 'cause it ain't thru yet.*

Two days later, Frank's battalion moved to Fawley on their last leg before Southampton and debarkation. The Third U.S. Army evacuation hospital and medical services followed. Before crossing the channel with supplies and blood, the medical teams checked each soldier, ensuring everyone was combat fit. Unfortunately, Frank had a setback.

*I don't know if I told you in my last letter, but I have to have the cast put back on my foot. It was taken off three weeks too soon. I hate the thought of sleeping with that cold piece of plaster again, but the doc says if I don't, I will have a sore foot the rest of my days.*

For the past ten days in Lobscombe, the soldiers had not gotten their mail, their lifeline to home. The mailbags were somewhere between Cottesmore and Fawley. Frank worried that he would leave for France without a word from Catherine. He wondered if his letters even had gotten delivered to her.

*Our mail has been all messed up again, and I have not had a letter from you for ten days, and each day now makes a lonely day. When your mail comes in regularly, it seems I can keep from missing you, but when it is cut off, it's like being cut off on a telephone.*

\* \* \*

Catherine was beside herself. Frank's letters had arrived sporadically before D-Day, then stopped altogether, and now she hadn't heard from him in over two weeks. Pouring over his last letter, she looked for clues where he might be. *Somewhere in England,* was all he had told her. The news at home talked about the buildup of troops in Normandy and the Germans retreating. Frank's letters told her so little, mostly asked about the baby, talked about the weather, joked about her sisters and the Irish, sent congratulations and good wishes, complained about the mail service, and wished he were home.

The warm days of Los Angeles summers felt good, almost too good, making Catherine feel guilty thinking about the gray weather of England. She glanced at the rocking chair in the corner, imagining

Frank sitting there with their baby on his knees. *John will be walking before Frank's home.* She prayed he'd come home soon, and they would have a baby girl that Frank talked about and hoped for in the future. Each month, Frank had been tucking forty dollars in his letters, which Catherine put in a tin box to buy war bonds, save up for a house, and leave enough to give her parents money for rent and food.

Dada, in his pin-striped navy-blue suit, came through the door after a long day working on the Redline streetcars. As usual, he had two bags of groceries in his arms. He did the shopping for the house since Mama often was ill or in bed with back and leg problems, which she contributed to having carried heavy loads of laundry as a child in Ireland. Catherine set the baby in his crib and greeted her father, taking his hat for him and hanging it by the door. As much as Catherine loved her parents and tried to be a good help, she worried she and the baby were an added burden to the household. A visit to her sister Mary and her three children served as a respite for Catherine, and hopefully, the house would be quieter for her mother.

Clouds swirled in her mind with so many unknowns. *How was Frank going to manage with a cast on his leg? Has he gained any weight?* In his photos, his clothes seemed to hang on his frame. He still looked handsome with that boyish grin she had fallen in love with, but so much thinner. In his letters, Frank had assured her he was eating fine, just couldn't put on weight. *Is he cold?* She made a mental note to get a package ready for him, perhaps add a woolen cap to his request for coffee and the LA Times. *And his brother, George. Why does Frank even bother with him when he never writes or keeps in touch with anyone?* Baby John started crying. Catherine left her thoughts to tend to him. She was doing her best to keep him healthy while Frank was away, but she wished he would come home soon to help.

\* \* \*

*Well, goodnite, Kitty. John will soon be four months old by the time you receive this letter. Don't let him grow up too fast, darling. Here comes the hit parade on the radio. They're talking of California now. It's a long way back to you, but I will be there soon.*

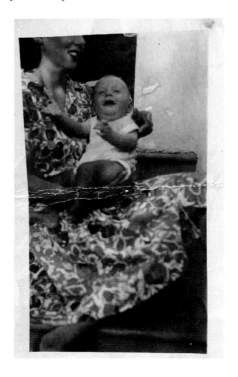

Catherine and John at four months, folded to fit in Frank's pocket

On July 11, Frank's letter was upbeat.

*Just sittin' around waiting for the show call and methink I better get a letter off to my better half. Have done nothing for the last three days but rest and more rest, hope it keeps going that way. The news from the front sounds especially good at the rate things are breaking.*

Within a few hours, everything changed. Frank never got the cast put back on. Not enough time. The "show call" arrived. It was time to move on, time to go to war. The trucks and flatbeds loaded with combat equipment fell into line heading out of Fawley. The soldiers grabbed their gear and met at 1900 in the marshaling area. The full convoy left at dusk and drove without lights till 0200 when they arrived in Southampton. The soldiers emptied out of the trucks and jeeps, found their duffle bags, and located a spot to lie down and wait. The port soldiers made final checks of weapons and equipment and filled the trucks and tanks with fuel and oil. The drivers moved the trucks and vehicles onto large nets lying on the ground. In the darkness, large cranes lifted the jeeps, tractors, and tanks and slowly placed them on the landing crafts or into the holds of the vast number of transport ships in the harbor while the military police and merchant marines stood guard.

At daylight, a loud blast of a horn roused the men from their sleep signaling to meet at the marshaling zone. Following orders, the men removed all patches and insignia that identified their unit as part of the U.S. Army in case the enemy captured them. Each man received K-rations, a small box with canned soup, crackers and cheese, water purifying tablets, sulfa pills, and extra portions of cigarettes and candy bars. The postmaster handed out the last bunch of mail and took the letters to be mailed. The payroll sergeant changed money from pounds to French francs, which was not real French currency, instead "invasion money," valid throughout the war.

Once organized and all troops accounted for, the 546th Battalion moved to the docks to get in line to board the transport ships called "Liberty Ships." It took several hours to get all the units boarded on the four-hundred-foot vessel, cramming the soldiers on the deck, with the trucks, equipment, and tanks already below. At 1900 the ship moved slowly south through the opening of the harbor to shelter to the north side of the Isle of Wight in the company of other Liberty Ships, all fully loaded with troops and their equipment for the combat zone.

Since the German planes flew at night, the ships waited till morning to cross the channel. The crew of civilian merchant marines, plus naval personnel, operated the guns on all sides of the vessel and monitored radio communication. The air filled with excitement and nervous tension, keeping most soldiers awake and alert for the journey. They smoked, joked around, and played cards.

Down below deck, the officers gathered for a few hands of poker. *I was a little lucky at poker on the way across the channel,* Frank wrote and tucked a few extra dollars into his letter he would mail from the continent.

By dawn on July 14, their ship moved into the open channel and joined the large convoy of other Liberty Ships protected by Navy destroyers on all sides. Frank scanned the horizon and, as far as he could see, were transport ships, freighters, minesweepers and destroyers, and above them, hundreds of fighter jets. Filled with awe and anticipation, Frank wondered when he would return but left that up to God.

The convoy covered a distance of approximately 150 miles in close to fourteen hours. When the transport ships anchored offshore, small landing craft and amphibious trucks transported the equipment and soldiers ashore through shallow water.

The men debarked with their duffels, guns, and tents onto the firm sand of low tide. The Army Corps of Engineers had used old ships to create a harbor and salvage metals to build reefs and bridges that floated on tires, making the land accessible to the tanks, trucks, soldiers, and medics.

Frank looked up at the German bunkers riddled with bullet holes lining the cliffs and huge chunks of cement falling into the sea. Shelled-out tanks, shrapnel, and pieces of equipment littered the beach. The bodies of the fallen soldiers had been taken away and buried nearby in temporary graves. Patton had ordered that all signs of graves be removed from the beaches and tops of cliffs so as not to shock the incoming troops and deflate their morale. But that didn't disguise the loss and destruction that hung heavy in the sea air. The smell of death mingled with the scent of grasses and weeds. A helmet was half-covered in the sand, bearing the U.S. Army emblem. Shredded shirts and clothing caught in bushes defiled the trail. Craters from bombs made a moonscape out of what once was a favorite French resort for the Parisians. At the top of the sandy path, the men of the 546th struck out on the road to St. Laurent-Sur-Mer where they bivouacked in fields and pastures until their equipment was unloaded, checked, and all vehicles dewater- proofed.

*Hello Darling,*          *Monday, July 16*

  *At last we are away from the buzz bombs, safe in France. Should I add, wish you were here? We are pastured out in a field with about a hundred head of cattle. Surprising to say they are sleek, fat, and apparently happy.*

  *It has been nearly two weeks since I've had a letter from you. They sent for the mail again but don't know if they will be successful. I told the Captain that I couldn't keep going until I received some more baby pictures. He says he fears baby pictures more than the German planes. Course we haven't seen any German planes.*

  *This is of necessity to be a short letter. So be seeing you, darling.*

# CHAPTER THIRTEEN

# Normandy

Within twenty-four hours of landing in Normandy, the 546th proceeded in convoy a distance of fifty miles to the vicinity of Bricquebec, a few miles northwest of Patton's Third Army headquarters at Nehou. Trucks and jeeps, filled with soldiers carrying rifles, grenades, and handguns, traveled over the narrow, crowded roads with tanks and flatbeds with the big guns interspersed in convoy.

Frank went with Kuret and another officer in a jeep. A rifle hung across Frank's shoulder, and his handheld a pistol, ready in case they came across a stray unit of Germans hiding among the bocage. The bocage, or hedgerows, were fields delineated by bushes five meters high intertwined with brambles and planted on top of four to six feet mounds, tall and dense enough to keep the cows and animals from straying, as well as marking property boundaries for the many apple and pear orchards.

While the Germans occupied France, they used the hedgerows to hide their weapons and to wage war on the incoming Allies from D-Day to August 1944. The bushes were not only impenetrable but blocked all view of what was on the other side. Thousands of soldiers lost their lives in the first month of fighting in Normandy. It could have been worse except for the ingenious invention of the tank spade, two husk-like metal pieces attached to the front of the tank, which tore through the hedgerows like a knife through butter, thus exposing the enemy and clearing the way for the Allied troops.

"Le Bocage," the hedgerows in Normandy, July 1944

If it were not for the war and the sounds of artillery and bombs, Frank observed an idyllic and alarmingly beautiful countryside. Along the road, he saw large wooden crosses garlanded with flowers, now decaying, and altars to the saints and the Blessed Mother.

*Kitty darling, France appears to be a very Catholic country with all the churches and shrines throughout the towns and countryside.*

The scenery changed, and the sense of false serenity left. Frank traversed the winding roads through towns where the homes, if standing, had windows blown out, and most shops shuttered. It was noon, and a few villagers moved furtively through the streets, carrying baguettes. A young boy with a small, wrapped package ran out from what appeared to have been a meat market. In St. Lo, the church at the center of town had been blown apart and shards of glass and bits of stone lying on the ground. Buildings and homes had gaping holes where bombs had exploded. The destruction caused by fighter planes strafing the streets made Frank's stomach churn, knowing that their bullets had torn apart families in the mayhem. With the intent of clearing the way for the invasion, the Allied fighter pilots had also struck the villages and destroyed so many innocent lives to flush out the Germans.

The 546th convoy arrived in Bricquebec on July 26 at 1800. The sun, covered in clouds and mist, shed a dull light across the terrain. Guns and guards surrounded the perimeter of the encampment. Frank and his men camouflaged their trucks and artillery with leaves and branches then dug slit trenches to burrow down in.

Very little light was left when Frank wrote Catherine.

*Hello Darling,*                 *Thursday, July 20*

*I'm writing this in my little old pup tent very untidily built over a slit trench. It's dark and raining now, so if some of the words I write don't add up to what I started out to say, blame it on the war.*

*Been rather busy as yet but hopeful we will settle down to the old slow time routine very shortly, so I can take time to write and dream about my wife.*

*I can hear the artillery barrage and bombing off in the distance, as of yet it seems remote and unreal. Everyone seems hopeful of an early end of hostility, could be, hope so. Who knows, maybe even by Christmas.*

*Have not heard from you since Sunday, so I have kind of lost contact again. How's our little man, Kitty? I seem to live from the twenty-fourth to the twenty-fourth. Well. If everything goes well, we will be able to celebrate his birthday together.*

Frank folded his letter and put it in his chest pocket, where he found Catherine's last crumpled letter. He read her words, kissed her message, and said his prayers. It was a rough night for all the men. In the morning, they left the field.

Moving only a mile away, they set up camp with the other units which had arrived earlier at the Command Post in an old apple orchard. Patton kept himself secluded, wanting the Germans to be surprised when all his troops were ready.

For the past seven weeks, the First Army had been fighting the Germans in Brittany. The Germans, already weakened, brought troops from their eastern front and increased their attacks. When the Third Army arrived, they worked together with the First Army. Patton and General Bradley of the First Army had similar fighting styles and mutual respect. They planned to integrate the armies, sending troops to the north and others to cover the flanks to the south. Another armed force moved west to free the ports with units covering them to the east. Patton recorded in his journal, "the two armies danced."

Aviation played a central role throughout the Normandy campaign. Not only did it provide troop support, but it also dislodged enemy troops from their caches. The most memorable event was *Operation Cobra,* when the two armies, the First and Third, in addition to the XIX Tactical Air Command combined all under Patton's command. "It was love at first sight," Patton declared, referring to the XIX TAC.

The soldiers settled into a routine for the moment.

*Hello Darling,*               *Saturday, July 22*

*Just a quick note to let you know I'm still operating but have the devil of a time getting a letter mailed thru. I just dropped by to see Hub at the officer tent and to borrow another sheet of paper so I could write to you. We're getting along pretty well now. The people we meet are delighted to see us. It is a much better reception than at first. I hope to go to mass in a French church this*

*Sunday. Every church I've seen has a shell hole thru the
tower, but they're operating again.*

The villages around Bricquebec had not suffered from the bombings as severely as those near the landing beaches. The arrival of the
Americans brought a ray of hope to the villagers. During the four years
of occupation, the Germans displaced the French from their homes,
stole or destroyed their possessions, raped their young girls, and killed
their men. Neighbors disappeared in the middle of the night, possibly
killed or sent to concentration camps. The French resistance worked
underground with the villagers to find safe places to hide the Jews in
attics or basements. Whenever the Germans came through a town,
they tore up homes and barns looking for Jews and resistance fighters.
Young children, especially the scouts, aided the resistance by running
messages and later helped the American soldiers by collecting gas cans
and other useful items that had been discarded by the Germans.

On the first Sunday in Normandy, Frank attended mass in a
nearby field. The army priest stood behind a makeshift altar, and one
of the soldiers served as an altar boy. The soldiers, armed with rifles,
knelt in the mud in a slight drizzle with the roar of guns and airplanes
overhead. About sixty men filed up the middle aisle to receive communion; their heads bowed, accepting the host placed on their tongues.
"Body of Christ."

How could one reconcile all the killing and believe in Christ's
teachings of brotherly love? As in most wars, the soldiers felt that God
was on their side. And practically, Patton, a religious man himself,
preached the more Germans you kill, the sooner the war will be over,
and the fewer will die.

*Hello Darling,*                  *Sunday, July 23*

*Things have slowed down, at least I'm stationed where I can find enough time to write to you daily again. I hope the story about the rupture in the German government is true, and if it is, it sounds like the beginning of the end. It seems only too good to be true. It won't take long when they start fighting among themselves.*

*Tomorrow is John's fourth month, one of these days I'm going to be home for that day. Soon he will be crawling around pulling tablecloths off the table. In the next eight months, I think he will be at his cutest stage. I don't want to miss all of it. Goodnite darling.*

Once settled near the Command Post in Nehou, the soldiers and army personnel got better food, B rations with some red meat, and with the PX rations being free, they got all the cigarettes and candy one could want. The weather changed for the better too. When the sun was out, everything seemed improved. The four lieutenants, Kuret, Hubbard, Carlson, and Frank, celebrated in the sunshine by taking a bath in the nearby river for the first time since they left England.

*Hello Darling,*                  *Monday, July 24*

*It is a beautiful warm day, the best day we have had since coming to France and another day closer to you. Today is John's birthday, and we celebrated by taking a bath. It was the coldest water I have ever been in. I believe we are now members of the Polar Bear Club. I was a bit on the dirty side.*

Back at camp, the fellas kept joking and horsing around, until the mosquitos came out. Then they started cussing and slapping at the bugs, a funny sight if you weren't the one getting bit.

*Kuret claims they climb on his chest and turn his dog tags over to see what type blood he possesses. I told him they must like Kosher blood because they don't bother me as much as him. His reply was, "you can't get blood out of a turnip." Well, goodnight darling-love to you and John*

Kuret lying next to their jeep July 1944

Kuret was a Jew, fighting a war against the extermination of Jews, putting himself at risk of being taken a prisoner and treated like the other Jews. On the back of his dog tags was an "H" for Hebrew. The Germans didn't adhere to the international rules protecting POWs, and Kuret wasn't safe as long as there were Nazis. Frank was well aware of what this meant, even if he joked with Kuret. Humor hid the tension and his fear of losing his buddy.

The next morning the skies were an azure blue with a clarity reminiscent of the winter days Frank had spent in the desert. Puffy clouds dotted the sky, and the air was crisp with a slight breeze rattling in the trees. Frank let the wind blow across his face, thinking of Catherine and their future when he set out with his driver on reconnaissance to locate where to position the guns. The news from the fighting front had been exceptionally bright, putting them all in a better mood. Frank whistled, *Take Me Home Again, Kathleen,* only he changed the name to Catherine. *Across the deep blue sea.*

On the horizon, a black line appeared in the sky moving forward at a fast pace, and a roar of thunder echoed off the hills. An armada of American fighter airplanes, P-47's and P-51's, passed overhead. Jeeps, trucks, and tanks stopped in the road, and the men cheered. The power of the Army Airforce was an impressive sight to behold, sending chills down their spines and filling the men with pride and hopes of victory. The Allied bombing raid continued for the next three days, clearing the way for the artillery and foot soldiers.

*Hello Darling,*                  *Tuesday, July 25*

*The news from the fighting front sounds especially good now. Today, we watched 3,000 planes go over this morning. They really started things humming. The Germans don't seem to have much in the way of planes to send back. Could be that they are saving them, but I don't know what for. The German planes never come over in daylight. This clear weather will be of value to our boys up front because in this weather our planes can put in their strong arm and it will help the advance*

*considerably. Everyone seems overflowing with optimism*
*which I hope it isn't too soon. This slaughter can't con-*
*tinue indefinitely.*

Frank and his driver continued along the road, littered with German equipment.

*The Heinies left quite a bit of horse-drawn*
*artillery, also the horses! I've been trying to catch one to*
*ride around on. My driver roped one the other day but*
*couldn't hold him, dragged him right along till he let*
*go. The country is beginning to show signs of life again.*
*More Frenchmen are coming back to take care of their*
*farms. Be seeing you soon, darling, maybe I will get a*
*chance to help you with those diapers yet.*

Later that evening at dusk, Frank and his buddies played horse-shoes, wagering cigarettes and phony francs. Hubbard left for night duty to check the guns, while Frank and Kuret headed to their tents.

*We have some new neighbors now, a group of cows*
*just wandered in. They would be welcome but, unfor-*
*tunately, can't find the latrine and make a miserable*
*mess. We will have to run them out in the morning. I*
*hope they don't mistake our humble abode for a stable.*
*It's raining lightly again now. It came up suddenly out*
*of a clear sky. Well, goodnite darling, looks to be a busy*
*day tomorrow.*

The next morning one could hear the heavy artillery barrages and continual bombing, which preceded the ground attack, resulting in substantial Allied gains. The U.S. Airforce applied the strategy of carpet bombing. Over three thousand tons of bombs blanketed the ground. Unfortunately, due to the proximity of friendly forces, over a hundred U.S. soldiers had been killed that day and 500 wounded. The good news was that by nightfall of July 27, it was evident that the enemy's left flank was collapsing, and the intense bombardment had opened passages between the German lines to pierce the front in the direction of Brittany and the vital ports.

The Third Army was in a position to roll on August 1st with Patton in charge.

# CHAPTER FOURTEEN

# The Push

*Hello Darling,*             *Saturday, July 29*

*We have not heard any news today, so I don't know how the big push took hold, but I am quite confident things will start moving. I did a little touring today. You don't have to go too far to cover this area. You remember I sent my galoshes home? Well, I bought a new pair today—getting sick of wet feet.*

*Nothing much new here. We have settled down to a routine. We call it E.T.I. now instead of E.T.O., otherwise known as the European Theater of Inspection. Everybody and his relatives are inspecting us! I guess it's better having our own chewing on us than having snipers winging away. We haven't heard our news broadcasts as yet today, but it is rumored that it is continued good.*

*You asked if I gained any weight. Well, I have not been near any scales, but am pretty sure I haven't gone up or down. I still have hopes of developing a little old pot belly—but that will have to come a little bit later. At least now we get bread and a little red meat without the tin around it.*

*I have to go in and have my foot ex-rayed again.*
*They decided not to put the cast back on. It doesn't bother*
*me as long as I keep the elastic bandage on it.*

Saturday evening, the men from the other "fire units" got together and made a baseball diamond and had a lively ball game. Frank ended up as umpire on account of his foot.

*What a life! I'm fighting a war but can't even*
*play baseball.*

The weather turned, and Frank woke to a beautiful morning, clear skies and sunshine.

*Typically, one would think what a day for a ride*
*into the country. But during the war, it was "what a*
*beautiful day for bombing." It depends on one's point*
*of view.*

Sunday, Frank attended another field mass. Patton, even though an Episcopalian, went to the Catholic masses and encouraged other soldiers to practice their religions. Kuret was at a service the same day led by the Army Rabbi. It seemed like everyone was on his knees that day. Patton believed, "a man must plan, work hard, and pray. A man prays to God for assistance in circumstances that he cannot foresee or control." Patton believed that without prayer, his soldiers would "crack-up" under the unrelenting pressures of battle. "Prayer does not have to take place in a church but can be offered anywhere. Praying is like plugging in on a current whose source is in Heaven. Prayer completes the circuit. It is power."

Earlier in the week, Lieutenant General Bradley, the Commanding General, had given Patton orders to ready his Third Army to drive roughshod to the south of Normandy, knowing the enemy was already demoralized and rapidly retreating. Patton conferred with the other commanders of the XX Corps, 5th and 35th Infantries, the French 2nd Armored Division, and the XIX Tactical Air Command before going into battle. Patton believed in teamwork, not micromanaging his officers. He figured if you gave a soldier the goal, he would figure out the best way to achieve it.

Frank and his men were ready and waiting for the starting bell. Over the last couple of days, Patton had visited the troops in the region, inspecting them and giving encouragement in only the way he could do. "Nobody ever defended anything successfully; the only way is to attack and attack and attack some more. Whenever armor and air can work together, the results are sure to be excellent. Have confidence in the air while you are on the ground, and push incessantly and ruthlessly forward. Remember, a pint of sweat saves a gallon of blood."

Patton took official control of his Third Army on August 1, 1944. The first mission was to secure and maintain a bridgehead over the Selune River between Avranches and St. Hilaire de Harcouet.

Confident that his troops were well prepared and advancing as directed, Patton stopped at the Command Post at high noon and took a shot of brandy with Colonel Harkins to celebrate the birth of the Third Army. By the evening of August 1st, the Third Army had taken the town of Pontorson.

*Hello Darling,*                                    *August 1, 1944*

> *I'm going to have to write to you while on the run. Things are moving so fast over here that it looks like we will spend most of our time on the road chasing these Heinies back to Berlin (I hope). It's a beautiful day again and it's really fun traveling around in this weather. The only drawback is the food—it means going back on K-rations and that I don't like. Wish those Heinies*

*would stop long enough for us to get a good meal. Looks like we'll hit Paris before we know it. Like the rest of these towns, Paris will probably be off-limits for us.*

*We will hopefully get some mail sometime today. They are doing a good job of it, considering so much movement.*

*The 546th convoy in a French town in Normandy*

The 546th surged ahead of Patton, clearing out enemy and their booby traps, and setting up a defense perimeter around Headquarters. In preparation for the Battle of France, the 546th had moved to Beauchamps on July 31. The next morning orders came, and Frank and his boys moved south, inching their way to Avranches, the lynchpin of Brittany. Frank's guns protected the Quartermaster location of Allied supplies. At that point in the war, gasoline was already at a premium with not enough to go around. The enemy was also running low on petroleum, thus limiting the use of their tanks. Each other's supply garrisons were targets.

The relentless aggressiveness and wide-ranging sweep of the Third Army offensive caused havoc in the enemy forces. In desperation, the Germans continued to enlist very young and inexperienced soldiers, as well as the older soldiers who were no longer of much use on the Russian defense line. The Third Army secured the crossing of the Mayenne River, captured Vannes, and continued to Le Mans.

The planes filled the sky overhead as Frank's jeep rumbled on the bombed-out roads below. The fighter bombers covered the armored divisions from above, maintaining constant air protection by rotating eight fighter-bombers over each armored division. The Tactical Air Corps (T.A.C.) had the double duty of preventing attacks by enemy air and knocking out anything which might hold up the armored column on the ground. By attacking the approaching Panzer tanks and armored columns of the enemy, they opened a corridor for the infantry. The XIX T.A.C. and the Third Army worked closely together, talking to each other by radio. The port of Brest to the south had opened, and the new supply lines could bring in more supplies to the war zone. The brave black men of the Red Ball Express operated the trucks delivering the supplies. Their service was the lifeblood of Patton's fast-moving Army.

*Hello Darling,*                                    *Sunday, August 6*

*Just a quick note to let you know I am still operating but having a devil of a time getting a letter thru. We're moving along pretty well.*

*We got in this evening at 10 o'clock after being up at 8:00 am for Mass and Communion. We made a cook's tour of France. Wish I could tell you about it but will have to save it for the fireside.*

*The French we are now meeting are really cor-*
*dial and glad to see us. They say, "We have waited soooo*
*long!" My French is improving slowly but it sure is a*
*struggle.*

*After our mission was accomplished, we pulled off*
*into a little apple orchard to wash up and have chow.*
*We no sooner had our shirts off than we had an audi-*
*ence of about 20 women and children, boys and men.*
*There were six of us, so they brought us some hotcakes*
*and eggs and stuff. Then the conversation started, and*
*my French paid off. I have my French book thumbed*
*hollow looking up words. This has all been different than*
*I expected and am really enjoying France now—more so*
*than England.*

*Goodnite, darling, it is too dark to do much more*
*writing.*

"Mission accomplished" could have been meant defending and protecting a bridge, shooting down enemy planes, or reconnaissance into enemy territory. August 6th had been the most massive enemy air bombardment since the Third Army arrived in Normandy. Fortunately, Frank had been a good thirty miles south of Beauchamps, when the German planes strafed and bombed headquarters, destroying their ammunition depot. There were no casualties, but the explosions continued for three days. Luckily, the U.S. army freed the port of Brest, and more ammunition and new supplies could now arrive on the Red Ball Express.

The Luftwaffe became more aggressive carrying out night raids, even bombing and strafing the P.O.W. enclosures that housed their soldiers, killing twenty-one Germans and two U.S. enlisted men. The Americans opened the cages to release the P.O.W.s during the raids.

After the bombing, two-thirds returned, preferring to surrender to the Allies rather than return to Hitler's Army.

By August 8, the enemy appeared scattered and disorganized, the situation obscured by an unusual lull. Were the Germans giving up? Or were they preparing for a siege?

# CHAPTER FIFTEEN

# The Rocking Chair, the Apple Orchard, and the Organ

*Hello Darling Tuesday,*        *Tuesday, August 8*
*Missed writing to you last night, just couldn't get*
*around to it, and every chance I had today to stretch out,*
*something else happened.*

Frank and his battalion had traveled thirty-three miles by truck and jeeps in convoy to a new location just north of Rennes, where the massive bombing had flushed out the Germans. Before bombing the city of Rennes, the American planes flew over, dropping pamphlets and letters telling the citizens to seek coverage or evacuate. The Germans in occupied France had the opportunity to surrender, and many chose to hang white flags out the windows.

Frank's jeep bumped along the heavily trafficked roads, inundated with the citizens returning to their homes in the liberated towns and cities, carrying with them what belongings they had. Horses pulled carts with children dangling their legs out the back, and the older men and women sat on top of sacks of wheat or what crops they had saved. Men with shovels and rakes walked beside the wagons. Remains of German tanks and jeeps, clothing, helmets, and the detritus of war cluttered the roads. People swarmed around the vehicles pulling off the sides of sheet metal, emptying the carcasses of planes, trucks, and jeeps, taking what they could use. The soldiers participated in the feeding frenzy, searching for souvenirs and possibly something of use to them.

*Kitty, I have finally found myself a nice soft rocking chair. I got it out of a German vehicle, with blue and red upholstery. Really snazzy. Everyone is picking up German vehicles and equipment which litter the countryside.*

Frank loaded the chair onto the back of his jeep. Kuret found a German helmet and dagger that he neatly stashed under the seat. What they picked up was not all that practical at times. Still, the scavenging put the men in high spirits and the stuff left behind signaled that the Germans were on the run.

*I hear by the radio that in the States, they expect this war to be over in two weeks. Sounds good, but I think it may be a bit longer.*

*The weather! Well, the last three days have been marvelous, perfect days, nice warm sunshiny days, and cool, damp nights.*

Even though bombs dropped from the sky, exploding in the near distance, at least it was friendly fire, and Frank felt safe in the caravan of French and American soldiers.

*It hardly seems possible that there is a war waging in the beautiful and apparently peaceful country, only for the continual stream of planes overhead and the refugees on the road would you know anything was amiss.*

When they arrived at the camp, Frank threw his chair onto the grass and sat down in its leather folds to finish his letters. Hubbard was all over him about such a stupid thing to take.

"Foster, how the hell are you going to lug that thing around, let alone send it home?"

"Doesn't matter Hub, I'm in my rocking chair now, dreaming of the one waiting for me back home."

The next day Frank had to leave his little apple orchard to go back out on reconnaissance. When he returned the next day, he reclaimed his rocking chair under the big oak tree.

*Missed writing yesterday, out touring. So here I sit in my old easy chair under a big old oak tree, and quite cozy and comfortable. I'm sitting around waiting for a rumored speech by General Eisenhower in which it is said that he was going to make a very important announcement. It may be idle and rumor, but a soldier lives on rumor. I hope the General's speech has something to do with me getting back to you before John is many months older. I mailed a pair of wooden shoes for him; the kind people wear here in bad weather.*

Eisenhower and Patton met at headquarters and concurred on the war plan. After the breakout on the Cotentin Peninsula at St. Lo, they decided to head east and cross the Seine. German resistance was crumbling, and the Wehrmacht was in full retreat. Patton's message to the men of the 546th battalion was encouraging, but also meant a long war, not what Frank had hoped for:

"Men, we have a great opportunity to drive the Germans into their homeland before the end of the year. The war will be fought on a broad front, across France from the north to the south, all moving east."

New troops were coming through the freed Mediterranean ports to replenish the Third Army from the south of France. Unfortunately, the supplies could not keep up with the fast-moving armies on the ground due to the delaying tactics of the Germans.

Frank's battalion settled into a camp among the apple orchards in Mountours. Once they stopped for more than a day, the cooks set up a kitchen and fed the men some hot food. The ground troops had out-run their supplies again, and their gas was low; otherwise, they would not have stopped. Over the next few days, supplies arrived through the newly freed Brest port in Brittany. As the German armies retreated, they attempted to cut off the Red Ball advance and interrupt the sup-ply route by leaving tanks and obstacles in the road. The ground and air commanders coordinated plans, and the XIX T.A.C. planes swept in and blew up the tanks clearing a path for the supply trucks and the Third Army to advance.

It was a slow day, waiting for supplies and the Jerries hadn't been bombing or strafing them. After checking the gun crews, Frank roped himself a stray horse and took off across the field riding a mare bareback, his youthful days blowing in his face, sun shining, lost in thoughts of when he would return home. He got back to his apple orchard and reclaimed his chair.

*Hello Darling,*　　　　　　　　　　　*Thursday, August 10*
　　*Another day and another letter to my gal. I'm sit-ting here under an apple tree with Kuret beside me play-ing the organ. What a setting—what a scene! An organ set up in an apple orchard. We have neighbors too, cows and a couple of horses. By their glances of apprehension, they wonder if we are just plain crazy or what. Anyway,*

*we borrowed the chaplain's organ and are having quite a time. This afternoon we had about 10 French children gathered around with mouths agape. About an hour ago a war correspondent wandered in and said, 'now I've seen everything!' He said it reminded him of the Scotsman with bagpipes landing on Normandy beach.*

The instruments they brought to war! On D-day, the" Mad Highland Piper," dressed in his traditional kilt, played the bagpipes as the men came ashore, encouraging them to fight on. Frank had wanted to bring his accordion but now realized it would have presented some difficulty transporting. He told Catherine that Hub had the right idea of bringing a harmonica, much easier to carry around, but *he played so poorly, that it lowered the men's morale.* Now, sitting in the apple orchard, Kuret played the organ to the amusement of the French. Frank busted a gut laughing, leaning so far back in his chair that it nearly tipped.

The next morning Kuret woke up screaming at Frank, who had rolled out of his tent moments earlier.

"Dang you! Why'd you throw water on me!"

The look of the calf's eyes surprised Kuret. Frank stood laughing as the little guy mooed at Kuret.

"Ah hell, Frank. Would you look at this? Some damn calf has licked my face, so it's dripping." Kuret looked so hopeless half-awake with his head sticking out of his pup tent and the spindly-legged calf eyeing him, ready to clean that stubbled face. He had a hard time living that one down and was the brunt of more than a few cow jokes.

Orders from the Command Post came in daily. Patton believed in plans, but also to be flexible enough to change on a dime. Until they had orders to march, the men took care of camp business as usual.

The 546th was a 172-man battalion, with 40mm Bofor anti-aircraft guns, and M50 and 51 anti-aircraft weapons on quads. The M51 could shoot 3200 rounds a minute, which took a lot of ammo to keep things going. The advantage of these small anti-aircraft cannons was that they were portable. On the other hand, their 155-mm had to be towed by a tractor.

Frank was in charge of a fifteen-man crew to operate the 155mm "Long Toms." A full crew manned the guns day and night aware of the night-bombing German planes. Frank spent the night roving among his guns. *I'm turning into a night owl, stay up most of the night and try to sleep during the day. It doesn't work.*

The 546th A.A.A. Battalion Battery B, France 1944

The next day the 546th left in convoy to move closer to the new Command Post at Saint-Jean-d'Assé, about six miles north of Le Mans. Frank positioned the big guns in defense of the Command Post to bring down enemy aircraft in the area surrounding Le Mans.

On August 14, the gunners tracked a plane flying low in the distance, a P-47, the most common American fighter plane in the war. The P-47 started coming at the gunners as if the pilot was saluting them, flipping his wings, but he didn't veer and was heading straight towards them. In a split second, the first lieutenant shouted to get him out of the sky. The gun crews jumped on it and shot the plane, knocking him down. Frank's heart sank that they had commanded their men to shoot down an American aircraft. The pilot was dead, his body removed from the wreckage. The pilot on the ground wore a U.S. American Airforce uniform. The first officer removed the downed pilot's watch and dog tags and put them into a bag to identify him, then called the medics to take him away. The men of the 546th, sullen and stunned, feared they could be court marshaled for shooting down an American plane. Other friendly fire had taken lives throughout the war, so they shook it off and got back to work.

That same day, Patton reported that the Third Army had advanced farther and faster than any army in history. He felt confident that the Germans were slowing and noted in his journal that the night of August 14 was the first night the Germans had not bombed them. Then Patton got the news of the downed American plane, and announced, "This morning we were attacked by an American plane which got lost. Unfortunately, our men had to take it down."

With reluctance, Patton got into his plane to fly to Le Mans to check out what had happened. "I had been assured the Germans would fail to get me from above, but I fear the Americans would get me from below, as they were trigger-happy, due to the considerable Wehrmacht bombing." His premonition of impending death did not materialize that day as he flew across the battlefields, but it was the first time he had voiced such thoughts. He landed his plane and surveyed the war-torn area.

Months later, after a full examination of the accident and the soldier's death, the truth came out as to what happened the day the 546th struck down the U.S. P-47. It was not an American pilot; instead, he was a German pilot. The Nazis had recovered an American plane after shooting it down and repaired it. The uniform and dog tags were taken from the dead American pilot and given to the hotshot German bomber pilot with the mission to kill. At first, the morgue thought they had identified the downed pilot from his dog tags but then found the size of the American was different than the body on the slab. They tried to match the fingerprints, but they didn't match.

By mid-August, the Third Army had nearly encircled the enemy. As if in a chess game, once the Germans moved forces, Patton took the next move, always a step ahead. The liberated area included northwestern France to the Seine River in the east and the Loire to the south. Along the coast of France, the U.S. artillery fired on the enemy ships sinking them, thus opening more ports and taking St. Malo. Another artillery barrage hit the German Command Post with a direct hit on their ammunition dump. The XIX T.A.C. destroyed armored columns and knocked out seven of twelve ME-109, German fighters that were the backbone of the Luftwaffe. The Third Army troops fanned out across Brittany towards Paris and could attack in any direction without crossing each other. The Third Army raced across France. *At this rate, we'll be in Paris in no time,* Frank wrote to Catherine.

# CHAPTER SIXTEEN

# Vive l'Amérique!

*Hello Darling,*             *Friday, August 18*

*The people of France are quite jubilant now, and it looks like they will have all of their country back shortly. France amazes me with its great number of forests, it's marvelous way they have preserved the woods. I located a chateau or castle today, complete with a wall, moat, towers, private chapel, and everything.*

*It's a great thrill to pass through towns just liberated. We are greeted with flowers, fruits, handshakes, and kisses. Everyone lines the streets and cries "Vive l'Amérique!" Great stuff! Only bad part is you have to be careful when they throw, you have to be looking in all directions in order to avoid being plastered. I fell asleep going thru one town and woke up just in time to avoid a tomato, two hard pears, and a big chrysanthemum. As the boys say, 'life is ruff in the ETO.'*

*The beautiful countryside, hot weather, and crystal-clear rivers and streams are as near to idyllic as one could wish for, except there is one drawback and that is there are too many bees around here, and at mealtimes, they swarm over your food and it's just about impossible to eat jam without swallowing a dozen bees or so. Well,*

*I'm back under another apple tree, they never seem to ripen. We keep moving into orchards, always hopeful the next orchard will have some ripe ones.*

It seems the analogy of *bees in the jam* and *apples that never ripen,* describes what war was like, something always messing up a beautiful day and a war that never ends.

The next morning Frank took advantage of being near a stream to wash his clothes, hang them on some tree branches, then take a swim. The only problem was he didn't have his swim trunks.

*Funny, I left my trunks in my footlocker in England. Never used them all the time I carried them around with me, and now I have plenty of use for them. Well, every time I go swimming now, I get my shorts washed.*

Kuret joined Frank by the river, and they built an open fireplace, boiled their clothes in a big pan, then rinsed them in their two helmets, dipping their shirts up and down, Frank humming what he called a washerwoman song.

"Hey, Kuret, you ever heard of the 'The Irish Washerwoman'?"

Kuret laughed, "No, but I could use one now."

Frank shook his head at Kuret's ignorance of Irish dancing. "It's a jig! When Dada, Kitty's dad, plays the violin, those Marren girls dance the jig like nobody's business, especially Peggy." Frank stood up and imitated the girls dancing the jig, throwing one leg in the air with a hop, skip, and a jump.

"Reminds me of the Hora, all of us dancing in a circle, going faster and faster…Hava nagila, hava nagila…" The men got to belly-laughing as Kuret bounced up and tried to teach Frank the hora.

Once they finished their wash, they dumped the dirty water from their helmets and put them back on.

"These helmets are the handiest gadgets," Frank remarked as he slapped Kuret on the back.

Kuret grinned and punched him back. "Let's just hope they're just as handy in battle."

The shirts were barely dry, still stained with the telltale gray of overuse, when the troops got orders to march to the outskirts of Le Mans. An unusual and dangerous mission had developed after the XV Corps had passed through Le Mans and turned north, exposing the railroads. Because of the speed with which the Third Army's attack was progressing, supplies brought into the Le Mans vicinity by rail did not get disseminated but were kept either as a reserve or were waiting to be unloaded. The boxcars of supplies made a lucrative target for the German Air Force. For the next few days, the 155mm guns stayed positioned in defense of the supply depot.

In between surveillance, Frank found time to go into Le Mans to see the cathedral.

> *I went to confession in a French cathedral yester-*
> *day. The priest couldn't understand English, but we got*
> *along pretty well with the help of my French book. I wish*
> *you could have seen the church. It had a central altar*
> *and about fifteen chapels in alcoves along the sides of the*
> *church. It was immense and awe-inspiring. I hope to go*
> *to Mass on Sunday.*

Frank missed Mass on Sunday at the Cathedral of St. Julian of Le Mans due to orders to advance and attack. On Saturday, August 17, they loaded up to move closer to the Seine River. Patton had argued with Bradley to keep on the move. "Wars are won by crossing rivers. It is evident with these crossings, the Seine and Yonne rivers will become useless to the Germans as barriers." It took a few days to convince the other generals to allow Patton to send his troops across the rivers at several locations. Even Patton felt worried, but he told himself what he had said to many soldiers, "Do not take counsel of your fears."

The 546th moved quickly into position along the Seine River, where the soldiers would cross. The anti-aircraft artilleries became operational on defending the territory from the ground as well as the air. In offense, the 546th shot large shells across the Seine, clearing the Germans out and exploding their booby traps before the infantry arrived. Patton pushed his Army to the Seine, knowing the river was the lifeline to Paris. He was impatient with the other Generals, especially Montgomery, who had the 'wait and see' philosophy until the time to attack was ripe. Even though Eisenhower agreed with Montgomery, mostly for political reasons, Patton wanted to push forward. "There is no reason to wait for the other armies to cross if the Third got there first." Bradley disagreed and again wanted to delay the crossing, but Patton convinced him to let him proceed.

Patton fanned out his Army to cross at several points. For only the second time, the German Air Force returned to the sky in the day in tremendous strength, only to be matched by the U.S. forces. On the first day, over one hundred XIX TAC planes flew over the area bombing the enemy, and in two days, they shot down more than sixty enemy aircraft. The 546th fended off the enemy attacks and shot down six enemy aircraft. With support from the XIX Tactical Air, the Allies conquered the Seine. After the terrible beating, the Germans decided to change their activity from solely nighttime raids to continued daytime operations as well. Full of hope, Frank wrote to Catherine:

*From the news, those darn Heinies are beaten to the pulp, but they don't seem to realize it yet. I hope they see the light soon. I've seen enough of the world. Anyway, it's a cinch they can't last the winter out.*

*I still haven't heard from George. I hope he comes through all right.*

There was little damage to the bridge over the Seine at Mantes, so some divisions of the Third Army crossed it readily and moved on to the northeast of Paris, while the 546th and other battalions spread to the southeast, securing Chartres. Heavy fighting took place in Versailles on August 22. With the Third Army's success in Versaille, Orleans, and Fontainebleau, the Nazis evacuated those cities, and the Allies moved in. On the 23rd, the Allies entered Versaille and recovered much needed medical equipment left behind by the fleeing Germans.

*August 24, another anniversary day for John, that makes five months, maybe by the next one this war will be over. This morning's news sounds like Bulgaria and Romania are all through. I was on the go all day yesterday so I couldn't write. We had quite a trip yesterday, wish I could tell you about it, but it can wait for the fireside. We were caught in the rain last night, and a jeep is no place to be in the rain. It has resulted in nice cool weather for a change. It was getting a little too hot for comfort.*

Patton heeded reports from special missions and military intelligence to be aware of German delay tactics. He sent advance troops to blow up booby traps, tanks, and vehicles, even streetcars, the Jerries used to block the roads. Frank and his men pushed on further east, traveled 80 miles, crossed the Seine, engaged the enemy, and defeated them in one day.

The artillery had sunk four enemy barges on the Seine River and proceeded to seize and secure the Yonne bridgehead at Sens, southeast of Paris. Disregarding the bad weather and low fog, the XIX Tactical Air Command destroyed twenty more German barges and damaged ninety-one others. It was a red banner day for the Third Army who successfully traversed rivers and cleared roads and airstrips across France. The first shipment of supplies came in by air at the freed airfields near Le Mans, and the same day fifty patients were air evacuated from the battle zone hospital.

As of the end of the first three weeks in France, casualties of the Third Army were one-tenth of the losses the Germans endured. The Third Army had lost a total of 15,000 men: 1,700 killed in battle; 8,000 wounded; 1,700 missing; and 4,000 non-battle casualties, whereas the Germans had total losses of 110,000 men.

The problem for the Third Army now was that they did not get enough replacements. Rather than a loss of morale because of being understaffed, Patton noted fewer men with battle fatigue, no AWOLS, and fewer going to the infirmaries for psychological ailments. When asked how this could be, he replied, "My men love being on the winning team."

Patton and his troops had long wished to enter Paris as victors. In advance, he sent a letter to his men, emphasizing the extreme punishment imposed on those who committed crimes and violence against the citizens. When in another country, soldiers and visitors often leave their good manners, respect, and law-abiding behavior at home, thinking there are other rules to play by, giving themselves liberties not allotted in their own countries. Patton knew that once they reached Paris, the streets would fill with the newly freed French, and the champagne and celebration would continue for days.

But Patton and his Third Army did not get the glory of entering Paris as victors.

Having encircled Paris and cut off the routes to Paris by road and river, the Third Army provided an opportunity for the French to take back Paris their capital, symbol of liberty and beauty to the world. The journalists and photographers had followed Patton, assuming he would lead the troops into Paris. Still, the Supreme Commander Eisenhower thought it politically correct to have the French Army enter Paris victoriously. Strategically, Eisenhower reasoned he did not want to become embroiled in the political disputes of governance that would follow the liberation of Paris, nor did he want his soldiers in hand-to-hand street fighting with the remaining Nazis and sympathizers. Also, the Supreme Headquarters Allied Expeditionary Forces (SHAEF) did not want the burden of feeding the millions of people in Paris.

The French officers pleaded with Eisenhower and Bradley that together they would enter Paris victoriously with the Americans. Eisenhower relented and allowed the First Army to join the French. Undoubtedly, Patton's soldiers were more than disappointed after having opened the way to Paris and anticipating the grand celebration.

Church bells would ring with townspeople cheering, singing, and dancing and drinking the bottles of wine and champagne hoarded for the occasion. Frank and his men would miss this historic, almost mythical event.

On August 23, the French 2nd Armored entered Paris from the west, and the American 4th Infantry Division of the First Army came from the south. From the north, Major General Leclerc and his French Army didn't "dance its way to Paris," as expected, instead they fought German resistance along the roads. The overly excited French crowds lining the accesses to Paris caused further delay, throwing flowers and kisses and pouring wine on their heroes, slowing them down.

On August 24, the British Broadcasting Company announced that Patton's Third Army had taken Paris, which was not the case. "This seemed to be poetic justice," Patton lamented, "as I could have taken it had I not been told not to." In respect and appreciation to Patton, when the French 2nd Armored Division led by General Leclerc entered Paris, they told everyone they belonged to the Third Army, not the First Army, who marched with them. By midnight of the 24th, the Germans surrendered to General Leclerc.

Amidst scattered shots from snipers on August 25, General Charles de Gaulle made his official entry into Paris through the ornate L'Arc de Triomph, down the Champs Elysee, and to the Place de la Concorde. Paris erupted in celebration of their liberation, and as imagined, the streets filled with people kissing the soldiers, drinking champagne from the long-hoarded bottles. At the same time, the media had a frenzy as to who would be the first to record the event and get it to press.

The stupendous encircling thrust by General Patton's Third Army had caused *the capital to fall like the proverbial ripe plum*, as recorded in the After-Action Reports of the Third Army. Another phase of the war had ended, but not as Patton and his boys had dreamed.

The 546th bypassed Paris and settled in the shadow of a chateau outside of Paris on the road to Metz.

# CHAPTER SEVENTEEN

# A Day with General Patton

After a great romp across France, mopping up and freeing the French, it seemed unimaginable to have not allowed Patton and his Third Army the honor of entering Paris, but that was the politics of war. The day after the liberation of Paris, Patton visited all of his troops to spur them on. He first drove to Fontainebleau, extolling the men for their successes and decorating several with Distinguished Service Crosses. By jeep and by plane, he stopped at each command post and field location. Patton mused in his notes, "Perhaps someday, I shall figure out the number of miles I drove and flew that day to direct the campaigns of the Third Army. I'll bet it was about a million." As he passed in his jeep with his dog, Willie, upfront with him, the men recognized him and stood up in their tanks and vehicles and cheered. They admired and respected him, knew that he was fighting alongside them, and they were ready to fight with him.

> *Hello Darling,*                   *Friday, August 25*
> *I'm at the Battery Post waiting for the mail, so I borrowed some paper from Hubbard so I can get this off in tonight's mail. Everything is the same as usual, the weather fine, the countryside is changing but still France. We are still getting "Vive l'Amérique" more*

*fruits, vegetables, and handshakes. In fact, when we came back from reconnaissance yesterday, we had enough groceries in the jeep to have a lunch of scrambled eggs, tomatoes, pears, and it was one of the best meals I've had in France.*

*I'm now sitting under a pair of giant cedar trees at least 200 feet high, and we estimate their age to be over five hundred years. They are located in the back-yard of a chateau, the occupants have disappeared. They were friendly with the Germans and are frowned upon a bit. The place has a moat and a drawbridge still operating.*

*Well, goodnight, darling. I'll be seeing you soon.*

It's an understatement to say those who collaborated with the Germans were "frowned upon a bit." As the Americans freed the French cities, they also took French prisoners who had been on the Axis side. The French government punished these collaborators, depending on the extent of their participation. During the liberation campaign, France executed 9,000 collaborators and sentenced 40,000 sympathizers to prison. Frank only knew that the inhabitants were gone, perhaps they escaped or faced the French punishment.

On Liberation Day, August 25, Frank traveled seventy miles from Fraze just southwest of Chartres, bypassing Paris, to Vrigny, just outside of Reims to the northeast of Paris. They circled south then turned abruptly north, and covered the southern flank of the Third Army, removing obstacles and chasing the Nazis further east.

Once in Vrigny, Frank and some of the men took time on Sunday to go to Mass.

*Hello Darling,*                              *Sunday, August 27*

*Went to Mass this morning in a nearby village church. There were about 60 G.I.s there, and the priest wouldn't accept any money from the Americans. So, one of our boys took up a collection in his helmet, and the Padre really did all right! Well, I must be off to work, be seeing you and John soon.*

On the following days, Frank went south to La Chaume to confer with the other officers before the Third Army pushed further east towards the Rhine. The much-needed supplies of gasoline and ammunition came in by air now, and the coordination of which division got what was a "snafu" (situation normal all fouled up). Officers commandeered supplies meant for other divisions. When Patton discovered that the gas destined for his Third Army had not arrived, he thought it was a backhanded way of slowing up the Third Army, but that was not the case. The delay was due to a change of plans by the High Command to redirect the supplies, which in Patton's opinion was General Montgomery's influence over Eisenhower. Patton pleaded that his army would be given the needed gas and ammunition for a rapid advance to the east to cut off the Siegfried Line before the Germans could staff it. Eisenhower denied his request, which infuriated Patton and strengthened his negative feelings towards Montgomery.

As if diverting supplies wasn't already a dire situation, Patton discovered that the airlift, carrying army rations and food, went to feed the Parisians and hundreds of thousands of refugees detained in the Third Army zone. The last straw was when the truck companies moved headquarters, thus slowing delivery to the Third Army, and the airdrops went to the Twenty-First Army Group led by none other than Patton's nemesis, Montgomery. In the meantime, De Gaulle attempted to detach the 2nd French Armored division from the Third Army, which was badly needed to guard Patton's right flank.

In true Patton fashion, he told his officers, "Continue east until the tanks stop, and then get out and walk because it is mandatory to get crossings over the Meuse River." The Third Army was not going to be held up by a few setbacks.

By August 27, the Third Army had seized control of the bridgehead in the vicinity of Reims. Frank and his boys set up their 155 howitzers and turned their guns towards the enemy across the river. The Germans had slowed down their air attacks, so now the anti-aircraft artillery focused more on land warfare. In Patton's eyes, the men of the A.A.A. battalions were the real soldiers who met the challenges as they arose and not only performed their duties as taught but could change to fit the situation. When needed as foot soldiers, some of the artillery enlisted men switched to infantry. They marched alongside the tanks, sweeping into a village on foot armed with their rifles and grenades. The anti-aircraft artillery, tanks, and trucks adapted to the new warfare and fell in with the infantry as they marched towards Germany.

> *Hello Darling,*            *Tuesday, August 29*
>
> *It's been raining all day today, and Captain Howell, Lt. Hubbard, Lt. Carlson and I had to ride 80 miles in an open jeep. What a ride! I hope it stops raining cause we have to go again tomorrow, and once is enough.*
>
> *On our trip today, Captain Howell and Lt. Carlson and I went on a jaunt. On the way, we picked up our groceries but brought our own beef steak. We set up in a forest and cooked our dinner, and it was really a spread of steak, scrambled eggs, tomatoes, jam, bread, coffee, and pears, surprising what you can whip up*

*with a couple of mess kits and an open fire. Our stove was a piece of armor from a nearby wrecked German plane.*

That evening they returned to camp on the grounds of the chateau.

*Well, I'm writing to you by the strain of "Kerry Dance" on the radio, makes me feel like I'm at home. I wish you could see this setting under the 500-year-old trees alongside the chateau.*

The violin music drifted into the trees. The Irish tenor sang:

"Oh the days of Kerry dancing, Oh for one of those hours of gladness, Gone alas like our youth too soon."

The following day the entire unit moved to La Chaume, the eighty miles Frank had just traveled.

*Hello Darling,*      *Thursday, August 30*

 *Missed writing to you yesterday but it just wasn't possible to do it. Here I am under another apple orchard. After this is over, I'm going to have to buy me an apple orchard or at least an apple tree cause I won't feel at home without them. The pity is those darn apples never seem to ripen.*

 *The news sounded good this morning, looks like Czechoslovakia has come to life and is going to be on the winning side, the more, the merrier.*

Frank had traveled over rutted roads, dodging sniper shots, and watching the sky for foreign planes. The Germans had pillaged villages and towns, and when they escaped, they left debris and roadblocks to slow down the Allies. It's no wonder that a few vehicles got wrecked.

Somewhere between Vrigny and La Chaume:

> *My jeep got wrecked the other day, and yesterday*
> *I had to use a German jeep one of the boys picked up.*
> *We were driving thru a town, just got to the outskirts,*
> *and the right wheel came off and rolled right on ahead*
> *of us, setting down with a thud. We calmly unloaded*
> *our equipment into another truck and took off, leaving*
> *it with a bunch of excited Frenchmen. I laughed for the*
> *next ten miles. Two days, two jeeps. Now I've got one*
> *borrowed from Headquarters till mine gets back.*
>
> *If you are in the sending mood, I wish you would*
> *send me some coffee and canned milk. We're really short*
> *on supplies. How's our boy doing, Kitty? Won't be too*
> *long now.*

Not only gas and ammunition were on short order, but the men had also resumed eating K rations and going without the perks of a commissary, like coffee and cigarettes.

Frank's men in the field

CHAPTER EIGHTEEN

# Champagne and Silk

*Hello Darling,*                  *Friday, August 31*
    *I have some French buttons I picked up in town today. They are wooden and hand-painted. We are beginning to pick up a number of souvenirs, some we can send, some we cannot. I saw some flimsy silk blouses and French items in town today. I would have gotten you some but didn't know what size blouse and gloves you take. I bought you a scarf, blue silk, and some more buttons and have them all wrapped up ready for the mailman but you better figure on about two months in transit, cause the traffic is heavy We can buy quite a bit in these towns but don't like to send too much because of the risk.*

    *I wish I could send you some of the Champagne I have but we can't mail it. It's stuff the Germans couldn't carry while running! The captain just brought in a bottle of Champagne into our tent and I'm working on him for the past hour to open it up and see if it is drinkable.*

The road wound through the French countryside of Champagne, over gentle slopes with chateaus on the distant hilltops and vineyards on all sides. The neat rows of grapevines hung heavy with fruit. The vendange had already begun. Women hunched over clipping the grapes, while the men carrying the large paniers collected the fruit and dumped the produce into buckets at the end of each row. A large farm truck stopped, and the driver got out and threw the grapes into the back and continued. Frank quizzed some of the French workers about working in the fields during the occupation and war. He studied the deep sandy soil, chunky clods of dirt, and the precision of grafting the vines and stringing them to the charming old branches from last year's crop. The irrigation ditches slanted slightly, and the water flowed smoothly. *Very efficient use of land,* Frank mused thinking one day he may want to plant a vineyard, maybe even in the Coachella Valley, if it weren't so hot.

The road passed through several towns and villages. Frank and the men took the opportunity to shop in the specialized boutiques: the *boulangerie* for bread, the *poissonier* for fish, the *charcuterie* for cured hams, sausages, and salamis, *and alimentation* for staples, all tidy little shops with bells on the door. Frank and his officer friends wanted to find something for their wives.

"Bonjour Messieurs," greeted the young shopkeeper of ladies' fine apparel. The officers smiled back a bonjour, feeling slightly out of place in such a feminine shop. Captain Howell found a few blouses for his wife while Frank lamented not knowing Kitty's size. The diminutive saleslady saw the American soldiers touching the clothes with their rough hands, a definite no-no in France, but she allowed them to roam the store before asking in her broken English if she could help.

"Oui," Frank attempted his French. "Je ne sais pas," he motioned with his hands how tall Catherine was. "I don't know my wife's size, s'il vous plait." Frank lifted the peach-colored silky blouse.

"Perhaps a scarf?" suggested the sweet girl.

Frank agreed and chose a sky-blue silk scarf to match Kitty's eyes. The clerk wrapped their bundles neatly in brown paper and attached a ribbon. The men pulled out their wallets, and the young girl called her grandfather from the back to meet the soldiers. He had tears in his creased eyes, maybe from age, but his voice showed his gratitude. He held out a bottle of Champagne for each of them and said something in French.

The young girl translated. "Please, accept this as our gift. You and your wives have suffered much for us." The men insisted on paying for the merchandise but gladly accepted the Champagne as a gift.

Frank's battalion was one of the critical units in the Liberation of Epernay on August 28, 1944, and of Reims on August 30. The townspeople greeted them with joy and relief, literally dousing them with Champagne at every turn. Much of the Champagne had been walled up in cellars or hidden in walls since 1940. The people of Champagne felt tremendous gratitude towards the Americans, their liberators. The Germans had stolen more than two million bottles of Champagne from merchants' cellars, not even accounting for the thousands of bottles that were left in personal vaults by inhabitants who fled before the invasion. In late August 1944, due to the speed of the Allies advance and the help of the French Resistance, the Germans hastily evacuated the region leaving behind their bounty of Champagne. During the occupation, the Nazis spared the region of Champagne and allowed the harvest to continue. They set up lavish headquarters in the regional capital, Reims, and sent the Gestapo out to clean up the city. They deported Paul Chandon-Moet to Auschwitz, and ruthlessly, arrested and executed other Jewish vintners or systematically used them until not needed. Those who were deported safely or escaped returned after the Liberation to find their chateaux in shambles, broken bottles, furniture turned over, and cabinetry burned. If the Nazis had time as they fled, they threw grenades through the beveled windows out of hate and spite.

\* \* \*

Catherine finished reading Frank's letter.

*I picked up some perfume yesterday. I don't know much about perfume, but they told me it was the best. As soon as I get it packed, I'll mail it to you. Hope you like it.*

Catherine thought about all the niceties, having a silk scarf, a fur hat, hand-painted buttons to sew on her clothes, lace, and French perfume. She set down his letter and wept, hoping no one would hear her. She wanted her own home, her family together, and for the baby to stop crying. John had been inconsolable while teething. She tried to get out of the house, but that didn't help either. Her mother Sarah was bed-ridden again, and Agnes worked all day at the department store and was gone every evening with Dick, who might put a ring on her finger anytime. Catherine hoped Frank might make it home in time for Agnes's wedding. She thought back to last week.

She and baby John had spent a week in Riverside with her sister Peggy. Seeing a photo of Peggy's new husband, Steve, in uniform, made Catherine sad. "Do you think Steve will be sent to the Pacific or European Theater?" she asked Peggy. It was uncertain where he'd go, but they both girded themselves knowing their husbands would be at war as long as it lasted.

Peggy lamented. "For a while, it seemed the war would be nearly over, but then it flared up. Steve worries that he'll be shipping out soon. Mary's the lucky one, three kids, and a husband at home."

"Oh, Peggy. It's not easy for Mary. Horace is working overtime to make ends meet and then volunteering at the fire department during the night. Frank is a little worried Horace is overdoing it."

"Perhaps you're right. Did you hear what Horace did last week?"

Catherine braced herself, hoping no one was ill or hurt. "No, what?"

"He got a late call that a gas station had left their lights on during the blackout. He grabbed his keys and roared down to the station only to find out the other volunteers had already axed open the door and broke a few windows in his father's gas station. To hear Horace tell it, you'd think it was a joke."

Catherine giggled, picturing Horace standing there with his big grin, apologizing to the other fellas.

The baby started fussing, and as natural as if John were her own, Peggy picked him up, cooing at little John, hoping for a child of her own.

Back home, Catherine folded the last letter, only two weeks old, and put it in her tin letterbox. She relied on Frank's messages, which were always encouraging until they weren't. He talked about soon changing diapers, helping with the baby's teething moods, and teaching John how to walk. Then she'd get a letter, and he wrote about the Heinies (she hated when he used derogatory terms for people) and chasing them back to Germany. When things weren't going well, he told her not to get too excited about the war ending anytime soon, but usually, he signed off, *will be seeing you soon...* The unknown was so hard to bear.

Dada opened the front door, hung his hat, and walked into the room, set down the groceries, and asked Catherine to help put them away. He quietly lit his pipe and walked to the living room to read the newspaper. When Catherine walked back in, he set the LA Times down. The news wasn't so rosy.

"The war seems to be escalating again. Getting nearer to Germany. What do we hear from our boy Frank?"

# CHAPTER NINETEEN

# Violin Concerto in the Forest

*Hello Darling,*                            *Friday, September 1*
       *Somewhere this week I lost a day, I don't know just which day, it's funny how sometimes you lose track of time. The weather threw us a curve yesterday and this morning, and rung in some cold weather, maybe to remind us that winter is just around the corner, and so it is. I hate the thought of spending the winter in this country, at least out in the open space as we are now. From the looks of the war map, Germany should already have quit, but the darn fools keep going on.*

Frank and the other officers had traveled 100 miles from their camp to meet with the commanders in the war tent at the Command Post. They studied the map, showing the positions of all the army corps in the Third Army. The blue squares fanned out from Metz to Nancy in the north and farther south along the German border. The U.S. forces had pushed the Germans to the edge of the Fatherland. The Allied aircraft flew over German territory bombing the cities, the villages, the roads, and the ammunition depots to clear the way as General Patton's Third approached the borders of the Third Reich. By the end of August, the battle for France had ended, and the battle for Germany had begun.

After the meeting, Captain Lowell, Hubbard, Carlson, and Foster climbed back into their jeeps. It would be another hundred miles in the dark before they arrived back in camp.

> *Hello Darling,*                    *Sunday, September 3*
> *I missed writing to you yesterday, but it was unavoidable. We took another one of those long jeep rides in the rain, covered about 200 miles, and when I got back, it was dark, and I was ready for bed.*
> *We saw one funny instance in a large town. A group of Frenchmen rounded up three German prisoners, one a member of the regular German army, the next a sniper, and the third, a member of the Gestapo. They marched them up thru the town to the hoots and hollers of the excited populace. They were a sad sight. Funny, so many of these so-called Supermen are little shriveled up weasels and many nothing but children.*

The curtain fell away, and Frank saw the soldier behind it, like Oz, he was a little man, feeble and exposed. Frank couldn't help but feel sorry for these poor souls, especially the children soldiers who knew no better. When the enemy is a figment of evil, war lacks emotion. But when you look into the eyes of another human being, empathy and sorrow filters to the bone.

The next day the battalion packed up and traveled by convoy northwest to Marson. Patton had received word that at least half of the available supplies would be coming to the Third Army, so he gave orders to cross the Moselle, and force the Siegfried Line.

*Another rainy day, but the war news is good so that we won't cry about a little rain. It doesn't seem possible that the Germans can carry on much longer. They seem entirely disorganized and making a beeline to the Fatherland. I won't be sending any money orders this month because I want to have a little capital if this war comes to a close.*

The closer Frank got to the Siegfried Line, the more apparent it became that the German army had splintered, and their soldiers were now hiding in towns and farmhouses. The enemy faced serious recruitment problems, employing inexperienced units to the front line. Cooks and bakers, clerks from stores and offices were thrown together into a military unit, given weapons, or put on tanks to patrol the countryside and villages. The Allied commanders received reports that indicated the enemy would make a determined stand at its fortified borders along the Siegfried Line.

September 5 Morning Report: Captured and wounded one German soldier. One German killed by guards.

*We are all gathered around the radio waiting for the six o'clock news, we usually gather after dinner for it, and now everyone is avidly awaiting each new broadcast, everyone is momentarily expecting the end to come. We captured a prisoner yesterday, and he was entirely out of contact with current news. Lt Kuret asked him if he thought the Germans were going to win the war. His answer was, "There was never a doubt." We told him where the Americans had advanced, and you should have seen his face. He sure was a sad sight.*

Then an unfortunate turn of events happened. Frank's battalion was held up by lack of gasoline and supplies, as well as bad weather, which kept the planes from flying, leaving the ground troops with no protection or advance reconnaissance. After covering thousands of miles and liberating the villages and cities of France, the history-making pace of the Third Army and the XIX Tactical Air came to a near stop in early September. The 546th battalion had run out of fluid and fuel, so they had to shut down for three days with only enough fuel for their 155 howitzers, which they kept running with an electric motor. Their trucks barely had a quarter tank left in each of them, so they waited. They were so far ahead of the Red Ball express transports that SHAEF ordered them to stop until the supplies caught up with them. Once the supplies arrived, as a high priority, they filled their tanks and carried extra cans of fuel to keep them moving.

Allied reconnaissance reported feverish construction activity by the Germans on the West Wall, the German border, also known as the Siegfried Line. The Nazis forced their citizens and prisoners to work under dire conditions and the threat of death, constructing booby traps and setting up roadblocks. Nazi guards stood above them, pushing with their rifle butts to hurry them along, no one was allowed to take a break, and if they tried to escape, they were shot. The slave prisoners built rows of square-pyramidal fortifications, called dragon-teeth, interlaced with anti-personnel and anti-tank obstacles and explosives. The Nazis' artillery units targeted their big guns across the Moselle River, along the border, and directly at the cities of Nancy and Metz. German observation points and radio communication kept a close eye on the Allied movement.

Even though their advance had slowed, Patton still commanded the Third Army to maintain an offensive position between Metz and Saarbrucken.

Icy rain flooded the U.S. army camps, and the men worked and slept in the freezing weather without heat or proper clothing for the early onset of cold weather.

> *I've been working on a German blowtorch trying to make a stove out of it, without much success and am about to throw it away as so much junk. Our tent is full of smoke now. Will write later.*

Try as he might, Frank couldn't find a solution to the mud, rain, and cold. Either he could lie inside his wet pup tent or stay out in the rain and mud.

> *Hello Darling,*          *Sunday, September 10*
> *Try as I might I don't seem to be able to get a letter written every day as I promised, my intentions are good, but things don't work out that way, but I will do the best I can Kitty. The weather is terrible, rain and more rain, and the outlook is that it will continue so. What makes it worse is that it slows up our advance, because it keeps our planes out of the sky, and they are one of our most potent weapons. Everyone is waiting for the big day then we can smile long and loud. We're going to get a little time off, and have some movies, one of them is Bing Crosby in "Going My Way." Did I tell you I caught a glimpse of him, and Doris Day being photographed in front of some tanks? I haven't yet got to see one of their U.S.O. Shows.*

The dry, dusty roads became sticky with mud. Tanks got stuck, vehicles slipped off the thoroughfare, and small streams and rivers swelled up flooding the towns and passageways. Fighting was limited to reconnaissance patrols and light exchange of gunfire.

Once again, Frank left the camp early in the morning on a clandestine mission with the other officers. He headed north to Verdun, close to the battle line. The Germans had retreated and set up their defense on the other side of the Moselle River. *Battles are won by crossing rivers,* Patton's words rumbled in his mind. The rain obscured his vision magnifying the sound of interspersed gunfire and confusing his senses as from which direction the fire came.

Occasional bombshells exploded in the distance, perhaps from belly cans full of gas dropped to ignite a fire in a supply depot. Allied planes didn't fly in bad weather, so the low humming of a motor was sure to be a stray German plane flying overhead. In training, Frank had been taught to identify enemy planes by how they looked, but over here, with poor visibility due to the constant rain and low clouds, the engine's sound identified the enemy planes.

Passing through the towns on narrow roads and blind curves, Frank held his rifle cocked, alert to the danger lurking in corners and around bends. Without air protection overhead, the jeep was on its own with machine guns handled at the back, and each soldier equipped with rifles and grenades to protect against snipers and possible run-ins with panzers or Nazi soldiers on the road.

They stopped along the roadside to investigate a turned over German jeep, knowing it could be a ploy or even booby-trapped. Kuret checked for wires and explosives. They had no use for the vehicle but took a few items, guns, and some warm clothing.

Frank and the other anti-aircraft artillery officers had to get north to size up the territory ahead of their units to find positions for their guns and possible sections of rivers to set up protection for bridge-heads. The anti-aircraft crews were needed to protect the Navy Corps of Engineers as they constructed pontoon bridges. At Headquarters in Etain, Frank and the other officers prepared for the next offensive, crossing the Moselle.

> *Hello Darling,*                    *Tuesday, September 12*
> *I missed writing to you again yesterday, had to go on one of those trysts and didn't get back till dark. I haven't received a letter from you in four days, so I'm expecting a stack of them tomorrow. Good news is I'm all set for the winter now, we have some equipment captured from the Germans-fur caps and big heavy fur coats, wish you could see them. How the Germans can keep going with the enormous loss in personnel and equipment is beyond me.*

The officers got word that the German's had built up their defensive position along the Moselle and Meurthe in the vicinity of Nancy. Fortunately, the weather cleared, and a C-47 flew into Reims and delivered an unexpected supply of 11,000 gallons of gas. The XIX Tactical Air took advantage of the fair weather and concentrated heavily on attacking military installations along the Siegfried Line, the "West Wall" of Germany. After 470 sorties and 39 air missions, which damaged 28 German gun installations and 136 German military installations, the XIX T.A.C. cleared a path, and the Third Army continued to advance.

Bradley and Patton concurred that the Third Army should persist and cross the Moselle and continue into the Rhineland. Still, Patton's antagonist, Montgomery, once again convinced the High Command to move all supplies to the First Army, leaving the Third to hold position and defend. Patton would have nothing of that. His men wanted to fight, not wait. On September 14, the Third Army took Nancy. The

546th set up in protection of Nancy, a major city and prize conquest within reach of the German border. Patton moved his Command Post to Etain, outside of the highly fortressed Metz, another plum he hoped to capture.

By the end of September, Montgomery, now known pejoratively as "Monty," once again convinced the Supreme General Eisenhower to slow down, even stop the American troops from entering Germany across the Rhine so that he could make a "dagger thrust at the heart of Germany." Bradley concurred again with Patton that it would be more like a "butter-knife thrust." The higher authority commanded Patton to assume a defensive position, giving the cause of "lack of supplies," which all knew would go to another division.

*Hello Darling,*                    *Thursday, September 16*

*Missed writing again yesterday, was kept busy with little details, and the consistent rain discouraged any attempt to get down to business. I'm writing this by candlelight. I had just sat down to write and had to take off in a blackout to locate a film, but now we can't get the projector to work. We are sitting around waiting for the 9 o'clock news. The news was awfully good last night, hope it continues so. Most all the talk among the boys now is how long is it going to take them to get back home. Well, anything can happen, so I'll keep my fingers crossed. I pray we will not stay over here as an army of occupation.*

*Kuret is also writing, and every five minutes, we get into a discussion of what we will do when we get home. It's fun thinking and planning now.*

Kuret opened his box of candy his wife sent and passed it over to Frank.

"Thanks, pal." Frank unwrapped the shiny gold wrapper and took a bite. "These are the best candies I've ever had! Where does your wife get these? I'm going to ask Kitty to send some."

"Tell her they're Almondettes and she can get them at I. Magnum's or Lundy's on Wilshire Boulevard. You want another?" Kuret passed the candy box.

The wind picked up, and the candles fell over spilling wax on their letters. The night was clear, with a low fog blowing through the trees, and high clouds passing in front of the quarter moon. Frank got up from where he sat writing letters on top of a crate.

"Got to do my rounds." He sealed his letter and handed it to Kuret. "Make sure this goes out with tonite's mail." He ducked going out through the tent flap and checked on his guns. The light of the men's cigarettes led him to each position.

"Everything okay, boys?" He peered through the site finder and adjusted the position.

"No action, sir." Frank continued to make his rounds to each gun. He stepped over and around puddles, still his boots were soaked by the time he finished. With no action, he understood the ennui of his soldiers and worried about them falling asleep, fighting among each other, or taking off, and just like that, some damn German plane would fly over. *War is a waiting game. Boredom sets in, and then all hell breaks loose.* Glancing across the encampment, he surveyed the tents, making sure all lights were out, in case the Germans flew overhead. He didn't want to illuminate their target.

The next day Frank and his battalion moved to Etain Command Post (C.P.), where they would remain defending the territory already taken.

*Hello Darling,*          *Friday, September 17*

   *Kuret and I just opened one of our bottles of Champagne to see if it wouldn't give a little inspiration writing our letters tonite, but so far it hasn't done anything but take the chill of the air out of our bones. We have a nice big pyramidal tent now for our C.P., that is why we have been able to evade blackout and get our letters written at night. We are kept pretty darn busy during the day and heretofore if we didn't get the letter written during the day-no letter.*

   *I have a fur hat to send you as soon as I get clearance to post it. It is part of some German equipment that was captured. I don't know what you can do with it, but it might turn into a winter hat if you can do a little altering on it.*

The soldiers had picked up "souvenirs" that the Nazis had left in deserted buildings or taken them from prisoners or off dead soldiers. It was a common pastime for the boys to collect things, especially anything with the swastika: Nazi helmets, flags, belt buckles, daggers, badges, weapons, or anything useful to them, like the coats and fur hats. As the Germans retreated from an area, many attractive souvenirs were left about purposefully, then booby-trapped with grenades or explosives in hopes of baiting the G.I.s. Many soldiers paid the ultimate price in their quest for the final war trophy.

*Dear Kitty,*          *Thursday, September 22*

   *I just got back from taking the mail around to the guns, that's one time they're really happy to see us captains.*

*So far, I have seen a good many towns but as yet*
*have not been to Paris and it doesn't look likely that I will*
*see it before the war is ended, well I would rather see Los*
*Angeles anyway. I was in the heart of the Champagne*
*country not long ago and got pretty well acquainted with*
*the industry. We were in Chalons-sur-Marne and went*
*over to Epernay. I'd like to get back there again as my*
*supply of Champagne has dwindled to almost zero. We*
*went to a cathedral in Chalons, it is still whole but was*
*damaged a bit. We sent some boys up to Reims, I missed*
*that trip but plan on going back sometime. The churches*
*here are amazing, both in size and beauty.*

*The weather has been very nice the last three days,*
*no rain, just a little fog. I don't know what winter will*
*be like here, but so far, the weather has been like the*
*Midwest states.*

Frank was back writing a travel log, no complaints, and at times
even enjoying himself. He and Kuret had an on-going repertoire of
jabs and jokes. If they were in school together, the teacher would have
separated them. The imposed slow down allowed some respite. The
soldiers amused themselves around camp, listening to the radio, playing music, and occasionally getting in a game of volleyball or toss-
ing the baseball around. Frank's jeep driver had picked up a ukulele
and was playing it while the boys sang the old-fashion songs of their
youth, "Yankee Doodle Dandy, Old Aunt Jemima, She'll Be Coming
'Round the Mountain…" Everyone seemed to join in belting out the
words as if it were their last. Frank had picked up a violin from Special
Services, the entertainment unit, and gave it to one of the sergeants
who played pretty well. Every evening after grub was served, which
had improved since they got fresh vegetables from town, the sergeant

played the violin. The night settled in over the forest, and after Frank checked his guns, he sat on a log, lit a cigarette, and let the music sink in. What irony to be in a war zone with glorious and peaceful music. The sergeant slowly moved the bow across the strings, emitting sweet sounds that floated among the trees. The soldiers listened, lying on the ground, looking out from their tents, or hunching over a letter. They didn't want to be there; they had had other plans for their youth. Frank stubbed out his cigarette and let the melancholy settle in his heart.

# CHAPTER TWENTY

# War is Hell! Especially War in the Rain

*Hello Darling,*           *Wednesday, September 27*

*Another month is coming to a close, when will it end is the big question, the war I mean. We can feel the breath of winter close on to us, but then too, the Germans can also feel it, and they will suffer more than we.*

*We've acquired a stove for our tent, and it's now between the smoke or the cold. It's a British stove, and I don't think it quite understands our accent, as emphatic tho it be.*

*Another day and no mail from you, this can't go on. Aggravating, isn't it?*

*We had our daily rain again today. I guess we just have to figure on it on a daily basis and adjust to it.*

*Bing Crosby's on the radio, it's just like home now, just no you. Are John's six-month photos from Jose Reyes done yet? There should be quite a change now since the last portraits were taken at three months. Give my love to your family.*

On the outskirts around the Command Post, the anti-aircraft battalions were taking extreme caution in case of an air attack. The

Luftwaffe had been uncommonly quiet, creating even more tension and need to be vigilant. Undoubtedly, the Germans knew the whereabouts of Patton. Frank's unit's primary operation was anti-aircraft, but their secondary mission was to be alert of any nearby enemy activity and attack if confronted both on land and from the air. Germans sent spies in civilian clothing to check on American positions. It was nearly impossible to identify the infiltrators, so all citizens were suspect. Frank made his rounds checking the 155mm, on the lookout for snipers and any unusual behavior in the vicinity. They remained vigilant, ready to use their handguns and rifles, if necessary.

The German tanks and artillery lined the other side of the Moselle, launching shells and missiles. Explosions could be seen and heard in the near distance as the Germans volleyed across the river. The Allies responded with sudden bursts of gunfire called "flash-bang," a counterbattery procedure that effectively destroyed the enemy or silenced them by driving its gunners to cover. When not actively engaged in combat, the U.S. artillery focused on known enemy encampments and supply depots.

Verdun was a few kilometers from the 546th outposts in Etain, only twenty kilometers from the German-occupied Metz. By early September, the Allies had liberated Verdun, and the Germans retreated, but the Wehrmacht retaliated by heavily bombing the city.

Frank's battalion set up in the existing WWI fortifications in the area to ensure the Germans didn't use their advantage of proximity to retake Verdun. Unknown to Patton, the Germans had no interest in Verdun; instead, they concentrated on building up their war arsenal and holding Metz.

*I picked up some postcards of Verdun I'll send you.*
*I spent a little time in and around Verdun. It's beautiful.*

*I saw the fortification and battlegrounds of the last war,*
*as a matter of fact, we used some of the dugouts.*

Frank sat outside his tent, cleaning off his boots caked in mud. The water-soaked leather wouldn't shine the way Frank wanted. Patton insisted on shiny boots and well-appointed uniforms. He demanded that his soldiers were clean-shaven, wear buttoned shirts and well-fitted pants, along with the right accouterments of war, a belt with grenades, a gas mask, his rifle oiled and ready, and the helmet. A soldier not wearing his helmet could be court-martialed. Patton believed if a soldier took pride in his appearance, it showed that he would take pride in his actions. Patton was the model soldier and expected the same from his officers on down to the enlisted men.

Frank got the shine on his boots he desired. The following day he met with other officers in the war room at the Command Post. Captain Howell and the First Officers studied the map, pinpointing the location of their battalion in respect to the area where the other companies were positioned. The forces kept each other informed via radio as to any action or detection of enemy planes or artillery.

The XIX Tactical Air Command had made sorties over enemy territory and relayed the enemy positions to the Commanders who drew plans showing the Allied Armies' line of defense along the Moselle from north of Metz to the south of Nancy.

The plan was to keep the Third Army in the defensive position, even though Patton reinforced the importance of maintaining the offensive spirit of the troops by attacking whenever the means permitted, or the opportunity arose.

The 546th repositioned in defense of Patton's Command Post at Etain. Using long-handled shovels, the men dug a triangular gun pit, then manually pushed the 155mm into it, extended the support beams, lowered the gun down, leveled it, then built rows of sandbags filled with the dirt from the pit and piled them around the hole two-and-a-half feet high. Metal ammunition boxes with shells were at the back of the pit. They worked well into the night to get the guns ready to fire. Frank didn't get much sleep, nor did he have time to write Catherine.

Unfortunately, the Third Army had inadequate means to advance and possibly could not even hold their defensive position. A few divisions were even diverted up north to Belgium to aid in unloading and hauling supplies to the First Army. "This shortage of troops is scandalous!" wrote Patton in his notes. "Now, we are faced with an enemy with equal or superior forces in an excellent defensive position."

The German Army had retreated to the east side of the Moselle, where they dug in for a stubborn defense of Metz. The enemy had a second defense line a few miles east of Metz, known as the French Maginot Line. The stand-off only gave the Germans the advantage. Patton convinced Eisenhower to let him attack Fort Driant, the mainstay of the German hold on Metz. Frank's battalion remained in defense of Etain to the south while other forces and troops stormed the fort of Metz with little success. After seven days, Patton realized it was a futile attempt to capture Metz. At the same time to the south in Nancy, the Third Army lost control of a hill above the city. Now, Nancy was in favor of the Germans as they rained down shells on the town. Patton decided to move the Command Post to Nancy, leave Metz to the Germans, and enter the Rhineland through the door of Nancy.

*Hello Darling,*                    *Friday, September 29*
    *No letter from you, but I'm not alone at that, none of the other officers have had any first-class mail for four or five days. There must be more important mail.*
    *Thank you for the pictures of my mother and father and family. I heard from my little brother Ralph last week. He's in Texas lamenting the fact that he isn't*

*overseas, wish I could trade with him, I wouldn't cry atall. Ralph hasn't heard from George either. I just need to hear from George now.*

*The forecasts for the peace are becoming a little pessimistic of late. I hope they are not true. It looks like the Germans want to do a little fighting on their own ground for a change.*

*The picture of John was sad. Maybe Jose Reyes can get him to smile next time. I hope for an early end to this nonsense over here so we can be together again.*

The next day, Captain Howell, Frank, Hubbard, and Carlson drove south to check out the situation in Nancy, taking the same route Patton took a few days earlier. Patton had been shelled on that road several times and wrote: "Seems probable the enemy has good observation in the mountains or else a radio detecting our whereabouts." Whatever the reason, Frank and the officers knew of the shelling and possible strafing as they drove in the icy rain.

*Kitty, Took another long ride and nearly froze to death. The jeep is the coldest thing you can ride in. I've got a big sheepskin coat which kept me pretty warm, but the wind cut my face to ribbons, and nearly froze my ears. It's only early October, and I don't know what I'll do when winter comes, guess I've spent too much time in the desert.*

Once again, the men had to wait. Orders to stay on the defensive left the officers and enlisted men with less to do, more time for diversionary activities. They kept their competitive skills sharpened by challenging other units to ball games, as encouraged by Patton. "Men need to fight, play to win, and when not fighting, they should compete in sports, and play to win."

*Darling, I had a big day today, athletically speak-
ing. We played touch football this morning. (You asked
about my foot, and it has healed fine). Then we played
three rounds at volleyball after lunch, and again after
dinner. News is on now. Nothing much new on it, things
seem to have slowed down considerably. Played a little
poker last night, had a good time and didn't lose any
money. Still eating well and feeling swell so don't worry
darling, I'll be with you again soon.*

Things may have slowed down, but the rain didn't; it kept falling with a little sunshine in between just to confuse the situation. The
nights dipped down to almost freezing. Frank settled cozily in a large
tent with Captain Howell, Hubbard, Kuret, and Carlson and lit a fire
in their renovated stove and let it blaze with some ersatz coal. They left
off the lid, mesmerized by the heat and burning coal.

While sitting around the stove, their hands toasting over the
glow, Frank remarked, "Looks like it's a toss-up between rain and snow."

Captain Howell was quick to place a bet. "How much do you
wager on snow? I'll take the rain."

Carlson laughed. "Captain, what the hell are you doing wagering on the weather when you're damn near to having to pay up your
last bet about the war ending."

"Right," Captain conceded. "All bets off about the weather. Just
wish I'd win the bet on the war ending early."

The conversation changed from weather to war. Patton gave
orders earlier in the day to be ready to move at a moment's notice.
It was futile to stay in Etain when the other battalions were actively
defending Nancy and could use their help.

"Things are heating up, and it looks like we're leaving early
tomorrow for Nancy. We'll be there by the thirteenth, which is in two

days from now," the Captain spoke earnestly without his usual smile. His handsome face had a few more lines than last year at this time when war was still a game in the desert. They left the fire burning, and in the morning, the embers had died out, and frost-covered their blankets.

> *Dear Darling,*                    *Wednesday, October 11*
> *The war seems no nearer to ending than a month ago, but with the Russians pushing on the other front, something is liable to give. Captain Howell bet $100 that the war would end by October 19 but looks like he stands to lose it. The men have all gathered around after listening to the B.B.C. news, and it has turned into a songfest. You can't mention a song Kuret doesn't know. I have to stop writing every so often to join in one or a few I know. They're getting into Christmas songs now, it'll end up with "I'll Be Home for Christmas" with a nostalgic tang. Well, goodnite darling. I'm chomping at the bit to get home to you.*

On October 11, Patton abandoned the attack on Fort Driant, the German stronghold outside of Metz. The ammunition supply was extremely precarious, averaging about seven rounds per day for the 155's and not much more for the 105's. On the thirteenth, they moved the Command Post to Nancy.

The soldiers stood shoulder to shoulder in the trucks, and the tanks lined up with a guard on top, the tractors towed the big guns, while Frank and the other officers followed in jeeps. They traveled in convoy over the uneven bombed-out roads, swerving to miss dead cows or abandoned tanks. Once in the city of Nancy, the citizens looked dour, unsure if it was safe to be out in the rubble-strewn streets, beaten down by the war and both sides bombing and strafing their once beautiful city.

The Third Army settled into a German barracks that the French had occupied before the takeover. After leaving the barracks, the French had requested the Americans to bomb the Germans who had relocated there. Fortunately for the Third Army, the bombing had not been effective. The Commanding officer Spaatz surveyed the untouched barracks and hoped to hell that Patton wouldn't tell anyone how poorly the American bombers had performed. "At least, the men have a roof over their heads and beds to sleep in thanks to the poor results." That night, the enlisted men ate K-rations and found a place in the barracks to throw down their duffel bags and get some rest on wooden cots. The officers billeted in houses, a relief from the tents and outdoor latrines dug in the dirt.

CHAPTER TWENTY-ONE

# In Defense of Nancy

Catherine had returned to Silver Lake after visiting her sister Mary in Ontario. Having caught up on family news, Catherine learned that Peggy's husband, Steve, was soon to be shipped to the Pacific Theater. Like other Americans, the wives stoically accepted that their husbands had a duty to go to war, and they had a responsibility to prop them up with correspondences and understanding. On the home front, women took jobs men had done in the past. Victory gardens sprung up in backyards, and families used ration stamps for food, sacrificing butter for colored margarine and rarely getting meat now destined for overseas to feed the troops.

The mail from the war zone had slowed again, leaving Catherine to wonder what was going on. The newspapers had reported on the significant advances and strides that had given everyone hope in early fall 1944. Now, the papers focused on the upcoming election.

Catherine opened a pile of letters that her parents had collected while she was gone. She settled the baby for the night and sat down with a cup of tea to read.

*Hello Kitty,*          *Friday, October 13*
*   It's finally happened, I slept in a house and on a bed, what luxury, but alas I tossed all night and never did get to sleep till early morning. Well, maybe I'll get used to it again. It looks like we will be fortunate enough*

*to be housed for a while. The most appreciated tho, I believe, are those gurgling water closets where one can sit and think in comfort.*

*We have an enormous mirror at the entrance of the house. It's been so long since I've looked in one, I saw myself the first time and checked my impulse to say hello to the long drawn out figure reflected in front of me.*

Catherine murmured aloud, *oh my!* Immediately, she made a mental note to send Frank a care package as soon as possible. She'd get those candies that Kuret's wife had sent, then make the fruit cake she made early in the fall for Christmas. And the coffee and powdered milk. She tapped her forehead, trying to remember what else he'd asked for, what else she could send. It worried her that he had lost more weight and could barely recognize himself in the mirror. Her forehead tightened, and she made the sign of the cross, a childhood habit when things were out of her control.

*Unfortunately, when the Germans departed this place, they ruined all the radiation and the electrical system. We now have lights but no heat.*

The ink changed from black to blue.

*I just had to take out time to play a little game of cards, made back the eight dollars I lost to Kuret about a week ago. How's John doing, Kitty? Is he still the little angel? It won't be long before he will be learning a few little tricks.*

Catherine took a sip of tea with the letter on her lap. *I wish he wouldn't drink so much and play poker, he smokes too much and has lost weight again. Why can't he be home to help me with John?* She stopped herself from going off the deep end of worry and self-pity. At least he was safe, for now, and out of the mud for a while. She picked up the next letter that was dated a month earlier.

*Hello Darling,*             *Sunday, September 19*

> *Today has been a blue Monday on a Sunday. Rain all day and no mail tonite. I'm sure getting anxious to get home and see you both. I begrudge every minute of this time. I did make it to Mass this morning, and our Chaplain said the Mass so I could understand the sermon. The cathedral had been bombed by the Germans, all the stain glass windows were blown out, and much of the building shattered, but they're still celebrating Mass there. Kitty, I always feel closer to you in church.*

His melancholy tone ripped at Catherine's heart. There was some solace that he could make it to Mass. She felt closer to him at church, as well as when she held John, who so resembled Frank.

> *It's going to be funny to be a civilian again, just think to be able to go where you want to go, buy what you to buy, no worry about whether the town is off-limits. It's really going to be an experience.*
>
> *I wonder if you read Elanor's statement on hints to housewives. She says the major post-war problems of American women will be to adjust themselves to their returning soldier-husbands. She says we have or will have deep-seated fatigue that may take months to wear away. Well, well, well, and well. I wonder what she's talking about.*

The look on Catherine's face was a mixture of confusion and concern. Her lip quivered, and her cheeks reddened, like when she was upset as a little girl. Did Frank feel that deep-seated fatigue or was he making light of the situation? And what did that mean to adjust to a soldier-husband? She imagined her tall thin husband dragging himself through the door, barely giving her a hug or kiss, only a pat on John's back then going into a dark room. She didn't understand, nor did she want to think about it. The photos in the newspapers had shown soldiers elated and kissing strangers on the street. Isn't that how it's going to be? *Only he will be kissing me.*

She put down the letters to make some notes and remembered he said, *I wish you would buy me some mantles for the Coleman lantern, just as quick as you can send them.* That letter was dated October 9. Now on October 13, he was in a house that had lights. She decided to send them anyways, along with more photos and his other requests. She continued to read.

*I have not looked at any lace or blouses, had forgotten it for the time. I intend to take a day off soon and look around the local department stores, they seem to be well-stocked.* Catherine wished he didn't feel obligated to buy her things when all she wanted was for him to be safe, to take care of himself, and to come home.

> *I just received two letters this evening, so saved them for dessert — one from you and the amazing thing, one from your sister Agnes. I read her description of John to the rest of the officers, and they get quite a kick out of it, then they all bring out their baby pictures in self-defense.*

Catherine giggled, thinking of Frank showing off his child that he barely knew and how all those strong men carried around their babies' photos. *They're good men fighting for a good cause,* she thought to comfort herself. Catherine put his letters in the tin box, turned out the lights, and went to her tiny room behind the kitchen. She stood above the crib, watching John breathe, then covered him with a blue baby blanket and got ready for bed.

> *Hello Darling,*             *Monday, October 16*
>
>     *Don't feel much like writing, just wanted to let you know I'm still kicking. We've gotten a few stories on the election, seems to be a lot of mudslinging. We've not kept up on the progress of it, seems far away and remote.*
>
>     *It only took one night to get used to sleeping in a bed, and I'm doing all right. I can't get over the business of living in a house. I'm just about housebroken again. I took my weekly bath just before dinner. What a luxury to stretch out in a tub full of hot water. You know this has been the first hot bath since I was in England. I have taken most of my baths in my helmet and a number of times in the numerous cold rivers of France.*
>
>     *Really knocked off late last night, didn't mind the sag in the middle of the bed. Good nite, it's late.*

Frank and his boys stayed late into the night setting up the Long Toms, getting them positioned on the enemy in defense of Nancy. Reports coming across the wire said the Germans were intensifying their positions on the hill above town, raining shells down on the city. Worse than that, the Luftwaffe started flying both night and day again. As predicted, once Patton left Metz, the Germans repositioned to attack and take back Nancy that the Americans had liberated in September.

On October 14, Eisenhower gathered all Corps and Army Commanders to have lunch with King George of England. Afterward, he delivered a pep talk, rallying support to keep up the spirit of the offensive even while defending. Eisenhower's two-pronged assault was to capture the Ruhr and Saar industrial regions that fed the Third Reich's belly. It was just what Patton had wanted to hear. Patton leaned back in his chair and called out, "Fair enough. The Third Army is ready." The next day Patton took the Supreme Commander's message to his officers.

"Men, touring France was a catch-as-catch-can performance where we had to keep going to maintain our primary advantage, liberating every goddam town along the way. Now, in our situation of inadequate fuel and ammunition, our operation has to move forward from an initial disadvantage. As I see it, we are fighting three enemies. One is the Germans, the second is the weather, and the third is time. Every day of delay means more German defenses to attack. The weather is our worst enemy. For the first time, our sick rate equaled our battle casualties, and the weather isn't getting any better. There is not enough ammunition to supply all the armies, but there is enough to supply one army, and that will be the Third Army. Sirs, get ready to attack in five days."

With his signature salute, he left the room, and the officers continued to discuss the next steps to be taken to prepare for the advance to the Siegfried Line.

*Hello Darling,*              *Tuesday, October 17*
*Another rainy, muddy day. I'm beginning to hope it gets cold enough to freeze. It would be better than this slimy mud. That's one of the things I'll always remember about France.*

*We're finally getting settled down again, I am hoping for a chance to look around here, it's a beautiful town with lots of history. I just got finished playing ping-pong with Hubbard. The other officers and I have a makeshift table that serves the purpose.*

*Captain Howell loses his bet in two days, the one he made five months ago when he bet the war would be over October 19. It's really over, but these Heinies won't believe it. They seem to want to inch the last bit of misery out of it. Well, goodnight, darling, keep that rocking chair oiled up for me, and I'll soon be home to take over where we left off.*

Low clouds hung over the city, disrupting the gunners' vision, but they heard the unmistakable roar of Messerschmitt engines. The site finder scanned the sky, and once the nose or wing of a plane appeared, Frank shouted, "Ready, aim, fire!" The shell shot ahead of the aircraft. One pilot flew his plane into the shell, and spiraled to the ground, while other aircraft swerved or dived. The shooting from the gun battalions echoed in the low ceiling of clouds for over an hour while the enemy planes made passes. Frank's anti-aircraft gunners shot down three *certains* and three *probables,* without any American casualties. It was unknown why the aircraft flew over that night without dropping any bombs. Was it a scare tactic or a warning of more to come?

*Hello Darling,*          *Sunday, October 2*
*Another Sunday evening slipping by, one of those evenings when I should be sitting by the fireside with my wife. Instead, here I sit holding my own hand trying to keep it warm enough to write. There's a good music program on the air now, and it sets me dreaming of home and you. Have you heard "Kitty Blue Eyes?" Reminds me of us.*

He hummed a few lines as he wrote them down.

*That's why she'll never*

*Hear anyone till he'll shout,*
*"I'm here, pretty Kitty,*
*Here pretty Kitty blue eyes."*

By the end of October, the weather turned bitter cold and wet, and the supply situation was terrible with limited rations, insufficient gasoline, and only enough ammunition to be used sparingly. As the Third Army freed cities, they become responsible for feeding and sheltering the refugees and displaced persons, draining even more of their resources of clothing, shoes, and soap. A major epidemic of trench foot broke out among the men since there was little to no sunlight to dry out their boots after mucking around in the rain, and no new socks to put on. One wondered if the supplies were going to other armies or stolen en route, or maybe there just wasn't enough to go around with all the people in need of the basics, food, clothing, and shelter.

*The plumbers and electricians are still over-running the house, we've been feeding them, and they seem to like it especially well, in fact, we're wondering whether they will ever finish the job. Maybe we better start feeding them C rations. By the way, how is the meat situation at home? Are you able to get any?*

The Germans took advantage of the apparent weak position of the Third Army. In the early morning of October 24, they opened fire on Nancy, blasting the buildings with howitzer shells until 0445. As the explosions whistled through the buildings, subsequent screaming could be heard from people caught under the rubble of their homes. The American soldiers, alongside the French citizens, pulled people from under the wreckage and sent for the Red Cross ambulances and doctors. Patton was among the soldiers helping out. Frank could say very little about the incident.

*Nothing much new today, pretty much the same
routine. Had a little excitement last night, but it was
over as quickly as it started. The Germans don't seem to
have much Air force left, at least they don't care to risk
much at a time over our territory.*

That day the American retaliation was minimal. The crew fired a
few shells at an errant German plane but missed hitting it. The aircraft,
which the officers assumed had been on surveillance, left quickly, and
did not return. There was no replacement for the daily expenditure
of ammunition, so the men used shells and gun powder only when
attacked. The rain and low clouds kept the American planes from flying; therefore, the XIX Tactical Air could not make their bomb raids
or assist the troops on the ground with telecommunication. Mud filled
the roads and seeped into everything. Tanks and trucks got mired in
the sludge, unable to move the soldiers or the guns effectively. Knowing
the situation was dire, Patton contracted 100,000 "duck feet," webbed
connectors that attached to the ends of the tank tracks, enabling
the tank to secure erratic flotation through the sticky mess but still
ensured better progress. Patton continued to press for more supplies
and more troops.

*We just received our cigarette and candy rations
this evening and just in time. We receive seven packs of
cigarettes each week, along with 5 bars of chocolate and
a few miscellaneous toilet articles.*

Where were the socks, the warm jackets, the earmuffs, the gloves?

*The plumber still hasn't fixed the furnace, so we
are sitting around with our coats on, and still cold. I
picked up a cold in the last two days. I think it's from
sitting around in this icebox.*

The Luftwaffe and enemy activity waned. Frank and his boys kept up surveillance as usual, with only a few hostile strikes to keep them busy. The enemy appeared to have gone elsewhere. The men of the Third Army fell into a lethargy of inactivity after the race across France. Holding the defense left the men with idle time.

*Hello Darling,*        *Sunday, October 29*

*Not much new to report. Just had a chicken dinner with dressing and cranberries, it's not Thanksgiving or any holiday, I don't know what the occasion is, but it sure hit the spot.*

*The sun shone all day today, couldn't have had anything to do with it being my birthday, or could it? Anyway, it was much appreciated by all in the vicinity. We had another excellent show, tonite, "See Here Private Hargrove." It isn't often we get a picture that pleases everybody.*

*I just took time from letter writing to play a game of ping pong with the Captain. The last few nights, Kuret, Hubbard, and myself and the other officers have been engaged in a few poker jousts. Been playing for low stakes to pass the time away. Some war, isn't it? I had hoped to teach John to walk, but it doesn't look too promising at the moment.*

*Kuret, Hubbard, and I are growing mustaches. I don't know how much longer I can carry on. I'm trying to get it long enough so I can twirl it over the ends, it's getting there but slow. I had it trimmed the other day because it was getting mixed up with my food, and it doesn't taste too good, even with catsup on it.*

Hubbard's mustache was a bushy blonde mess, not at all sophisticated to match his good looks and brill-creamed hair. Eventually, he got a string of lip hair to twirl then shaved it off. Kuret trimmed his dark mustache into the style of Cary Grant, earning him the reputation of *Hollywood*. Tall, lean, and handsome, Frank twisted the ends of his mustache, mocking the others with caterpillars growing on their lips. Catherine had suggested he try an Errol Flynn mustache.

Captain walked in on one of the boys' arguments and shook his head, "Really men, you have nothing better to do? And Frank, you're going to scare the hell out of that young son of yours with that growth on your upper lip."

"Right captain, I figured it would be a good tool for disciplining him when I get home."

The Captain made a few remarks about setting a good example for the boys outside. Frank hemmed and hawed then said, "Captain, I was just heading out to check our guns."

The enemy continued his defensive tactics digging in and hoping for a winter stalemate, giving them time to rest, refit, and reorganize its battered divisions. The Nazis concentrated on a defensive reorganization between the Maginot Line and the Siegfried Line, a buffer to stop the Allies from entering Germany. They built anti-tank ditches, communication posts, fire trenches, pillboxes, and minefields. Barbed-wire was used extensively around the perimeters of sensitive buildings and communication towers. The recent German prisoners of war reported that dugouts and foxholes were being winter-proofed, a sign they planned to stay awhile. The POW's cooperation signaled a weakening in the morale of the Nazis, a surrender of sorts.

The U.S. Generals had another idea for winter, to smoke the Nazis out of their lairs.

# CHAPTER TWENTY-TWO

# Burned Letters

*Hello Darling,*              *Wednesday, November 1*
*Missed writing to you last night. The colonel called*
*a meeting that started at 7 o'clock, and the monologue*
*continued till I fell asleep on the floor at 11 o'clock.*

Patton and Bradley had met in Nancy in preparation for the renewal of the offensive, getting supplies of gasoline, ammunition, and rations to the Third Army for a planned attack and forward thrust to the Siegfried Line. Montgomery's British troops weren't ready, but the Third could jump off with a twenty-four-hour notice. An air raid was set for November 7, and if that were not possible, due to the on-going bad weather, then the XII Corps of the Third Army would still attack November 9.

Patton spoke briefly in no uncertain terms. "Men, the honor has been given to the Third Army to attack alone. I reiterate the use of marching fire, and all supporting weapons will be in force."

Patton's orders went down the ranks till every man was informed and ready. Patton asked a radio representative to announce on-air that the attack and forward movement was for the limited objective of straightening the line for winter occupation. He wanted a surprise element in his attack. The Germans believed what they heard and counted on a cease-fire over the bitter winter. Patton was pleased with his deception. The Third Army was ready to move into Germany and finish the war.

> *Hello Darling,*                    *Tuesday, November 7*
> *It's election day, wish I could be there to file my vote for you. From the sounds of things, it looks like it will be all Roosevelt again. The news from the Pacific sounds good. Everyone over here was worried that as soon as this was finished in Europe, we would have to pack up and work in the other end of the world for a while. It's just possible now that they both may end together. I have not been able to locate George as yet, and the prospects of finding his outfit are remote. I imagine he is in the south of France or at least came in from the south.*
> *We have some more captured wine, brandy, and cognac, which we can pass out to the gun crews. It sure helps in this miserable weather. It was thoughtful of those Heinies to have so much on hand for us. I'd like to get a hold of some more Champagne. It is really the king of drinks. I have two bottles left, which I'm going to save for the end of the war.*

Captain Howell briefed the 546th on the planned attack. Frank prepared his crew and coordinated their targets with the other battalions. Everything was ready. On November 8, at 0500, despite floods, rain, and fog, the Third Army opened the Battle of Germany with a barrage of artillery that woke every living thing in the area. All artillery was used on the ground to clear a path for the infantry and foot soldiers. "The discharge of over seven hundred guns sounded like the slamming of so many heavy doors in an empty house, while the whole eastern sky glowed and trembled with flashes."

"I even had a slight sympathy for the Germans, who must now have known the attack they had feared had, at last, arrived," Patton noted in his journal on his bed stand.

The American infantrymen poised in the frontline recalled that day. "Suddenly, we were awakened in our foxholes, chilled hands reaching automatically for our weapons, then slowly relaxed, as we realized that the greatest, most God-awful artillery barrage we were ever to hear was outgoing. Our troops. For two hours, our big guns pounded incessantly while the enemy didn't believe any division, much less one new to combat, could attack after living in a 36-hour rain in water-filled holes."

With no German infantry ahead of them, the first U.S. platoon walked into German territory, sweeping the roads as they went. After the U.S. soldiers crossed the Maginot Line, the Germans counter-attacked from their newly built defenses and within houses in the villages, causing casualties and injuries to the Americans. The U.S. Medics quickly attended to the wounded and also captured German medics who worked side by side with them. The U.S. infantry plowed through the countryside and villages and kept the Germans on the run.

Frank took a tour of his gun crews, pushing them to keep the firing up. "Scare those Heinies back." He walked to a soldier reclining after letting loose a volley of ammunition. "Here, have a hit and get back up there."

The young crewman smiled at the bottle of cognac and gladly tossed it back, burning his throat as it trickled down. "Woooo-eeeee!" he smacked his lips. "Thanks, sir, that hits the spot." He jumped to his feet and relieved the next gunman who eagerly took a hit of the bottle and passed it around.

"Carry on men. Run those Krauts out of their foxholes, the bastards." Frank checked the marks and set the next target. Frank's boot stuck in the muddy quagmire around the gun. He lifted his boot out and shook his head as he squished through the slurry and headed to the road leading to the next position.

By 1000 the skies cleared, and fighter-bombers appeared in force and attacked the enemy command posts. In communication and synchronization, the XIX Tactical Air and the Third Army reignited and sent the Germans scrambling with casualties ten times that of the Allies.

"This day was the brightest and the best we had had for two months," Patton recorded in his notes.

But the next day was disheartening. Many of the U.S. protected bridges had collapsed under the barrage of fire and rising waters. Floodwaters marooned U.S. Army trucks, airplanes, and a platoon in enemy territory. Tanks bellied down when they skidded off the road into the drainage channels filled with slow-moving mud and debris. The weather had gained the upper hand.

By November 10, the Moselle River and tributaries had receded, and the submerged bridge at Pont-a-Mousson and other bridges were again usable. Bridging activities resumed during November and exceeded those of any other month, even though unusually heavy rainfall fell and twice flooded the Moselle Valley washing out bridges and inundating the approaches. The Army Corps of Engineers reconstructed Bailey bridges, set up Treadway bridges of linked together tires, and built substantial pontoon bridges. Rafts ferried the infantry and heavy equipment across the swollen rivers and inlets. The Third Army surged on under enemy fire advancing further into enemy territory.

The Germans had turned every village into a defensive strongpoint. They used their dwindling supply of artillery to fight the U.S. infantry as they marched in combat and rolled through the towns on the support tanks that had made the crossing without sinking or getting stuck. The best the Germans could do were delay tactics, leaving their tanks, trucks, and even trolley cars overturned in the roads. They employed demolition tactics with dynamite strung across roads and bridges, and mines planted along the soldiers' paths. Their anti-aircraft artillery turned away from the air to aim their weapons against the ground troops as the Third Army continued their progress to the Siegfried Line.

The U.S. soldiers fought and maneuvered through rainwater and mud, and forged swollen rivers, while the *Ack-Ack* gunners operated their big guns in the torrential rains that seemed never to stop. Another enemy reared its head that could not be stopped by gunfire, trench foot. Of the near five-thousand severe cases of trench foot, ninety-five percent of the patients would be of no further value for combat during the winter months. Patton could not afford this loss. He ordered prisoners to dub, oil, and waterproof all of the soldiers' boots. Each day, along with their rations, the men were to receive a pair of dry socks. The marching infantry received overshoes, and even if it slowed them down, it was mandatory attire. But the most effective action was the reorganization of the corps so that some divisions could rest and dry out while others pushed forward. The rate of trench foot went down considerably to less than a hundred cases a day.

> *Good morning Kitty,*          *Saturday, November 18*
> *It has turned really cold now, and we are looking for a little snow soon. I will have to cut this short now so I can get out to check my guns, it's like going around in a circle, day in and day out. We are starting to send a few men in at a time to Paris. It's a new policy the army has put into effect. It will be a long ride, but the boys are all for it. One officer out of 35 or so can also go. We played a hand of poker for our battery nominee, and Lt Kowoski won, I was third. Unfortunately, in the final showdown*

*with the battalion, one of the Headquarter's officers got*
*the nod. One of my Section Chiefs got to go too, and is*
*he excited.*

November saw a further decrease in hostile air activity over the
Third Army zone. Frank and the boys in the 546th had shot down and
destroyed sixteen planes and eleven "probably" destroyed. The infantry needed more riflemen and foot soldiers since the situation of foot
soldier replacement was determined to be extremely bad. Patton issued
the order to cannibalize the non-essential units, which now included
the anti-aircraft battalions, and send those men to the infantry.

He reorganized the officers and transferred some of the enlisted
men of the 546th to another division on the frontline.

*Hello Darling,*        *Sunday, November 19*
    *We have lost Captain Howell, and he is now on*
*the Battalion Staff. He doesn't like it, and neither do we.*
*I hope he gets transferred back. All the rest are still with*
*us. Hub, Carlson, Kuret, and I are sulking around writ-*
*ing letters and cussing out the army in general. What a*
*marvelous bunch of civilians we will make. Good night*
*darling, and more tomorrow.*

Captain Howell and the four lieutenants, Foster, Hubbard,
Carlson, and Kuret, had all been together since the Desert Training
Center. They spent hours in the jeep racing over the bumpy roads,
riding through villages with crowds cheering them, seeing and smelling
death along the way, and always in fear of losing a friend to gunfire,
bombs, mines, or sheer accident. When Captain Howell left, it was like
losing a limb.

Since the race across France began August 1, the Third Army
had lost, to injury or death, over 40,000 men and now had only

30,000 men due to the scarcity of replacement troops. Patton suggested to take over more corps, but Eisenhower refused him the human resources. Patton had to reorganize his forces; Captain Howell went to Headquarters, and Captain Cook took charge of the 546th battalion.

> *We keep pretty close tabs on the news programs now. It isn't possible the Germans can hold off much longer unless they want to commit suicide, and race suicide isn't a German trait. We all expect it to end suddenly, and it can't be too sudden.*
>
> *We are on duty 24 hrs. a day that is subject to be called at any time, not actually working. It makes the soldiers awfully mad when they hear of strikes for more wages or double pay for overtime. Time doesn't mean a thing over here, it's just get the job over with. What started all that? Let's change the subject. How's Agnes's romance? Sounds pretty darn serious.*
>
> *Today was a beautiful day, hope it keeps up. The bombers were out thick and heavy, looks like they were really giving those Jerries hell. I'm anxious to get moving again, cause as long as we are static, the longer the war lasts.*

The next day the weather was back to its groove, more rain, and more mud. Captain Cook was their new chief, and even though he was fair, he was tough and a lot less fun than Captain Howell. The poker sessions came to an end, and no one seemed to care to play anymore. Frank stuck to himself on his time off, studying French and occasionally cajoled Hubbard to practice speaking French with him, which didn't last long. They always ended up saying how much they resented their time in the army. The men missed Howell and lamented the fact that that's the deal you make with the military, you go where they tell you, without consideration of the person. *Another good reason to get this war over with and become a human again.*

> *Dear Kitty,*          *Tuesday, November 21*
> *Here it is two days before Thanksgiving, and we are already having turkey, 21 ounces per man. Tomorrow we will have chicken. Looks like we get all the good food at the same time. We have been having a lot of Spam and Vienna sausage. One boy received a can of Spam in the mail, and he nearly blew his top.*
>
> *I do have something to be thankful for. I have you and John home waiting for me. Also, I received three letters from you, and tonight I indulged in the luxury of a hot bath. I never told you about our beautiful marble bathroom, did I! It's really nice, has a shower attachment in a deep tub.*

> *Hello Darling,*          *Thursday, November 23*
> *Thanksgiving today, we had an excellent turkey dinner with cranberries, sweet potatoes, salad, pie, and all the trimmings. More importantly, our drive is progressing in the direction of Germany, and soon we all will have something to be thankful for.*

The days dragged on with round-the-clock surveillance, a tag team of worn-out men, tired of the rain and mud, homesick, and just plain sick. Early on Friday the 24th, the Red Cross girls made their rounds of the gun positions in Nancy, bringing the men coffee and donuts. The young enlisted men happily took the coffee, grabbed some donuts, and hung around the young girls in uniform, their grey coats and skirts, the hat with the Red Cross emblem, and fresh faces was a relief from the tedious work of war. The "non-fraternizing with the citizens" rule kept the soldiers away from the local women. Still, there was no cultural connection with the townspeople, no understanding of their habits or language in a foreign country. Along with the donuts and coffee, the American girls engaged the boys in conversation, asked about their homes, teased about their girlfriends waiting back home, and generally kept up the banter, filling the void with familiar chatter with someone who understood their loneliness and brightened the moment.

Frank returned to his cold apartment; the gilded ceiling and marble entry didn't raise his spirits. No one else was home, so he took advantage of the vacant writing desk to write Christmas cards. From his coat pocket, he took out the package of cards wrapped carefully in brown paper and tied with a string. As was his habit, he had ten or twelve letters from Catherine folded and put in various other pockets. On the dreary night watches, he would take the notes out to read, getting a warm feeling of closeness from her words written in sweet Catholic school cursive. Catherine never had a bitter thought or wrote a sharp word. Instead, she saw the goodness in people and prayed for those who had difficulties. It wasn't that she tried to be good or flaunted it or even judged others by her standards of kindness and understanding; it was just part of her nature.

The Christmas cards laid wrapped on his desk while Frank began to reread all of Catherine's letters. One by one, he carefully unfolded each of them. A smile crossed his face as he read about John, his early stages of teething, his cute antics standing in his crib, and throwing his toys over the side. He could almost hear Catherine's lilting laugh. In his mind's eye, he picked John up and bounced him on his knee, singing the "Grand Old Duke of York." Instead of writing Christmas cards, he sat down to write to Catherine.

*Hello Darling,*           *Saturday, November 25*
*No letter tonight, but I guess I hadn't better kick, as this has been a good week on letters. I even got one from my Grandma's sister who lives in Staffordshire, England, and that's where I was a good bit of the time while in England, and traveled all over the country, but didn't know the folks existed. Too bad, I would have liked to visit them*

*I purchased some Christmas cards today and will send out ten to fifteen. More rain today but a beautiful evening.*

He stopped, unwrapped the cards, and began to address them. Something was eating at him, a raw gnawing feeling of loss, something he couldn't express to Catherine. He got up and walked over to the fireplace and made a small fire. Looking into the flames, he could see only sorrow. He went back to the table and picked up the twelve or so letters from Catherine and walked back to the fire. He tossed each one in separately and watched the edges tinge in red, yellow, then flame into blue curling till consumed into shiny black leaves disappearing into ashes.

He returned to his desk to finish his letter to Catherine.

*I just reread about ten or twelve of your letters that I have been carrying around in my pockets, (a bad habit), and then burned them. They make me too sentimental and dissatisfied.*

CHAPTER TWENTY-THREE

# Bad Weather and Short Days

Frank and his gunners had twenty-four hours off, an opportunity to take his crew to a movie and explore the town. After the show, he wandered around Nancy, got a haircut, and did some Christmas shopping, that is, he shopped for himself. With all the reports of a cold winter, Catherine had implored him to buy a heavy coat and forego looking for presents for her. She had received the wooden shoes, the hand-painted buttons, the lace, a blouse, and the fur hat. Knowing that the hat had belonged to a German soldier, she put it on a high shelf in the coat closet so as not to be reminded of the messy business Frank had to do.

The snow was coming down in big snowflakes the size of half-dollars that melted as soon as they hit the pavement. White patches remained on the eaves of the buildings, and frost stuck to the sides of the windows. If it hadn't been wartime, Frank might have gotten into the Christmas spirit. He pushed open the door to a haberdashery.

The bell atop the heavy door jangled, and a thin, well-dressed man appeared. "Bonjour Monsieur," he said in the typical sing-song voice of a clerk.

"Bonjour," Frank replied.

The man immediately changed to a guttural English. "How may I help you?' His tone was reserved, not friendly.

There was a mistrust of American soldiers in the Alsace-Lorraine region bordering Germany. The people held on to their Slavic roots yet spoke the French language, even though the Germans had occupied them. They divided their allegiance between France and their German heritage, not Nazism. During the four years of German occupation, the Nazis forbade them to speak French and conscripted many of the citizens into the German army to use as informants. If they did not cooperate, the Germans threatened their lives and their families' lives.

"I'm looking for a winter coat," Frank said.

"Bof! You Americans brought us this horrible weather. Never before has it been so cold so early in the fall."

He motioned to Frank to follow him to the rack of heavy coats then pulled a few out that looked his size. For practical reasons, Frank chose a combination of raincoat and overcoat in a deep navy blue, almost black. The clerk measured his arms and took the coat to the back, where the tailor altered it on the spot. When he walked out of the store into a wet blizzard with icy snow swirling around his head, he pulled the coat up around his ears, grateful Catherine had insisted he buy himself some warm clothes.

The next day, Frank returned to town to check on his gun positions. After walking a couple of blocks, he discovered a pipe shop with beautifully hand-carved pipes in the window. Upon entering, the rich smell of pipe tobacco reminded him of Catherine's father, who smoked a pipe with cherry tobacco in the evening.

*Hello Kitty,*                    *Tuesday, November 28*
    *While wandering around town visiting my gun positions, I ran into a pipe shop, have been looking for a pipe ever since I hit France. I'm trying to get away from cigarettes. I hear there is a cigarette shortage in the states. American cigarettes are such great demand that*

*the prices have gone up to 100 francs (to you $2.00). In fact, in buying some articles, things are priced in terms of cigarettes or francs. And I need to thank you. Yesterday, I bought a coat, your Christmas present, I mean from you to me. I like it a lot.*

After Thanksgiving, the men's spirits fell. There was no hope they'd be home by Christmas, and the weather kept them confined to their posts or indoors. Frank had a plan.

*I took about twelve of the men down to the gym, and we had a session of basketball. We are going to work up a team and play a few games with the outfits nearby. I suppose just about the time we get organized, we will have to be on the move again. But the sooner we get moving, the sooner this darn war will end.*

Catherine was pleased that Frank could get back on the basketball court, the game he loved most. She had an inkling that Frank was part of a bigger team, a well-known army. She pieced together information from his letters and guessed he was with the Third Army since he had written about traveling so fast across France, liberating the townspeople, and by-passing Paris.

*I can now confirm your guess as to which army I am in. You guessed the 3ʳᵈ· and that is right. I wish I could find out which army George is in, and I would have some basis to work on finding him. As yet, he has not answered my letters. Can't figure him out.*

Now Catherine could follow the route of the Third Army and get an idea where Frank was and if he were in a battle. What was to come would not be a consolation for Catherine.

The LA Times reported that the Third Army had taken over the German strongholds, capturing of Nancy in late September, surrounding the forts around Metz in November, and capturing Metz by early December. By December 8, after one month of fighting, the troops of the Third Army had taken 873 towns, captured 30,000 prisoners, and killed or wounded 88,000 of the enemy. Frank was alive, and that was all Catherine cared about.

On a livelier note, Frank teased Catherine about how the French celebrate her feast day. *Did you know St. Catherine's Day is a big holiday in France? In fact, it's the French equivalent of "Sadie Hawkins Day." The shop girls parade around in predatory bands, pouncing on hapless G.I.s and kissing them. Unfortunately, it seems it is only in Paris that they take it seriously.*

He happily reported the poker games reignited, and Captain Cook joined in.

> *It's getting so we stay up late every night playing poker. Last night Hubbard was the big winner, in fact, the only winner. We went over to another battery's C.P. to engage in a friendly game of poker, it was a long hard fight, but we came away with a good share of their money. This poker is getting to be a habit, and I suppose you will be putting your foot down soon. Anyway, it passes away some of the evenings.*
>
> *I'm enclosing a sixty-dollar money order. Let me know when you receive it. Tomorrow is payday again, another sixty dollars to carry around with hope of not spending it. I have ceased trying to buy French merchandise as it is priced way out of line. And they are now watering down their perfumes and selling it off to the G.I.s.*

*You will likely receive this letter very close to Christmas, wish I could be with it. Don't know whether I will be here for Christmas. We would like to stay in the same place with steam heat and everything, but the longer we wait, the longer this mess carries on. Wherever we are, I'll be with you in spirit. My fear is if we get out in pup tents again, I'll freeze to death.*

Frank signed his letter, *See you soon as...Merry Christmas to the family and love to you and John,* then sealed it and headed out to check his guns. He had the all-night duty, which they split among the officers. Every fifth night, one of them stayed awake at their command post, ready to answer a call or receive radio messages. Frank had his feet up at the Command Post, the alert radio popping and buzzing away, and on his other side another radio playing Dennis Day's Christmas songs from Ireland. The telephone to the gun line was at an arm's length in front of him. It was raining outside, and Frank was cozy warm inside.

*They're playing "Take Me Home Again Kathleen" on the radio, making me homesick,* he wrote.

At 2040 the alert radio static ceased, and a message came across that enemy aircraft was seen flying low over the city. The Germans typically flew just above the trees to avoid radar detection. Frank reached for the telephone to alert his gunners then ordered them to fire their guns. A hundred rounds of ammunition shot into the sky, the explosions knocking the gunners back. The German planes had made one final sweep then took off. Frank reported in the morning reports of December 4, "low-flying E/A (enemy air) engaged by gun section No.4 at 2040. Ammo expended-100rds 50cal. No casualties. Fired in defense of Nancy."

Over the next couple of weeks, the inspections doubled, causing more work for Frank and the officers, and harsh words demanding they keep things in top shape.

> *Hello Darling,*                *Wednesday, December 6*
> *There is little new to tell you, same old routine, only more inspections that worry us to death. More trouble with them than the German planes. The brass think we're not doing enough to earn our money. Saw Captain Howell at Headquarter, and he's not happy either. We all miss him and wish he were back, been together so long now. That's army life, none of it is too happy.*

Christmas packages started arriving, and Frank got his share of gifts from Catherine and her parents and sisters, fruit cake, cheeses, crackers, coffee, canned boneless chickens, a hand-knit sweater, more than he could use.

> *I brought the fruit cake out during a poker game, and Captain Cook dug up a hidden bottle of champagne, needless to say, both disappeared before I could raise the ante. The cheese and crackers will come in handy on my night watch. Still haven't had a letter in weeks. How are you getting along on groceries now? Is meat still rationed? They can't say we are getting any of it. We are receiving chicken about once a week, but little or no beef, quite a bit of pork.*

The weather continued to stress the troops with torrential rains, followed by sleet and snow that only turned the streets to a sloshy mess. The roads, or what used to be roads, were ruts of clay and mud, the asphalt having been worn through by tanks and trucks and the punishing rains.

Frank's driver drove him to Headquarters to go to confession and attend an evening mass in a large auditorium that had once been the German Headquarters. The army chaplain gave the sermon in English, which was a relief from trying so hard to understand the French priest.

> *Hello Darling,*          *Saturday, December 9*
> *I went to Mass yesterday afternoon at Headquarters chapel, went to confession also. The chapel is in a large auditorium in a former German headquarters. It was nice to have Father O'Neil give the sermon in English, the French priests are difficult to understand. They must speak something different than what they write.*
>
> *I saw a baby this afternoon when I picked up my laundry, he was just about John's age and cute as can be. Played with him for a while, couldn't stand it very long, starts a guy to getting sentimental, and I start worrying about how much I miss you both.*

After getting his laundry, Frank walked on to the post office and mailed the parachute he had been carrying around and another fur cap. *Now, please don't ask me what you are going to do with them, anything you like.*

> *Glad to hear you finally received the perfume. I had just about given up hope. I've been looking around for some more perfume, but it is getting scarce now. I imagine about every soldier has sent some home. I was looking at a radio today, thought seriously about buying one, but they are scarce and much too high. Even a very*

*small one cost at least a hundred dollars. Needless to say, I don't want one that bad.*

That night Frank and the boys finished off the champagne.

> *Finally gave up saving our champagne for Victory day, and we drank it all up last night. We had a merry little songfest with it. Kuret calls it soda pop. Only fifteen more days to Christmas and no chance of spending it with you. I've finally given up, now we will have to plan on our wedding anniversary—what a reunion. We will be getting into that Virginia Ham you're saving.*

By early December, the men were battle-weary from the weather as well as the fighting. *I wonder how many times I've said that the elements seem to have been against us all the way thru this campaign. The war would have been over by now if it had stayed clear a little bit longer.*

Bad weather and short days kept the planes from flying, and the anti-aircraft battalions had less to do. Whenever possible, Frank got films for the men to watch in the evenings and took advantage of his free time to catch a U.S.O. Show.

> *The captain and I went over to a U.S.O. show this evening, just heard about it by chance. It was really good called "Five Pips and a Dip." Had five lovely American girls, we sure appreciate our own women after being gone from home this long.*

The U.S.O. Troupes, called the "Foxhole Circuit," performed near the front lines in France and Germany. When not performing, they adhered to military rules and lived very similarly to the troops, eating the same meals, wearing uniforms, sleeping in similar conditions, and following the same protocol. They signed an oath of secrecy, promising not to divulge sensitive information about their tour or their location. "You're in the Army now," the contract read. And they faced the same dangers of war; some got captured, and some died in service to their country.

Patton continued to push his army east despite the weather. His plan was on December 19 to have the Third Army break through the Siegfried Line and proceed to the Rhine. "While we were all accustomed to rapid movement, we now have to prove that we can operate even faster."

Besides the Germans, another obstacle, the continuing bad weather, was wearing on Patton's mind. Being a religious, if not a superstitious man, Patton ordered the Army Chaplains to pray for good weather. Upon returning to the Third Headquarters at Nancy, he met personally with Chaplain O'Neil.

"Chaplain, I want you to publish a prayer for good weather. I'm tired of these soldiers having to fight mud and floods as well as fighting the Germans. See if we can't get God to work on our side."

"Sir, it's going to take a pretty thick rug for that kind of praying."

"I don't care if it takes a flying carpet! I want the praying done."

"Yes, sir. May I say, General, that it usually isn't customary among the men in my profession to pray for clear weather to kill their fellow man."

"Chaplain, are you teaching me theology, or are you the Chaplain of the Third Army?"

"Yes, sir."

The prayer was created and published on a small-sized card. Being close to Christmas Patton included a personal Christmas greeting to those under his command.

*Hello Darling,*     *Wednesday, December 13*
 *I slept the whole day through, got up a 4:30, then*
*had dinner. This staying up all night isn't worthwhile,*
*although I seem to get more sleep that way. After dinner,*
*we settled down into a poker game, and it is 11:00, and*
*I'm not sleepy but will go back to bed soon as I finish this*
*letter. I am figuring on a trip tomorrow.*

Frank preceded his troops along with other officers on reconnaissance before major moves. His "trip" coincided with Patton's excursion on the same day, December 14. They drove to the front of the combat line to analyze the situation before the blitz that Patton planned for the 19th. Patton always moved forward, even under fire, visible to the troops, stopping to encourage them, yet the soldiers never saw him retreating. At the other end of his journey, a plane would take him back to Headquarters in Nancy.

Frank and his driver headed towards the Siegfried Line, passing the Maginot line with little trouble. Frank could not report to Catherine what he did or what he saw, but most likely, it was as Patton wrote that day in his diary. "The fighting was very tedious as the combat was from house to house. The Germans had made the ground floor of the houses into veritable forts with reinforced concrete about twelve inches thick with machine gun openings just above the sidewalk level in practically all the cellars. The Germans are certainly a thoroughgoing race."

After the reconnaissance trip, Patton determined the Third Army had a chance to make it to the Rhine. He gave orders to Captain Cook: Depart Nancy December 17; relocate to St. Avold, on the German border.

Once Frank had left his post in Nancy, he could tell Catherine about the city.

> *Nancy is the best town I've seen since we have been here. It's practically intact. It's a large town with department stores, streetcars, and everything. I wanted to get on a streetcar and tell the conductor to let me off on Silver Lake Blvd, Los Angeles. Nancy is very much like the towns in the states. It's a town of churches, there seems to be one on every corner and all of them big.*
>
> *We were all sorry to leave.*

# CHAPTER TWENTY-FOUR

# The Prayer

*Hello Darling,*          *Monday, December 18*
*I missed writing to you yesterday. We were out on*
*the road most of the day, and the rest of the day busy*
*chasing around. Finally, have a breather to settle down*
*again to a normal routine.*

On the 17th, Frank drove over fifty miles in a jeep in a convoy of trucks carrying troops and supplies, tractors pulling the 155mm guns and other howitzers, and reconnaissance vehicles. The rain seeped through the plastic windows of the jeep, and Frank's jacket barely kept the icy wind out. Trucks veered and slipped off the icy roads, some overturned into ditches and were either abandoned or pulled out with ropes and tractors. The slow-moving caravan was an easy target for snipers that lay in wait in the villages. The infantry moved ahead of the group to clear out what renegade soldiers they could find by throwing grenades into the basements and taking shots at the attics and church towers where Germans could be watching them. The bomb squad preceded the convoy checking for mines and booby traps, detonating what they found.

Frank's battalion reached St. Avold on the border of Germany by mid-afternoon. The XIX Tactical Air Corps had already blown apart the German vital communication center in St. Avold, where the vast network of enemy defenses had guarded the western border of the Third Reich. The Nazis retreated under fire, leaving the town in utter despair and wreckage. Under dark skies, Frank positioned the guns, billeted the men for the nights ahead, reassuring them of their abilities to perform, and making sure they had what they needed to perform their duties, proper clothing, guns, ammunition, food, and shelter. Once everyone had settled into the new routine, Frank could finally sit down.

> *Darling, We are in a building now, but all the windows are broken. We make our own electricity, so we have lights. Tomorrow we will get some stoves so it will be lots more comfortable. The place was really a mess; it must have been a German army headquarters of some kind because it was full of records and junk. I thought winter was here to stay, the ground had become frozen almost solid, but now it's like a spring thaw, a warm wind got by the mountain and started the water going again. According to the French, we should have snow on the ground.*
>
> *I still haven't heard from George, and I know he can't be far from us. I can't understand why he doesn't write.*

Frank and his men worked into the night setting up for the defense of the bridge where the U.S. troops would cross the Saar River into Germany. Equipped with automatics and grenades to protect against snipers, the gunners kept surveillance around the clock for possible ground and air attack. A close watch was held on the river as it rose, threatening to flood and submerge the bridge.

They never did have the time to settle into a routine at St. Avold. The mission to cross the Siegfried Line and continue to the Rhine was suddenly aborted. The Nazi High Command had effectively surprised the Allies and launched its counter-offensive in the forests of the Ardennes. The Germans attacked the American troops installed on the borders of Luxembourg and Belgium. With the German panzers bearing down on the roads and blocking the only outlets, it became apparent the Germans would recapture most of Luxembourg and Belgium towns. The U.S. 101$^{st}$ stood their ground in Bastogne and soon became trapped as the enemy surrounded the city, cutting off all deliveries of food, medical supplies, equipment, weapons, and replacements.

German spies, wearing U.S. Army uniforms of captured or dead soldiers, had snuck undetected through the streets in Luxembourg and Belgium, disrupting communication by cutting telephone wires, changing street signs, and seizing the bridges. Once aware that the Germans had infiltrated their cities, the citizens put out the German flag and flew the swastika in order not to be identified with the Allies. The Germans had broken the Allied line, and as a result, tens of thousands of citizens and soldiers lost their lives. Hitler had amassed all his resources for this battle, his last effort to take back Europe, and he had the advantage as the Wehrmacht moved west.

On December 18$^{th}$, Bradley called Patton to Luxemburg to brief him on the situation. "The German penetration is much greater than we thought to the north, in the vicinity of Ardennes," he told Patton as they studied the war map. Unfortunately, due to weather, air supplies could not be dropped to aid the soldiers surrounded by the enemy. The 101st Airborne Division continued to hold out in Bastogne, not willing to give up the city. The Germans relentlessly attacked the town from the west and northwest with artillery fire being extremely heavy mid-December. Unprepared for fighting in the snow, the Allied soldiers in Bastogne dressed in dark camouflage, which was like flashing black targets as they ran and ducked for cover in the snow-covered fields. Until supplies arrived, they used white sheets offered by the villagers and sewn into capes to cover up their uniforms.

A request for 1,200 gallons of white paint and an equal amount of thinner for use in painting helmets, raincoats, and leggings for snow camouflage purposes was sent to Communications Zone to be disbursed to the armies heading into winter combat. The military requisitioned yards of white cloth from local French civilian sources and delivered it to a salvage repair company which in one day completed 700 tunics. Once the supplies arrived, the Army Engineers hurriedly snow camouflaged the vehicles and tents.

After the meeting with Bradley on December 18th, Patton realized he had underestimated the Germans. The Germans had concentrated their forces in the thick forests of the Ardennes. The war turned in their favor.

Eisenhower called the U.S. Commanders to Verdun on the 19th to decide how best to defend the liberated cities of Luxembourg and Belgium, and the vital routes to the port of Antwerp.

He asked General Patton to take command of the battle in the Ardennes. "When can you get your troops organized and ready?"

Patton replied, "By this afternoon, sir."

In an unprecedented maneuver, in less than 24 hours, Patton turned his Third Army divisions 90 degrees from the German West Wall to the north to attack the German's southern flank in the Ardennes. The weather still was not cooperating, and the XIX TAC could not drop their bombs to clear the way for the troops. If his forces were going to fight and liberate towns and rescue the 101st trapped in Bastogne, then Patton demanded that his tanks and infantry were given priority in POL (petroleum, oil, and lubricants), ammunition, rations, and replacement soldiers. The roads were too beat up and icy to truck the supplies, so Patton ordered the Quartermaster to commandeer a

French freight train to get the supplies and men to the front. Once in position with adequate supplies, the Third Army went into battle. Patton was hell-bent on defending the liberated territory at all costs.

The higher echelon lauded Patton's ability to attack successfully with three divisions on short notice. Patton retorted, "I doubt the Heinies even knew that the Third Army was moving. Hell, these boys can turn on a dime and keep firing. I maintain my contention that it is better to attack with a small force at once, and attain surprise than it is to wait and lose it."

Reported in the *After-Action Reports: The offensive movement necessary to throw the Third U.S. Army's striking power to the north was a large and complicated operation involving a switch of the Third Army's divisions and their supporting troops. Some of the most rapid troop movements in the history of warfare were required and combined with a high degree of precise timing and coordination. Not only did the tactical units have to be faced at right angles to the Western Front but the entire supply organization had to follow.*

Patton praised the all-black troops that operated the Red Ball Express and carried machine guns and grenades to protect the supplies and to deliver them on time.

On the morning of December 19[th,] General Patton gave the 546th orders to leave their post in St. Avold and reposition forty miles northwest in Pont-a-Mousson, the southern flank. Once again, Patton cut up the 546th and sent many of their enlisted men to the front to replace the dead or wounded soldiers.

With minimal gunners, the 546th positioned their guns in defense of the bridge across the Moselle River. Enlisted men were taken daily from the battalion and sent north to fight in the infantry which meant more hours on the guns for Frank and his men.

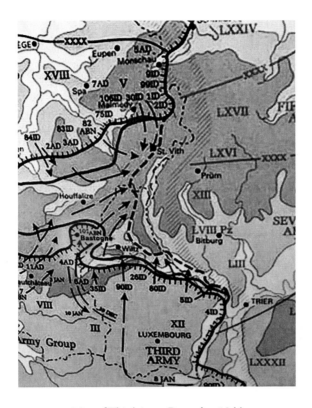

Map of Third Army December 1944

The snow, sleet, and rains had not ceased. The army slogged north to engage in the Battle of Ardennes, soon to be known as the Battle of the Bulge. On the twenty-second, each man received the prayer and Christmas Greeting from their Commander, General Patton. Even if the invocation was written for another battle, the prayer arrived timely for the most significant struggle ahead.

After a long day mucking around in foul weather and firing the big guns across the Moselle River to intimidate any German Panzer or ground troop, Frank and his men received the prayer written by Father O'Neil, the army chaplain, at the request of Patton.

*Almighty and most merciful Father, we humbly beseech thee, of Thy great goodness, to restrain these immoderate rains with which we have had to contend. Grant us fair weather for Battle. Graciously hearken to us as soldiers who call upon Thee, that, armed with Thy power, we may advance from victory to victory, and crush the oppression and wickedness of our enemies, and establish Thy justice among men and nations. Amen.*

On the back of the card was Patton's greeting of a Merry Christmas, encouraging the men with his confidence in their courage and devotion to duty. *May God's blessing rest upon each of you on this Christmas Day.*

# CHAPTER TWENTY-FIVE

# Christmas 1944

*Hello Darling,*           *Friday, December 22*
*Just a short note before I take off this morning to make my rounds. Couldn't write last night. It's snowing now, looks like it's heavy enough to stay. I don't know where we will spend Christmas day, but we already have our turkeys ordered. Found a shower house in town here yesterday, tile showers and real hot water, and as soon as I can shake loose, I'm going to take advantage of them. What a luxury! I'd like to hear some of those boys in the states cry about extra pay for overtime. Our boys here barely get time for a shower.*

Patton had orchestrated the Third Army to cover and protect the Saar, the Moselle, and the Rhine rivers. At the same time, the infantry and armored tanks fought towards Bastogne and the north, where the Germans had created a "bulge" around the area of the Ardennes forest by pushing through the American defensive line.

The weather continued to hamper the troops' movement. "Pray harder," Patton told his clergy.

Friday evening at Pont-a-Mousson on the Moselle River:

*Nothing new happened since this morning, just the usual running around to positions. Now the sky is*

*clear again with a half-moon shining very brightly. The
Red Cross girls came around to our boys again today,
bringing coffee, donuts, music, and some laughs. They
are doing a swell job. Haven't heard from George. Have
you? He's due for a trip home. He has been overseas for
almost two years. I don't understand that guy.*

Miraculously, the next morning on the twenty-third, the weather
cleared and remained so for six days, enough time to turn a temporary
setback into a crushing defeat of the German army. Patton's prayer had
been answered, and he immediately acknowledged Chaplain O'Neil
with a bronze medal. "Chaplain, you're the most popular man in this
Headquarters. You sure stand in good with the Lord and soldiers."

For the next few days, there was a break in the lowering skies
which had prevented full air support by XIX Tactical Air Command,
and now the clear weather was indeed a godsend in halting the enemy's penetration. Christmas dawned clear and cold, and the sun shone
brightly for the first time in months.

"A good day for killing Germans," Patton wrote in his diary.

Seven groups of fighter-bombers took off in the clear skies destroying bridges and German supply depots while the P-47 Thunderbolts
attacked the German troops in the Ardennes forest. Cargo planes
dropped food, blankets, ammunition, and necessary surgical instruments and medical supplies, including whole blood, penicillin, morphine, and dressings. Subsequently, glider planes dropped a team of
Red Cross doctors and nurses, as well as infantry replacements, coming
to the aid of the beleaguered troops that held Bastogne. Thousands of
jeeps, tanks, trucks, and howitzers from the Third Army continued on
their journey to the southern flank of the Ardennes, fighting through
snow and ice, and preventing the enemy from sealing off the corridor.
Rather than take the defense or use roadblock tactics, the Third Army

attacked and destroyed panzer units and the German infantrymen. Patton believed that the way to save his own men's lives was to attack as continuously and aggressively as possible. "The sooner you beat your enemy, the more lives you save."

The Allies expected German retaliation. Frank's men were on high alert twenty-four seven for German planes.

Despite the fighting, Patton had made sure every man in his army had a hot turkey dinner on Christmas eve or day and for those on the frontline at least a turkey sandwich with dressing and cranberry sauce.

*Hello Darling,*                       *Sunday, December 24*
*It's seven o'clock Christmas Eve, we have been through dinner some time, and some of us are writing home. I went to Mass this morning in a parish hall, the church itself is still standing but pretty well beat up, or I should say down. We are to have a midnite Mass in the church tonite at eleven-thirty. The radio has been playing Christmas carols all day, but nobody can get into the mood for them because this is a Christmas unlike any other we have experienced. Fortunately, the Mass is still the same.*

Frank left the barracks around ten and made his rounds of his gun positions, bringing some turkey sandwiches and liquid cheer for the boys. He wished them a Merry Christmas adding, "It's one hell of a Christmas, isn't it?" He pulled his coat up around his neck and walked down the cobblestone street to the open plaza in front of the church. The soft lights from inside flickered through the blown-out windows. He found Hubbard and Captain, and together they went inside the church. Candles glowed from candelabras that lined the aisles up to the altar. Candlelight lit the altar surrounded in red poinsettias. The altar boys in white robes escorted the priests, one who carried the chalice and the other two who wafted incense from the golden thuribles. The organ sounded a long note, and then the chorus broke into "Oh come, oh come Emmanuelle," in Latin. Once Mass began, Frank joined in reciting the Latin responses and singing along the familiar cantons of High Mass. The stars showed through ragged openings torn in the ceiling. The thought went through Frank's mind, *with so much beauty, how can there be war?*

> *I went to Midnight Mass, and the French put on a real spread. One thing I liked was the singing and everyone joined in on the responses. The hymns are the same and so is the Mass in Latin.*

That night at 0230, a German plane flew low over Pont-a-Mouson. One could hear the whirring of the two propellers, then the rat-a-tat-tat of the front-mounted guns of the enemy plane heading toward the bridge as it sprayed bullets across the water. The night was bright enough to detect the Messerschmitt ME 210 as it flew below the radar. One of Frank's gunners engaged the plane with the *"ack-ack-ack"* of the 155 Howitzer piercing the night sky.

In the Morning Reports noted, "Low flying ME 210 engaged by Gun Position 5, at 230, no casualties. Fired in Defense of the bridge across the Moselle."

The Germans continued to counter-attack and batter Bastogne from the north. On Christmas Day, the Germans sent in a white flag group demanding that General McAuliffe surrender. All that the general wrote back was, "Nuts." Even though confused, the Germans got the message that the Americans were continuing to defend the area. The next day the valiant Third Army successfully punched through and opened a corridor, arriving in Bastogne with replacements, tanks, ammunition, and the spirit of winning.

The day after Christmas, the German siege ended in Bastogne. Forty trucks filled with supplies entered the town. Ambulances were finally able to evacuate the wounded Americans. Evacuees returned to their homes, to their Christmas trees and unopened presents. The Americans once again liberated them.

> *Dear Kitty,*                         *Sunday, December 24*
>     *I have only received one of your December letters, and I'm getting anxious to hear some more of John, also to get some pictures. He is nine months old today. I suppose you are all fussed up tonite with Christmas things and wishing John were old enough to understand what is going on.*

* * *

The house on Silver Lake Boulevard had a gayly lit Christmas tree with tinsel and shiny bulbs standing in the front window, and an evergreen wreath hung on the door. Indoors the fireplace had a small fire going. Catherine lit the fourth candle on the advent wreath in the center of the dining room table. It had been four weeks since she'd heard from Frank and the news in the papers wasn't encouraging. The soldiers suffered from frostbite while fighting in the coldest winter on record, some even trapped in a town. *Oh, where was Frank?*

Grandpa played with John, tickling his toes with his violin bow in between playing a few ditties. John reached out and touched a red lightbulb on the tree and let out a scream.

"Catherine, come here, the baby's wailing like a banshee, burned his little finger."

Catherine came running and scooped Baby John in her arms, cooing, "It's okay, Momma kiss it. All better." John caught his breath, hiccupped a few times, then reached his arms out to grandpa. "Here, Dada, he seems to like your fiddle playing."

Grandpa put John on his lap and looked up with furrowed eyebrows and asked Catherine, "How's your mother doing?"

Catherine wiped her hands on her apron. "Dada, I don't think she will be joining us for dinner. Agnes is in with her now, Momma's in pain."

In his last letter, Frank wanted to know more about Catherine's frequent trips to Ontario, where her sister Mary lived.

> *Darling, is it a visit or a move? I hope everything is alright at home. You probably explained it in one of your letters, but I haven't received it as yet. Is your mother feeling any better?*

Catherine was torn between being a good mother and a good daughter staying home to take care of her mother, who had *gone to bed with an aching back* months ago. The doctor prescribed the usual dosage of morphine, but the pain persisted, and her use increased along with the alcohol. As long as Agnes was home, Catherine could escape to Mary's house and occasionally to Riverside to be with her sister Peggy whose husband was away in camp, still waiting to be deployed.

The next day, Christmas Day, the whole family gathered at the Silver Lake house, bringing presents for everyone, especially the children. Mary and Horace's little girls, Shereen and Nola, had on pretty red dresses and big bows tied in their curly blond hair.

Catherine made a fuss over them. "Oh, Mary, when Frank comes home, we're hoping to have a little girl cousin for them to play with."

Terrence, their third child, had on pressed shorts and a white shirt with a bowtie.

Horace teased, "Can't figure out why Mary dresses Terry like Little Lord Fauntleroy. Bet you, Frank won't allow John to be dressed like that!" He picked up John and threw him into the air catching him and making him laugh.

"Stop!" Mary and Catherine cried in unison, and of course, Horace threw him in the air again.

"Going to make a man out of him, Catherine. Frank's not going to want a sissy!"

The joking and teasing continued throughout the day, pictures were taken, and presents were opened, lots of toys, and games. After the midday dinner, everyone said their good-byes.

It would be a month before Catherine read about Frank's Christmas.

*Hello Darling,*          *Tuesday, December 26*

*Christmas has come and well on the way to start pointing for the next Christmas. We had another big dinner at noon on Christmas, but in all other respect, it's been the same routine as any other day. We did take some pictures of the guns and crews. It was a beautiful sunshiny day, brisk and cold.*

*I'm anxious to hear how you spent the day and what John did about it. I suppose he received a lot of presents and none from his Daddy. This being daddy by proxy isn't so good, is it Kitty? It's goodnight again, darling. Keep praying Kitty, and we will soon be together again.*

*Frank, Hub, and Kuret*

CHAPTER TWENTY-SIX

# Moonlit Nights

*Hello Darling,*         *Wednesday, December 27*
*No mail yet, just lots of packages coming in now.*
*We would trade the packages for letters any day.*

*The weather is clear now, as yet no rain or snow*
*for about five days, it is the longest spell in several months.*
*I don't like these bright moonlit nights, it's about the only*
*time we get much work, it's up and down all night. Jerry*
*doesn't venture out much during the day. The nights are*
*bitter cold now, and not much fun waiting around in*
*it. Saw Captain Howell today at headquarters. Haven't*
*seen him in some time. Only had time for him to ask*
*about you and John. Have you heard from his wife?*

Frank looked outside the window as if watching a movie.

*Wish you could see the scene outside our build-*
*ing tonite. Across the street there is a very large building*
*with a gaping hole in the roof. Alongside is a bombed-*
*out bridge. From my view you can see the moon shining*
*down on the river below, rushing through the ruins. The*
*white foaming water picks up the moonshine making the*
*water foam like champagne. Across the river is a church,*
*still standing, with everything around it completely*

*demolished. Last night one of our machine guns was popping tracers off the church steeple, also popping into a hapless Jerry plane. (A tracer is live ammunition embedded with chemicals to create a bright line showing the trajectory of the tracer in the night sky.)*

Hearing the thrum of German planes low overhead, the gunners in the church steeple shot tracers into the night. On the other side of the river. Frank and his boys followed the streak of light, then let off a volley of gunfire from the big guns. A fiery flash burst as a plane spiraled down, crashing into the river.

More low flying planes circled back towards the bridge about thirty minutes later. The 40mm and the 155 engaged the plane and destroyed the enemy aircraft. No American casualties were reported the next day in the Morning Reports. Night after night, the Germans attacked, night after night the anti-aircraft gunners shot them down or turned them back.

*Dear Kitty,*                    *Friday, December 29*

*Another night of full moon probably means work for us. Kuret, Hub, Captain and I will probably sit around and play poker, sweating it out as they say.*

*I spent the last two hours fixing the stove in our room, it is the smokingiest thing I've ever come across. In fact, we are beginning to believe they are some of Germany's secret weapons, left to wear down our patience. I punched out a part of a window and stuck the stove pipe out that way and it works pretty well. Only the draft makes it cold again.*

*Hello Darling,*           *Saturday, December 30*
*It's snowing again tonite, this time it will stay because the ground is frozen solid. I'll be betting on a white New Year. Tomorrow is Sunday and I plan on going to Mass and Communion, be looking for you.*

*Darling,*                  *New Year's Eve*
*In the morning we start a new year. I wish it could be New and different year, but it looks like the same old rotten business is the order of the day. It is rumored that Adolph is going to give one of his speeches 5 minutes after midnite. I hope the filthy beast has had enough.*

* * *

As the clock struck midnight, lights illuminated the Fuhrer's headquarters in Berlin, where Adolf Hitler gave his wartime proclamations over the radio to the people of Germany and his army. Sequestered in his bunker, delirious from drugs and power, he vowed, "Although our enemies have proclaimed the collapse of Germany every New Year since 1939, and in particular hopes this year 1944, we will never again allow what happened to us in November 1918."

The radio blasted across the courtyards where Hitler's Army and Youth had gathered, arms raised, and yelling "Heil Hitler," after every proclamation. The citizens celebrating the New Year stopped their festivities for the obligatory salute. Adolf's voice quivered and rose to a crescendo.

"Never before did victory seem so close to the Allies as in those days of August of last year when one catastrophe had followed another. At one time the enemy said that the war would be over before the leaves fall; another time that Germany would be ready to capitulate before the next winter. Like a phoenix from ashes, so strong is the German will, all the more, we will rise up anew from the ruins of our cities."

The soldiers and Nazis raised their arms again, "Heil Hitler." He spoke for over an hour, blaming a Jewish-international conspiracy for spreading lies and demanding the extermination of the German *Volk*. At the end of his speech, Adolf roared, "A German capitulation will never come, only a German victory."

Patton had another idea for ringing in the new year. At midnight on the night of December 31, all guns fired in rapid succession for twenty minutes. When the gunfire ceased, the forward observers stated they could hear the Germans screaming in the woods.

On New year's Day, the men went to church services, to atone or to be grateful for their conquests. To observe the holy day of obligation, Frank went to Mass then later to the synagogue to check on an incident. Someone had targeted the synagogue.

> *Dear Kitty,*           *Monday, January 1*
>
>      *I went into a synagogue this afternoon. Kuret and 5 others had attended services there this morning. During the services, someone was peeking in through a shell hole, and either threw a rock in at them or else accidentally knocked one in. Unfortunately, they didn't catch the culprit. The German gunners had used the synagogue for a storehouse. We found the covering of the Torah, like our Bible, all ripped to shreds and evidence of a burning. If those walls could talk, they would probably have a long horrible story to tell. There is a Synagogue in a town north of us that the Germans used as a house of ill-fame.*

Frank left the synagogue more determined than ever to stop the beast, Hitler. The Allies had not yet discovered the extent of torture and murder of the Jewish people. What Frank knew then was that he had five members of his battalion who were Jewish, who wore the letter H on their dog tags, who were targets when they attended Jewish services, and if taken as prisoners, they'd be sent to the concentration camps. And one of them was his best friend, Kuret.

In the evening, the men assembled after chow to hear Patton's New Year's message to his troops. "Men of the Third Army: From the bloody corridor at Avranches to Brest, thence across France to the Saar, over the Saar River into Germany, and now on to Bastogne, your record has been one of continuous victory. Not only have you invariably defeated a cunning and ruthless enemy, but also you have overcome every aspect of terrain and weather by your indomitable fortitude. Neither heat nor dust nor floods nor snow have stayed your progress. The speed and brilliance of your achievements are unsurpassed in military history."

Patton further acknowledged his troops at a later ceremony in his honor by saying, "The Distinguished Service Medal bestowed on me, is not for what I have done but for your achievements."

In early January, Patton was returning to his C.P. when he saw an endless parade of ambulances taking wounded men back from Bastogne. He passed a truckload of soldiers, nearly frozen in place. They stood and cheered him in the bitter cold. "It was the most moving experience of my life, knowing what the ambulances contained made it still more poignant."

The first days of January were not the success that Patton had hoped for. At the beginning of the year, the Germans began bombarding Luxembourg with a peculiar rocket-like, long-distance shell that killed a Commanding officer, among others. The novel projectile was

shot from a weapon a distance of thirty-five miles. The war again escalated. The Germans continued to attack as they retreated, and the conditions of the roads made it nearly impossible for the Third Army to
advance and attack.

On January 4, a weary Patton who felt he had done everything
correctly in lining up his army, wrote in his diary, "The flashes of our
own guns and those of the enemy in the gathering darkness against the
white snowfields were very beautiful, but not reassuring. I'm afraid, we
can still lose this war."

The enemy also had to contend with the rough Ardennes terrain and the heavy snow. Their tanks rolled in single file in narrow
passageways with bottlenecks at the bridges. The extreme cold forced
the Germans to hole up in the small villages, making them an easy
target, but also strengthening their defensive tactics. The Germans cut
communication wires as they fled and set fires and booby traps along
the roads. The seventh day of the new year marked the most intensive
firing in the operational history of the Third Army.

Frank had been up most the night with his men in the same position, defending the bridge across the Moselle. At 0302, one low-flying
enemy aircraft engaged the gunners. They expended six rounds from 40
mm anti-aircraft gun as well as 110 shots from the 50 caliber machine
gun, bringing the plane down with no casualties to the U.S. soldiers.

Orders came in over the wires. More A.A.A. battalions were
needed up north. The fighting had increased endangering Luxembourg,
Belgium, and the route to the principal port in Antwerp. As the
Germans retreated, they destroyed roads and bridges and set up their
defenses along the Siegfried Line.

Late afternoon on New Year's Day, Frank left Port-a-Mousson in
his jeep alongside the 546th convoy of trucks. They traveled 27 miles
along the Moselle and reached Toul after dark.

About a foot of snow covered the roads, and more was coming down. The bomb reconnaissance team went ahead in the twilight. Knowing that mines buried or frozen beneath the snow would be a danger in the spring thaw, they detonated or removed what they could find. Most of the mines that the Allies had set were also frozen, with the triggers locked up.

The convoy stopped. Shouting up ahead alerted the officers who then passed the trucks by driving along the side of the road. Frank got out to talk to the men upfront.

"Sir, we're taking extra caution before entering the next village. It should be just a few more minutes before we move on."

Temperatures had dipped below zero, and Frank could see the men riding in the open trucks had burnt-red faces from the blizzard and cold. Frank, not much better off, stepped back into his jeep and wrapped his trench coat around his ears.

*Hello Darling,*          *Tuesday, January 2*
    *Missed writing to you yesterday, we were on the move again. I think it was the coldest I have ever gotten. Never did get warm even when I finally rolled into my bedroll. We are located in a big barracks now, but I'm afraid it won't be for long though, it's too comfortable. There are some hot showers somewhere close by and I'm going to look for them tomorrow and partake of that luxury once again.*

*Dear Kitty,*          *Friday, January 5*
    *I missed writing to you last night, was busy making a pair of woolen shoes, worked on them till midnight. I cut the sleeves of my big sheepskin coat, and I wish you could have seen the result. They fit inside my overshoes,*

*I even sewed zippers on them. Kuret is on duty tonite and he is doing the same. I can sew the rest of it into my trench coat and make a pair of fleece lined mittens then I will be fixed for the cold weather. It's snowing tonite, and really beautiful, but cold.*

*I took that hot shower today, the windows were out of the building, but the water was hot. Hubbard says, "Hereafter I'm just going to just change my clothes!" The next group of soldiers didn't even get hot water. Looks like we may go back to bathing with our helmets, at least we can heat the water.*

*Some of our boys are still in tents outside. I found some lumber to at least build them some floors. Once we get comfortable, we'll be on the move again.*

*Hello Darling,*                               *Sunday, January 7*
*Another Sunday down, got to the 11:15 Mass, it was celebrated in a small chapel adjoining the Cathedral, an enormous church, all beat up. I would like to have seen inside but it is all boarded up, too dangerous to enter.*

Monday morning at 0700 Frank reported to the operations room for a twenty-four hour tour of duty, with no sleep. The soldiers getting off duty briefed him on the previous day's events and signed out. Frank stoked the fire in the pot-belly stove in the corner then added a few more pieces of wood trying to get the chill out of the room. He huddled up next to the stove but kept his coat on. The darn thing just wasn't throwing off enough heat.

*In this snowy cloudy moonless weather being at the command center is a rest cure, as there are no planes flying.*

He checked the radio channels to make sure he had a signal, then sat down with a book. The radio picked up static; then messages came across about the movement of the troops. Usually, this information was coded, so as not to spread classified information around so every German could hear. Later Frank found out that the SHAEF had intended to deceive the Germans about the army's positions. Subsequently, captured documents showed that this deception had worked.

In the quiet of the night, Frank wrote a letter to Catherine.

*Hello Darling,*            *Monday, January 8*
*I've all night watch in the operations room. I've spent most of the evening reinforcing my sheepskin gloves and boots. Tried them out in the cold yesterday and they really are marvelous. Seems funny to be living in a real winter climate, after living in California so long. We sure miss that steam-heated home we had a month ago and those amazing gadgets called toilets with` water and flush.*

Back in the barracks, the boys gathered around a table to engage in *a little game of chance.* Frank had to miss the game for the first time due to night duty. The guys were grumbling about Foster checking out of the game with all his winnings, but they knew he'd be back to joust the next evening. They all agreed *it's a*n excellent way to pass those jittery moonlight nights.

# CHAPTER TWENTY-SEVEN

# Not Over Yet

*Darling, I hope the present war news has sobered
up the civilians to the fact that this mess isn't over yet,
and there is still a lot to be done.*

On the front page of the LA Times was a photograph of Nazi troops capturing and marching American soldiers down a snowy, deserted road in the Ardennes. The title was in bold caps: **GERMAN OFFENSIVE IN THE ARDENNES.** *Disastrous trapping of the 101ˢᵗ Airborne in Bastogne in horrible weather conditions, thousands die, and the surge of the German army has alarmed the Allies. The Battle of Ardennes is the bloodiest of all.*

Battle of the Bulge, Ardennes

The alarming news panicked the wives and families of the soldiers. With mail being three weeks to a month out, no one knew where their loved one was stationed or fighting, if alive or dead. Frank had cautioned Catherine not to look for him in the newspapers, or to think every battle she heard about included him. The fact was many soldiers didn't see the front; many were in replacements camps keeping in shape at a reasonable distance from the action or in defense of cities and bridges already won over by the Allies. Still, the escalation of the war meant more men would die, and more replacements would go to the front.

By the middle of January, it became evident that the end of the Bastogne operation was in sight. The enemy had thinned, their attacks were on a shoestring, and they did not have enough replacement troops. XIX Tactical Air Corps destroyed much of the Wehrmacht equipment, tanks, guns, and ammunition storages, as well as bombed and strafed the retreating Nazi troops. The unleashed Third Army had forced the Germans to relinquish their stronghold on Bastogne. At every escape route out of the Netherlands, Belgium, and Luxembourg, the U.S. Army fired upon the Germans in a harassing barrage of gunfire. The effect was psychological warfare as much as an intent to kill. The artillery subjected the Germans to random, unpredictable, and intermittent artillery fire over an extended time, undermining their already low morale and increasing their stress levels.

Patton rejoiced in the demise of the Wehrmacht. "During this operation, the Third Army moved farther and faster and engaged more divisions in less time than any other army in the history of the United States and possibly in the history of the world. The results attained were made possible by the superlative quality of the American officers, American men, and American equipment." The Allies regained all the territory lost in the Battle of the Bulge from December 18 to January 28.

The Nazis withdrew behind the Siegfried Line to defend Germany from their home position. More A.A.A. battalions were sent up north in case of a counterattack and to help route the Germans back to their homeland.

Frank was asleep when word came to pack up. It was time to move. At 0805 on January 12, the 546th convoy was rolling. They covered 57 miles and arrived in Baroncourt, the western route to Luxembourg in line with Thionville, one point in the Saar Triangle. Patton estimated this would be one of the paths the Germans would take.

> *Hello Darling,*         *Saturday, January 13*
> *Like the proverbial thief we picked up our tents and disappeared into the night and here we are set down again and huddled around a fire. Couldn't write to you last night as I was too cold, too tired and also too busy. I wish you could have seen me in an open jeep (yes, we still keep the top down, why? I dunno.) I had on my long drawers, a pair of wool OD's, and pair of combat pants, which are heavy wool covered with Kaki, then a sweater, a field jacket, and an overcoat, a pair of fur-lined boots, fur-lined hat, then a heavy sheepskin coat for a robe. Was I cold? No, Kitty.*

The day was beautiful when they pulled out of camp. Big bombers filled the sky like silhouettes against the azure sky, leaving long jet streams marking their paths. Frank looked up and yelled, "Thank God we're on the winning side!"

Kuret grinned and pointed to the fighter planes. "Looks like our Pygmies leading the way, got them Heinies on the run, covering our asses on the ground." As he looked up, he swerved and couldn't adjust the steering wheel to avoid getting stuck in a snowbank.

"God damn it, Kuret, what the hell!" Frank jumped out, got on his hands and knees, and started to dig the snow out from around the tires while Kuret gunned the engine, digging the tires deeper. A group of about twelve French kids gathered to help while one fetched a shovel. With a team effort, the jeep skidded back on the road. Frank tossed the kids some chocolate and a few sticks of gum he had in his pocket. The older ones let the little ones grab the goodies, so Kuret tossed them some cigarettes. They sped off to catch up with the convoy while the children ran after them, waving and crying, "Vive les américaines!".

*Hello Darling,*                                      *Sunday January 14*

*The weather is still clear, really nice for the third day in a row, hope it stays that way. The planes (ours) were out as thick as mosquitos. Again, if the weather stays clear it is very much in our favor.*

*We're getting pretty well settled in our new home, it's not too bad, at least it's a house. There are so many quail and rabbits around here, I wish I had enough sense to bring along a shotgun and some shells. They'd sure make good eating. They really look funny, waddling around in the snow. I don't see how they can get much to eat, but they sure do look fat.*

*If you can find a rubber bedroll mattress, don't hesitate to send it. Mark it, "Military Equipment." And I've been trying to buy a radio, but they are hard to find. If you come across a small set, I wish you would send me one. Send the tube separately. I don't know if they are available in the states now or not. If we only knew*

*what we know now, we would have brought plenty of*
*things along.*

The men needed more protection against the cold. They were ill-prepared for the coldest winter on the books, and it was only getting worse. Those who worked on the bridges, those who dug themselves into trenches, and those who spent long hours in the night firing guns, all suffered, and many had trench foot and frostbite, a casualty that took them out of duty. At one point, there were more non-battle casualties than casualties by enemy fire. By late January, the army flew in seven hundred tons of warm clothes, mittens, and fur-lined boots and distributed them to the men on the front. Frank worked on getting his men their share of the clothing, as well as insulating the larger tents by putting in wood planks and rigging up stoves that worked. But as Frank had predicted, they had to move.

*Once we settle down and begin to enjoy life, it*
*will be time to move because we're getting too comfort-*
*able. It wouldn't be so bad if we could stay in one place,*
*but when we move, we have to leave the accumulated*
*comforts behind then spend a couple of frantic days dig-*
*ging up some more stuff in a new location. We have lived*
*in everything from mansions to hovels. Our boys are liv-*
*ing in tents, and lumber for flooring is hard to find.*

The weather vacillated between the cold of clear skies with sunshine, which melted the snow into a muddy mess or the cold and snow, which made the roads slick with ice. The Third Army pursued the Germans while also racing the all-out Russian drive on the Eastern Front, who were now less than 150 miles from Berlin. Patton was as eager to beat the Russians to Berlin as he was to beat the Germans. He feared the Russians would grab the land for themselves and not liberate the people, and he intended not to let that happen. As much as Patton hated the Nazis, he had respect for the German people as an industrious nation and even admired their generals for their ability and appetite for war. It was as if Patton were in a sort of sports competition or a chess game with the Germans. He wanted to beat his opponent in strength as well as intelligence. To win, Patton read the histories of wars, especially the writings of the German generals, to know how they thought so he could determine how they would act.

Late in the afternoon on the nineteenth, the 546th convoy arrived in Jeandelize, France. Frank and the officers took over a little house that must have been two hundred years old with at least 30 years of accumulated dirt. Kuret wouldn't put his duffel on the bed until the mattresses were thrown out on the snow and thoroughly beat with a broom. Carlson took his arm and cleared off the table in the kitchen of dirty dishes and rubbish, then dropped his stuff on top and set to work scrubbing the sink and floor. They put the filthy bedding outdoors and made it into a bonfire. Frank cleaned out the fireplace and started a roaring fire, filling the room with heat and only a minimal amount of smoke. *We scrubbed it up pretty well, and the house is quite livable.*

They hadn't moved far that day, the roads were slick with ice, and the sleet spiked their faces. Still, they covered twenty-one miles, getting closer to Metz in an effort to squeeze the Germans back to their homeland and to protect the main cities and routes.

Frank had an all-night duty, and in the morning, he went to Mass in the village church less than 100 yards from the Command Post. Afterward, he slept all day and played poker that night. Overnight, it had snowed over two feet, giving the streets and houses a fresh look, almost fairytale. The war action had moved to the east, and a few of Frank's boys got leaves to go to Paris. *They are all excited at the prospect, lucky boys they leave tonite, and have 48 free hours in Paris, just think to be able to sleep in a luxurious bed, take a bath three times a day, have your meals in bed, no one to tell you what to do for two days. Must be a dream. One officer from our battalion is allowed to go, know it won't be one of us.*

By the end of The Bulge, Frank and the other officers had earned Bronze Stars for exemplary conduct in ground combat against the enemy, but they were not to be awarded the medals until after the war. The Third Army had successfully turned the war back around in favor of the Allies. "So ended the campaign of The Bulge, which cost us, 50,630 men," Patton recorded in his diary.

Having worked with Kuret during their early training days and through the war, Frank was thrilled when his buddy Kuret received recognition for his outstanding performance as an officer. *Kitty, Kuret made First Lieutenant today, and as to be expected, he is tickled pink. I'm sure glad to see him get it as he sure deserves it.*

# CHAPTER TWENTY-EIGHT

# Little John

*Hello Darling,*                      *Saturday, February 3*

*Just got back from a long trip and now must sit up the rest of the night as I'm the duty officer tonight. You know when you think of France, you picture it a certain type of people, whereas it is not. The country has been different all the way across with characteristic changes in the people as well as how they do things. A tourist would never notice the different kinds of gates, each section in fact, every move we made brought us face to face with a new contraption and method of locking a gate, never dreamed there could be so many methods of keeping cattle in.*

*We have another south wind blowing and the snow is thawing and running away. The bad thing is it brings back the mud.*

They flipped a coin to see who would be in the lead jeep, always the most vulnerable position due to mines, ambush, roadblocks, and booby-trapped German vehicles. It was a dark winter morning at 0600 when Frank, Kuret, and Carlson hopped in the first jeep while Hub and Captain Cook followed behind in their vehicle. The driver kept his eyes forward and focused. Entering the Ardennes forest, the driver swerved off the road to miss the fallen trees, the handiwork of the retreating

Germans, and his wheels slipped side to side as he maneuvered through the mud. They came to the first gate with barbed wire twisted around the posts and top tier of wood to secure it. Frank jumped out, took the wire cutters they carried under the seat, and clipped the wire only to find that the gate didn't budge. Shivering in the icy wind, he cussed and kicked till Kuret jumped out. Studying the two wood crossbars that fit into the post, he slid one out, then the other.

"Well, I'll be damned Kuret. You son-of-a-bitch ain't so dumb after all."

The driver continued over the rutted road and off-road through fields covered in blankets of melting snow with what looked like rocks or small boulders dotting the ground ahead. When they approached the area, they stopped. The snow was pink with drained blood from the carcasses of horses and cows that lay stiff and motionless. Up ahead were several abandoned German tiger tanks blown apart to be of no use to anyone else. Once upon the wreckage, they discovered hundreds of frozen bodies strewn across the field, soldiers contorted in action and riddled with bullets, their faces a ghoulish black, stripped of their outer clothing and anything of value.

The stench was unbearable as they continued on the country road climbing through the densely forested and mountainous terrain until it widened and opened up to rolling hills and farmland as they entered Luxembourg. Tanks and artillery ringed the city, and the military police escorted them to the meeting hall. Inside the cavernous building, war maps covered the walls indicating the current positions of the Third Army. The plan was for the 546th anti-aircraft artillery to move into Belgium in the following days in defense of the Ardennes and the surrounding cities. The Germans had left the villages destroyed and weakened. Studying the maps, Captain Cook made notes as to where to position their guns to prevent enemy air counterattacks and to protect the vital channels of transportation, the airfields, railroads and train depots, bridges, and the main roads leading from the west coast. They would set up camp in the vicinity of Bastogne, fifty miles or less from the German border, with orders to protect the western flank, while the Third Army tanks and infantry fought to take over Trier and Saarburg and to break the Siegfried Line.

Upon returning to the Command Post in Jeandelize, Frank went on night duty and could barely keep his eyes open as he sat close to the stove, reading the daily reports and making notes on their reconnaissance trip. He learned that the officers had planned a dance for the boys the following night, their last night in France. He wrote to Catherine, leaving out the unsavory details of war.

> Hello Darling,          Sunday, February 4
>
> We had a movie last night, it was Edmond Love in "The Girl in the Case," a comical mystery and was much enjoyed. The church has a small hall with a stage, and the priest let us use it. It had been some time since we had a show.
>
> Tomorrow night we are having a Battery dance, it is really going to be good to watch some of those boys try to carry on a conversation in French. All this sounds like war, doesn't it, what with dances and movies etc. One of the Batteries had a dance the other nite and invited all the girls who could come. It so happens that these people are somewhat on the German side but still French. Well, they had a big turnout with Momma, Papa and the children too. They all danced for an hour until the food was served, after that they all disappeared except about six of the girls.

*Good night my darling, take care of yourself and John.*

The closer the battery got to the German border, Frank found the people were less friendly and somewhat hostile to the "invading Americans," as they saw it.

Frank announced to his troops that it was time to pack up and move north in defense of the territory gained in the Battle of Ardennes (The Bulge). The boys grumbled as usual, then packed up.

*Hello Darling,*            *Monday, February 5*

*The news continues to be good, could be sometime this mess will end, but sometimes it seems it will go on forever. When the boys ask me when I think it will end, I always tell them "Tomorrow," and someday, I will be right.*

*It's our last night, and we've gotten our little place so comfy it will be hard to leave. We have a beautiful log fire in our fireplace now and it's throwing up purplish-blue flames, wish you could be here to cuddle up and watch it. With that thought, I'll say goodnite to you darling, may we soon cuddle up in front of our own fireplace.*

At 0800 on February 6, their convoy of trucks left Jeandelize and arrived in Libramount, Belgium, at 1300 in the vicinity of Bastogne. Frank and the other officers had gone ahead in jeeps, radioing back the road conditions as well as forewarning the convoy of obstacles. At one point, the road submerged underwater from the overflowing river that ran alongside their route. Tread marks showed the diversion of other trucks across a field to rejoin the road up ahead. The Army Engineer

Corps had laid down boards that supported the heavy vehicles over the sludge.

Their convoy reconnoitered in the next village. Signposts redirected the route to a new road that the engineers had corduroyed with stringers and cross-pieces spiked onto the wood. It was a temporary fix to an infrastructure of roads destroyed during combat with the heavy tanks and trucks driving over the frozen streets.

Entering Belgium

Once in Libramont, Frank set out with Carlson to locate positions for the big guns as well as to survey the situation of billeting the men. Pulling up in front of a farmhouse, Frank jumped out and with another armed soldier to search the premises. The farmer emerged from the barn with a friendly wave. "It's all been cleared! Welcome, we've been waiting for you."

The Belgians were so grateful to the Americans that they readily opened their homes to the soldiers. Still, they had their concerns about billeting men and implored them to behave around their young women. Some of the G.I.s, who initially liberated Libramont, had taken undue liberties with the young girls. Patton had instructed the officers to enforce the code of conduct, and some of the boys found themselves reprimanded, court-martialed, or worse, on the frontline.

It wasn't until two days later, Frank wrote to Catherine.

> *Hello Darling,*　　　　　　　　*Thursday, February 8*
>
> *I'm somewhere in Belgium. Missed writing, just couldn't get around to it. I was on the road, and on reconnaissance the first day, then yesterday we were just too busy to do anything.*
>
> *Kuret and I are billeted out with some Belgium people. They are nice, and if we could stay here a while, we would learn to speak French, but I'm afraid it might not last too long.*

After the long hours of getting his men either in tents, farm-houses, or homes, Frank and Kuret settled in a modest but comfortable room in the back of a Belgian family's house. Frank unpacked his duffel bag and found a pound of coffee he could bring to the family as a gift, not much compensation considering they took over their back room with its private entrance. Kuret used the outhouse and came back in shaking off the cold. Both men cleaned up and soaked their feet in what looked like a urinal with a faucet. After settling, they walked around to the front of the house and knocked on the door.

The Monsieur greeted them at the door with a booming voice and exuberant handshake. The living room had a couch, and two over-stuffed chairs, a piano in the corner, a playpen, toys on the braided rug, a bookshelf with more framed photos than books, and lace curtains on the windows with knick-knacks on the hand-carved shelves above each portal. Adjacent to the living room was the kitchen. The family sat around the kitchen table next to a wood fire, burning in a blackened stone fireplace. The children sat quietly, their eyes round with curiosity. Jenny was ten years old with long braids that she kept twirling. John, who was eight, stood up and saluted, triggering a salute back from the two officers. The rosy-cheeked mother held their youngest child, Joseph, who had just turned one. Frank handed her the coffee and introduced himself and Kuret in his best French. Before standing to boil some water, Madame gave the baby to the father, who held him like a rugby ball.

Frank laughed and told them his son was almost one, but he hadn't held him since birth. He showed them his most recent picture of John, and they squealed and howled, thought it was marvelous. "His name is John too," Frank beamed. There was no holding them back. The little boy John stood on the bench, peering over the adult shoulders at the photo of his namesake. The moment pierced Frank. Would he return home to see his John grow up? Would he and Catherine have the little girl he prayed for?

The smell of fresh coffee filled the room, and Madame served a steaming mug to the men. Putting the baby down on the floor, the father went to a cabinet and brought out a fine cognac. "The Boche didn't get this bottle. Hid them under floorboards in the bathroom." He motioned and told his story in broken English with a smattering of French. The mother sent the children to bed, and more war stories ensued.

German forces had invaded Belgium on May 10, 1940, and the occupation lasted until the Allies arrived in September 1944. Over the four years, as in all occupied Europe, food, clothing, fuel, and materials for livelihoods were rationed or not even available to the civilians. A black market existed in the country, supplying food illegally at very high prices to those who could afford it. The Nazis raided their homes for loot, especially their alcohol, and took over their houses, leaving the families to find another place, perhaps with a relative, it made no difference to the Boches (slang for dirty Germans). Like the angel of death, the Gestapo went from door to door rounding up Jews and citizens who opposed the regime, taking them as prisoners of war and sending them to labor camps to work in forestry, road building, man-ufacturing, and farming projects with little or no compensation. The living conditions in the camps were deplorable with inadequate hous-ing and barely enough food to survive.

The Gestapo sent nearly thirty thousand Belgian Jews to con-centration camps, most to Auschwitz death camp, and subjected them to the inhumane treatment and brutality under the Third Reich. Fewer than 1,000 survived.

Over 400,000 Belgians had collaborated with the Nazis during the war; some enlisted in the Wehrmacht; others received favors for giving Allied information and cooperating with the Secret Police (S.S.), informing on their Jewish neighbors. After the war, the War Tribunal prosecuted 56,000 Belgian collaborators and executed 250 sympathizers.

To flush out the Germans, the Allies, both the British R.A.F. and the United States A.F., had bombed occupied Belgium, often missing their targets, causing high civilian casualties. The war touched all the Belgians; everyone had lost friends or family, and many were still miss-ing when Frank arrived.

Monsieur showed them a current French newspaper from December 20, 1944. Frank translated the best he could. *This time, German armored units have encircled the U.S.A. forces in and near Bastogne. More German armored units have crossed the River Our. Libramont is in German hands.*

"After being liberated from *les sale Boches*, they came back at the holy season of Christmas." Monsieur's eyes teared as he explained in broken English that they were still fearful of returning to German rule.

All roads, leading to the port of Antwerp, crossed through Bastogne and Libramont. Both cities took the brunt of the Battle of the Bulge. Germans assaulted the neighboring land with heavy tanks rolling through towns, machine-gunning down whatever moved, to regain the territory. Projectiles and shells exploded in the fields and villages nearby, and the people took cover in cellars, or away from windows, locked in closets and storage rooms.

It's no wonder that when the 546th rolled into Libramont, the Belgians greeted them with open arms. The Americans had liberated and saved them once again.

*The country here is very similar to France, the people even more enthusiastic than the French, probably because of their recent experience with the Boche. They have all kinds of stories to tell.*

*Our hosts started serving us coffee and cognac at nine o'clock, I'm not sure when we got to bed. We each have a large bed with a box spring mattress, the first I've been in since home. Sleep! Never been better.*

*The weather is still fairly warm, it looks like winter is really over, we only had two months. Now it rains every other day and mud, mud, mud.*

*I was in Luxembourg a couple times last week, it's a very beautiful country, and above all, they have good beer, the first real beer since I had my last bottle of Millers.*

The rain pattered against the window, the weather had become wishy-washy again, rain, snow, then sunshine all in one day. That evening, Frank took off his overshoes that Catherine had sent him last month, shook off the water off his clothes, and hung his coat before entering the living room. He tiptoed so as not to disturb the sweet scene of Kuret teaching Jenny "Twinkle, Twinkle Little Star" on the piano. Kuret played some notes, and Jenny smiled and sang, "Ah! Vous dirai-je Mama," a French nursery rhyme put to the same music by Mozart. She was so endearing and sweet and motioned Frank to come over. They played and sang, Jenny in French and the big American soldiers in English.

> We finished an after-dinner session of poker and came back home to write to you. I just broke in on a piano session by Kuret and the little girl Jenny. She is really cute, and we are trying to talk them out of a picture of the kids. I'll send you one if we succeed. In any event tomorrow we will take some of our own.

The next night at the family home, Frank and Kuret sat in the living room listening to a man who was in the F.F.I., French Forces of the Interieur, the official name of the French resistance fighters. *He's telling long yarns about rescuing pilots and sending them back to England by the way of the underground. Also, a Belgian lad was there who was captured by the Germans during the Battle of the Bulge and then escaped. He also has some tales. On top of that Madam started serving cognac and coffee with some cakes and cookies. You just can't refuse the things they offer as they do it in such a good spirit. We give them things and they just won't be outdone.*

In the morning, Frank asked if he could take Jenny, being the oldest child, to Mass with him. She had a bad heel and couldn't walk, so John begged to go even though he had already gone to an earlier Mass. How could Frank refuse the little guy? "Go ask your mom. I'll wait here." He ran inside, put his Sunday clothes back on, and with the biggest grin, took Frank's hand and accompanied him to Mass. *Was he ever proud! Kitty, I wish you could see these people, it would warm your heart. It's like an oasis in the desert of war. Little John has a bit of a record as part of the F.F.I. even. He used to carry ammunition for the resistance right under the German nose, and he is only nine years old! The parents gave me a photo of them which I will send you. It is really cute.*

That evening, like other evenings, Frank and Kuret spent time with the family after being in the muddy fields all day spotting positions for their guns.

> *Last night we didn't get home till ten-thirty, and they were all waiting up, with John sound asleep in the armchair. His mother tried to waken him, but it was impossible.*

On their last evening in Libramont, they made sure to get over to see the family early enough that the children were awake.

> *John is sitting right under my nose, waiting for me to finish this letter, he is very well-behaved and just patiently sits without a peep.*
>
> *It will be hard to say good-bye tonight, but we leave in the morning.*

# CHAPTER TWENTY-NINE

# Belgium to the German Border

As the snows melted in the mountains and the meadows, the rivers and streams overflowed, and the fields turned into muddy pits. The rivers were wider, deeper, and flowed faster than had been estimated, creating a death trap for troops ferrying across the Sauer River, and for the engineers building the bridges.

On the far shores, the enemy was firmly entrenched in pillboxes and natural rock formations, firing at the troops like in a shooting gallery. Besides dodging enemy fire, the Third Army assault troops often fell into the water as their floats and boats overturned. The bridge construction troops worked under the double handicap of the swift-flowing streams and enemy artillery fire. A dozen bridges were lost, but despite these handicaps, the U.S troops got across the Sauer River and continued their advance to the Siegfried Line.

Remarkably, the Army Corps of Engineers erected more bridges in February than in any other month of Third Army's operations. Towards the end of the month, after the deplorable weather conditions let up for a few days, the railroad and air transportation became the primary means of supply delivery to the divisions. Once again, the Third Army charged to the Rhine.

The 546th had moved northeast through Belgium closer to the German border, passing through towns whose structures lay in rubble, their roads impassable, and the citizens without means to get medical supplies or food. Frank and his boys positioned their guns in defense of transportation and bridges. Ground maneuvers became the main focus since few enemy planes were flying in the area due to the disorganization of the Germans and lack of forces and supplies. Only two enemy aircraft made attacks, both strafing attempts but with no known damage.

*Hello Darling,*                    *Thursday, February 15*

*I missed writing to yesterday as we were on the go again. Finally have a break in the weather, yesterday was as beautiful a day as I've seen since leaving California, like a perfect winter day on the desert, blue sky and everything sparkling. I spent most of the day walking around spotting positions. The mud is still with us, but maybe a week of this weather, even that will be gone. We passed through Bastogne, what a mess it is. We'll take the camera out today and see if we can get some good shots.*

*Thanks for getting the air mattress, if you can get any more, please send it. I told Captain Cook about you finding one, and his wife has been tearing her hair out trying to find him one.*

*I spent an hour wandering around town today looking for a gift for our wedding anniversary and John's first birthday. On the surface, the city appears to be well-stocked, but as usual, it isn't. There are lots of knick-knacks and souvenirs but little worthwhile. I was looking at some lacework, but I don't know enough about it to figure out what to do with the stuff. I got a couple of letters from you today, they are coming in much better, but I have received only one L.A. times to date, it was*

*December 17th issue. The news here has a different slant,*
*so even if it's old news, I like receiving the paper.*

*I'm enclosing a picture I want you to put away for*
*me of John and Jenny, the children of the house where*
*Kuret and I billeted. I wish we could have stayed with*
*them a little longer.*

*It is just a month now till our second wedding*
*anniversary, and then John will be one year old, it doesn't*
*seem possible that I have missed all that. These years are*
*too precious to be wasted wandering around this dis-*
*contented miserable continent. Tain't right, is it Kitty?*
*Goodnight, darling, love to you and John.*

Frank was now in Arlon, near to the German border. Their new
quarters met their basic needs, and much better than tents. In the last
town, Kuret and Carlson had picked up a radio in an electric store that
still carried a few miscellaneous items. That night, the old group got
together to play some poker, *the first session we've had in this position.*
The radio played the hit parade, Hub sang along, and Kuret pounded
away on the piano that had been left in the house. *Our new radio helps*
*to while away many otherwise empty hours.* The days dragged on as they
continued the same routine of setting up the gun positions, censoring
the mail, getting in a few poker games, and a few nights on the town.
The beer halls were open and doing good business with the G.I.s, but
not much else was going on.

*I visited a few of the local bars, the ones we vis-*
*ited were very much like our own at home, and they*
*play American records for us, good ones. The beer is just*
*fair, a bit better than the English, not nearly as good as*
*our own.*

Kuret and Frank got into a discussion over a few beers about their future after the war. Kuret had his heart set on going back home to San Francisco, settling down with his wife and having a family.

Frank agreed. "Yeah, I want to settle down too, have that baby girl, but I don't know what I'm going to do for work after we get out of the army. For the life of me, I can't decide what I would like to engage in."

"Me neither, but I'm going to make some money whatever I do. Might stay in Los Angeles, get a job in the movies, taking photos of those starlets, maybe even film a movie."

"Ha! Good luck. I worked at Shell, selling fertilizer, but I don't think I would care to go back to Shell again. At least, not in the desert. I feel that I've spent too much time down there."

"My fifteen months in the DTC was enough desert for me, that's for sure!" Kuret had hated the long days in the desert sun.

"It would be alright there but for the summer and the gnats. Don't think it's a good place to bring up children either. It's going to be quite a problem not knowing what to do in the future, and I hope it will be in the near future."

"Where does Catherine want to live?"

"Probably Los Angeles, but I don't like the idea of living right in Los Angeles. Looks like we'll have to toss a coin to decide."

"Yeah, let's pray we get the chance to toss that coin."

Hub interrupted to see if they wanted to place some bets on playing the pinball machine he found in the back room. Frank was all for a game. "Pinball machine in war-torn Belgium! Let's have a go at it." The three friends made such a ruckus betting, playing, and splashing beer at each other that the bartender stuck his head around the corner to see what the commotion was. Exasperated, he exhaled and said, "Oh la la, les américaines sont fous." Just crazy Americans.

*Hello Darling,*                    *Sunday, February 25*

*Went to Mass this morning in a very large and beautiful cathedral. I wish you could see some of these places with me. Maybe after we put away our first million, we can come over and see some of these places together.*

*The news sounds good again on all fronts, let's pray it keeps going so. Glad to see the progress made in the Pacific, that's what worries all the G.I.s over here. Not much future in the C.B.I. The weather has turned for the better again, and when the sun shines, it always seems like the war is close to an end.*

*Captain Cook and I met a really nice family here and it's really fun visiting them. It's about the best chance to learn French. These people know quite a bit of English too and are very jolly. In fact, the man of the family reminds me of your dad, he likes to kid a lot. Then too, he has a lot of stories of the German occupation. He tells how the Germans confiscated everything they wanted, even bicycles and radios. I've been trying to find out the political feeling among the Belgians. Most houses I've been in have pictures of the King and Queen and they seem to think quite highly of them.*

*They always seem to bring out their photo albums, and as a proud poppa, I show them John's photo, I carry it in my shirt pocket, and it comes out at the slightest provocation. Maybe we'll get to practice our French. I wish we had been able to stop along the way in our earlier hurried trip across France, and we would have been*

*pretty good at the language by now. They served some red*
*wine that was really delicious.*

*It's the first time in a long time we've had such*
*a nice setup, and we're taking advantage of it. I hope I*
*don't jinx it by telling you.*

Well, Frank did jinx it. Word came over the wires that the interrogation of a prisoner of war elicited advance information of a strong enemy counterattack in Prum. The army needed more troops at the northern border of Belgium and Germany. Frank got orders that night to move out. The 546th left Arlon and traveled sixty miles north to Gouvy, nearer to the fighting in Prum, Germany.

*Hello Darling,*                    *Tuesday, February 27*
*The last letter I wrote was Sunday night. I told*
*you we were very comfortable and that it couldn't last,*
*well it didn't last ten minutes more, were we mad, but*
*as the French say, "It's the war." We are in a mud hole*
*now and have to wear our overshoes all the time. We had*
*a hard time finding a Command Post but finally moved*
*into a fairly nice place.*

Patton reported from Prum: "There are quite a number of pillboxes on the far side of the river, one camouflaged like a wooden barn. When you opened the door through which the hay was supposed to be stored, there is a concrete wall nine feet thick with an 88mm gun sticking out. Another was completely built inside an old house, and when it became operational, the outside walls were knocked off! The amazing thing is these defenses produced no results."

Patton gave orders to blow up the pillboxes with the 155mm guns, which proved to be a successful tactic. Frank's A.A.A. battalion had joined the XII Corps battery, which reported nine pillboxes destroyed in one day. Despite the weather and flooding, the German delay tactics, and the continual enemy shelling, the Third Army continued to cross the river into Germany.

Frank and his boys mucked around finding gun positions to aggressively defend the town of Gouvy and the surrounding roads, depots, railroads, and bridges. Throughout the night and day, they shot off shells across the river, if nothing more than to instill fear in the enemy, known as a "harassing program." The German planes weren't flying, so they focused on ground patrol. No enemy artillery fire was received, and no enemy counterattack developed.

> *It's payday today with no place to go and no place to spend it, no place to howl, and I don't feel like howling anyway. All I want is to see you and John. It's been a long time, and I'm getting awful lonesome for you. The town we are in (I say town with reservations because there isn't much left) has no stores open. I haven't even found a café.*
>
> *More rain and the town is pretty muddy, can't even step out of the house without sinking into this sludge. The house we are in was used by the Boche during their last spree, and they sure left their mark on it. They shot up the inside with pistols scarring it terribly, it had been beautifully furnished, but it isn't any longer. I received your letter saying you found a mattress for me. I sure could use it now. We finally got some canvas cots issued to us, which will be a great help.*

The town of Gouvy had little infrastructure left, and there was a general lack of civilian medical personnel and facilities, which put a heavy burden on the military medical units. To eliminate or reduce the problem, they improvised military hospitals and relocated civilian doctors and salvaged medical supplies. The primary health issues among the soldiers were trench foot and lung problems exacerbated by gasses used in warfare, as well as the ongoing cold and wet weather. After treatment for pneumonia and bronchial ailments, the men rested a few days then went back to duty. The infantry and foot soldiers had more problems. The rough terrain and fast-flowing rivers made rescuing the injured soldiers a harrowing experience. When brought to the Red Cross tents, there were minimum supplies for the seriously wounded. Handicapped by poor road conditions, the military medics innovated a plan to use railroad cars for the evacuation of casualties rather than the slower ambulances.

Patton bestowed the well-deserved Bronze Star on the Red Cross nurses and medics that worked tirelessly throughout the Battle of the Bulge and other campaigns under dire combat situations without having enough supplies to do their job. Delivering a short speech, Patton recognized that no war could be won without the Red Cross nurses and medics, and because of their selfless work, more soldiers would return home.

Frank found the Red Cross set up in the once tree-lined *centre ville,* the plaza in front of the cathedral. He walked over to chat and found that they had the cinemobile there where he could get some movies for the boys. He talked with the ladies and charmed them into visiting his boys across town at their gun positions. They obliged and took hot coffee and donuts to the men, always a welcomed sight. Frank borrowed two movies and left to set up the projector for a movie night after dinner. It was such simple diversion, but the soldiers enjoyed the Bing Crosby movie. Frank closed his eyes, dreaming he was in his easy chair at home listening to Bing croon.

Even though enemy resistance was stubborn throughout February, it was nowhere near strong enough to stop the driving power of the Third U.S. Army. By the end of the month, the Third Army broke the Siegfried Line and passed through most of the army zone. At the end of February, there was nothing between the U.S. Army units and the Rhine River, except rough terrain and a badly mauled, retreating enemy force.

Every day, Frank witnessed German soldiers surrendering with their arms over their heads, hoping for mercy from the American soldiers. *This war must end sometime, and it might just as well end now.*

CHAPTER THIRTY

# The Beginning of the End

*Hello Darling,*          *Thursday, March 1*
*Missed writing to you again yesterday, pretty hard*
*job writing in a jeep, so I gave up. The mud is back*
*again with a vengeance, and you can't imagine how*
*gooey it can get after these trucks break down a road. I*
*got my jeep stuck on a high center made by trucks when*
*out on reconnaissance the other day. We lifted it with the*
*boys but had no luck; finally, another jeep came along*
*and pulled us out.*

Catherine visualized Frank in his overshoes, slipping in the mud as he pushed and pulled, trying to get his jeep over the ledge. She remembered the time in the desert when their car got stuck in the sand. He wouldn't give up, pushing and yelling at her to step on the gas when she didn't even know how to drive. Finally, the wheels dug in so deep that they had to wait for their friend Bert to drag them out with his truck.

John pulled himself up on the coffee table and grabbed at the lace doily under the flower vase. Catherine caught the vase and put John in his playpen while she finished reading Frank's letter. She spoke aloud to no one, "And he said he doesn't know what lace is used for.

My, my, it's all over this house, on tables, chair arms, and draped over the chest of drawers." She wiped a tear and thought, *I don't need any more lace or perfume, I just want to see him walk through that door.*

Last month in the L.A. Times, she was sure she had found a photo of Frank riding in a jeep through the rubble in Bastogne. She cut it out and sent it to him a few weeks earlier, and now he commented on it.

> *I received your letter of February 12 today, the one with the clipping. No, the picture was not of me. The only picture of me I want you to see is that one coming up the stairs to greet you, so don't be seeing things in the newspaper.*

It was already March, nearly their second wedding anniversary and John's first birthday. Why was it so difficult on the days when milestones appeared on the calendar? On her wedding anniversary, they'll celebrate St. Patrick's Day with her family, but it will feel so hollow without Frank and his joking. They'll not be doing the jig till after he comes home. John won't miss his father on his first birthday since he doesn't even know him. What does John think when he is shown his daddy's photo and told, "This is your daddy." He doesn't have a concept of what a father is or isn't. Catherine thanked God for her family, who kept her buoyed and hopeful, but no one could take away her sadness.

\* \* \*

The 546th left their post in Belgium, drove through Luxembourg and continued south, crossed the Moselle River, and positioned their guns to protect the infantry as they crossed the Saar River into German territory.

Frank got out of his jeep, his clothes sopping wet and with mud splattered from head to toe. It was impossible to keep anything clean. It was useless even washing his clothes since one ride in the jeep would negate any cleaning. He had left early that morning on reconnaissance to check out the locations of the small towns along the Saar River. He drove along rutted roads, dodging sniper bullets, passing through dark forests like those in a Grimm fairytale where wolves roam. *Werewolves,* the name given to the Nazis youth trained in guerilla warfare, now roamed the forest. More often than not, the American soldiers would come across German soldiers that wanted to surrender; even then, it was hard to tell if they were genuinely surrendering or luring them into their den.

After taking the G.I.s across the Moselle and Saar rivers, the evacuees filled the barges on the return trip. Men, women, and children fought to get aboard, fleeing the final days in their war-torn country, trying to get back to their homes or escaping captivity.

Driving into a small village, Frank felt a pang of shame and sadness as he watched a German woman with two children and a suitcase fleeing the area bombed by the Americans. As awful as the bombing was, the Nazis only understood force. White bedsheets and flags hung out the windows, billowing in the wind, drenched in the rain, yielding to the Allies. The desperation was palatable.

*Hello Darling,*                    *Friday, March 2*
  *It's late, and I'm going to make this rather brief.*
*I've been jeeping all over the countryside and am kind of*
*sleepy. I just finished taking a bath, the first in two weeks*
*or more, kind of dirty, wasn't I? This wasn't much of a*
*bath, one of those out of a helmet, but it gets the outer*
*layer off anyway.*

On March 4, the 546th A.A.A. Battalion attached to the 65th Division of the 12th Army, a consolidation of troops under Patton. The final thrust into Germany focused on crossing the Saar River, breaking the Siegfried Line, and ultimately crossing the Rhine, the last natural defense of the Germans.

At each river crossing, the anti-aircraft artillery launched their 155mm shells across to the other side of the bank, blowing up the pillboxes and making a pathway through the dragon teeth and other delay obstacles.

On the other side of the Saar river, there was one command pillbox that was a three-story submerged barracks with toilets, showers, baths, a hospital, laundry, kitchen, storerooms, and every conceivable convenience plus an enormous telephone installation. Identical diesel engines produced electricity and heat, yet the whole offensive capacity of this installation was two machine guns and a 60mm mortar operating on hydraulics by remote control, lifting the guns through cupolas. The extravagance of the German bunkers far surpassed their capabilities of defending their country. The pounding of Allied shells made only dents in the structure, but one dynamite stick broke open the door.

Frank returned late at night and laid his clothes out to dry. A bulletin arrived that all soldiers were to be issued a new uniform, a uniform that Patton took particular care picking out.

"I spent a long time inspecting uniforms and came to the conclusion that the best uniform for war is combat boots properly made of leather with the flesh side out, heavy woolen trousers cut not to exceed eighteen inches at the bottom, a woolen shirt, a helmet and helmet liner, and for winter, a modified trench-coat with a liner and gloves, and two weights of shirts. It was the best-looking and most useful uniform." Patton was a man of style, as well as a warrior.

The men were issued new uniforms and new orders to move. Patton planned to spread his army out to the north and south along the Rhine River and gave commands to attack as soon as possible, believing that time was more valuable than coordinating with the slow-moving Montgomery. Bradley was aware of his plan and encouraged Patton and the Third Army to strike before Eisenhower knew they had crossed the river.

Frank's battalion crossed the Saar River on March 7 and camped in the area of Saarlautern. The enemy fire hit their corps daily, sending soldiers to hospitals and evacuation tents. The war was now being fought on the enemy's fatherland, an affront to German autonomy and dignity. At this time, the enemy still did not indicate that he was abandoning his "defend and delay tactics," nor withdrawing beyond the Rhine River, even though the Wehrmacht was steadily losing ground. Thousands of German troops were being bagged daily as prisoners. Some replacements were reaching the enemy's frontline units, but not enough to replace their losses. The Nazi troops had diminished, and they now depended on recruiting citizens, very young men, women, and older men. Hitler refused to surrender or relinquish territory, and if a subordinate suggested capitulation, he would declare him a traitor and have him shot in the head.

German firepower had not been exhausted, and shells landed in and among Frank's battalion, but they only suffered injuries from shrapnel. The U.S. Third Army lost trucks, equipment, and a few buildings occupied by the Allies and minimal lives. Frank worked around the clock checking on his guns and going out on reconnaissance missions surveying the area to advance the men from the Third Army infantry who now rode in the trucks of the 546th. The enlisted men slept in tents or on the floors of schools and public buildings while Frank and the officers located a house for themselves. Still, they barely had enough time to sleep, let alone wash their clothes, an ongoing concern.

> *Hello Darling,*                 *Friday, March 16*
>
> *I didn't get a chance to write to you; we managed to keep a little too busy, one of those days. The weather is just about the funniest I have ever seen. It rains, it shines, it snows all in fifteen minutes. We've learned when we leave the house always to take a raincoat.*
>
> *This Sunday, I have no chance to get to Mass but hope you can take care of that for me. I'm afraid I'm not going to be able to get you a present for our wedding anniversary, but I am too far away from any stores to purchase anything. Instead, I'll send you all my love, darling, that's what I have the most of.*

Over the next few days, Frank and Kuret set off on their own for reconnaissance, unfettered by the higher brass. They hadn't seen Hub, Carlson, or Captain Cook for days. That night, camped in the forest, Kuret and Frank reminisced about this time last year, those peaceful days seemed so far away.

"You know Kuret, when we were in the desert, I'd debate if I would go see Catherine on a short leave. I'd reason, well if I were overseas, I would give all the money I had just for one day, even one hour to be with her. I'm so glad I did go visit her every chance I got."

Kuret nodded and agreed he'd give all the money in the world to see his wife. "Just hope I get the chance to see her again, Frank."

The next morning Frank and Kuret were hell-bent on finding an advanced position to place their 155mm howitzer guns along the River Saar to blow up a few more pillboxes and clear the way for the soldiers on foot. The XIX TAC planes flew above them, strafing areas where Nazis could be hiding. When the strafing intensified, the refugees and freed prisoners trudging along the roads and highways would scatter and duck for cover. Frank pitied the poor souls that had been held captive and now released by hundreds of thousands as the Germans retreated.

Other refugees fled from the Eastern countries to the west, fearing the reprisal of the Russian soldiers. Innocent families, young girls, even nuns, were not safe from the Russian soldiers who took possession of their homes, raped the women, and killed the men. According to Stalin, it was the right of the conquering army to have their way with women, and if they needed to eliminate the men, so be it. The Russians behaved so ruthlessly that the Germans surrendered to the Americans rather than be caught by the Russians.

The number of prisoners of war increased beyond the capacity to care for them. The U.S. Army took photographs of over two hundred thousand German prisoners of war in cages. The SHAEF never published the photos because it was degrading to the men, especially the last one who held a sign, "I'm the two hundred thousandths P.O.W."

> *War is hell, as Sherman says, there are a lot of people over here who agree, but what I can't understand is what keeps these damned Krauts going on in this hopeless situation. Oh well, we'll just keep plugging away.*
>
> *PS I haven't heard from my brother George at all. Can't understand him. My letter was never returned, so I guess he is still around here somewhere.*

# CHAPTER THIRTY-ONE

# Nord de Guerre

Frank's battalion was moving fast, the towns lumped into the category, "North of the War." They stopped only when necessary to fight, then pushed eastward to the Rhine.

> *Hello Darling,*                *Sunday, March 11*
> *It won't be long, and we will be out in the field sleeping on mother earth. I'm still looking for that air mattress. I sleep on it every night in my dreams. Not much time to relax moving all the time, and I sure miss my poker games. My platoon picked up a German motorcycle yesterday and has it all fixed up like new, so we have a little more transportation. Most of the vehicles left by the Germans that we find are beyond repair.*

German vehicles littered the roads, and with American ingenuity, the soldiers fixed them up and rode alongside the convoy. Gas cans were used and thrown to the side of the roads. Patton thought this was wasteful and misuse of gasoline and put a stop to it. He sent the order to confiscate unallocated vehicles from the soldiers and to return them to the civilians who were in dire need of transportation. Patton raged to only use the gasoline for fighting. And fight they did.

> *The weather has changed for the better, warmer, and some sunshine all day for a change. I had a ringside*

*seat watching ten planes peel off and bomb and strafe a German railroad. Wasn't a shot fired at our pilots. If the weather holds, we'll see a lot more of that and get this mess over with. Typically, the fog lifts by noon, and the water is dried up, very little mud to fight. You know, sometimes it was harder to fight against the mud than the Germans.*

*We came across some propaganda leaflets today, very raw and coarse.* One German leaflet, appealing to American troops to surrender, depicted a passionate kiss between a man and woman. "FAREWELL Remember her last kiss? Gee were you happy then! Together, you spent marvelous times ..., lounging on beaches ..., dancing, enjoying parties galore ..., listening to the tunes of your favorite band ..." The leaflet's backside reminded the soldier that his loved one is longing for him and that most of the men he had come with are now dead. Whatever flyer Frank had picked up, it disgusted him.

* * *

*This week whizzed past in a hurry for some reason or another. Half of March is gone already, and I should have been home with you two weeks ago. I am rather anxious to get away as we haven't really been able to relax since leaving the States. Had one day off this year, and that was at Nancy when I just took off. That's what gets me when I read about these guys that are striking for double time or overtime in the States.*

*Sometimes the things they argue about and stew the most over seems to us unimportant. For instance, the stories of rehabilitation of broken down Vets, what a rosy picture they paint, homes, jobs, security. Wait until they have 8 or 9 million cascading home, we'll be a dime a dozen then.*

\* \* \*

In the first two weeks of March, Frank's battalion had traveled through Belgium, Luxembourg, and France, and now they were racing through Germany, attached to the newly arrived 65th Division, "Battle Ax."

*Dear Kitty,                          Wednesday, March 21*
*Haven't been able to write for a couple of days, sorry but it couldn't be helped. We were pushing so fast it wouldn't do any good to write. We even hit some towns before the infantry. Everything seemed to collapse at once, and the Germans let their prisoners go, and they are begging to be picked up. They keep milling down the highway toward the rear of our convoy, forlorn as can be. They claim to be Polish, Italian, or Russian and claim they wouldn't touch a hair on our head. Don't know how to take these German people, they seem bewildered and dazed, we don't even look at them though, just look through them. As we pass through these towns the people line the streets, nudging their children to wave, but no one waves back. I saw refugees cutting up dead horses lying along the side of the road. If this pace keeps up, this war will have to run itself down.*

In each town Frank came to, the Third Army liberated the people, took prisoners, and left. A few Nazis tried to defend their cities, but it was useless as the tanks rolled through. German snipers secreted on perches and roofs and shot at the soldiers, threw grenades at the trucks, which caused some casualties, but the impact of the Third Army was much more significant. In Patton's words, "If the war ceased at this moment, troops under my command would have had the best and most successful campaign in history." As of March 19, the total losses for the Third Army, both battle and non-battle, were eight hundred, whereas they captured over twelve thousand Germans in addition to the thousands killed. By the twenty-second, they were bagging eleven thousand prisoners a day.

One tactic to get the Nazis to surrender was to send projectiles of leaflets telling the people to surrender or risk destruction. If the burgomaster did not come out within the allotted time carrying a white flag and claim that no German troops hiding in the town, then the Third Army would send a volley of rockets into the city, or the XIX Tactical Air would "drop their eggs." In this way, American soldiers could enter a city without battle, take prisoners, and force every citizen to give up any arms they may have hiding in their homes. They confiscated piles of guns, swords, daggers, and grenades, keeping some as souvenirs.

By the end of the war, Frank had collected several German rifles and souvenirs of war. He carried them around until he could mail them to his long-time friend.

German sword Frank sent back

*I packed up a rifle and a few souvenirs and am*
*mailing them to Bert Ripple. I didn't want to send them*
*to you as you wouldn't know what to do with them. I'll*
*ask Bert to put the gun together and keep it for me. There*
*is a chance it won't go through. I don't know what I'm*
*going to do with all this junk I have, but it was sure fun*
*collecting it. Incidentally, you don't have to be afraid of*
*the parachute, it was brand new, in fact, some of the boys*
*who had them used them to sleep in.*

Frank's anti-aircraft battalion arrived in the vicinity of
Oppenheim on the Rhine, *still sweating out the war.* Frank attended
Mass on Sunday afternoon for the first time since he entered Germany.
It was during Lent and Catholics were obligated to fast during the
day, but the priest gave the soldiers general absolution for their sins
and dispensation to disregard the fast. Only those in Allied uniforms
and the Red Cross attended the Mass. The Supreme Commander had
ordered a no fraternization decree, and therefore the soldiers were not
allowed to attend Mass with German civilians. Frank lamented the
fact he couldn't speak to the civilians, other than to order them to do
something. He couldn't imagine what the Occupation would be like
without having a conversation with the people.

*Hello Darling,*          *Friday, March 23, Krautland*
*Here it is a day before John's birthday, and I'm*
*still helping chase the Krauts back over the Rhine. It's all*
*been so fast that it's hard to believe. I guess even harder*
*for these people around us. They are all seeking sympathy*
*now. When we move into a home, out they go, it seems*
*pretty harsh, but I think back on what they did to the*
*French and Belgians and what they would do to us and*

*our homes and families, and I can't feel sorry for them.*
*It's a pity the young children have the same load to carry,*
*but if they are allowed to do the same things as their*
*fathers did, the future indeed will be bleak.*

*Our bombing has been terrific now that we can*
*see the results firsthand. Communication and railroads*
*were knocked out completely all along the route.*

*The news remains good. Let's pray this will be*
*the final march to end this mess. It's time to get home*
*to my darlings. It's goodnight Kitty, be seeing you some*
*bright Tuesday.*

That evening the captain caught up with Frank and his men and brought the mail, three letters from Catherine, and the rubber mattress. The captain pulled out a bottle of Scotch Whiskey he confiscated from a home where a German general had billeted during the war. With the boys, they took a swig of the good Scotch to toast the end of the war and that soon they would all be home with their wives and children. The liquid burned as it went down Frank's throat and melted his weary muscles. The bottle was shared, and their hopes were high.

He inflated his rubber mattress, a gift of incomparable value, and laid down protected from the cold cement below him in the school auditorium.

The Third Army captured a railway bridge and crossed the Rhine to the north at Mainz, where the Germans expected Patton and his men to pass. Instead, Patton and his troops moved south to Oppenheim and crossed on pontoon bridges and rafts. Engineers laid a smokescreen to hide the crossings along the Rhine. As the soldiers passed, the German's gunfire overhead sounded like freight trains. Like shooting skeet, Frank's men shot at the enemy planes, sending one spiraling down. The massive German air attack on the bridges could have been disastrous except for the actions of the XIX Tactical Air Command and the anti-aircraft guns protecting the bridges and knocking out the German defenses and downing Jerry planes. The Third Army quickly crossed the Rhine with few casualties.

Third Army crossing the Rhine

Patton called the Third Army's fast crossing of the Rhine, "magnificent" and headed for the river to cross in grand style. His jeep stopped on the pontoon bridge, and he got out mid-river. In his knee-high boots, crisp uniform, pistol on his hips, and the sun reflecting off his highly shined helmet, Patton pissed in the Rhine. Emulating William the Conqueror, he stopped on the far side of the river and picked up a clot of dirt symbolic of taking possession of the land. Besides being theatrical, Patton believed he was the reincarnation of past great warriors. Who is to say he didn't have their blood churning in his veins?

*Hello Darling,*                    *Friday, March 30*

*Being in Germany so suddenly not only amazed the Germans but also amazed me. It reminds me of the time the dentist was drilling away at what he thought was a good tooth, all of a sudden, he went thru the crust and down to the nerve, then calmly said, "I guess it will have to come out." Well, that's what all this reminds me of.*

*These have been lazy restful days with perfect sunshine weather, hope it continues. We have a nice house with steam heat, hot and cold running water and electric lights and the radio going all the time. I wish you could see my bed, I sleep on mattresses with eiderdown covers which have been almost useless to the Germans. One fact stands out, these people really prepared for war and prepared for bombings with thick-walled, deep cellars where they lived.*

Frank and other officers billeted in castles and wealthy estates that boasted of fine wines, champagne, and specialty foods, like caviar. When available, the men enjoyed these niceties of bourgeois life knowing it wouldn't last, and they'd soon be back in the field tents. The men explored the extensive cellars and underground hallways decorated with elaborate furnishings and stocked with expensive liquor.

*I wish you could have seen the scene in our officer's mess tonight. We were seated in a sumptuous living room with beautiful china and silverware. An orderly pranced in with a trayful of plates full of army C-ration stew, it wasn't very filling but quite funny. We're still hungry, so Kuret and I brought some eggs and C-rations back to*

*our room, and now we're going to eat. I must have a*
*tapeworm because I am always hungry. Remember you*
*couldn't get me to eat, well I've been cured of that.*

> *I can't understand their war mania, it's bred*
> *into even the very young with military lore and tokens.*
> *Saw something funny yesterday. An officer slipped up*
> *behind a German civilian and bellowed "Heil Hitler."*
> *Automatically, the guy turned around, clicked his heels,*
> *and answered, "Heil Hitler." He darn near got his skull*
> *cracked. It was a good laugh but without humor.*

The German civilians, the released prisoners and slaves, and
those fleeing other countries from Russian control created a human-
itarian crisis. The bombs had destroyed their towns and cities, their
factories and railroads lay in ruin, and no set government was in place
to organize reparation or to take care of the refugees.

> *It is really going to be a job to get Europe on a*
> *normal basis again. So far, Germany hasn't been hurt as*
> *badly as France and Belgium (at least the parts I've seen),*
> *but what was knocked out was done very thoroughly, like*
> *nearly all the railroads and communication centers.*
>
> *They are making the Germans tear down the*
> *fancy roadblocks that they have so carefully built along*
> *the West Wall, totally useless. Goodnight, darling, keep*
> *up those prayers.*

By morning Frank was on the move again. His battalion fought
their way through towns and cities, not stopping at times even to sleep,
and not getting enough to eat. *The food hasn't been too good or too bad,*
*a little too much Spam and cold cuts, but after seeing some people picking*
*the ribs of a dead horse, I guess we are pretty well off.*

After days of traveling, Frank was finally able to get a letter off to Catherine.

> *Hello Darling,*                    *Thursday, April 5*
> *This is the first attempt at writing a letter in the jeep, but I have been doing everything else in it, including eating, sleeping, writing etc. Four of us had to sleep in the jeep night before last, and of course, it was raining, all kinds of rain, thunder lightning, sleet, the works. Needless to say, there was no sleep, but we made every attempt. Usually, when we stop, we get ourselves nice fluffy beds and take over, the trouble is we don't get to stop very often. For three nights running, we averaged two hours of sleep each nite, but we're getting places. Last night we found a city that still had electricity and beer, we enjoyed both, but as usual, when dawn broke, we took off again.*

From the time they left Saarlautern, Frank and his platoon had little contact with the others in his battery.

> *At Saarlautern, we had a pretty hot spot. We were never inspected by the big brass there, in fact rarely saw anyone. Just about every time a vehicle parked near our own C.P., the shells would come, and down in the basement, we would go. We lost one 40 mm on the bridgehead, but fortunately lost no personnel, a couple got a bit of shrapnel. Then we raced across Germany attached to the Field Artillery, carried the infantry in our trucks all the way across Germany. We crossed the Rhine right after the armor broke through then headed for Berlin.*

Frank stayed in command of his small platoon as they chased the Heinies across Germany, only stopping a day or two at a time to set up their guns, then continued on a mad dash across Germany. Gunfire whizzed over their heads as they loaded the big guns and shot off hundreds of shells. On April 1, there was an increase in enemy air attacks. Frank's battalion retaliated and shot down a few planes, and the other planes retreated. Amazingly, there were no American casualties reported. Like the finale of a fireworks show, the Germans released their last gasp of ammunition.

> *We have been getting lots of practice with our pea-shooters now, and the boys are really in top form.*
>
> *Every town we enter is filled with Polish, French, Russians, the refugees, slave laborers, and prisoners of war. From the looks of things, the whole French Army was in German hands. The German homes and their houses are well kept and stocked. The Nazis have robbed the rest of Europe and taken mighty fine care of themselves.*

Kuret and Frank passed Captain Cook in a small village, honked, and kept going. When Hubbard and Carlson pulled up alongside them, they gave each other thumbs up. The separated friends had confidence in their men's shooting abilities and survival techniques as they forged on single-minded to get the enemy. Frank barely even noticed the big moment they had been pushing for.

> *We crossed the Rhine some time back, don't even remember the date or even the day. I thought it would be quite a thrill, but I was so cold, hungry, and sleepy that night, I hardly realized we were over. It was pitch black, so couldn't see anything anyway.*

One day blurred into the next as they raced along "Hitler's Highway," the autobahn had been built for fast movement of the German troops and connecting all of Hitler's residences from Berlin through Nuremberg, Munich, to Salzburg and Linz in Austria. As the Germans retreated or surrendered, they destroyed the overpasses and parts of the autobahn or left tanks and debris to delay the Allied Armies.

Frank's jeep swerved around the obstacles and bounced across the detours until back on the smooth highway. He finished his letter and hoped it would get to Catherine.

*Well, darling, adios till I can write again. Please don't worry about not getting letters every day, but you will be in my thoughts all day and every day. Take care of yourself and John. I'll be home taking over one day.*

# CHAPTER THIRTY-TWO

# Concentration Camps

Frank was with The 65th division when they neared Berlin, the prize city where the Allies hoped to capture Hitler and bring him and his comrades to justice. With little warning, Eisenhower, the Supreme Commander, ordered the Third Army to change directions and move southeast to Bavaria, the German Redoubt. The Russians were to be given the jewel city of Berlin, much to Patton's dismay and disappointment. Patton felt strongly that the Russians were not to be trusted and would take over the countries for themselves. He wrote in his diary:

"It was April 4 when we got to the boundaries and halt line. Nothing was in front of the Third Army that could not easily be overcome. We were opposed to stopping, but as prescribed by a higher authority, we practically had to stop or at least slow-down in order for the others to catch up. However, we continued to push along several miles a day to prevent the enemy from digging in."

The Russians pushed from the east and the Allies from the west, cornering the Nazis in Bavaria. The Supreme Commander could not risk the Russian troops and Allies fighting on the same ground and possibly mistaking each other as the enemy; therefore, the SHAEF drew boundaries as to where the Third Army was to stop. As ordered, Patton and his Third Army stopped, turned, and headed south along the Danube, leaving Berlin to the Russians. The chain of orders took a few days to reach Frank.

*Hello Darling,*                    *Friday, April 6*

*Yesterday, I wrote to you in my jeep, as I finished the letter, we got a call on the radio to pick up some ammo for our guns. We picked up the stuff, distributed it, and went back to our place in the column.*

*We stopped, and my driver (answering the call of nature) went over to the edge of the road looking down into the ditch. Immediately he ran back to the jeep yelling, "Give me my G.D. Tommy gun, there's a bunch of Krauts hiding in the ditch." We ran over and yelled for them to come out. Reluctantly, a civilian man and woman came out. We could still see a soldier hiding in the brush. Finally, we worked the brush with a better persuader, and out came five more soldiers, one didn't make it out. After searching them, we found we had two officers, two spies, and a couple of soldiers. Also, we picked up some useful information.*

*I forgot to tell you we are with the 65th Division now, and really going to town and that town is Berlin. Today is the first in the last four days that we haven't knocked down a couple of Jerry planes.*

*We are in a pretty good size town now, and we are very comfortable with an adjoining bath and a good wine cellar and above all nice thick beds, quite a contrast to some of the previous nights. Hope it lasts another day or so.*

*Goodnight darling, it's time to crawl into my feather bed, I'm going to take advantage of it, never know when we'll be out in the mud again.*

When the order to change directions and move south came in, Frank and his boys had been in Mulhaussen, the closest American soldiers to Berlin. Once again, the Supreme Commander thwarted their plans of glory. No Paris, no Berlin, even though the Third Army could have taken both cities first.

Changing directions, Frank and his boys inched their way south, mopping up the towns, taking prisoners, and clearing the path for the infantry. They were stationed in Marksuhl when word came that Eisenhower and Patton had landed nearby. General Eddy had discovered looted treasures in a salt mine in Merkers, where the Germans had constructed over five hundred and eighty kilometers of tunnels from thirty to fifty feet high. The Generals, accompanied by several German officials, took an elevator and descended twenty-one hundred feet to the vaults where the Nazis had hidden paper money, gold bricks, and a great deal of British, American, and French gold currency. Hidden in rooms behind steel doors were suitcases filled with jewelry, silver and gold cigarette cases, wristwatches, silver and gold spoons and forks, vases, and strangely enough, gold-filled teeth. All were in unmarked suitcases, most likely the valuables gleaned from robbery and the Jewish prisoners. Eisenhower demanded the removal and labeling of all plunders and ordered the Rangers to take the loot to Reichsbank in Frankfurt for safekeeping before the Russians arrived on the scene.

The Russians had looted, raped, and killed the townspeople as they conquered German territories from the east. The Allies were not about to let them treat themselves to the spoils of war and taking over the land already liberated.

*Hello Darling,*                                    *Sunday, April 8*
    *Here we are another day in Germany, another day, these Germans have kept me away from you, they will never live it down as far as I'm concerned.*

*Another comfortable night last night. I took another hot bath just to get ahead on them. We are in a castle of some sort tonight, belongs to a baroness or other claim to have had Von Rundstedt and other Nazis big wigs as guests here, but we don't mind as long as they don't try visiting us now.*

The baroness on castle doorstep

Von Rundstedt was the Nazi field marshal who orchestrated the Ardennes Offensive and did nothing to punish his subordinates who in cold blood killed 84 unarmed American prisoners in Malmedy. Frank and the other officers were disgusted to hear his name. After an evening of drinking and listening to war stories, Frank made his way upstairs to a grand room with a soft bed of eiderdown.

*You know I have only had to use my mattress twice since being in Germany, we always manage to find a bed if we get to sleep. From the looks of things, the next*

*few days will be a bit of a rest. It would be nice to relax
and forget that the war is going on.*

*The Germans are taking it in the chin for a
change, I've seen it in their homes, and it reminds me
of France and Belgium but not quite as bad. I think the
ordinary run of Germans would like to quit now, but
their fanatics and S.S. troops keep the ball rolling.`*

Billeted in a castle, Frank and his boys took advantage of the
running water and cleaned off a couple of layers of dirt before going
downstairs to the dining room. After dinner, their stomachs distended
with a little extra food, and Frank reported to Catherine, *I feel better
and have a better appetite than ever before.* A beautiful river ran alongside the castle, and they were all set to go fishing, but as luck would
have it, they got a call into town. The prisoners were teeming into
the cities, and the Allies took extra caution that none of them were
Nazi infiltrators.

*The prisoners are still pouring in, you wonder
sometimes where they all came from. I hope soon they'll
run out and I can get home to my wife and baby, if I
don't get home soon, he won't be a baby any longer, thirteen months gone is a mighty long time, isn't it Kitty.*

The weather remained beautiful, the trees put out their blos-
soms, everything looked peaceful and lovely. Only the distant boom,
every so often, brought back the grimness and reality of war.

The next day they left their comfortable castle and moved into
a house in Catterfield, a little more humble this time, but the roof still
kept out the rain. Their Command Post was only a few miles from
Ohrdruf, where the 80th Infantry Division and the 4th Armored Division
had liberated the local townspeople. On the outskirts of town, the U.S.

soldiers discovered a concentration camp that had been abandoned by its commanders only hours earlier. The German SS had shot as many prisoners as they could before leaving, and the blood on the bodies was still warm. The horrors of the slave camp were beyond belief.

*Hello Darling,*      *Wednesday, April 12*
 *Yesterday's letter didn't go out, but I am writing another. I saw a horrible mess today, a German concentration camp complete with cremator, torture racks, and all the horrors. Something like12,000 people have been taken care of there in the last four months. You will probably read about it in a coming issue of Life, as the correspondents were here taking pictures.*

On the eleventh, Frank and Kuret drove through the pine forest to a large clearing. The other officers and men were already there standing in front of two rows of twelve-foot high barbed wire fences. A wooden guard tower stood fifteen-feet high. Correspondents and reporters from Life magazine pushed to get in first. Soldiers and M.P.'s were stationed at the gate checking identification and providing an armed soldier and possibly an inmate to guide them through the camp. Frank and the officers entered and walked down the unpaved road lined with one-story barracks in total disrepair with peeling green paint and tall narrow windows with tube-like metal chimneys protruding from them. Inside were four tiers of bunks with straw in burlap bags for mattresses. Discarded trash and ragged clothing laid strewn across the floor. The rank smell of urine and feces seeped from the floorboards. Frank took out a handkerchief to cover his mouth and nose, guarding against the stench. The prisoners had recently vacated the room, but the stories of human misery still hung in the air.

Outside the barracks, the gallows stood as a testament to the torture the guards subjected the prisoners to. The S.S. guards shackled the prisoners by the wrists above a platform and beat and whip them until they died or until the guards got bored and left them to bleed to death. The ex-inmate pointed to another set of gallows where they hung the prisoners by tying piano wire around their necks and kicked the boards out from under them, allowing their toes to dance on the platform until their throats were severed or their necks were broken. The ex-prisoner took pride in explaining the torture, almost gleefully. It turns out that he was an S.S. guard posing as a prisoner to save his skin. The MP's took him to a field and shot him.

Rows of whipping tables lined the dirt road behind the barracks. Stocks secured the victim's feet, and his body draped across the table with his hands held by the two guards while others beat him with clubs and sticks. A club lay beneath a table with blood crusted on it.

Weak-kneed, the group continued and came across a row of bodies recently shot in the back of the head, with blood still pooling around the corpses. When the S.S. discovered that the Americans were close on the path of finding them, they shot all the living prisoners before fleeing. A pile of partially naked bodies lay nearby in front of a barn-like shed. Opening the barn door exposed a stack of corpses, twenty maybe thirty high, completely naked and salted with lime to quell the reek of decomposing flesh. During the full occupation, the guards had thrown the bodies on top of each other until they amassed about two hundred from floor to ceiling, later to be removed and buried in a mass grave. Over three thousand prisoners had been buried there since January 1945.

Only hours before the Americans arrived, camp officials had been moving the Ohrdruf inmates on foot to Buchenwald Concentration Camp thirty miles away. The S.S. guards shot those who couldn't make the journey. The remaining German SS officers tried to cover their crimes by exhuming the inmates and burning them on giant grills laid on top of railroad ties encased in a brick foundation. They lit the fire then left to save themselves from capture. The attempt to rid the evidence was a failure. Frank saw the charred bodies lying atop the pyre. After two hours of seeing the terrors of Ohrdruf, Frank and the men had seen enough to fuel nightmares for a lifetime. The soldiers drove back to camp in silence. There was nothing more to say.

That day, Frank stood witness to unimaginable atrocities. In his letters, he kept the full horror from Catherine, but later, it became a family story. *I found a shed of dead bodies.*

General Walker informed Eisenhower and Patton of the carnage and told them to get there immediately to see for themselves. They arrived on April 12, the day after Frank first visited the concentration camp. Repulsed and sickened, Eisenhower ordered every American soldier stationed in the vicinity to tour Ohrdruf and bear witness to the atrocities. He commanded the citizens of Ohrdruf, the German officers, and the mayor to see firsthand what had happened within a mile of their town.

The mayor admitted, "We did not know what was going on, but we did know," then went home, and he and his wife hung themselves.

Generals viewing burned bodies at Ohrdruf

A few days later, the Americans discovered another death camp near Weimer, Buchenwald, less than forty kilometers from Ohrdruf. Buchenwald was the infamous concentration camp that housed political prisoners, Jews, slaves, and prominent doctors and scholars, one of whom was Eli Wiesel. Besides working in the V-1 bomb factories, the S.S. forced the slaves to select from their ethnic group who was to be tortured and executed. They then commanded the prisoners to perform gruesome acts, often ending in a fatality. The S.S. forced the doctors to carry out experiments on living humans, injecting them with typhus then inoculating them with an anti-typhus vaccine. Of the 800 subjects, only 100 survived the trial.

The S.S. officers had lampshades made out of the skin of Jews and even stretched swaths of their tattooed skin like canvases and framed them to hang on the walls. Ghoulish and unethical, it was hard to believe, but here was proof of the evil in the Nazi regime.

Despite their weakened bodies, the newly liberated survivors picked up the American soldiers onto their emaciated shoulders and paraded in victory.

The next day in the company of Colonel Walker, Patton visited the Buchenwald concentration camp even more heinous than Ohrdruf. Patton wrote, "The inmates looked like feeble animated mummies. If they didn't die of starvation, they were dropped down a chute where a hangman wrapped a rope around their necks with a grommet that clipped onto a meat hook and hung them from a clothesline, waiting until they died, and if not, he beat them with a club until their brains were mush and oozing from the cracked skulls. All the dead bodies in the camp were put on an elevator to the second floor, loaded on a tray, and rammed into one of the six incinerators."

Patton immediately called Eisenhower requesting that he send senior representatives of the press and photographers to Buchenwald to report the odious crimes historically. Eisenhower not only did this but also sent Congressmen to the concentration camp.

"Get it all on record—get the films—get witnesses—because somewhere down the road of history some bastard will get up and say that this never happened."

Eisenhower also ordered the townspeople of Weimar to view the savagery that took place under their noses. As a punishment for not doing anything to stop it, the citizens had to dig up the bodies of the dead and give them a proper burial in town. The civilians made coffins, children with shovels next to their parents dug up the shallow graves, teens threw the bodies onto wagons, and the men carted them to the town for burial. Chaplains of the Third U.S. Army officiated at hundreds of burial ceremonies throughout the last weeks of April.

* * *

Catherine had not heard from Frank in weeks, and by the time she got his letters, it was near the end of April. The news reporters had disseminated the news of liberating the concentration camps at Buchenwald and Ohrdruf, in photos, in print, and on the radio.

Catherine had a pit in her stomach as she walked home from Sunday Mass and up the outdoor flight of stairs, counting as she went seventy, seventy-one, and home. She took off her hat and picked up John, who was on the floor playing with his blocks. Her mother and father hurried out the door to attend the eleven o'clock Mass. Catherine was alone with her thoughts. She wrote to Frank daily, knowing that he may not receive her letters, but also knowing it was his lifeblood. He'd been gone over a year now, but it seemed so much longer. The war dragged on despite the hopeful news that the Germans could not last much longer. But what about Frank? Would he come home after the war, or stay in the Occupation Army, or worse would he be sent to the Pacific?

The Sunday LA Times was on the ottoman in front of her dad's easy chair. One correspondent who witnessed Ohrdruf Concentration Camp quoted General Eisenhower, "If America's soldiers didn't know before what they were fighting for, at least now they know what they are fighting against.

\* \* \*

Frank was unable to eat when he returned to his command post after touring the concentration camp. Inside the evacuated German home, he wrote a few words to Catherine. *I can't feel sorry for the Germans knowing what they have done. The amazing thing is that most of the civilians stay in their homes and claim it wasn't their fault. Funny people! Wonder why they keep up this hopeless fight. We have a beautiful program on now, just finished Schubert's, Ave Maria. The music helps, but it makes me melancholy and can't afford to be that way over here.*

CHAPTER THIRTY-THREE

# The National Redoubt

A rumor spread through the camp that President Roosevelt had died suddenly from a stroke on April 12. Frank had been on the move and didn't get the news until after attending Mass.

> *Hello Darling,*                    *Sunday, April 15*
> *I hated to hear of the President's death, it was very much of a surprise and a shock. At first, we thought it was propaganda, but later we heard it over the radio. I went to Mass this morning in what I believe was a Lutheran church. This is a very historical area. Luther was imprisoned in a castle nearby and we're near the birthplace of Bach.*

How unfortunate that the President didn't live long enough to see the great victory and end of the war, which all felt was imminent. In some ways, the soldiers thought his death was a victory for Hitler, which made it even harder to accept. President Truman took office as President and their new Commander in Chief.

\* \* \*

Since the Allies had encompassed the Germans, the SHAEF anticipated that the Nazis could derive certain defensive advantages compressing its strength and hoping for a stand-off in the Bavarian Alps where the Germans supposedly had built up their arsenal in underground

bunkers. Eisenhower tapped Patton and his Third U.S. Army to prepare for the operation of attacking to the south in the so-called German
Redoubt area.

Eisenhower was also eager to liberate Linz and Salzburg in Austria
and meet up with the Russians. His only uncertainty was fueled by
propaganda that the Nazis had an unshakeable grip on the alpine area,
the National Redoubt, that would make it impossible, or extremely
costly in lives, to dislodge them. General Eisenhower believed that
the Berchtesgaden area might be the scene of Hitler's last stand, and
this was one reason why the Western Allies fought their way across
Bavaria instead of hurrying on to Berlin. The Minister of Propaganda,
Goebbels, had created the myth of the National Redoubt to sow fear
that the Germans still maintained their grip on Bavaria and planned a
resurgence. Hitler had hoped to persuade the Americans to join them
in their battle against the Russians.

Frank's battalion turned southeast down the Danube River valley,
their destination Linz and Salzburg, Austria. This shift in the direction
of attack was comparable to the ninety-degree turn the Third Army
executed in December to rescue the trapped 101$^{st}$ army in Bastogne.

*Hello Darling,*              *Monday, April 16*
  *We are still mopping around, cleaning up, and
picking up stragglers. The only kick I have is that I'm
not home with you, and I'm always hungry. We finally
received our P.X. rations, missed the previous week, lucky
I was a week ahead, or I would have been wrassling the
refugees for cigarette butts along the road!*
  *Here I am again, been going since 4 a.m., it's 9
p.m. now, so this will just be a note to let you know
I'm still here and kicking about it. The weather has
been beautiful, just like spring in the desert, cool in*

*the morning and hot in the day. The chow is still the same, catch as catch can with little variety, everything is dehydrated.*

There was little German resistance until the army reached Nuremberg, where the American troops met fierce resistance. The Germans refused to surrender. The American artillery unmercifully shelled the old city damaging many of the old buildings, including the historic castle.

*Hello Darling,*                 *Wednesday, April 25*
> *Sorry I haven't been able to write in a couple of days. I hate to miss even a day, but the situation we've been having of late is not conducive to letter writing. It now has been raining and cold and as miserable as can be. I'm going over to eat now, haven't had anything since breakfast and that was ten hours ago*
> *Our bambino and I are pretty much strangers, and it doesn't look too bright a picture for the near future.*

After four days of intense battle, the Germans surrendered Nuremberg. After a constant shelling and bombing of the city, the U.S. trucks and tanks rolled through Nuremberg. Frank saw that the destruction was far worse than he had anticipated. The bombs previously dropped by the XIX TAC Airborne had destroyed most of the old buildings, decimated the rail and transportation systems, blew out all communication centers, and obliterated the headquarters of the S.S.

Frank stood at attention as the Third Army raised the American flag in Nuremberg's grand stadium, the Adolf Hitler Platz, where Hitler had once held his rallies, the arena where the Nazis paraded in goose steps and displayed their military vehicles.

U.S. soldiers, Nuremberg

Patton visited the city a week later and was astonished by the condition of the beautiful old city. "I think the most complete destruction of anything we had so far seen, but sadly, the artillery bombardment was needed in order to persuade the Germans to leave."

Frank left Nuremberg in his jeep alongside the trucks of infantrymen until they reached Regensburg on the Danube River. He and a few officers attempted to continue on the river to the fabled city of Vienna, but time didn't allow it. Instead, he remained in Regensburg for a few days until he and the troops crossed into Austria at Scharding Passau. The old town of Regensburg and its cathedral remained intact, despite the war.

*I went to Mass last in Regensburg, in a most beautiful cathedral. I can't understand all the stories of oppression we have heard. The churches all seem to be*

*open and attended, but I have not been able to talk with*
*any German people on the subject.*

Munich and southern Germany, even though Catholic, did not feel the oppression that the Jews and darker races felt under the Nazi rule. Being light-skinned and blonde meant they were part of the superior race that Hitler saw as ethnic purity, the Aryan race. Ironically, Hitler is believed to have a Jewish heritage. His unwed grandmother conceived his father with a young Jewish man. Frank didn't see the oppression in the cathedrals and Bavarian towns and cities, but by then, the cleansing had already removed most Jews and Negroes or driven them into hiding.

As the 546th moved closer to the border of Austria, the enemy troops surrendered along the front with only sporadic resistance. Four war correspondents caught up with Frank's reconnaissance party and asked Frank a few questions.

"Can you tell me what the situation is now." The reporter had his tablet ready to take notes, his overcoat flapping open in the cold brisk wind.

"I don't know what the situation is now. And if I did know what's going on, it probably wouldn't be news anymore." Frank was peeved that he didn't know more about what the other platoons were doing, how they were faring. Without a radio, he was pretty much left in the dark.

"Where you've been? Shot down some planes? Where are you heading to?"

Frank wasn't going to give out classified information, so he gave the reporter a rundown of what had happened, where they had been, and the cities they captured.

"We attached to the 65th back in March. It's been hell on wheels ever since Saarlautern. We didn't get very much shooting till we got around Mulhouses, then we really let go. We were even shooting while driving down the road!"

"Any tough spots?"

"Nuremberg gave us a little trouble, but after taking Nuremberg, we kept rolling and crossed the Danube 4 miles below Regensburg, and took that city April 26. On April 27, we entered Austria, seized Scharding Passau, crossed the Inn River, and here we are in Eferding."

The correspondent took a few photos of the men, and their 155mm then shook hands with Frank and said, "No wonder I couldn't keep up with you, boys!"

By the end of April, the Americans had destroyed or captured most of the German Panzers. The enemy replacement system had broken down, and their communications shattered. The complete collapse of the Third Reich was impending.

Still, the war was not over. Patton doubted the German's had remnant forces ensconced in the National Redoubt in the Alps, but he followed his commander's orders. The Third Army proceeded rapidly to the southeast to seize and secure Linz, Salzburg, and Berchtesgaden, the enclave of the S.S. and Hitler's lair.

Bad weather prevented the XIX Tactical Air from preceding the troops into the Alps. Snow and blown out roads hampered the tanks and troops but did not stop the artillery and infantry. As the army approached the narrow entry to the hamlet of Berchtesgaden, they came across S.S. troops defending the pass. The Americans backed off and set up their artillery and fired away until the Germans melted back into the mountains. The Americans proceeded with a few roadblocks and mines that, by now, were easily detonated. They arrived on the Obersalzberg on the morning of May 4, 1945, only four hours after the S.S. had set fire to the Berghof, Hitler's residence, then left the area.

As always, army politics entered the picture. Eisenhower had given the honor of capturing Berchtesgaden to the 101$^{st}$ battalion as a reward for their stand-off at Bastogne. Still, Leclerc felt the French should have the honor of seizing the last bastion of the Wehrmacht. Eisenhower conceded to the French and held back the 101st, but neither got there first. The Third Army had been in the best position to take the surrender of the German officers at their last stand in Berchtesgaden. The confusion led to hard feelings among the Allied troops as to who had captured and defeated the National Redoubt.

By the time the Americans arrived, the German officers and soldiers were ready to surrender. In the quaint mountain town of Berchtesgaden, they stood in their long gray coats, lining the streets awaiting orders from the Americans. They relinquished their arms, took off their belts with pistols and daggers, and marched to the fenced area designated for prisoners. A German officer signed the surrender then went inside a café for a drink with the American officer.

*Hello Darling,*          *Monday, May 6 Austria*

*I hope this hiatus in my letter writing hasn't worried you, but it has been practically impossible for me to write in the past five days. We've been going, going all the time, and have come into some funny situations. They say the war is practically over, I'll believe it when we hear no more artillery, and as of yet, the last round hasn't been shot.*

*The prisoners are pouring in like mad, we point to the rear when they come up to us and all file behind us like ducklings. This morning I got lost on reconnaissance and ran into some Krauts who hadn't quite decided to come in yet. When I pointed to the rear, they kept going the other way, so I didn't argue and turned around and went the other way myself.*

*The Austrians greet us somewhat as the French did, with flowers and "vivas" etc. but when you take over their homes, you find the same old swastika and army pictures of children and relatives in the German army, many S.S. troops to boot.*

*I've been taking pictures all this section, the scenery is beautiful, the snow-covered Alps off to the side reminds me of San Jacinto, only more snow.*

During those five days when Frank did not write to Catherine, he was on reconnaissance. Sometime during the capture of Berchtesgaden or shortly after, Frank and Kuret drove their jeep up the narrow circuitous mountain road to Hitler's lair. When they crested the hill, Frank took in the devastation of the recent British bombing. In front of him was Oberzalzberg, the enclave of the S.S. and Hitler's top men. Most of the buildings were damaged or destroyed, including the houses belonging to Goering and Bormann. The Berghof had been set on fire by the departing S.S. and only partly damaged. Hitler's mountain bunker system survived intact.

The Berghof in Oberzalzberg, May 1945

Frank snapped a picture of the Berghof, Hitler's second home, and the seat of government outside of Berlin, where he had planned his conquest of Europe and hosted heads of state. Every Allied unit had wanted to stake claim to the prestigious takeover of the Berchtesgaden; every soldier wanted a souvenir from the evil empire. Frank's jeep descended the long driveway to the Oberzalzberg, and he and Kuret went into the Berghof.

When they arrived, a few American soldiers were already inside looting. Some had gotten into the fine wines and whiskey and toasted the news of Hitler's death. The elated soldiers snapped photos of themselves on the deck overlooking the Alps. Inside, the feeding frenzy continued along the halls, and in the bunkers, the soldiers taking anything not nailed down and piling the stuff in their jeeps.

Kuret rummaged through an office and grabbed Hitler's secretary's typewriter, a bulky prize that remained in Kuret's house as a toy for his little daughter, which he later donated to the World War II museum in New Orleans. Frank tore a Nazi flag off the wall and salvaged a dagger made of the high-quality Solingen stainless steel and fastened into ornamental handles in a spiral swirl displaying the Nazi swastika and eagle emblem.

Nazi flag from Berghof

One officer later wrote, "We couldn't believe what we saw. The walls were covered with shelves, and the shelves were stocked with all kinds of wines, champagnes, and liqueurs. The food bins were well stocked with a variety of canned hams, cheese, and two-gallon cans containing pickles." Frank and Kuret took their share.

Frank had dreamed months earlier that he captured Hitler and *let his Tommy gun do the talking*, and now he rejoiced Hitler was dead. Looking down on the storybook hamlet, the soldiers stood victorious atop the mountain where Hitler had written "Mein Kampf."

# CHAPTER THIRTY-FOUR

# The War Is Over

With the announcement of Hitler's death and the capture of Munich and Berchtesgaden, Eisenhower ordered the troops to make no further advances but to remain in place on the defensive. Like dominoes, the Germans fell, surrendering in the towns and cities along the Danube. Their Commanders conceded their arms and instructed their soldiers to lay down their weapons. Rows of Nazi prisoners marched locked step down the roads and autobahn to detention centers or rode in trucks like cattle.

Hundreds of thousands of Polish, Czechs, Romanians fled west across the line of demarcation to the Allied side, creating problems as to where to put these refugees freed from under the German rule but not wanting to live under the Russian state. Carts pulled by horses and ox carried people and their belongings down the autobahn with American soldiers leading them to refugee camps. Patton was furious that non-military vehicles and people clogged the roads, delaying his jeep and other authorized means of transportation. But, there was no other choice, given the numbers of refugees and released prisoners of war.

The 546th held their position along the Danube River, not firing a shot, but ready and aware of isolated German troops and the young S.S. "werewolves" who waged guerilla warfare, not conceding defeat.

During the first week of May, Eisenhower devised plans to cer-emoniously meet the Russians along the line of demarcation in south-east Germany, where Patton's Third Army controlled.

On May 2, Captain Cook of the 546th received the Bronze Star for his role in liberating the towns of Germany and defeating the enemy at every turn. Patton later bestowed the Bronze Oak Leaf Cluster in addition to his Bronze Star, which Cook wore proudly on his uniform, a tribute to his entire battalion. At this time, Patton was elevated to four-star general and presented General Walker with his three-star pin saying, "Never in the history of war had an army moved so fast defeat-ing the enemy at every turn with so few casualties."

Frank and his boys were somewhat chagrinned with the self-con-gratulatory behavior of the upper brass. Frank knew his men deserved the honors and medals, not just the words.

*Hello Darling,*                         *May 7, 1945*

*As the Germans say, "All is kaput in the Deutschland," and it's finally true. They have been all thru for some time, but for some crazy reason or other, some wanted to draw more blood. We heard official word this morning, and we've been expecting it for so long that it dropped like a dud shell, and elation wasn't quite as expected. It's like a pause or intermission with the Japs still to overcome.*

*As luck would have it, here we sit in a dirty old Austrian farmhouse near a large city (Linz) with all modern conveniences. A fine place to end up in the cold, drafty rooms, after all the nice towns we have taken. If when I come home, don't be too amazed if I spend a couple of days in the bathroom pressing the buttons and watching the water flow.*

*We have a lot of catching up to do, haven't we Kitty.*

Kuret walked into the room and sat down on Frank's bed, bounced up and down to check out the mattress. "Hell, Frank, your mattress is as lumpy as mine. Why don't you drag out that rubber mattress and put it on top of the bed?"

"Not a bad idea. Geez, how'd we end up here after throwing out all those Germans and living in their castles? It's so damn cold, in here, it's like living in a barn. I could use a good dose of sunshine." Outside, the sky was blue but the winds from the snow-capped mountains blew the cold right through the cracks in the windows.

"Remember the good old days in the desert? What I'd give now for those warm winds."

"Ah, Kuret, it's been a long time since then."

They reminisced about the blue desert mountains with jagged brown peaks that looked like a silhouette standing at the foot of the range; the long jeep rides across the desert floor with no fear of the enemy.

The next day Frank and his boys left the 65th Division and reunited with their battalion in the city of Linz.

Word came in that the Russians and the Allies had agreed that the war would officially end at midnight on May 8-9. The SHAEF informed the Germans of the rules of surrender and set the boundaries for the Russian zones and the American zones.

On May 8, in the crepuscular light of spring, the Third Army met at the bridge over the Enns. On one side of the river were the Americans, and on the other bank, the Russian soldiers. The American and Russian Commanding Generals and their aides marched to the center of the bridge. American General Walker and Russian General

Birokoff saluted each other and shook hands. The two exchanged medals of honor. Cheers went up, having defeated the Germans.

*Hello Darling,*                                              *May 8, 1945*

*This is that day we have long awaited, now for that day when we will be reunited with our boy. It's been a long wait and possibly will be a little longer, but that day will be soon. It's a funny sensation to look out the window and see the windows glaring bright with festivities.*

*The boys have been celebrating a bit tonight but with a bit of reserve. We are back with our battery again, and we had quite a reunion, lots of tall tales passed around, we all had some funny experiences and now and again a few close calls, but on the whole, it's been one big chase since leaving Saarlautern.*

*I met my first Russian soldiers. A few wandered in while we were playing poker, an officer, and a couple of enlisted men. They were looking for a couple of their comrades, and they were rough-looking characters.*

*It's goodnight time again, my darling, hope very soon we can be together again. I'm getting kinda homesick.*

May 9, 1945 On the Danube with Kuret

Frank remained in Linz under orders from SHAEF "to remain in present positions," until the unconditional surrender of all German land, sea, and air forces in Europe was signed. The Russians were still in combat to the north and implored Eisenhower to wait until all German troops had surrendered. Eisenhower agreed and ordered the correspondents not to publish any news releases to the press, pending an announcement by the Heads of the three governments, United States, Russia, and Germany.

Of course, the press correspondents had snapped photos on May 8 and rushed to be the first on the wires to announce the historic moment: VICTORY in EUROPE; GERMANY SURRENDERS.

\* \* \*

It was early on May 8 when the news of the German surrender hit the press in the States. Catherine awoke to the bold headlines in the L.A. Times: FULL VICTORY IN EUROPE (with the caveat the ) "Allies to make the announcement today." The next day read: "Last shot fired, Europe at Peace, Stalin joins the Allies in announcing the end of the war." In New York, Wall Street's ticker tapes and shredded telephone books poured out of office windows. People across the nation jammed the streets, waving, shouting, and screaming with joy. Catherine turned on the radio to hear the stream of good news, believing Frank would be home soon.

\* \* \*

The next day the Austrian skies cleared, and for once in a long time, Frank didn't think, "a good day for bombing." He joined his fellow officers drinking the confiscated German wines, celebrating the end of the long six-year war. The only question was, "what now?"

Frank's battalion was stationed in the foothills of the Alps, an hour outside of Munich. His duties as First Lieutenant remained the same: set the guns in defensive positions, rotate his men through their guard duties, censor letters, and report events of the battalion, the names of who transferred out, and who replaced them. Jobs for the enlisted men were plentiful during the occupation: electricians, engineers, mechanics, medical staff, bankers, post office clerks, carpentry, bakers, cooks, truck drivers. The base ran like an independent city situated outside of hamlets and on the perimeters of the big cities. The soldiers' morale was the biggest problem. They had fought long and hard and wanted to go home or at least know when the army would discharge them. FUBAR (fouled up beyond all recognition) ensued, no one knew what to do with the hundreds of thousands of soldiers left in Europe without a war. So they waited. As their duties waned, the army kept them busy with sports, classes, and movies or sent them out of Germany on leave for rest. Being treated like high schoolers didn't sit well with the men. During the war, they had a purpose, and now it appeared, they were marking time.

How to deal with the occupation of Germany was contentious. Patton insisted that the German people get back to work and govern themselves. His priority was to enlist the Germans to clean up their cities and set up local governance. He trusted the Germans to return stability and lawfulness to their society but didn't feel the same way about the Russians who he distrusted immensely. Eisenhower disagreed with Patton. He felt the Germans were not to be trusted and sent a decree of non-fraternization with the Germans. The soldiers were not to intermingle with the Germans. The Americans would be in command and stay watchful of insurgence.

On his way into town, Frank stopped to read a sign posted on the corner of a bakery. Gruesome photos of the Holocaust plastered on the cardboard with signage that read: "Remember This! Don't Fraternize." Frank was conflicted. *These people want their lives back; their families have suffered enough. Let them hang the bastard Nazis sympathizers, not these farmers.* But the Supreme Commander of the Allies, Eisenhower, blamed all Germans for the atrocities of the Nazis. Was that true? As Frank continued down the road, he held his eyes forward so as not to have eye contact but he couldn't help but notice a young boy holding his grandfather's hand. *That man looks like Dada, and the boy must be near John's age.*

Over time, the soldiers needed to communicate and treat the Germans with respect as ordinary civilians since they no longer posed a threat. Life had to go on. The non-fraternization policy was loosened, first by permitting the G.I.s to talk to German children, then allowing them to speak to adults, but only in certain circumstances, and *not in affairs of the heart or salacious interaction.* Early in the war, if a soldier admitted to fathering a German or Austrian child, they could be convicted of aiding the enemy. With pressure from the U.S. State Department and Congress, the policy lifted in stages. It wasn't until the end of December 1946 that marriages between U.S. soldiers and German women were permitted. Still, Frank resented that

German couples and families were reunited while he remained away from his family.

> *Hello Darling,*                     *Tuesday, May 14*
>
> *Here we are out in the woods again. When the war was going on, we could take over houses, etc., but now it's different. It's funny we were much better off while we were fighting. When we moved into a town if any civilians were around, out they went and we took over. Every chance I got I kicked out the burgomeister or the richest guy I could find. Those were the days. Now we are out, and the Heinies are in, that's life.*
>
> *We are living in pyramidal tents in quite a beautiful setting. The good news is that we are all together again, in fact, here comes Captain Howell, seen quite a bit of him recently. I hear you all were having a conference call to find out what happened to your husbands.*

* * *

It was early May, and Catherine worried having not heard from Frank since April. She had been on the phone with Irene, Captain Howell's wife, who told Catherine that her husband hadn't been with Frank for almost a month. "Frank and his platoon set out on their own in late March. Lyle only saw him a few times as they passed each other."

"Oh my, I'm not sure if I'm getting all of Frank's letters. Sometimes, I get them within two weeks, but since he got to Germany, they come in sporadically. Have you heard from Kuret's wife?"

"Yes, she's biting her fingernails again. I told her not to worry." Irene took on the role of keeping the wives informed as best she could.

"I heard that Kuret and Frank were still together," Catherine said quietly and paused. "Well, if I hear anything, I'll call you, Irene. And please do the same." Catherine hung up, still holding the last letter Frank sent at the beginning of April. *Well, darling, adios till I can write again. Please don't worry...*

A few days later, Hubbard's wife called with the news that all the boys were back together since the war ended. They all had survived. Now the question was, when will they come home?

> *We don't know what is in store for us, and I guess we shouldn't be too optimistic, but all we talk about is going home. What a happy thought, let's pray it comes true.*

A few weeks passed, and a flood of letters arrived.

*Hello Darling,                    May 16, 1945 Germany*
> *We're having quite a time here, lots of athletics, a movie every night, and the Red Cross will be here tomorrow with coffee and donuts. We're near a river and I take the men swimming every afternoon. The river is a bit muddy, but it is rather fast flowing. I would give five bucks for a good hot shower or tub bath, the Inn River is pretty dirty.*
>
> *Funny how the weather has changed, it has been absolutely perfect since the day the war ended. We have an accordion, and you can imagine how much use it gets. Being in the woods is an ideal place for it, won't disturb anyone while playing it.*

Kuret picked up the accordion, and the other soldiers joined in singing and acting like lost kids in the forest. Frank was pretty good at the organ keyboard and put his piano lessons to use on the accordion. Like the Bremen musicians, more men joined in the cacophony, using sticks or rocks if an instrument wasn't handy. The war was over, and they let off steam. They played a raucous volleyball game; officers took on the sergeants. The officers lost but immediately set up a game for the next day, a rivalry without guns. *It was the first time we played since Nancy. The arguments were about as fun as the game!* The days had turned warm, and after the game, they all jumped in the river in their skivvies.

By the end of the month, the weather changed back to rain, and they still had no news as to what was happening. All the men were waiting to get points for the battles they fought, not so much for the recognition, but the more points they amassed, the better the chances of going home. *Everyone is counting their number of points and the possibility of discharge. I'm afraid I can only muster 76 points, and it takes 85 to make the grade. I sure begrudge the army another year, these years are too precious now.*

By the end of May, Frank had been awarded four battle stars and was hoping for a fifth. *We may not get our medal for the Battle of Ardennes, as only one battery was in the immediate "Bulge" area, although we actually participated in the battle. The others we got are "Battle of Northern France," "Battle of Normandy," "Battle of the Rhine," and "Battle of Middle Europe."* The fourth battle gave him 81 points. He warned Catherine not to get too hopeful. *The battalion is giving out Bronze Stars now, it's like something out of "Pinafore" or any of Gilbert and Sullivan. All the brass, that is the Captains on up got them, even though most of their time was spent around Division headquarters. As usual, the poor E.M. were let in on the fringe. Only two of my men received them, and both are sergeants. That's war, I guess, or is it?*

His question is left hanging. Who deserves the medals, the accolades, the benefits? Those who fight or those who lead?

*Hello Darling,*           *Thursday, May 24*

    *Here we are sitting around in the rain waiting for someone to make up someone's mind as to when we are going to move. Yesterday, we struck down the tents, and here we are still waiting. We hastily pitched a tent late last night, and we are all sitting around writing letters, have a fire burning in the middle of the tent Arab style, a bit smoky but comfortable.*

"Hey Hub, what you are you telling your wife now. For god sake, I can't think of anything new to say," Kuret said as he balled up his letter.

Carlson laughed. "Hey, I got an idea. Let's switch it up. Everyone writes to someone else's wife."

After a good laugh at what they would write, they took out their old letters and reread a few aloud to get the creative juices flowing. Then…

    *A funny thing happened, we started the fire and were short of paper so I asked if anyone had any old papers. Everyone threw in his old letters. Lt Carlson had just finished a letter to his wife, and when he started to seal the envelope, he discovered he had thrown the new letter along with the old into the fire. Now he is busily engaged in writing another letter.*

    *The next day, they broke camp and headed back into Austria near the Danube. Will tell you more about it when we get there. We still have no indication what our fate will be. I wish I could find out what is in store for us. We live on rumors that start in the latrines, all of them baseless. I'm getting awfully anxious to get home to you.*

Hello Darling,                                        *Thursday, June 7*

*I just returned from a jaunt to a town called Eggenfelden. We are to be split up for a while, and I will have just my platoon with me, and that's the way I like it.*

*We've taken over a large building, considerably better than living in tents. It has all the modern conveniences, except for a bath, sometime, we will locate a bathtub and I think I will live in it. It's sweltering hot, in fact, in our new location it's 100 yards from the Rott River, and I'm going to jump in to keep cool. I believe it was the hottest day I have experienced since the desert. I've been trying to get some ice cream made here, an armored outfit has the plant sewed up, but I think I can get some in a few days. It would be quite a treat for my platoon.*

*There are two of us here, Lt. Carlson and me. Hubbard started a vacation, eight days, and most of it will be traveling to Brussels. I'm holding out for the Riviera. Keep your fingers crossed. Kuret went to Luxembourg and was so happy to get back, and Captain Howell was in Paris and said it was too expensive.*

Two days later, Frank received orders to move back with his platoon to the battalion in "tent city." He had spent exactly 48 hours in Eggenfelden, billeted his men, and planned the routine when another A.A. platoon replaced him. *Now we are back to the old "spit and polish" and military B.S., and it really gripes me. If they keep the outfit over here under the same conditions as ours for very long the morale is going to be shot to pieces. They have lots of plans for us, but there is little other than wasting time going on now.*

Shooting craps

Nobody cared about anything but counting their points or winning a few bucks at gambling. *The officers spend their time recommending each other for Bronze Stars, counting their points, praying for leaves, and shooting craps. Of course, the Colonel wrote himself up a Silver Star, and now it sets two classes, as usual, the Haves and the Have nots. With the stories being passed around now about heroes, I feel sorry for the civilians who are to receive these stories second and third hand with flourishes and embellishments. Great life if you believe it.*

Frank was desperately in need of a leave of absence. He slept a lot and listened to the rain pondering how he was going to survive after the war.

*Here I am sitting in my tent, the rain pounding down as though it means to come through. As soon as I finish writing, I'm going to put the rest of the afternoon in the arms of sleep. I can remember not long ago when I would have given anything just to relax and sleep until I couldn't sleep anymore, but not now, it's boring, and I'm getting lazier and lazier. Soon our boy will be 15 months old, it's been a long 15 months, I wonder how much longer.*

CHAPTER THIRTY-FIVE

# Paris

Finally, Frank went on leave. On June 15, he and two enlisted men left for temporary duty for seven days in Paris, hardly enough time to travel.

*Hello Darling,*           *Paris, Monday, June 18*
    *Another day in Paris, it seems they have a parade every day in town and do the Parisians love parades. We got a big kick out of watching the crowd more than the parade. They started lining up on the streets last night at midnight in order to get points of vantage. We were walking down the Champ Elysees last night and were puzzled as to why there were so many people, so we asked, and it was hard to believe.*
    *Everyone is kicking about the inflation of prices in Paris. Prices are exorbitant. The French will offer as high as $2.00 for a pack of cigarettes.*
    *We had an interesting tour yesterday afternoon, The most interesting was Notre Dame Cathedral, but it is highly commercialized that it is actually disgusting. We went to Bal Taborin last night, hot, smoky and stinking, but they call it life. They're just like the nightclubs in the States.*

The young soldiers had a hoot watching the dancing girls at the Bal Tabourin, a cabaret near the famed Moulin Rouge, where they catered to a drinking crowd, rowdy and vocal. The girls came out clad in less than modest clothing, bustier, and frilly panties. Stage props lifted them in the air, and the girls did synchronized acrobats. The show ended with a rousing Can-can, legs kicking higher and higher. Frank had had enough and walked back to the Red Cross hostel along the darkened streets in oppressive heat at midnight. He had spent a week's worth of pay in the few days he was in Paris.

Paris, June 1945

His leave came to an end, and it took him three days to get back to camp. He and his driver stopped in Reims and picked up some more champagne, then on to Nancy, where they spent the night. Frank visited with Captain Howell and found out that he was coming back to the 546th battalion, which brightened Frank's mood.

When Frank got to Stuggart the next day, he was shocked by the terrible shape of the city. Once, a beautiful modern city, it was now reduced to rubble. *It's a shame that so much of the beauty has been destroyed needlessly. I would hate to have it on my head.*

Frank reported back to camp a couple of days late, and to his dismay, the army had transferred him to Regensburg, which meant another trip in the morning. He packed up and left early for his new post only to get another set of orders a few days later: *I just received a jolt today, was informed I am to leave for Paris this evening.* A jeep was waiting for him to take him to Munich then catch a plane directly to Paris. The army had chosen him to attend another school and this time for competitive athletics.

> *Hello Darling,*                    *V-mail no date*
>     *I have walked my feet off today, and the greatest part was this afternoon at the Louvre, one could spend two weeks going over the details and still not cover the exhibits.*
>     *We start school in the morning, and the whole week it seems we'll be playing games baseball, basketball. They issued us shorts and tennis shoes. Rough life isn't it? If only I had you here with me, everything would be all right.*
>     *I met up with the other officers from my outfit, spent the evening, and today together. After this session in Paris, I think it will enough for all times, too much champagne and too much money.*
>     *Everyone says I'm lucky, but the only thing I will consider in that category is getting home to you.*

The hardest part of being away from his unit was that he couldn't get any of Catherine's letters. *This is going to be a long week before I can get back to my mail. The novelty of big city life has worn off again, and I'm longing for the peace and quiet of a simple life with my wife.*

The sweltering heat of Paris and his meaningless classes and sports ate away at Frank's morale. He had his camera with him and passed the little free time he had walking the streets in Paris, hoping to take photos that he would later develop back at camp where the men had rigged up a black room. He just didn't have it in him to take too many photos.

One evening in Paris, after seeing couples strolling the streets, Frank wrote to Catherine, baring his discontent.

> *Kitty darling,*                  *Monday, July 2 City*
> *University Paris*
>
>     *How are you? I'm longing for you and John. I hope John when he comes of age, has more sense than his dad. If I can do anything about it, he will marry young, not too young, and not spend the best years of his life futilely marking time in the army.*
>
>     *They talk about non-fraternization not being workable. Well, every time I see a German walking down the street with his wife and son, I feel like slitting his throat for getting me away from mine. Rough, aren't I?*
>
>     *I brought my camera along to school with plenty of film, but as yet, I haven't even taken one picture. There are all kinds of beautiful sights and buildings, but everywhere you go they have pictures on sale, better than I can take, then I say to myself, what do I want these pictures for, I'll never look at them again, and that's that.*
>
>     *See you in my dreams and pray soon, you will be in my arms.*

After morning French classes and the afternoon on the athletic field, Frank dressed in the mandatory tie and blouse of the army, sticky and hot, and took an uncomfortable stroll down the Champs Elysee, stopping in the sidewalk cafes *to watch the world go by. It does seem like the world is concentrated in one spot.* Wanting company, Frank went to one of the many officer clubs on the streets of Paris. He sat down and had a cup of coffee and some donuts with the other officers and talked about the occupation, replacement troops, and points to go home.

"Hey, Frankie, better get going, it's nearly eleven," another officer from his group called from across the smoke-filled room. It was still light outside when Frank checked his watch, grabbed his hat, and raced outside to catch the last metro at 2300. The sun had set an hour ago, but the hues of pinks and purples stayed in the sky. He and his buddy dashed down the street, around the corner and flew down the metro steps only to be stopped in the crush of people. *That is the maddest rush of all, smashing, jamming, pushing, it seems to be an old Paris kind of sport.* If they missed the last train, it was an hour's walk to the university dorms outside of Paris.

The last evening in Paris, he went back to the officer club and was surprised to find his old friends. *I ran into Kuret and Major Walker the last night in Paris. I was sure tickled to see them. From the stories they told about our battalion, it will probably be broken up over here. Our battery commander has been transferred to an outfit that its due to leave in about a month. He had about 114 points, so he will probably be discharged by fall. As I understand it, everyone will be transferred out to other outfits. I prefer staying with my outfit. Not sure where I'll end up. Rumor has it, we'll be in the E.T.O. for a while longer.*

After the war, Frank received the temporary status of antiaircraft automatic weapons unit commander with another platoon. He liked his gig and wondered if it wouldn't be wise to try for a permanent transfer to his present job. *I think I would prefer it to another A.A. outfit, there is no telling where I would end up.*

School had finished, and Frank chose to drive back to Germany early Sunday morning rather than wait till Tuesday for a plane. *Frankly, I am glad to get away from Paris. If I were to tell someone that they would call me crazy.*

He hitched a ride with two other officers from his battalion at school who had a jeep and trailer. Frank dreaded the seven-hour drive in the back of the jeep, taking the same route as before through Nancy and Munich. He wanted to stop by his battalion in Nancy to find out what changes had been made. He had heard many of the men from his platoon and his officer friends already had been transferred out.

The same old feeling of being left behind crept into his head, recalling all the days he said good-bye. First, leaving his family home, then standing on the platform, waving to Ralph as the train rolled away from the station, being left alone in the orphanage. Trains always meant someone was left behind. In college, pretending to go home, he rode the train for hours and days so that no one would know of his loneliness at boarding school. His classmates all thought he had a place to go at Christmas and holidays. But the hardest departure was leaving the desert on the troop train, with Catherine and their new baby still in the hospital.

A carnival was going on in Nancy the day they pulled into town, so a few officers headed down to the main square. After a few beers, Frank and the men started gambling with the Frenchmen, all in good fun, with yelling and singing. The usual French joie de vivre permeated the town, music, games of chance, costumes, parades, and celebrations. Frank joined the circle to play craps, the French cheering him on. He won a bottle of wine, and the onlookers patted him on the back, crying, "Vive l'américain!"

The next day the summer heat was brutal as the jeep bumped along with no top, the trailer wagging at each turn. *We left Nancy this morning intending to go to Munich, but we got tired and are stopping to spend the night in Ulm where we found a nice billet and a good meal. Like most German towns, it has been pretty badly beaten up in spots. It has been very hot today, and my face is windburned and red as a beet.*

On the road to Germany, Frank ran into French Senegalese troops going to the Rhineland as part of the French occupation. Warily, Frank looked out the corner of his eyes as they marched by, not used to seeing African soldiers. *They are really rough-looking characters, and I wouldn't care to have them occupy anything near me.* The French colonies recruited the West Africans who fought alongside the French, but once they were no longer needed, De Gaulle *whitened* the French army and either sent the Senegalese back to Africa or put them in occupied territories of Germany.

*Senegalais Tirailleurs* corps of colonial infantry in the French army

The next morning, Frank arrived in Munich and stopped by the battery to see Hubbard, Kuret, and the other officers. They had already moved twice since Frank left them, and were about to move to another area. Everyone was preoccupied with packing up.

"No time to talk, no time for a little game of poker. What's the army coming to?" Frank joked with the guys.

"Grab your orders, Foster," the Captain said. He handed him an envelope.

"Regensburg?" Frank picked up the rest of his equipment, saluted, and said good-bye. "Typical, I got to be there in a couple of hours and already have duty till eleven tonight."

Kuret stubbed out his cigarette and wrapped his arm around Frank's shoulder. "This can't last forever, Frankie. Soon we'll be home with our sweethearts."

"It's not easy. I heard one of the officers just got married to an American nurse. They'll have about two to three days together, and then they will be miles apart. I feel for them. They have a lot of happiness and lots of heartaches ahead of them. Damn army."

Frank reported to duty along with a new set of officers.

"Of all the cockamamie ideas," Frank griped. "Up till eleven last night at the swim meet and now all morning writing up the results of the swim meet and tennis tournaments. I'd rather be firing that 155 right now."

Lt. Bruce laughed. "You're in the army now…"

"Aww, I've heard that too many times."

"The facts are you have to serve your time doing this menial athletic stuff if you want to go back to your battalion."

"I'm between the devil and the deep blue sea. Our battalion is already breaking up. Who's left if I go back. I don't know where to jump."

"Frank, there are worse jobs, so stop your bellyaching. At least the long hours keep you out of trouble."

The officers moved into a hotel with running water, hot showers, and flushing toilets. Their artillery battalion was only on duty in case the M.P.s couldn't handle a situation. Frank continued working in the athletic program, baseball, tennis, swimming, and track meets. *Next week is our big week. We will have our corps track meet. It will be two good days of work, then most big events will be over until fall.*

Other than the uncertainty, Frank enjoyed the time at the hotel monitoring sports events. The meals spoiled the men after eating rations in the camps. The German waiters and waitresses who had worked for the hotel during the war remained on staff. Perhaps, it was uncomfortable being around the Krauts, but Frank never complained if they served him or cleaned his room or clothes.

> *Our food has been excellent here. Tonight, for instance, we had steak, ice-cream, and cake. Hope it continues so I can put on a little weight. I weighed myself yesterday, totaled up to 149lbs, so I haven't changed one way or the other.*

\* \* \*

Catherine worried about his weight. *Over six-feet two inches, he should weigh more than that.* She wrung her hands and went about busying herself with the baby. *When he gets home, I'll fatten him up.* She opened the next letter and realized she had more to worry about than his weight.

> *Hello Darling,*          *Tuesday, July 17*
> *There is nothing new to report on the going home situation, it hasn't brightened up one bit. If only the*

*Bronze Star and those five points would come thru and get my total officially up to 86. I heard about one captain who had 83 points and was just transferred into C.B.I. (China, Burma, India) bound outfit and is he fit to be tied.*

There was still a chance Frank would be sent to the Pacific to fight. His points preoccupied his mind and set Catherine to worrying.

*You asked if I were in the Army of Occupation. No, not as yet, but if that Bronze Star doesn't come thru pretty quickly, I'm very liable to be stuck in it. All the officers under 85 will be transferred out of the outfit very soon. If that happens, I will probably get hooked.*

That evening Frank and Lt Bruce played a few games of bad tennis then decided to go to the stables and get the horses tackled for a ride. Frank was a little jittery getting on a horse after so long out of a saddle. He mounted the dappled mare, fit the stirrups to his height, and softly nudged the horse. It felt strange at first, but he got used to it in no time. The evening was like a warm summer night in the desert, the soft air filtering by his ears. He broke into a full canter blessed at the moment without fear or longing. The horses survived the war, possibly even more cared for than the people. When they returned to the stable, the stable boy took the heated horses and brushed them down. Frank and Lt Bruce headed back home and stopped to get a beer. Frank offered him a cigarette.

"How'd you get these?" he asked.

"My wife sent me a few cartons, just in time. Here, take a few."

They got to talking, and Frank pulled out the latest photos of John.

"Not the best. The photographer can't get John to smile. I could do better than that looking in the other direction."

"You do photography?"

Frank smirked, "Don't we all? There's a black room set up in every post now."

The conversation turned to how many points they had and who was getting transferred.

> *Hello Darling,*                                    *Thursday, July 19*
>
> *Another hot day, working hard, attended one baseball game between the 4<sup>th</sup> Armored and the 83<sup>rd</sup> Infantry Division. We're in the midst of the tournament for our Corps Championship.*
>
> *A group of our officers and enlisted men were transferred to a Quartermaster Truck Co. right near here. I haven't heard if I've been affected by it. I wouldn't know many of the officers in our battalion now. Everything is confused, and I don't know whether to run or walk.*
>
> *I haven't gotten paid this month, but I think I'll let it ride a few months. I haven't spent a penny since my Paris trip, and it's not likely I'll spend any until the Germans get some stores open.*
>
> *I didn't get any mail from you today, in fact, none came through for anyone. I will be on the lookout for those pictures of John.*

At the end of the war, over three million American Army men were in Europe, and additional soldiers were in the pipeline to be assigned to Europe, even though the war had been winding down. Army and Airforce units in Europe were classified in four categories. Category I consisted of units to remain in Europe in the occupation army. II were units to be re-deployed to the Pacific. III were units to be retrained and reorganize to be reclassified to either I or II. And Category IV units were to be returned to the U.S. to be inactivated and discharged. Only those soldiers who had enough points, 85 or above, were considered for discharge. Frank was sweating out his last 5 points. Bad news arrived.

*Hello Darling,*                                    *Friday, July 27*
  *Well, the rush is over, and I can relax a bit, but not as I planned. I was notified tonight that I am in another A.A. Battalion, one that is occupation, and in addition to that, I'm seven days AWOL as they neglected to send orders here. My Bronze Star failed to go through. It has bounced back three times because it wasn't sent in the proper form. So I got good and tight last night to celebrate Victory Europe, but the victory, like my poor stomach today, is hollow.*
  *If those people at the 546th get on the ball, then the 5 points might come thru, but until I have 85 points, I can't get a transfer in my present setup.*
  *I take off and report in at Munich and see what gives. I am slightly disgusted, as you may easily see. It's the old army game. What a happy day it will be when I get out of it and be back with you and John.*
  *It's goodnight again, darling. I miss you terribly, I really need you now.*

Frank reported the next day and immediately put in for a transfer and tried to straighten out the AWOL to remove it from his name. Like a caged animal, he attempted every move possible to get out the Occupation Army, which could mean another year in Europe.

*There's not much I can do until this mess is figured out. The talk of peace negotiations with Japan is heartening, but from here, it sounds like a will-o-wisp. I'm afraid the Japs won't sail for an unconditional surrender. I hope I'm wrong.*

Even though Frank's big apartment house was at the edge of town near parks and forests, he couldn't enjoy it. *I'll have lots of time on my hands. Days of nothingness are far worse than combat duty, boredom, and more boredom.* He toured the guard posts around Munich with an older officer, gnarled by war, still with his sense of responsibility intact.

"Not much to do here, just make sure you do your rounds daily, keep your men alert. You never know when they'll be needed."

"Yes, sir. What is expected of the men on duty?"

"The M.P.s cover all the skirmishes and incidents between civilians and soldiers, but it gets rough sometimes."

"How so?"

The old soldier pointed to a group of swarthy men, a few women in peasant clothes, and raggedy children. "Those are former slaves. Germans brought them in from all over, mostly from the Mideastern countries. They can't go back, or the Russians will do the same. Slave trade." He lit a cigarette and offered one to Frank. "Son, those bastard Nazis may deserve it, but these fellas get brooding on their lot and go on a rampage beating up on some luckless German. Your men are the back-ups. Pull out your guns, sit on 'em, get them controlled, and the M.P.s will put them in the slammer."

That night, Frank walked the streets of Munich, taking in all the damage. The factories had lights on, and he could see people working to restore it. New bricks lay alongside the crumbling walls. *Munich is pretty severely mauled, but they are cleaning it up rather quickly, using railroad cars and trucks. I admire their industry.*

Returning to his apartment, he had a cigarette and drank with his fellow officers, but it lacked joy, not like shooting the breeze with his buddies. *I wish I could be with Kuret, Hub, Carlson, and Captain. After living with them in the same outfit for two and a half years, it's hard to break away, and I don't care too much for my new friends. I wish I were transferred back to the 12th Corps Headquarters, where I was on temporary duty in Regensburg.*

Frank's Texan roommate, Jack, didn't see eye to eye about race discrimination. Frank believed all men in the service deserved equal respect, no matter the color or religion, so they avoided discussing segregation, just let it hang in the air. *That's the army. You don't get a choice who's your roommate.*

On Sunday, Frank and Jack took a stroll through the park near their apartment on the edge of town. The ground was soft with pine needles, and the trees offered a welcome respite from the heat.

Jack elbowed him. "Hey Frankie, look at those Joes and frauleins fraternizing. These women around here are really man-crazy."

Looking in the direction he pointed, Frank saw them. Dressed in army blouse and tie, the G.I.s held the women close, with no shame kissing in public; in fact, the soldiers made a show of it.

"If someone told me two months ago that I'd see all this cozying up with the civilians, I'd say they were crazy," Frank said. He couldn't believe the change in attitudes in the last few months. Rules of non-fraternization had loosened or the men just ignored them.

"You just can't stop human nature." They both agreed it was for the better if Germany got back on its feet, and the civilians were treated like anyone else, but the lingering feeling of distrust remained.

Jack veered towards a bar, and Frank continued to the Carmelite Church to attend a G.I. Mass where he found over 200 older civilians in the church and only a handful of soldiers and no young people. *This seems to be a very Catholic area, many road shrines, the houses are loaded with holy pictures and statues, but I'm afraid the older people hold the religion and that many of Hitler's ideas and teachings have affected the youth.*

*I'm praying for an early collapse of Japan, but there's no kidding ourselves, the prospect of getting home to you in the near future is diminishing rapidly. At the rate things are progressing, I'm going to see another winter here. I hate the thought of another winter without you, but I'm very much afraid that barring a miracle, that's what it will be. Three months ago, today, we stopped fighting, it seems years since then because I've been so many places and done so many different things. It's going to be heaven to settle down.*

Frank knelt in church a little longer after the mass, the place he felt closest to Catherine.

# CHAPTER THIRTY-SIX

# Don't Get Your Hopes Up

*Hello Darling,*                    *Wednesday, August 8*
*Another day of my sentence in Deutschland com-*
*pleted. I wonder how many more there are to go. If this*
*atomic bomb is all they claim it will be, it ought to*
*scare the Japs into surrendering and shorten our term*
*over here.*

On August 6, 1945, an American B-29 bomber dropped the world's first deployed atomic bomb over the Japanese city of Hiroshima. Three days later, **a** second B-29 dropped another A-bomb on Nagasaki, killing an estimated 40,000 people. Japan's Emperor Hirohito announced his country's unconditional surrender in a radio address on August 15, citing the devastating power of a new and most cruel bomb convinced him to end the war and stop the carnage.

Frank and his men gathered around the radio to hear the Japanese emperor surrender. The day they had been waiting for had finally arrived. The men stood silently, sobered by the fact that the atom bomb had killed so many innocent people, and the war had taken so many innocent lives along the way.

An enlisted man broke the silence. "Well, it's about time." Everyone nodded, a few cussed, and others mourned their buddies who hadn't survived to see this day. "I should be happy, but it just doesn't feel right."

> *Hello Darling,*            *Wednesday, August 15*
> *What a day! Well, it's over now, let's pray it stays that way or a good long time. We have been waiting so long for the war to end that the end was really anticli-mactic. I heard Hirohito's message this morning, and it reminded me of an aspiring heavyweight boxing champ who has been beaten but has in mind training and building up for another crack at being champion in the future. I think though that they will get a going over that will prevent that.*

The army had had practice parades daily, preparing for this day to celebrate a hard-earned victory. That afternoon in the rain, they paraded for the General. It went off very well with the infantry marching, the tanks and trucks rolling, and Frank in the front seat of his jeep. *The only walking I did was from the front of the jeep to the front seat, which suits me fine.*

Parade day wasn't a holiday, and Frank found himself touring Munich, checking his posts, on a rotation of six hours on, and six hours off over 24 hours. At the end of his guard duty, he took advantage of the hot shower at the battery since his apartment still didn't have hot running water. He got back to his apartment, put his feet up, and went through a stack of letters.

> *Kitty, finally, the mail is catching up, five from you and one from Mary Catherine, who still talks about having that ham I sent for a homecoming party that I'm really looking forward to. That ham is getting pretty old, remember I sent it while at Special Service School in*

*Virginia. Ha! While she was writing the letter, Bert was opening the box containing the rifle and dagger. I imagine he will get a kick out of the junk. I have another rifle I'm going to fix up as soon as I get in the mood. And a surprise letter from my sister, but nothing from George.*

Frank had almost given up finding his brother, George. He wrote to him often and assumed George had received the letters and didn't answer them. *I just don't get that guy. He's been here for over two years. Must have been sent home.*

Then word came from his sister. "George is stationed in Nuremberg, not too far from you. Here's his address." Frank immediately contacted his brother and put in a request to visit.

*Dear Kitty,                            Saturday, August 18*
*I finally have found George, and he's only about a hundred miles from here. I don't know when I'll get away to see him. They're keeping me busy now that I've been promoted to AA weapons unit commander. I spent eight hours in a jeep, riding around our area in Munich, surveying for billets, and locating units. Tomorrow, I'll have another 6 hours on a jeep security patrol. Still haven't heard any more about seeing George.*

George had not communicated with Frank during the entire war though he had sent a letter to Catherine and knew where to mail Frank. Frank never quite understood the dynamics between them. Frank was young when their parents died, and George had left home to live with another family. Frank never knew what happened to him until years later when George resurfaced as a disgruntled man. The family ties seemed to be forever broken, but Frank wanted family connections more than anything and wouldn't give up on contacting George.

*Kitty Darling,*          *Monday, August 27*
*I missed writing Saturday and Sunday on account*
*of I unexpectedly got a pass and went up to Nuremberg. I*
*met George there and spent the night with him and most*
*of Sunday. He is still the same.*

The two brothers went down to the local café to have a beer and something to eat. George smoked through the entire meal, saying very little, and when he did, it was to complain. Frank broke the ice with a few questions about his points.

"Why the hell aren't they sending you back home? You have way more points than most of the enlisted men in Europe. I can't understand it."

"Shit if I know. I've got 115 points and still sweating it out. You'll probably get home before I do, officers always get the breaks. I've been overseas since North Africa. Two years and counting. What the hell!"

"I got 83 points and going nowhere till my battle points come in. George, you'll be home first."

"What home? I don't have a wife waiting for me like you." The old jealousy rose in his red face as he took another swig of beer.

They finished dinner and walked back to George's barracks and played some poker with the guys. The next day was a warm August morning, and Frank asked George if he wanted to go to Mass with him. George stubbed out his cigarette. "You go ahead, Frank, say a prayer for me."

Frank left feeling like he always had around George, guilty for getting the breaks in life and regretful that George seemed to get the bum deal.

*Frank drove down to Regensburg to see if he could get stationed back there. His old captain told him they're still trying to get him back, but he needed more points. Points, points, points! That's all we think about. The good news is the Jap war is wound up, still waiting for official notice on points though. I imagine that will change the point setup considerably. Maybe we will get home before Christmas.*

A couple of Frank's old officer friends invited him to have a beer. They gave him the scoop. "Our old outfit is kaput, been changed for a Quartermaster Trucking Company."

"Now that's a sad fate for our gunners! I'll keep my mouth shut. I'd rather stay where I am in the A. A. I got a promotion last month to commander. It's just more work." Frank lit a cigarette and inhaled, blowing out a cloud of uncertainty.

"The army is a mess. Can't figure out what to do with us, yet they won't ship us home."

"I just don't want to get stuck here in the Army of Occupation. Hope they get some more replacements for us. I missed the last quota because no one could replace me. I'm due home." The creases in Frank's forehead deepened.

Frank returned to Munich to the same old routine, up at reveille, marching, and calisthenics, checking the guard positions, lie in the sun and wait, back out on duty from 8 pm till after midnight making sure the guys were either in bed or on duty, and not in the bars. The military exercises seemed useless without a war.

*Hello Darling,*          *Tuesday, August 28*
    *Another beautiful day in Munich. We're preparing for yet another parade. What a waste of gasoline.*

*Don't know why I'm here, my next assignment is to watch a football game between the troops and report on it. I'm still anxiously awaiting the call to go home. Each day passes, but I'm still just as far from home as the day before.*

*I've been drinking quite a bit of beer of late, we always have a case of it in the apartment. It isn't as good as ours, not quite as strong and heavier, but it's a good drink, would like to have your dad here to share it. Does he have trouble getting beer now?*

*Well, it's goodnight again, Kitty. I'm going to curl up in bed with a bottle of beer and a book.*

In early September, Frank's roommate got the call to go home. He had made the quota, but not Frank.

*My roommate will be in the States by November 1. It seems almost unbelievable to be going home sometime, and I'll still be in a daze when I get there.*

*Kuret was around today, and they're moving into Munich about two miles from me. He claims he has six horses he will bring with him. I've been wanting to get in some riding.*

*I just finished dinner and must get this letter off before Kuret, Carlson, Hubbard, and Captain Howell come by. That makes four of us who spent the war together! We're going to have a bit of a reunion!*

Like an old-time movie, the years passed quickly in his mind from the early training days at the Desert Training Center to the end of the war. They had been together on the Queen Elizabeth, landed in England, and raced through the French towns and cities as liberators.

They shot German planes out of the sky, forged through snow and mud in the Battle of the Bulge, and lived with Belgian families, and billeted in castles and farmhouses. In the dead of night, they crossed the Rhine, freed the POWs, liberated the concentration camps, and stood triumphant at Hitler's Berghof. They had traveled by jeep in inclement weather and under enemy fire. Miraculously, they all survived. With a twist of fate, they all got posts in Munich within two miles of each other. Another miracle!

Carlson, Kuret, Hubbard, and Captain burst through the doors of Frank's elegant apartment in Munich. "What the hell, Frank! How do you rate these digs?"

Frank knew they'd be jealous of his new situation, a lavishly furnished bourgeois accommodation, the spoils of war. "Wait till you see the piano, Kuret. I'm taking lessons too."

Kuret raced over to the instrument, sat down, and pounded out a ragtime toon that got the party going.

*I hope the furniture can stand the gaff. They will probably bring some of the liquid stuff and become rather exuberant.*

All the guys could talk about was going home. They were all in the same position as Frank, waiting, and going crazy waiting. The War Department had created a point system based on the simple principle of who had fought the longest and hardest should be returned home for discharge first. The officers automatically started with 70 points, and got one point for each month in the service, one more point for each month overseas and five points for combat awards, the magic number being 85 before being considered for redeployment. Still, it was uncertain, even with the adequate points, for officers to be since so few of them could be replaced.

Frank and the boys were waiting for their Bronze Stars earned in the Battle of the Bulge.

"If and when it comes thru, I will breathe much easier. I still don't know which way to turn. If only those five points would come in." Frank took down another bottle and opened it.

The men lit up cigarettes from the butts of the last ones, poured a little more whiskey in their cups, and continued to bellyache.

"If my bronze doesn't come in pretty quick, I'm very liable to be stuck here in the Army of Occupation. They aren't getting enough recruits over here to replace us."

"Don't get yourself tied in a bunch. I heard we're getting awarded another Battle Star for "The Bulge.""

"Well, if that's true, it'll give us five stars, that should earn us some points!"

"And there's a possibility of one more for the Battle of England."

"Well, hot damn, we might all make general one day, we're so great."

"Yeah, maybe, and probably get hooked in the Army of Occupation with the other brass."

"Damn, I'm going to miss you guys." Hubbard took a long swig.

"Let's make a pack. We'll all meet up with our wives once the last one of us gets home."

They all shook on the promise to stay in touch.

The night wore on with laughs about the good ole times in foxholes and being shot at by a sniper in the dense forest, or the time Kuret convinced the vicar to let him have the organ from the blown-out church.

"I'll never forget the look on that farmer's face when he heard you playing that damn organ in the apple orchard!" Frank got to laughing at the thought of it.

"Hey Kuret, what did you do with that typewriter you took from Hitler's office? Got it in your bag?"

"Nah, sent that home with the officer's dagger. Frank got a swell sword too, Swastika emblem and all."

"It's all safely boxed and on its way to California. I sent one of those parachutes too but not sure if Catherine ever got it. I still have that German flag."

* * *

Within a few weeks, the critical score went down to 75 points.

*Points, points, that's all we talk about, think about, and pray for. I can now sweat out that darn Bronze Star in peace, it will be a matter of time before they start shipping us home. Maybe I'll get home before Christmas. But don't get your hopes up."*

# CHAPTER THIRTY-SEVEN

# Repple-Depples

*Kitty Darling,*           *Friday, September 28*
*Well, it has happened again. I received orders today to report to a replacement center at or near Nurnberg. We're due there on October 4. I believe it's the same place that George left from. Don't let your hopes run too high, though, as the so-called "Repple-Depples" are a notoriously slow way to go home. I'd much prefer to go with a unit. Well, anyway, it's another step in the right direction.*

*I went to the movies with Carlson and Kuret, told them good-bye. Hope we keep in touch.*

*Did you get your portrait? The one I had enlarged and done in color, it's really a beauty. I know you will like it.*

*It's goodnight time again, darling. With a little luck now, maybe I'll be seeing you along about my next birthday.*

Before leaving Munich, Frank went to Meyer's Studio, where he asked the proprietor to enlarge a photo of Catherine that he had carried throughout the war. Frank gave specific instructions.

"I'd like the photo enlarged to 12X16 and tinted. My wife's eyes are deep blue, and her hair looks as though the sun is shining through a veil of dark brown curls. Oh, and her cheeks are rosy."

On Friday afternoon, Frank went to retrieve the portrait. When he arrived at the shop, he saw Catherine's portrait displayed in the window in a gold frame.

"She is lovely," Mr. Meyer said as he took the portrait down and handed it to Frank.

"Yes, that's my Kitty."

"You'll be happy to get back to her," the gentleman said.

Frank approvingly looked at the framed picture and asked the proprietor to wrap it carefully for mailing.

Tinted portrait of Catherine "Kitty"

On Thursday, October 4, Frank was relieved from assigned duties and attached to the 17th Reinforcement Depot, Vilseck, Germany, a replacement center or "repple-depple," about 50 miles to the east of Nuremberg. The base, built in 1938 for German soldiers, was captured in 1945 by the U.S. Army and used to house prisoners, as well as soldiers preparing to leave the ETO or waiting for reassignment.

> *I counted about 39 truckloads of prisoners today, and I didn't see all of them go by. They don't look so arrogant jammed in a truck. I like to watch the expressions of the German civilians as the prisoners stream by, but can't even tell if they are sad or glad. Most all of them have a son in the army, so I guess they are a bit depressed and anxious.*

Within a week, Frank boarded a train that carried troops across Europe to the staging area in the French port of Le Havre. The enlisted men crowded into the boxcars with standing room only and no food until the first stop at 10 pm, where everyone got a hot meal. The weather was miserably cold and wet, so the doors remained closed as they jostled along in the unfurnished boxcars. As an officer, Frank fared better by getting a seat in the first-class compartment, his feet on his duffel bag. He lit up a cigarette and bantered with the other officers.

The apprehension of what the future would bring hung heavy in the smoke-filled cabin. While in the military, the soldier had orders to comply with, jobs to do, and minimal downtime to think or question authority. The goal was to stay alive and kill the enemy, which permeated their psyche, making them jumpy, reactive to sounds, on edge. One of the men in the compartment broke out the cards, and others brought out bottles of whiskey from their bags. Playing poker broke the ice, the whiskey loosened them up, and for a while, they felt a comradeship with barely saying a word, a few jokes but no mention of the war.

Frank's homecoming was now within reach. How would he react, seeing Catherine and John for the first time in almost two years? What would he say? Would his son, now a toddler, let him hold him?

The train arrived the next morning in Le Havre, where a jeep picked up Frank and the other officers while the enlisted men poured out of the boxcars and into open trucks. They traveled in caravan two miles to Camp Herbert Tareyton, named after the cigarette company. Like other cigarette camps, it was a huge, temporary army camp that housed up to 35,000 men in tents. Nissen huts, the ubiquitous military structure made from a half-cylindrical skin of corrugated steel, housed the Red Cross station, the mess hall, and the Service Club for entertainment and relaxation for the troops. Frank rated the food, cooked by the German prisoners, as relatively good, but the sleeping accommodations left a lot to be desired.

Camp Herbert Tareyton, Le Havre, France 1945

Frank plopped his bags on his bed and surveyed the room. Four cots per side, no windows, only flaps and doors at the front and back. There was no heat or electricity in the tent, so he walked to the officer's club, where he sat around a wood-burning stove to read by a lantern. It was going to be a long wait, no matter how short it was.

*Hello Darling,*          *Friday, October 19, 1945*

    *We are more or less suspended in motion now. Just sitting around waiting, waiting. We read daily in the "Stars and Stripes" about how they are releasing men in the States with even as low as 50 points. To say the best, the boys over here are slightly chagrinned.*

    *I was quite surprised to hear that George was in France. I will be on the lookout for him, but France is quite large and full of G.I.s*

    *I passed part of the day at the Dentist's, had the barnacles scraped from my teeth. As of yet, we have no shipping date, we should get it in a day or two. The consensus of opinions now is that it will be about November 1.*

    *You know the thought about "civilian life" rather awes me now. It has been so long since I've done a lick of work, that I seriously doubt whether I'll be about to face it. Maybe I can work into it gradually.*

    *You asked about clothing. Yes, I have plenty, in fact, more than I need. I have the German sheepskin, my own overcoat, a short canvas coat, and three field jackets. After struggling with the French electrician and plumber today, we finally have electricity in our tents now, so we can spend some evenings reading and writing. There are eight of us squeezed into this tent, so there is very little room to move around. As of yet, I haven't visited the town of Le Havre. Maybe tomorrow.*

Frank checked the shipping schedule on the deployment board outside of the mess hall. His group had secured quarters on a ship set to depart November 5. Seeing the end to his time in Europe gave him a sense of urgency. He planned a trip to Le Havre, where he viewed the damage of the war.

It was unbelievable that the Germans had held out at all costs to keep Le Havre. The Allies had landed on the beaches of Normandy over a year ago in June and liberated Paris in August, but in September 1944, Le Havre still awaited liberation. The Germans had ordered the evacuation of civilians, yet, the majority of the people of Le Havre stayed, not believing the Allies would bomb them since most Germans had left. The Germans who controlled the harbor refused to surrender, and British RAF dropped a deluge of bombs on the city. The Allies continued firebombing the next day, destroying Le Havre, nothing left but ashes and rubble. After thousands of people had died, the Germans surrendered, and the Allies liberated Le Havre on September 5, 1944.

What must have Frank thought when he viewed the destruction? He stopped in the Church of St. Francis, which survived the bombing, the last remains of prewar Le Havre. *How strange, I was married in the church of St. Francis.* He left, having seen enough war and destruction. He was ready to go home.

He wrote his last letter to Catherine while on the continent: *No mail today. After I leave here, I probably won't get any more letters from you until I get to the States. It's good night darling, I hope it won't be too long before I'm in your arms.*

Frank shipped out from Le Havre on November 5, 1945. He missed his birthday but was home for the holidays.

# Acknowledgments

I am grateful to my cousins for trusting me with their father's WWII letters to their mother and allowing me to tell their story. Frank's words were my guide throughout the process of writing this book, "Darling." To unravel his adventures, I researched his battalion's Morning Reports, which recorded the date, the place, and the status of soldiers in the unit on that day, the transfers, temporary assignments, leaves, promotions, demotions, AWOL, illness, and medals. I mapped each location where Frank was stationed and correlated what happened there from firsthand accounts and primary sources such as diaries, letters, and speeches. I had troves of information, primarily from *The Third Army After Action Reports* released in 1948 and Patton's book, *War As I Knew It.* which gave detailed information from his journal and his other writings before he died in December 1945. I cross-referenced these sources with information found in Frank's letters, even though he could not say too much about the war. Knowing where Frank was each day, allowed me to write about the military events that took place in the same location.

Frank's letters directed me on what to write. If he mentioned a name, a battle, a popular song, or used military jargon, then I'd look it up to find out more detail and information. Writers talk about their Muse, something, or someone that takes over their writing. Well, Frank inspired me, his words, his photos, his friends, his family, all gathered at my desk as I wrote.

Special thanks to his first girl, Mary Foster, and her daughter Colleen for meticulously copying each letter and photograph and sharing them with me. His son, Joe Foster sent me a few of his father's letters and suggested I might want to write about the war experience.

Little did I know there would be over 200 letters. Joe and I talked about his family history, which he had researched. John Foster, Frank and Catherine's first child, asked his father about the war when they worked side by side. "Did you ever kill anyone?" Frank never directly answered that question but he told John stories about Patton, his driver, and the time he ran into the Germans in the forest. Tom Foster, Eddy Foster, and Patty Foster Davis sent photos and their memories, which didn't include a lot about the war. "The only time Dad mentioned the war was when we asked to go camping. Then he'd reply, 'I've done enough camping in my life during the war, so no thanks.'"

On the internet, I found a radio interview of an enlisted man in Frank's platoon, Ken Lubben. He was an enlisted man with the 546th since the Desert Training Center days and spoke of his time in England protecting the Cottesmore Airforce Base during D-Day and the Horsa glider flights carrying troops to Normandy. He recounted the story of the P-47 they shot down only later to discover that the pilot was a German. Patton corroborated the incident in his book. The obituary of Frank's best wartime friend, Marvin Kuret, gave information on his wartime service in the 546th. I contacted Kuret's daughter, who told me about the typewriter from Hitler's Berghof that is now in the WWII Museum in New Orleans, but like most children of the WWII veterans, their parents did not talk to them about the war.

The conversations in the book are Frank's words he wrote to Catherine. I conflated the information and attributed some of the dialogue to friends or people he met, but for the most part, they are Frank's words.

The speeches, songs, and sayings by famous people are historically correct, even though some of the addresses were written down after they were given. The pictures in the book are photos that Frank took, as well as photos from the Third Army After Action Reports, and the National Archives.

Frank lost contact with his war buddies, Carlson, Hubbard, Captain Howell, and Kuret. Perhaps, they wrote a few times, made a few phone calls, but the relationships didn't carry through his life. He did remain great friends with Bert Ripple, who brought him to the desert in 1931, and they celebrated his return from the war with the Virginia ham Frank had sent him in 1943.

Contrary to what Frank said in his letters about not returning to the desert, he did return to the Coachella Valley after World War II to work for Shell Oil Company selling products to Coachella Valley Farmers. In 1958, he started his own company, Foster-Gardner, developing new products and manufacturing liquid fertilizers.

Frank always worked close to the earth, growing crops of corn, cotton, grapes, citrus, and dates while providing other farmers with the needed soil products. More importantly, Frank and Catherine grew and nurtured a family of six children. The little girl he longed for, Mary Catherine, was born April 25, 1947. Their children and grandchildren continue to live in the desert, maintaining his company as well as developing new ways to grow products in the desert and branching out to other companies and innovations in farming.

On September 7, 1979, Frank was in his fields, driving his truck across the desert roads on his way to check on his friend's carrot packing house on the other side of the railroad tracks. He'd done these rounds checking on his customers and plants for over fifty years. Frank had had recent eye surgery, and his hearing hadn't been right since the war, but I never heard him complain about either, or would he. His son, John, then a grown man and married with two children, worked with his father and was out checking the irrigation in the fields that day. The AC blasted cold air inside Frank's truck, quite a difference from the open-air jeeps he drove during the Desert Training Center days. Still, it was the same desert, the hot winds, the perfectly carved Shadow Mountains in the background, the beauty of cactus and Joshua trees, and now the verdant green crops.

From where John stood, he could hear a train whistle then a noise like an explosion and saw a cloud of dust as if a bomb had detonated. He ran until he could see that the train had struck his father's truck on the tracks, and he knew that his father had died.

Frank left a legacy of hard work and generosity. He never forgot his younger days as an orphan. To him, family always came first, which extended to all his nieces and nephews. He had a soft heart for the ones left behind and today the Boys and Girls Club of Coachella Valley is named the Frank Foster and Palmer Powell Family Clubhouse in honor of him and his friend whom he was to have visited at the carrot packing house the day he died. The children and grandchildren of Foster and Powell still support and remain involved with the club.

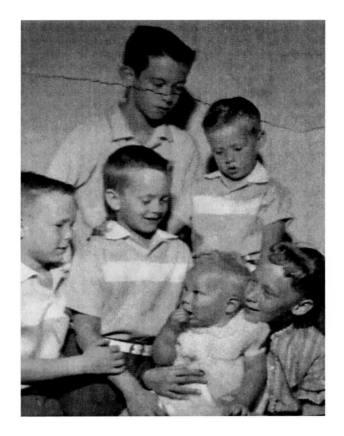

Frank and Catherine's Children 1957

# BIBLIOGRAPHY

Ambrose, Stephen E. *The Supreme Commander,* Random House 1969

*AntiAircraft Artillery, Brief History of Operations in Europe, 1 August 1944-24 September 1944, The United States Third Army,* United States Army, 1945

*Coast Artillery Journal,* VOLUME LXXXXI JULY-AUGUST 1948

Cummings, R.E., /Colonel, Adjutant General, *After Action Report: Operations of the Third United States Army in the European Campaign for the period August 1944 to May 1945*

Dougherty, *Steve, In Germany, War and Reunion,* May 26, 2010

Eisenhower, Dwight, *Statement to soldiers, sailors, and airmen of the Allied Expeditionary,*

National Archives, June 5, 1944

Embrey, William, Our Outfit, *Lanham's Wartime Experiences American Style* - 1940-1990

Gallagher, Robert F., *World War II Story,* Third Army, European Theater, 1939-1945

Gohn, Sandi and Case, Mike, *USO Camp Shows, D-Day and Entertaining Troops on the*

*European Front Lines in WWII*

Harding, Andrew S., *Patton and Eisenhower,* paper Manchester College, 2004

*Hommage Au General Patton,* 32 Avenue de l'Opera, Paris, France, 2007

Ike Skelton Research Digital Library, *XII Corps Spearhead of Patton's Third Army; After Action*

*Report: Third US Army, 1 August 1944-9 May 1945. Vol 1, the Operations*

Janus, Allan, *The Stripes of D-Day* Archives Division of Smithsonian National Air and Space Museum, June 6, 2014

Museum, June 6, 2014

Kelly, C.J., *Artillery Innovations in WWII,* "Owlcation," May 2018

Klein, Christopher, *Fooling Hitler: The Elaborate Ruse Behind D-Day,* June 3, 2014

Levine, David, "Remembering Camp Shanks," March 2010

Marshall, George C., Secretary Of War, The War Department Pamphlet No. 211 29 July 1941

National Archives Photos Public Domain

Patton, General George S., *War As I Knew It,* Houghton Mifflin Company, 1947

Province Charles M., *Unknown Patton,* San Diego, CA 1982

Rennison, John, *Wings Over Rutland* - Rutland Local History Society - Vol 4 in the Rutland

Seekatz, Sara, "Desert Deployment: Southern California's World War II Desert Training Center," March 16, 2015

Shulz, Eugene G., *"The Ghost in General Patton's Third Army: Memoirs of Eugene G. Shulz During His Service in the United States Army in World War II,* Xlibris Corporation, 2012

*During His Service in the United States Army in World War II,* Xlibris Corporation, 2012

Smith, Claude, *The History of the Glider Pilot Regiment,* June 2008

Stanton, Shelby, *Order of Battle: U.S. Army World War II,* 1984

Wesley Johnston, *1944 World War II Troop Ship Crossing,* Skylighters. org., 1999

# Frank's Route

Morning Report locations 546th Battalion

## ENGLAND

May 2, 1944
Staffordshire

May 20, 1944
Cottesmore

July 5, 1944
Lobscome Corner

July 8, 1944
Fawley

July 11, 1944
Southampton

JULY 12 en route

**FRANCE**

July 14, 1944
Saint-Laurent-sur-Mer

July 16, 1944
Bricquebec and vicinity

July 23, 1944
Néhou

August 1, 1944
Montsurvent

August 2, 1944
Beauchamps

August 3, 1944
Le Mesnil-Rogues

August 8, 1944
Montours

August 12, 1944
La Baconnière

August 15, 1944
Saint-Jean-Assis

August 20, 1944
Frazé

August 25, 1944
Vrigny

August 30, 1944
La Chaume

September 5, 1944
Marson/Francheville

September 9, 1944
Courtisols

September 15, 1944
Herméville-en-Woëvre

September 26, 1944
Étain

October 12, 1944-December 17, 1944
Nancy

December 17, 1944
St. Avold

December 19-December 31, 1944
Pont-à-Mousson

January 1, 1945
Toul

January 12, 1945
Dommary-Baroncourt

January 19
Jeandelize

## BELGIUM

Febraury 6

Libramont

February 14, 1945

Arlon

February 26

Gouvy

March 1, 1945

## LUXEMBOURG

Luxembourg

March 2, 1945

Kédange-sur-Canner

## GERMANY

March 7, 1945

Saarlautern

March 22, 1945

Neunkirchen

March 27, 1945

Oppenheim

March 28, 1945

Nieder Saulheimer

April 1, 1945

Wetterfeld

April 1, 1945

Ersrode

April 3, 1945
Sontra

April 4, 1945
Gros-Burschla

April 6, 1945
Treffurt

April 9, 1945
Marksuhl

April 11, 1945 (near Orhdruf)
Catterfeld

April 12, 1945
Stutzhaus (Luisnthal)

April 13, 1945
Frankenhain

April 14
Marlishausen

April 17, 1945
Gerach
Ober Krumback

April 20, 1945
Deinschwang
Lauterhofen
Hohenfels
Schönhofen

April 27, 1945

Regensburg

May 1, 1945
Eggenfelden
Passau
Scharding

## AUSTRIA

May 4, 1945
Waizenkirchen
Eferding

May 8, 1945
Linz

## GERMANY

May 13-July 3, 1945
Wiesberg

## FRANCE

June 15, 1945
Paris

En route
Nancy
Stuttgart
July 15, 1945

## GERMANY

Regensburg
September 7, 1945
Munich

October 4, 1945
Vilseck, Nuremberg

## FRANCE

October 19, 1945

Le Havre

November 5, 1945

En route to U.S.A.